Year
of the
Incubus

UNHALLOWED
LOVE SERIES
BOOK 3

TARA FOX HALL

To Mom, for always wanting to know "What happens next?" with Shaker and Co.

To Nancy, for helping what I thought was 1 stand alone spinoff become its own series.

CHAPTER ONE

January

"Kaitlyn, can you please show in Mr. Gray?"

"Yes, Mrs. Black."

Debbie steeled herself. *Remember, Vassago Gray is an incubus: charming, handsome, and a master seducer of women. Seduction isn't limited to sex.*

Vassago sauntered in, his smile easy and full of innuendo. "You rang, my Mistress?"

He looks like a male model straight out of GQ, except more amusing and accommodating...RESIST! "I'm not your mistress. I am your boss and the CEO of Pandora Productions, and you'll address me as Mrs. Black."

"Very well, Mrs. Black," Vassago agreed, sitting down on the edge of her desk. "I accept and acknowledge your authority." He winked. "If you wanted my complete submission, you had only to ask. What can I do to please you?"

Save me from demons who think they are God's gift to women, for starters. "Get off my desk immediately. You need to act more appropriately."

Vassago smiled wider, as he stood, slipping his hands into his pants pockets. "Perhaps we should meet in private tonight, and you can give me a lesson in manners? I promise to be a quick study."

Kaitlyn knocked on the door, then opened it. "I have a Brady Black on line one." She glanced at Gray, who met her gaze and winked, making her look away as she flushed.

"No calls, Kaitlyn," Debbie said loudly.

Kaitlyn withdrew, but the door remained slightly ajar.

Damn it. Debbie got up and went to the door. Gray blocked her, grinning impishly. "Shall we lock it, and begin my lessons now?"

Debbie's first urge was to slap him, the second to knee him in the balls. *No, he's a demon, but he's still an employee. I just need to take control of the situation.* "Vassago, either shut up and listen to what I've got to say or get out and don't ever come back. I can find another actor to do *Incubus*."

Gray drew back, bringing his head high. "Okay, I'm listening. What's so important that it called for a meeting this early, when I'm not even filming on set today?"

"You can't be connected to a new starlet every week!" Debbie exploded, as she slammed her door, then stalked over to her desk past her new leading star.

"I thought it was good for publicity," the incubus said mildly.

"You be flippant about this, and you're getting a holy water bath," Debbie threatened, lifting up a capped liter bottle. "I'm serious."

Grayson pouted, striking the same pose from the promo poster for *Incubus*, which did nothing for Debbie's anger. "I'm being safe."

"These starlets don't like being screwed, then left for the next babe in line. Who cares if you leave them not pregnant? Most of them are likely infertile anorexics, anyway."

2

"Oooh, hostile," he teased. "I can't help it if I'm popular."

"Damnit it, Gray. I mean it. You can't act like this."

He made a face. "Call me Vassago or Vass in private, please. I thought that was what was required of a male leading man, that you constantly romance starlets. Shaker told me to make sure to be seen with many celebrity women in my first year, and to make sure that the media took a lot of pictures."

"Dates, sure, but not full-blown orgies! *The Star* just ran an article saying you were engaged to Belle DeMadison, and how much she was enjoying planning the wedding."

"I only told her that I enjoyed our evening and would be happy to spend eternity with her. Pillow talk, as you humans say."

"Bullshit. She told the reporter you and she agreed on no rings because you were going to donate that money to the Peace Corps."

"She said it was her pet cause. I thought it would make for good publicity."

"Listen and hear me, ok? Good publicity can be exaggeration. It can be a lot of flash with almost no substance. What it can't be is outright lies that are easily shown to be lies. Right now, you are losing the fan base we've tried so hard to build you for *Incubus*'s premiere ad later this month! Women don't want to lust after a man who is a faithless liar."

"The women of America think I'm a faithless liar?" He had the good grace to look appalled.

Debbie nodded. "You need to make a statement later today that you're going into treatment for alcohol addiction. It's a more "friendly" addiction that sex or drugs, or straight mental illness."

Now he was incredulous. "But I'm not addicted to alcohol!"

"You need a scapegoat for your behavior, so officially, you are as of now," Debbie stated. "You will also call any women you've made promises to—don't give me any crap that you can't remember all their names—and apologize. Say that you are getting help but need to face your problems on your own. That will get rid of them in a socially acceptable way."

Something like awe flashed across his face.

Debbie buzzed her secretary. "Please get *The Star* on the line, offer them an exclusive interview with Mr. Gray if they agree to run it front page within the next forty-eight hours. Also we want all questions ahead of time, no exceptions." She looked at Vassago. "Go home and stay there. *The Star* will jump on this, if I know their editor at all. If possible, mess yourself up a bit. You look too perfect now for an addict. You need to look repentant and earnest, without losing all the sex appeal. Can you manage that?"

Vassago nodded. "Ok." He got up and went to the door. "You know, you'd have made an excellent demon, Debbie."

"That's Mrs. Black," Debbie called after him, the door shutting to cut off her words. "Ugh!" She sat down at her desk and took a deep breath. *Compose yourself, you've got the first important team meeting of the year next week, and you still haven't prepared. You've got to not only hold it together, you've got to inspire them, make them believe that the set accidents and deaths that happened here last year can't happen again. Which means lying. But most important you've got to find a way in the next couple months to make the lie true, unless you want Pandora Productions to end up like Titan Pictures: chopped up and sold off in pieces to pay outstanding debts.*

Sheila entered. For a moment, Debbie relaxed at the sight of her good friend, then she straightened, remembering who was really in the body before her. "How did the morning go, Song?"

"You should be calling me Sheila when I'm here," Song said demurely, handing her a stack of files. "And it went ok."

"I'm tired of the pretending," Debbie said, taking them. "What are these?"

"Some new projects, and updates on the movies in progress," Song answered, sitting down. "I don't know the name of the demon that inhabited Sheila for those couple of months last year, but she was decent at keeping appearances up. Everything is up to date, if missing Sheila's flair."

"Yes, she always used to write comments in the margins,"

Debbie said, paging through the folders. "These are all blank. But at least that demon didn't sabotage us further by screwing these new projects up. It would have been easy to do."

"Pretending to be other than who we are is ingrained in us," Song said with a mix of apology and pride. "It's the first rule of possession. Titus reminded me of it, when I took over Jett's sister."

"Now we are being too open," Debbie said, casting a look at the closed door. "Besides, you should get Sheila home, so you both can rest. I am glad though that you are giving her some...exercise." *I can't believe I said that.*

"I'll see you later on," Song said, rising. "And no, there's still no change, Debbie. I can't feel her at all, and she doesn't answer me. But I'm not giving up hope, and you shouldn't, either." Her expression became determined. "When she comes back, I want her to be able to resume her life and her career here. I know it's what she would...um, will want, too." She left, closing the door.

Debbie paged through the folders for a moment, then put them aside.

Sheila's body was fine, but her mind had been on hiatus for months now, ever since one of her two demons, Harp, had been ripped from her during an exorcism. The shock of it was usually fatal, or so Shaker had told her. Sheila had survived as she was still bound to her other demon, Song, but couldn't seem to find her way back to consciousness. "I'm going to have to contact Devlin," Debbie mused out loud. "Titus needs to take a look at her. I should have done that from the beginning. Fuck."

You don't need to go through Devlin. Titus is now your brother in law, remember? You can just call him up, Shaker said in her mind. *He has unparalleled skill in healing.*

Debbie shifted at the unbidden thoughts. *I remember all too well. Where have you been, Shaker? You said you'd be able to spend more time with me this year.*

I'm sorry. I've been trying to arrange some uninterrupted time with you. It's taking longer than I anticipated. Please, have patience, Debbie.

Well, when do you anticipate being able to see me?

There was no answer.

Damn him. But he is right, I should contact Titus. If he asks about Shaker, I'll either come off as insecure or angry, because hell, I am both for sure. But it's Sheila's life. In no world does possible embarrassment justify staying silent.

Reluctantly Debbie reached for the phone. Before she could grasp it, the voice was in her mind. *I'm here, Debbie.*

Titus? she answered mentally, surprised.

Are you alone? I will come now, if that is all right.

Yes. Debbie got up and locked her office door. As she was turning to go back to her desk, Titus appeared in front of her. "Hello, Sister Kin," he said formally, then a smile crinkled his flushed face.

"I have to ask, were you checking on me?" Debbie said curtly, giving him a look.

"No. You said my name aloud. I have a ward on mention of myself. It was easy to tap in."

"Tap in" to my head. God. Debbie shook her head but smiled, too. "I suppose you heard my thoughts."

Titus nodded. "Enough to know I needed to see you posthaste. I should take a look at Sheila. She is at home, with Song?"

"Yes. Can you please see her today? Do whatever you believe might be able to awaken her."

"Of course. I should have asked after her before now. But with all that happened last year, I didn't. My apologies, Sister Kin."

All that happened. Shaker possessing Jett, us getting married, my getting pregnant then losing the baby, the priest and his guardian angel pursuing us and exorcising Sheila, Jett's death and Shaker's return to hell, only to get out again bound to someone else. Sheila's possession by an enemy demon that almost killed me, before Myrrh burned its body and made it one of many in her murder of crows.

"You are safe now," Titus said, laying a comforting hand on her shoulder. "Please, do not relive the bad of the old year. This year is bound to be better."

"Thanks, but you can't know that."

"Yes, I can," he intoned. "Formidable enemies you faced are finally gone, you are safe, Pandora is a haven now for our friends, and Shaker is now positioned almost as well as me. Devlin is still your ally, Debbie, and his affairs are also finally set to rights, after a few years of nothing but strife. This will be an excellent year for us, and for Pandora." He patted her shoulder with his clawed hand. "I believe I can wake Sheila. It's better that you didn't tell me immediately, as that gave her time to heal and rest. It's also good Song has kept her body toned with exercise in the meantime. After shocks such as these, a human host's biggest problem is often regaining full mobility after extended bedrest."

That someone else besides her and Song thought that Sheila might make a full recovery filled Debbie with relief and gratitude. "Thank you, Titus." She hugged him impulsively.

Titus grunted, but there was a pleased note to it. "You are welcome. And yes, Shaker sends his regards."

"Is he being treated well?" Debbie said carefully. *Do not tell me his new Mistress has made him become her lover.*

"I wouldn't tell you that," Titus said, shifting uneasily as he read her thoughts. "That is not my business. But to my knowledge she has not, so I can say as much. But yes, he's being treated well. He's been busy on orders for her, but also in creating a small home for himself on Devlin's vast estate."

Debbie lost her temper. "Are you telling me he's not seen me in weeks because he's busy building a house? I already have a house!"

"It is not my place," Titus restated. "But my feeling is that he liked being able to give you things, as Jett. He can't possess anyone now, for danger to his present Mistress. The same goes for having a day job; it would not be permitted, save for working for Devlin, which is what he is doing."

"He's working for Devlin?" Debbie repeated, disbelief in her words.

"Hayden has been without a maintenance team for a few years now," Titus said carefully. "Lash used to head it up, but most of his men that were trained for such duties were killed within a two-year span. They couldn't be replaced except with new men and Lash himself had a period where he was very ill, so these new men only had a little training. I cannot go into details, but there are large sections of fence, walls, roofing, and other structures that need to be seen to, not to mention cemetery duties."

"Cemetery duties?" Debbie repressed a shiver.

"I am a demon, and you are aware of what needs I have," Titus said stiffly. "But I do not eat my colleagues."

He's offended. "I'm sorry, I didn't mean to imply anything."

"Many of Devlin's men fell in the attack last spring. They were hastily buried, with only temporary markers. Several more fell last summer in attacks, and several more this past fall and winter. Part of the contract they sign when pledging themselves into Devlin's service is that all their funeral expenses are paid, and their final resting place taken care of in perpetuity. It was a kindness on Devlin's part to add that last, but it makes for a large graveyard after several hundred years. This must be maintained, and new stones sculpted and engraved as needed, according to the religion each guard adhered to."

"Why did Devlin add that to his contract?" Debbie asked. "You told me you've been with him since he ascended to power in this country, so you must know."

"I advised him to, as it's a small matter to reanimate a corpse. Even males taught not to fear anything can and do likely run when a former friend they just buried shows up at the door. A mate or child might welcome a dead man in, glad that their loved one is not really dead. They never see the weapon in his hand until it's too late. Detonation devices can easily be carried in by such a being. There's also the ability to copy a body, if you have enough of their

8

flesh, hair, and bones. But mostly I advised it because there are magics that can be used on even a skeleton to see snatches of what the person once saw when it still lived. It was and is better that guards who fall at Hayden remain there, so that no one disturbs their rest."

Debbie groped for words but found none. *Is all that true? What kind of world have I married into?*

"I digress. Shaker is helping to sculpt the gravestones, training the new men in building, and doing some landscaping." Titus smiled. "He enjoys building structures, he always has. But this is also a rest for him, after his return to this plane, Debbie. What he did for you cost him, both in energy and in resilience. He will be visiting you soon, take it as fact. Now I must go, you always get me talking more than I mean to." He hugged her, then disappeared.

"Damn it," Debbie said, running her fingers through her hair. "I should have asked him about Latham's Landing." She pulled the file of the same name out of the stack and paged through it. "*Origin of Fear* would make a fantastic summer horror film."

Last year, Shaker had been against making *Origin of Fear*, his excuse that a true demon presided over the haunted island mansion featured in the tale, and that the house itself was real, not fiction. He'd also indicated that the author who had submitted it was a surname for someone of dark power that was attempting to play some kind of game with him, that whomever it was knew Jett Black was really Shaker in disguise. Debbie's instructions to Sheila had been that the project was to be put on hold for now, because of Shaker's information. But the project had been Sheila's favorite, and it was obvious from the notes in Sheila's handwriting that her friend had ignored her advice.

"She found the house," Debbie breathed, slipping an 8 x 10 color photo out of the folder. It showed the remains of what looked like a house listing to one side in the middle of a lake, only the top floor visible. The lower floors and base were flooded in water. *Shaker should be relieved at that. It would be impossible to use this site for shooting a film. It's dilapidated.* Debbie scanned further into the folder.

There were copious notes on legends about the house from interviews, and excerpts from local papers on drownings and disappearances. Sheila had contacted several people, trying to find out who had rights to the house and the lake. There were scribbled out names and numbers, then finally a listing for a Mr. Staahl along with a couple exclamation points, and the notation "the retired police chief?" and "How'd he afford this? Who *really* owns the island and the lake?" But there was also a string of curse words, and the note that Staahl had refused her offer of money to let them so much as film the house from land for the film. That was the last note in the file.

I'd worry that the demon who possessed Sheila had something to do with Latham's Landing, but that entity didn't touch this file in all her time here. Debbie quickly flipped through the stack of other projects; each movie file had notes more recent than this in a stranger's hand; the notes were just on a separate page in the back of the file, not in the margins. Progress had been made on all of the others. *Just not this one. Either the demon took seriously my order to leave it alone, or she was also leery of the island.*

Debbie grabbed a pen and a Post-It. *Either way, if Sheila…when Sheila comes back, she'll want to resume work on this. So the next step is we need another house to stand in for this one, someplace we can flood as needed, preferably at adjustable water levels. We can make the movie closer to home, maybe up north in Oregon? Use the legends to make the film intro, lead into the college kids script we bought called Origin of Fear for the main plot, then end it with shots of the clippings, to give it a real-life scary ending.* "Good as the *Blair Witch*," Debbie said in approval, jotting down her thoughts.

She flipped down to *Hell to Pay*, the movie she was planning to bank the new end of the year around. As Song had said, this was also up to date: actors and actresses had been cast for the major roles, the script rewrite she'd wanted was done, and filming was set to begin in early February. She put that folder aside to take the script home to check out the differences for the one she'd scanned months ago, then looked at the last few folders.

""*Everlasting*"? What is this?" Debbie scanned the first few pages, then the back notes. "A mortal woman sells her soul to create a lasting legacy through art for her brother and his family? You have got to be kidding me." By the acquired date, this was a script that the demon masquerading as Sheila had bought. There were copious notes on the film: ideas for casting and for fleshing out of the script, which looked at best rudimentary. Ideas for setting. Ideas for affordable locations. "Must have been her pet project." Debbie put that on the pile with *Origin of Fear*. "I guess I'll have a couch weekend. But it's not like I'm doing anything else."

Two of the remaining three were the movies Sheila had talked to her about before, *What Matter's Not* and *Sacrifice*, both of which had been bought by Angel Pictures. Debbie flipped through both of them just to check that they were what they appeared to be, then recycled them.

The last was another film she had never heard of, *Dare to Tell*. "Wait, I do remember this. I had asked Sheila to find me a movie that we could use this name for." She opened the file folder. In that same stranger's handwriting, she saw copious notes, and a complete script, as *Everlasting* had. But this also had casting and location done. The last note said that shooting could begin in summer, if not sooner.

"Damn that bitch had a set of balls on her, to go ahead and cast, book location, and everything else without even showing me the script for approval," Debbie mused. She skimmed the first few pages.

A woman was being visited by a ghost of a dead friend who kept asking her to intervene to save her child. "Well-written, but not very exciting." She flipped to the synopsis. "An urban career woman denies her psychic abilities until a horrific near-death experience leaves her seeing ghosts and dreading death. She relocates to a remote location, leaving her boyfriend, friends, and family to run a bed and breakfast in an old estate on behalf of a reclusive dying man. But the place has ghosts of its own, some of whom have witnessed murder. When local teens begin to go missing as they did ten years prior, she must decide if she dares to tell the police what happened to them." *Wow. Definitely has possibilities!*

"Probably *Dare to Tell* can begin shooting in the summer if these actors and location are sound, possibly before, depending on what budget we have to work with. I need to go over the numbers, and also read the entire script." Debbie rubbed her eyes. "Sheila, you'd better wake up 'cause I need you."

That night, Debbie relaxed with a glass of wine, the scripts to *Everlasting* and *Dare to Tell*, and her three hellhounds on the couch, as Song paced the carpet, clearly worried. Titus had told Song not to enter. He was in Debbie's guest bedroom with Sheila's unconscious body, sequestered with the door closed.

Song made a nervous noise. "He's still in there after five hours. What could he possibly be doing?"

"You know more about this that I do. What could he be doing?"

"Okay, okay, I know it's nothing bad, but I'm nervous."

"She's not going to blame you for fucking a stranger and not realizing it wasn't her," Myrrh said bluntly, entering from the deck, one of her crows on her shoulder. "She's just going to be happy to wake up."

"You don't know Sheila," Song said darkly, then pushed past her into the night.

"Aren't you tactful," Debbie said snidely. "How could you say that? You know she's anxious. I'm anxious myself about the same thing. I let a bitch from Hell invade my friend and use her like a puppet."

"You didn't know."

"I should have known. She was acting so bitchy–"

"Yes," a voice came weakly from the doorway. "You should've known, Debbie. But that's not going to help us now." Sheila stood there, supported by both the doorway and Shaker. The hellhounds scrabbled, bolting into the shadow of the couch and disappearing.

"Sheila!" Debbie set down her wine, slopping some over the edge in her haste, and ran to hug her friend. Sheila hugged her back weakly.

"She'll be fine, but I recommend a long restful weekend," Titus said, coming from behind Shaker. "She's as healed as I can make her. What she needs now is a little TLC, and a lot of interaction."

Debbie looked at him oddly.

"She remembers parts of the last few months, but not everything. Tell her what happened, all of it. I must return to Devlin."

"What do I owe you, Titus?" Sheila asked, turning to him. "I know your help isn't free. I would still be comatose if not for you."

"I'd ask for a bit of your soul, but it's still healing," Titus said. Debbie smiled at first, then realized he meant it, and dropped her eyes. "Instead I'd appreciate if you would give my wife a job."

Debbie's gaze snapped back to Titus, and Sheila's mouth dropped open. "Your...wife?"

"You met her at Debbie's wedding, remember?" Shaker prompted. "Her name is Leri."

"She is Devlin's sorceress, isn't she?" Myrrh said, making it more of a statement than a question. "Her place should be at Hayden then, protecting him."

Titus flicked his red eyes to her but didn't answer.

"There was a falling out of sorts," Shaker supplied. "This has happened before, and Leri will likely go back to working for Devlin in time. But for now she needs to hide in plain sight, so to speak. Working here on the opposite coast would give her a means to exist independently while his temper eased."

"Wait, um…"

"Look, I don't want to offend you," Sheila interjected, talking over Debbie. "But if Leri has run afoul of Devlin, we can't hire her, or we risk he may pull his support for Pandora."

"Devlin is a current investor, our largest one. He's going to pay for two of our future pictures," Debbie added. "What would Leri do at Pandora, anyway? You can't want her to be a janitor?"

"You said you had staff openings," Myrrh said quickly. "Could she fill any of those vacancies?"

What's her interest in this? "Marketing, Location Scout, Security Manager."

"Leri could do locations," Titus said quickly. "She knows this country well, and Europe, too."

"Can she take the initiative? Negotiate for good prices? When we choose a location for a film, we are trying to shoot not only in-state, but as close to our headquarters as possible to save costs. We also try to shoot most of any particular movie in one site, again to save costs. I know Leri can do magic, but as much as it would be fantastic to use her teleportation power to grant us access to sites all over the world, something tells me it wouldn't be prudent to let the entire company know we have an actual sorceress on the payroll."

"I see your point," Titus said gruffly. "Yes, she can negotiate, and she could also teleport to view and book locations, saving you her travelling fees. She could also do a little magic to make locations that were inexpensive and nearby…more a perfect fit for a particular film."

"Will she cause trouble?" Myrrh questioned. "I know what she is capable of, Titus."

"You should, you are alive because of her," Titus said, again staring at her steadily with his crimson eyes.

"I hadn't forgotten," Myrrh concurred with a nod. She turned to Debbie. "If she will agree not to kill and to do her best to fit in, I think she could be an asset."

"Good. I'll tell her tonight, and ask her to come herself, to pledge assurances," Titus said, relieved.

"Wait one Goddamned minute!" Sheila said.

"We didn't agree to this," echoed Debbie. "She can't stay here with us."

"I'll get her a local place," Titus assented. "I don't see why this isn't good for everyone. You said you needed personnel, specifically ones not afraid to work at Pandora. Leri will not only work hard, she'll be an asset in any attack. Though with her and Myrrh around, you're not likely to get attacked at all."

"Is she a demon?" Sheila asked. "We can't supply her sustenance, only a paycheck."

"No, Leri is a dark faerie, like Myrrh," Shaker chimed in. "I'm sorry, but I need to get back, as does Titus." He blew a kiss to Debbie, then the two brothers disappeared. The three hellhounds immediately crawled out of the shadow of the couch, and jumped back up on the couch near Debbie, setting themselves down with happy sighs.

"That's just fucking great," Debbie said, tossing down the files on the coffee table. "Thanks a lot for—" She trailed off, seeing that Myrrh had left. "Damn it, she's always doing that."

"Come and sit down," Song said, guiding Sheila to the couch and helping her sit. "I'm so glad you're well again."

"How can you be here?" Sheila asked her. "Our bond was broken."

"I inhabited Jett's sister Rhonda for a while. You remember, before you…well, she's pretty crazy now from our time together, so she's in an institution. I got her to agree to be my Mistress in one of her lucid moments, in return for leaving her alone, which let me manifest by myself. But now that you're back, I'll go possess her and we can be together again." Song put her hand over Sheila's.

Sheila recoiled, taking her hand away. "I'm…I'm going to need some time, Song."

Song bit her lip. "You're blaming me for what happened to you. Debbie didn't know that you weren't you, either!"

"Yeah, but she wasn't fucking me! You were! How could you not know, Song?"

"I thought you just…decided that you liked new things. It's not like we were married for years, Sheila, and knew everything there was to know about one another!"

"Look, I should let you, um, talk," Debbie said, trying to extricate herself from the dogs and the couch.

"No, I'll go," Song said sadly. "If you don't want me here, I need to go decide what to do." She disappeared.

"I'm sorry," Debbie said. "I should've known you were possessed, Sheila. You're right."

"I'm sorry," Sheila said, coming to the couch and hugging her, as she began crying. Both women cried for a few minutes, then just hugged each other. Debbie pulled a blanket from the back of the couch to cover Sheila and the dogs, then went to the kitchen and got them both a pint of ice cream and spoons. "Here, Magnum Cracked Vanilla. I got it for you, I've been saving it for months."

"Probably ice-crystals galore," Sheila retorted with a huge grin, accepting a spoon. They both dug in.

"Where do you want me to start?" Debbie said, scooping out another spoonful. "I have no idea where to begin. After Henry hit you?"

"Just give me a quick overview," Sheila said. "I'll ask questions from there."

"I'm so glad to have you back," Debbie said in pure relief. "Okay, I'll start in August. Henry got sent to jail for assault, but he's out on parole I think already. But I have a restraining order against him my lawyer Catarella arranged, so he can't come near Pandora or here, ever. Titan Pictures' huge movie *Escalation* flopped after their president was outed for dogfighting, and their stock fell to almost nothing. They got eaten by corporate raiders over the holidays. The studio is gone, which is a huge relief. Titan and Henry created most of the problems we faced last year."

"And Myrrh?"

"She saved me from the demon who was inhabiting you. I thought you were just becoming evil, so tried to get help, but Titus said there was nothing to be done. Myrrh and Shaker helped me get you to a convent, but it didn't do anything."

"It did," Sheila admitted. "I was able to break the hold the demon had on me. I told the sisters, but they wouldn't listen, and they had no phone or internet, so I couldn't contact anyone. Then a priest came and got me out, but as soon as I stepped off the grounds, the demon got me again." She began crying. "I killed him, Debbie, the demon made me. He's buried in an unmarked grave."

"So you remember it all?"

Sheila nodded, sniffling. "Even that you tried to kill yourself."

"I did," Debbie murmured. "I was stupid and weak."

"Don't be too hard on yourself. I tried to kill myself, too, but the demon just laughed. I couldn't move my own body at all, it was awful." She took a deep breath. "That's why I think Song and I aren't going to work. Knowing possession from the point of the person being taken over, I can't condone it being done by my partner. I also don't want ever to be a mark for demon hunters again."

"You might be able to work something out," Debbie said vaguely, at a loss for words and feeling loyal to Song, who she was already missing. "She did take care of you for months."

"I know. I still love her, and I feel guilty, too. I don't know what to do. Which is why we need some space." She sighed. "I'll send her some flowers tomorrow. Is she still at the Black Rose? I should've been more explicit: I remember everything the demon did when it had me, what it said, etc. I have two gaps though, from when I got severed from Song by Henry's attack, until the demon possessed me, and from when the demon left until now. But both seem to be only a few weeks, maybe? You hired that guy Gore to kill the priest then."

Debbie nodded. "Yes, that priest can't hurt either of us again, not that he'd want to now."

"Did you keep my house?"

"Song didn't sell it, no, she was worried you'd be upset when you awoke. But I'm not sure what the demon might have done in her months as you. They were living at the house, or so Rack told me. I think Song kept it up after the demon left you, though when she found the time, I'm not sure." Debbie paused. "Look, you probably need some time to think about everything that's happened. If you aren't ready to go back to Pandora, then take some time off."

"Thank you, but no," Sheila said stubbornly. "I need to take back my life, and it's not going to get easier. I've missed enough time."

"Um…you're still married to Rhonda, too," Debbie mentioned reluctantly. "Although you probably could divorce now that she's been declared insane."

"I did that," Sheila said, rubbing her eyes. "That wasn't just the demons, it was me, taking the easy route. I owe Rhonda an apology and to talk to her, find out what she wants. I'll give her a divorce if she wants one."

"Is there anything I can do to help?"

"Yes. Get dressed and come home with me," Sheila said, staggering to her feet. Then she looked at Debbie. "Sorry, I didn't mean that the way it sounded. I just need to see my place and I'm worried about going alone."

"Of course," Debbie said, groaning mentally as she threw off the throw.

CHAPTER TWO

January

Debbie checked in the rearview mirror uneasily as she drove. There was no sign of a crow escort, something she'd been so used to with Myrrh. *It sounds ridiculous but I don't feel safe without some being of mystical power as an escort. How pitiful is that?* She let out a breath. *Remember, neither of you is bound to a demon now. You don't have anything to fear.*

Debbie pulled into Sheila's driveway. There was a car already in the driveway, and lights were on inside.

"Whose car is this?" Sheila asked Debbie.

"Rhonda's," Song answered, coming out with her arms full of clothes. "I'll be out of here in a few minutes."

"Look, you don't have to leave." Sheila sighed. "Yes, I'm upset about what happened, but I know you wouldn't have done it purposely. You can stay, we just can't be intimate…now."

"Um, we should go inside," Debbie prompted, watching a light come on across the wide street. "Your neighbors live a lot closer than mine do, and it's close to midnight."

Song carried her load back inside, followed by Sheila and Debbie. She put it down on a bunch of boxes.

"You packed fast," Debbie commented, then flushed.

"Sheila told me that we might move to better digs in the new year," Song said softly. "This was after Jett died and Shaker got sent back to Hell. She said that there was a good chance that you'd decide to resign, Debbie, and she'd be asked to step into the CEO role. She asked me to pack. I just haven't gotten around to unpacking."

Debbie narrowed her eyes. *What else had the demon who'd possessed Sheila promised Song? Had Song had an inkling of the possession and lied?*

"I know that demon told you that," Sheila said slowly. "But it's not going to happen."

"I'm not angry," Song said, shifting uneasily. "She told me she wanted other lovers, male lovers. When I offered to be male for her, she…she said I made a better female. She said Harp couldn't come back, either, even if he was free, as he'd failed you." She bit her lip. "She made me watch."

Debbie didn't know where to look, and wished she could leave, but stayed silent.

"I'm sorry for what she did to you, and to us," Sheila said. "Please, just stay tonight in the guest bedroom and go to sleep. We'll talk in the morning."

Song tried a hopeful smile, then let it fall as she moved away, the door shutting behind her.

Sheila looked around. "At least she kept the walls the same color, even if she replaced most of the furniture. I hope my credit isn't wrecked."

Debbie looked around, searching for words that wouldn't offend. "It looks like she copied an ad from a magazine. She must have gotten a decorator."

"It's not bad," Sheila managed. "I hate that. After what she did to me, this place should look like a cheap skank's lair and instead it looks nicer than when I left it."

"But you saw it like this when you were possessed," Debbie said slowly. "You said you were able to see what she did as you. So you should've known that the house looked this way, Sheila. Why did you really want me to come here?"

"Sometimes I didn't want to see," Sheila said with a shudder, leaning out to grab the back of an easy chair. "Sometimes I closed my eyes and covered my ears. There's a way to...um, log off, so to speak, when you're possessed. I see why people go insane now like Titus said they did last year."

I need to stop being so paranoid and start being a friend. "Look, don't think about that," Debbie said urgently, taking hold of her shoulders. "You came through it and its over. You're a strong person, Sheila, and you're not going to be possessed again. Whatever chinks you had in your armor from being bound to a demon are gone."

Sheila blinked back tears, then coughed. "You're right. I have to move ahead. The first thing I should do is go talk to Song, and not put it off."

Christ, I'm trying to comfort her and instead I'm pushing her too fast. "Maybe you should rest."

"I've slept enough," Sheila said raggedly. "Please go home, Debbie. As much as I'd like you here, you need to rest, too. I can do this. I wasn't sure I could, but I can. I'll call you tomorrow."

Debbie wavered, unsure of whether she should leave Sheila alone with Song. *Funny that I never would have considered that dangerous before tonight.* "Okay, but first I'm going to go with you around the house and check no one else is here, then make sure that you set the alarm after all the windows and doors are locked. Then we're going to call the alarm company and have your password changed, and make sure only you and Song are still on the list of people who can okay a tripped alarm. Then I'll go."

Sheila began to cry and hugged her. "You're a good friend. Did I tell you that already?"

"You are, too," Debbie said, tearing up. "You are too."

～

Debbie drove home, weary but glad the night sky was still dark. *I can sleep in, and it will be fine, tomorrow's Saturday. Then I'll read those scripts.*

She turned into the driveway. *Weird that the demon hadn't changed the passcode or added anyone else's name to the account. She must not have had any demon friends she trusted, even with all the allies she attacked me with the night she abducted me. She probably wanted to keep control by not letting any of them share her power as VP.*

Debbie parked, then unlocked the front door, almost bumping into Bawdir.

"Good evening," the man with large black crow wings said, as he bowed.

How does he do that and not overbalance with the weight of the wings? Ah, they unfurled a bit at the ends. "Hi. Why are you, um, in human form?"

"My Queen asked me to watch over you. She left with the murder to check on her home, a magical alarm was triggered."

"Oh. I'm going to bed after I shower, so you don't have to stay."

"Should I assist you. You look very tired."

Debbie did a double take. "Did you just ask to take a shower with me?"

Bawdir folded his arms in front of his chest, then smiled tightly. "I'm offering to stay nearby as you shower so you don't hit your head if you slip and lay there all night. My wings can get wet, but they would be useless to me if I allowed soap on them, which would remove the natural oil and make me unable to fly if I changed to crow form."

Debbie blinked at him, then flushed slightly. "My apologies, you can see I'm tired and I'm not thinking straight. Sure, if you would, please stay within hearing distance so that I can tell you when I'm done."

"Of course."

Debbie hurried into her room and shut the door, then started the water running. She showered fast, then rubbed on a little lotion, enjoying the relaxing scent. Turning off the light, she called for the hellhounds. "Baroness, Pitch, Pike!"

The three dogs appeared beside the bed from out of its narrow shadow, then leapt up onto the bed, happily stretching out.

"Hey, I need room too," Debbie said, pushing them over so she was able to lay down. "Bawdir, I'm safe in bed. Thanks for watching over me."

"Of course. Goodnight Debbie," came his polite reply.

∾

Debbie awoke with a yawn, belatedly realizing it was still dark. *What the hell? How can I be fully rested when it had to be two in the morning when I went to sleep, if not three?* She rose partway and looked at the bedside clock. "This says it's close to nine. Damnit, have I slept all the way through to Saturday night?" *Wait, the dogs wouldn't have let me do that.* She looked around, noticing that they were missing. "Baroness! Pike! Pitch!"

There was no answer.

Stymied—and wondering if the dogs' absence meant that Titus had returned with Shaker—Debbie left the bedroom, looking through the rooms for her dogs and calling. Finally she opened the sliding glass door to the deck, the sliver of the moon leaving shadows everywhere.

"Baroness! Pike! Pitch!" *This can't be right; they would be here. I must be dreaming.*

"They aren't here," a polite voice whispered. "Only I am."

Debbie gave a start, then let out a huge breath. "Damn, you scared me, Bawdir."

"Did I?" he said with a small smile. "Or were you perhaps looking for me?"

"I was looking for my dogs."

"You need to go back to bed." With a graceful deft movement, Bawdir swept Debbie literally off her feet and into his arms. He used a wing to slide the door shut, then locked it.

"I don't think—" Debbie began, but he covered her lips with his. The kiss was almost chaste at first, but then his lips began searching hers, his tongue teasing her closed mouth until it opened to his questing tongue. *He tastes like mint and flowers.*

The crowman lay her on the bed in the utter darkness, slipping off her pajama pants, revealing her naked flesh. Eagerly, his hand sought her thatch, parting the lips. "Too fast," he whispered, then came the touch of his hands parting her thighs and the warmth of his tongue as he teased her lips before slipping between them to circle her clit in slow motions.

Debbie was moving all over by now, unable to keep still, an almost physical pain in her groin aching from needing to be filled. She could feel her channel moisten in hopeful readiness. She arched up, her firm nipples tenting the front of her pajama top.

Bawdir tasted her sweet excitement. With a grunt of pleasure, he moved off her, then she felt his hands on her hips, turning her even as he pulled her to all fours. With an eager groan he thrust the tip of his hot, hard prick into her wetness. His hands reached up under her pajama top, grabbing a breast in each hand. With excruciating slowness he pushed inside, his huge cock slowly stretching her.

Even in her lustful excitement, Debbie paused, a slight twinge of panic in how gargantuan the crowman's penis was. *This is a dream, just enjoy yourself.* She made herself relax, then let out a little gasp as the crowman ran out of room inside her. Carefully, he began to move his rigid organ,, in and out in easy languid strokes, squeezing her breasts possessively as he kissed and licked her neck.

Debbie moaned, wanting it to go on and on but yearning already to come. Still, it was strange, as he hadn't said anything to her at all. *This is my dream, I should be able to make him say something sexy, shouldn't I?*

Bawdir pushed hard against her suddenly with a moan of such desire, breaking her thought as she let out a cry echoing his need. At the sound, he thrust faster, burying himself in her with each plunge. Debbie felt her orgasm coming and begged him silently to wait as she reached for it, feeling the white light coming closer, then bursting over her.

"Yes! Yes! Yes!"

Bawdir plunged deep one last time, then his hips spasmed against her as he came. He sagged slightly, then withdrew. Carefully he got off the bed and padded into the bathroom. There came the sound of water running.

In a moment he was back, laying something into her hand. "A wet washcloth."

"Thanks." Debbie used it to clean herself, then he took it and went back to the bathroom. He returned in a moment, sitting beside her in the darkness.

Why wasn't the dream ending? "I'm surprised you didn't say anything." She extended her hand toward him.

He clasped it. "I was afraid if I did, you might reconsider. I've not had a woman in many, many years."

Debbie chuckled. "I'm glad to be the one to break your fast."

"Thank you," he said, kissing her hand.

"Is this goodbye?" *Damn, I thought he'd give a repeat performance, at least.*

"I'm afraid I held out at long as I could," he apologized. "I've not a lot of stamina. But if you are still aroused, I can offer you…others."

Debbie's breath caught in her throat. "Others?"

"Others of the murder. I sent them away to be alone with you tonight, but they aren't far. Myrrh left three of us to watch you. They would be…more vocal, as you indicated you would like."

Debbie chuckled. "Why would they want me? I'm not a young girl, Bawdir."

"No, you're not. You're a lovely voluptuous woman that any man would be eager to bed, if not die for." He kissed her hand again. "I only wish I could raise my cock again to service you."

Debbie's lust stirred again, hearing the desire in his voice. "What are their names?"

"Fenrir and Everyn. Do you want them to come? If so, say their names."

"Fenrir. Everyn."

Bawdir kissed her hand again, then rose. "I'll go out to stand guard. Enjoy yourself." He left, leaving the door open. In a few moments, there came the sound of two people entering, then shutting the door.

One sat on the bed near her. "It's Fenrir, Debbie. I hope you don't mind if I go first?"

At his words, Debbie felt suddenly tawdry. *Stop it. This is a dream, not real life. You want to be faithful in real life to Shaker. Having sex in dreams is the best way to do that, and he's already said as much. For all you know Shaker is tuned into this dream watching you, enjoying himself.*

"Debbie?" Fenrir said, touching her shoulder. "Have you reconsidered?"

"No," Debbie said, gripping his arm with her hand. "But I want you to say sexy things, ok? But no swearing or stuff like that."

"Of course," Fenrir said. He kissed her hungrily, his mouth crushing hers in a kiss far different than Bawdir's, then dropped his head, nipping at her breasts through her pajama top.

The erect nipples were tender, and Debbie arched her back, letting out a cry.

"Oh, eager, are we?" Fenrir grabbed a nipple lightly through the cloth, then pulled gently, mouthing it. Debbie let out another desperate cry.

"Are you ready for me to slide in?" he murmured, kissing her throat as his hand slipped between her thighs. "My Goddess, you're soaked."

"You're a liar," Everyn growled from the corner. "You're just saying that because you know I'm already hard as a rock over here waiting my turn."

"Come, brother and feel her."

Debbie knew they weren't lying, she could feel it herself, how excited she was. *Why not, this was pure sex, with no inhibitions, just wanton wanting.*

Everyn climbed onto the bed, a second hand slipping between her thighs. "Shh...mm, you're right. Even her flesh is swollen." He slipped a finger gently inside her. "Mmm, yes, you're going to feel so good, Debbie. I only hope I feel as good to you."

"Hey," Fenrir protested.

Everyn moved on top of Debbie, taking her hand and putting it on his erection. The flesh was slick and hot, already slippery with precum. "How do I feel?

Debbie dipped her hand between her thighs, then circled her hand and ran it up and down the shaft, lubricating the swollen flesh as Everyn twitched and moaned. "How do I feel?"

"Too good to wait a second longer." Everyn parted her thighs, lifting her hips as he pushed inside, sliding in easily. He began pumping hard. "You feel so good, Debbie, you're so wet and warm, I'm sliding so deep into you, God, its fucking wonderful!" He let out a sharp cry. "God, I'm trying so hard not to come, please please come for me, I want to hear you come!"

God he's as big as Bawdir. Debbie wrapped her legs around him, with every thrust he filled her to bursting, enjoying the feel of his root pushing against her clit every time he drove himself home.

"Come for me," he murmured raggedly, thrusting. "Please I want to hear you come."

"Make me," Debbie teased, kissing his throat. "Rub that big cock of yours against my clit and make me come."

Everyn let out a cry of almost pain, then stopped thrusting. "I can't, I can't move, I thrust one more time inside your luscious body and I'm going to spurt."

"Get off her then," Fenrir growled, pushing at Everyn. "And go. If you can't please her, you aren't worth her time."

"Roll on your back," Debbie instructed. "I'll come easily then." Before Everyn could protest, she moved her hips, his penis slipping out effortlessly as she slid out from beneath him.

Everyn eagerly rolled on his back, a whisper of his wings as he settled. Debbie mounted him eagerly, impaling herself all the way on his erection. She began to move at once.

"God yes, work me, do whatever you want to me, but please, please let me hear you come!"

Debbie was almost there and in a last push of his body into hers she felt the climax wash over her. Everyn felt it and grabbed her tight against, him, bucking wildly against her, shouting over and over. He held her tight against him, until his spasms finally stopped. "I don't want you to leave me," he said almost shyly, when she moved to dismount. "I think if you'd only grind against me, I'd get hard again, and we could…"

"Get out," Fenrir grumbled. "You're done."

Everyn grumbled, but he kissed Debbie's hand quickly, then left. Debbie then felt another washcloth being pushed into her hand. Again, she cleaned herself, then Fenrir moved over her, lying beside her. "Are you sure you want me?" he asked gently, touching her wet thatch. "I'll understand if you can't again."

"If you're gentle, I can," Debbie said, reaching for him. "But only if you want me, too."

He hugged her, then guided her hand down to his groin. The phallus was engorged and hard, throbbing slightly. "You can feel I do. Do you want me on my back, too?"

"Yes," Debbie breathed, as he moved her atop him to straddle his hips. "Fill me."

"Gladly." Fenrir pushed up gently, filling her fully. Debbie bore down, taking him in completely so there was not an inch between their joined bodies.

"I'm going to move," Debbie said, doing just that, so his penis within her stroked just the littlest bit. "You thrust up into me as deep as you can. I want all of you, every inch. I want it slow and deep and hard, for as long as you can last."

"It's yours," Fenrir murmured. "Take it. Take me."

Debbie took him in again and again, loving the feel of being so aroused, so wet, so full. When she came the first time, he came right after. But when she went to dismount, he stopped her, beginning to move again. After they came again a few moments later, he stopped.

"Please, if you'll roll off, I'll clean you." Debbie did as he asked, feeling the gentle strokes of the wet washcloth on her still very swollen flesh.

Fenrir returned to her after disposing of the washcloths, and lay beside her, pulling her into his arms. "Thank you."

"Thank you." Debbie kissed his cheek. "It was wonderful."

"Do you mind if I lay here, until you fall asleep? My brother crows are watching over us."

"Are you sure they are in any state to keep watch?" Debbie said with a yawn. "I'm going to pass right out."

"Probably not," Fenrir said, chuckling. "But they will force themselves to remain vigilant. We'd be in enough trouble with our Queen if she found we had indulged our lust with you. Adding falling asleep on watch might get us punted right into Hell."

Sleepy as she was, Debbie snorted with laughter. "For being part demon, Myrrh is kind of prudish, isn't she?"

"Taken in comparison with other dark fairies and demons...yes. But she's had to be an adult from a young age, because of her great

29

power. Being locked in rock for decades gives you a tendency to really watch your words and actions after you get out."

"She Who Waits, Song called her. That name, that was because of that imprisonment?"

"Yes," Fenrir said reluctantly after a moment. "But also because even when she was released by Torren, her soon-to-be husband, she stayed out of public life, for the most part. I have been with her for close to fifty years now, and she's always gone her own way. There was speculation from others who had power that she was biding her time, waiting for something. But that was mostly from people who asked for her support against a foe, and she refused."

"Why is she here defending Pandora, then?"

"Why don't you ask her?"

"I did, she said it was for the money."

"And you think it isn't? Her estate she has in Pennsylvania is large and needs a lot of funds. It's beautiful, yes, but there's a lot of upkeep, even as we souls do what we can to help out."

"Why keep the estate, if it's so large and there's only her and you, especially as it seems most of the time the murder remains in avian form? I don't understand."

"Torren and she were happy there for a couple decades. It was his ancestral home; his family died out. After he was killed, another vampire came to claim it. That was the last time she really showed her power, when she took it back, and made Devlin recognize her as an acting vampire lord for the city it resided in."

"She's not a vampire. He did it?"

"Yes."

"Why would he recognize her as a lord? How could he have, the other vampires must have had a fit."

"They grumbled, but they saw all the ashes of the vampire and his entire clan who had tried to take her home. Devlin's not afraid to fight, but that doesn't mean he'll choose a fight if there's a better option. Myrrh did her part, that county, of all the United States, is the only one where no non-human has been murdered since she took control."

Debbie began to speak, but he held a finger to her lips. "You need to rest, its nearly morning and you've been up all night. Please sleep. Know that none of us are here to harm you, Debbie. We are here to protect you."

~

As soon as Debbie woke in the morning, she slipped her hands down to her mound. *Still slippery, even onto my thighs.* Suddenly worried her lustful dream hadn't been just a dream, she hurried into the bathroom and looked in the hamper. Her clothes from last night were there, but no washcloths. Debbie cleaned up, then threw that washcloth into the hamper, relieved also that all her other washcloths were clean and in place in the cupboard. *It was a dream. Yes, an out of control slutty dream, maybe, but one I really enjoyed.* Blowing a kiss to her reflection, Debbie went to her closet and dressed in sweats, then made her way to the kitchen.

Myrrh was there, sipping some coffee. "Are you cooking breakfast?"

"Is that your way of telling me you want some?" Debbie replied with a laugh.

"Sure, if you're cooking," Myrrh said, smiling.

"You're in a good mood this morning." Debbie got down some pans, then rummaged in the fridge. "I'll have to go shopping, its eggs and toast only."

"That's alright," Myrrh said.

"Where's the murder this morning?" Debbie said, then flushed crimson.

Myrrh seemed not to notice. "They're at my home."

Debbie's flush deepened. *What Bawdir told me in dreams isn't likely true, or it could be, about them helping out at Myrrh's estate. I can't remember for sure if she ever mentioned the name Torren to me, I think she did. She told me he died, that she loved him.* "Please thank Bawdir for watching out for me last night. He was the perfect gentleman."

"He should be," Myrrh commented. "He's near redemption."

"I remember you changing that spirit haunting me into a crow, and the demons who attacked me, too," Debbie said slowly, as she sat down. "You said they would die or redeem themselves in your service. Can you tell me how that works?"

Myrrh studied her for a moment, then nodded once. "You've likely heard from Shaker that demons are fallen angels, at least some of them. Others were born demons. All true demons can trace their roots to fallen angels though, if you go back enough generations. So all true demons have the potential to become angels again."

"True demons"? She must mean intelligent ones like Shaker or Harp versus the kind he called base evil that weren't capable of reasoning, only chaos. He called those Homeless or Takers. "Shaker said there was no way that he could ever be what he was," Debbie blurted, then bit her lip.

"He probably said he couldn't ever be forgiven, with all he's done," Myrrh corrected. "But think about the Bible, what is the New Testament's core message? That everyone who is repentant and believes in Jesus and God can be saved, a.k.a go to Heaven. Does it really make sense that some beings would be denied forgiveness?"

"I don't know," Debbie replied. "I stopped believing in God when I was young and saw how nasty people in the world were. I only began believing again when I met Shaker, because if demons and Hell are real, God and Heaven have to be, too. But after meeting that angel, Rafael, I'm not sure if it's a place I'd want to go. He didn't seem to me like a being that really represented forgiveness, only strict rules and punishment."

"There are a lot of descriptions of what Heaven might be like," Myrrh said slowly. "All of the demons I have ever had in my flock were late generations, less than a hundred years old. They only knew one way to be, and that was evil, which is how they were treated themselves. I offered them a different path. It's a hard path, though, because angels are infallible tools of God. You're right that they seem to be held to a pretty narrow path versus human beings."

"How does working for you make them redeemed? I apologize if this is presumptuous, but you don't seem to know God or Shaker's master personally, so you can't know what their rules are for who gets into Heaven and who gets sent to Hell."

"I don't, and you're misunderstanding me. I don't pronounce my souls redeemed and poof, they go to Heaven. I simply give them a way to exist out of Hell, and a choice to serve me. Aside from helping me, they are given freedom from having to serve Hell's agenda, as in going from Master to Master advancing evil. They have to decide if they want to redeem themselves. You might call it the ultimate free will."

"How can you protect them from Satan?" Debbie whispered the name nervously.

"I use the hellfire to burn the devil's taint out of them. He's got tons of demons, and I guess that he doesn't miss them. The spell I do, it's one I created from scratch. I believe like you that the world is a hard place. No one should be made to serve eternity as a slave. No one should be denied forgiveness, either."

This is a new side of her, one at odds with who I thought she was. "Thank you for being so forthright."

"I have to be," Myrrh said, getting up and putting her cup in the sink. "I needed you to know that my souls aren't immortal, Debbie. They are mortals with high regenerative properties, much like a shifter. They retain much of their strength and any magic they know, but they can be killed."

"Were any of them hurt rescuing me?" Debbie asked. "I'm sorry, I thought they hadn't been hurt, that only my dogs Charon and Lazarus were destroyed."

"Your two former hellhounds are in Heaven, like I told you back then. But yes, several of my crows were hurt badly. They are at my estate healing, which means growing back lost limbs."

"I'm sorry. What can I do?"

"Understand what I've said to you now. I will be around if you need me, but I won't be around as much. I'll leave at least one soul here at all times, likely Bawdir, in case something bad happens."

"That's not an answer to my question. Why do you have to go?"

"No, you can't do anything for those hurt. But be more careful than you were last year. I don't want Bawdir to die saving you because you make a rash decision."

That stung. "Why do you have to go?"

"Because you have a husband and a life to get back to," Myrrh said, reaching out and clasping Debbie's hand. "You're not bound to a demon anymore, and your soul is clear." She laughed, her eyes sparkling. "Well, not clear exactly, but there's no evil taint. Sheila's also more or less clear, and from what Bawdir reported, she and Song are taking some time apart. People freed from possession usually have second thoughts about their life direction."

As much as that's judgmental, she's right. "I think she and I both are. We can't undo what we did. But that doesn't mean we can't move forward in a new direction. Thanks also for leaving Bawdir here. Do you want to work out some kind of payment schedule for this year? We haven't talked about it."

"The only payment I want is for you not to bind a demon to yourself this year," Myrrh said with sarcasm. "You've been given a second chance, Debbie. Use it and be happy."

Debbie glared at the faerie. "Where do you come off as so condescending? Because you're older than I am, even if you look young enough to be my daughter?"

Myrrh blanched and glared back. "Because I didn't expect things to work out as well as they did." Her face softened. "I just want you to be happy. And I believe in Pandora. I think that you could use it as a place to create movies that might really impact the world. I believe in you."

I just cannot figure out this woman. "Thanks, I guess." Debbie let out a breath. "You don't have to be concerned about any demon binding. Shaker and I are still bound by the loyalty vow, but he's another woman's demon now. Titus reports that he's secure. She's probably another high-level vampire, like Devlin."

Myrrh nodded. "That would be good." She folded her arms across her chest.

"You said the crowmen were mortal. How can you transform them from demon to human?"

"Not human. Mortal."

"Ok, mortal."

"Magic."

What happened to all her being forthright? "So they work for you and die of old age or defending you and then what? Bawdir, in my humble opinion, is civilized enough that he could pass for an angel and go back to Heaven."

"I forget how astute you are," Myrrh assented. "Yes, he could likely try at least. But he has told me he would prefer to stay with me. Most of my souls do that."

"Why do they choose to do good instead of evil?"

"You are full of questions this morning. I think because they don't have a master hounding them to do evil. Evil begets more evil, always. I put them back at zero, to make a good euphemism. They can think about what they did in their former life and choose something new. I'm not saying it always works. I have had demons I transformed serve grudgingly and then revert to their evil ways in a short time. I burn them back to Hell when that happens. If they don't want the opportunity of a second chance, I see no point in delaying the inevitable."

"I agree." *You have put me back at zero, too. And you're right that it's made me think a lot about where I go from here.*

CHAPTER THREE

January-February

"THANK YOU ALL FOR COMING THIS MORNING. I'M SORRY ALSO that this meeting didn't take place earlier in the month." Debbie beamed at her assembled team. "I have some announcements and an overview, then I would like an update from all of you."

"As you all know, we had a great year last year. We called it Year of the Demon. You're also aware that this year we have only one film currently in progress. I'm pleased to share that *Destiny in the Ashes*, the third Smoke and Ashes series film, is complete except for a few non-speaking scenes that remain to be shot. We have arranged Jett's younger brother, Brady, to stand in for these, and he's agreed. This will be slated for a Christmas release like the second Smoke and Ashes film was last year. Sheila?"

Sheila stood. "As you know, Jett is up for a posthumous Academy Award for best Actor in an Action movie. *Smoke and Ashes II: Out of the Ashes* was also nominated for Best Action movie. Jett's acting ability aside, it's unlikely that we'll win any awards, given the movie is a sequel. But the film was a major success at the box office, and it will likely garner us a lot of downloads and rentals this coming summer."

"I want to add," Shelia continued. "That *Immortal Confessions*, the vampire tale many people here today discounted, surpassed all expectations and was an even bigger hit than *Smoke and Ashes II*. We expect downloads and sales for that also to be high this coming spring, we have already gotten inquiries. Adeline is already setting our website up for preorders now. Adeline?"

"The website is clear of viruses, and we have additional security in place to protect guests logging in and also corruption of the website by ransomware. What happened last year won't happen this year."

"Yes," Debbie added forcefully. "As you all know we had some bad accidents last fall and winter here at the studio and in the offices, one of which claimed the life of my husband. We have upgraded security, and will be hiring a replacement for Mr. Minor, who its rumored was working to sabotage Pandora on behalf of Titan Pictures."

There were a few sharp intakes of breath, and some of her team looked around at their neighbors.

"We have vetted all remaining employees. You may notice Nelson is also gone. He was also found to be compromised." *Possessed. Killed in my rescue, the demon who possessed him now one of Myrrh's murder.*

"We plan to interview people this coming week for the areas of Marketing, and Security," Sheila added. "Mark has said he prefers to promote one of his team from within to fill Nelson's role overseeing filming."

"What about Location?" Stacy asked. "We never got a replacement for Joshua."

She always had a crush on that cute young vampire. I hope Nathan was able to discover who killed him, there was that other murder up north that was attributed to that killer, but I never heard anything further. "We do have someone doing Location. Her name is Leri."

"And I'm here," a commanding female voice intoned. "Leri White, but just call me Leri, please. I spoke to everyone here ahead of the meeting to introduce myself, to save us time."

Debbie blinked. There opposite her at the end of the table sat Leri, her attire a simple black dress with a black blazer over it. Her brown hair was back again in an elaborate braid, her earrings black shiny stones. "I'm glad you were able to get here for this. We didn't expect you until another week." *I had no idea when to expect you and even if you'd really show at all.*

"I had to give notice," Leri said primly. "My former boss told me I should leave, so I did. Thank you again for making me part of your team. I'll do my best for Pandora, and for you."

She certainly seems like she means it. But is this an act? "Thank you. We're kind of jumping around here, but please meet with me and Sheila after the meeting to go over our current needs."

Leri nodded. "Of course."

"Okay," Debbie said, looking around at her team. "Back to stats. We have solid backing for two movies, and with the success of last year's pictures, we plan to release three movies this year, tops, based on how fast we can shoot the pictures. As I said, we only have Smoke and Ashes III close to finished right now. I know you've all looked over the scripts for the other 2 films by this time, so let me officially announce them. They are *Hell to Pay* and *Dare to Tell*."

Sheila shot her an incredulous look.

"I know everyone here has also heard about another film called *Origin of Fear*. Let me say that we DO want to begin shooting this picture this summer if we can. Yes, it was originally slated to be shot and launch this year. But I was and am hesitant to try to get out a movie that is nothing more than an unfinished script at this time, when both of the other films I mentioned not only have had script revisions done, but they also have casting pretty much done. We are just waiting now to hear back from a few actors and actresses. *Hell to Pay* pretty much takes place in a few easy to shoot locations: an isolated house in the country near a pond and some forest, a hospital, a city street, and a bar. All of these should be easy to shoot here in the studio except the street, we'll need to use a film lot for that. We'll need some location shots for the beginnings of each scene; Leri, please look into that and see if you can secure some sites."

"On it," Leri said, writing on a pad of paper.

She's either doing real shorthand notation, or she's writing in some other symbol language. "*Hell to Pay* is a gangster movie, with a paranormal twist. A group of assassins—all of them paranormal in some way—go up against an evil spirit sent by a demon. Only three survive, but the thing they fought, a kind of sorcerous spirit called a Spiritwalker, keeps hunting them. It kills off another of them before the two that are left flee. They find a badass who has his own group of men and pledge their service to him if he'll help them destroy the spirit. Now the script originally left this open ended, the author intended to finish it in a sequel which was too complex to add given time constraints. We asked for a rewrite, so she added a finale, and simplified it."

Sheila sat down, her face now neutral. "The characters include two werewolves, a witch, a vampire, some kind of being that's half demon-half angel, and a wizard. And a villain demon."

"Are we no longer pro-demon?" Stacy asked.

"We want to open up our offerings to include more paranormals other than demons, after the success of *Immortal Confessions*," Debbie supplied smoothly. "We hope to slowly grow, and we can't limit subject material. That said, I will give ongoing preference to movies with some kind of paranormal slant, provided the scripts are solid and everything else lines up." She paused. "Caroline, you have free reign on the costumes for *Hell to Pay*. There's no year given in the script. Based on scenes it takes place sometime after the invention of cars and before the internet. We might also be able to set it in present year or close, if we add in cell phones, etc. and modify the script some. I don't see why we couldn't do that to make it more modern, but it's up to you, Nicole, after you consult with Caroline. My only request is to make the costumes hardy and long lasting, there's a lot of action. We'll also need special effects for the spiritwalker."

"It's some kind of floating skull head demon thing with smoke," Nicole said, "It's too bad it's destroyed really, I think it's a great antagonist."

"I agree," Caroline interjected. "I plan that the poster will have a picture of the skull and smoke, with maybe the team in front of it, or their heads near the bottom. Reminiscent of the first *Scream* poster."

"Too many heads," Bart complained. "Keep it simple, just the skull and smoke. It'll cut costs and also be less confusing."

"I'm glad you're all excited," Debbie said, both happy and relieved. "Please go ahead and start on this picture first. If we can finish it, we can release it first, hopefully midsummer. We will meet in a month for progress reports, I hope to begin shooting end of February."

"That's ambitious," Bart stated, then shrugged. "But if we don't have issues like last year, maybe we can make it."

Thanks so much for your support, Master Chief. At least you didn't call yourself that ridiculous nickname, like you managed to do in every other January meeting. "Good. Now we should talk about *Dare to Tell*. An urban career woman denies her psychic abilities until a horrific near-death experience leaves her seeing ghosts and dreading death. She relocates to a remote location, leaving her boyfriend, friends, and family to run a bed and breakfast in an old estate on behalf of a reclusive dying man. But the place has ghosts of its own, some of which have witnessed murder. When local teens begin to go missing as they did ten years prior, she must decide if she dares to tell the police what happened to them." Debbie paused. "I really think this is a great haunted house story with a new twist. I think if we could find a small town to shoot this in, we could likely complete it in a matter of weeks, if the town has a mansion on its outskirts."

"Like in *Salem's Lot*?" Leri asked.

"Exactly like *Salem's Lot*," Debbie replied. *Wow, she's a quick study. And here I was worried we were being asked to carry her.*

"I'll find something perfect," Leri promised, jotting more notes.

"We can shoot the initial intro and catalyst accident here in the studio, and the rest at the small town. This should also be easy to complete. Like *Hell to Pay*, the total number of characters don't number more than ten, though we will need walk-ons for shots around the town. Locals will likely be willing to help us out there for a fee. I have sent offers to some actors and actresses for the main role and the ghosts, including the missing teens, and we're waiting to hear back. The only issue is that we are going to need some serious CGI to do the spiritwalker concept justice, as well as some of the spirit interaction the medium experiences in *Dare to Tell*. We also want to showcase the paranormal aspects of all the assassin team members, which means more extensive hair and makeup than we usually use. But we can use CGI for that, too, if we need to cut costs down. Bart, take a look and give me your feedback. I will look into hiring someone who can give us good CGI."

"That would be good," Bart said. "Jett did all his own stunts, but most of the movies we've done until now just have actors playing paranormals with effects added later. We are probably going to need greenscreens for at least a few scenes, like the part where the spiritwalker attacks the moving van and peels the metal side off by biting into it. But I'd like to limit the CGI as a whole in both movies. Most viewers don't mind a little of it, but when its most of the movie, the movie usually doesn't do well with audiences because they know those scenes are fake."

"Good point, Bart. Please try a few shots and let me see the finished scenes, and we can go from there. Now, I'm obviously hopeful that we can get *Dare to Tell* ready in time to release in October, to take advantage of Halloween. But if we can't, we'll save it until next Halloween. We will have another progress meeting in two months' time, to go over how far along we are on *Hell to Pay* and see if we can start filming alternate weeks. I have booked ads for the fall season already, but I can switch the content of those until about a month ahead of time." Debbie took a breath. "I want to thank you all for staying with the company, I know when Jeremy left, he tried to talk at least a few of you into going with him. Thanks for staying and for believing in me and Pandora."

Everyone clapped as Debbie sat down.

Sheila stood. "We pretty much went over everyone's immediate focus. Is there anything else anyone wants to say?"

"Will there be a sequel to *Immortal Confessions*?" Nicole asked. "Working in Continuity, I was curious. I heard Devlin, the investor, remark to you that he might see if whomever penned it would write one."

No, he said that he would talk to the other vampires he knew and see if they had a story to tell as good as his life story, which was what Immortal Confessions *was. But without Devlin's involvement and power behind the picture, it's unlikely that a new vampire epic will make even half the money that its predecessor did. Sequels usually don't; Sheila's right on that.* "All I can tell you is I haven't heard from him in regards to a sequel." *I haven't heard from him at all.* "I'll let you know if anything changes."

"You haven't mentioned *Incubus*," Bart chastised. "I have to say I thought that was my chief focus until this meeting."

"I'm sorry," Debbie said, standing again. "You're right, Bart. I left *Incubus* off as it's not a movie. It's a serial or series."

"What?" Bart said, apoplectic. "Serial? I only have the one script which is pretty thin. I've been thinking of ways to try to drag it out to an hour and a half movie."

"It can be an hour and a half movie," Sheila said, standing. "And my apologies also. I was working on this, and when I got hurt last year, I didn't get as far as I planned. The script you have Bart is for the pilot episode. Doing a serial was an idea I proposed to

Debbie last summer, to take advantage of the direct online streaming market. All of you know that movie attendance is down across the board. Couple that with the very low marketing budget needed to launch a streaming-only movie, and I thought it was worth contemplating, if we could find the right star. You will have seen the posters with Gabrial Gray, our new male lead. He will play an incubus, a demon who visits women at night and steals some of their energy through making love."

"Sex," Bart corrected. "Lots of it, from what I've seen."

"This isn't porn," Debbie said staunchly. "Yes, we hope to include a bit more skin and detail than would be in a normal movie because this would be streaming. No, it's not a romance story, either. We need excitement, sex, and the unconventional. Gray has to be someone women desire and someone men would like to be. My take on that—and what you'll get from the script—is dangerous, well-dressed, and sexy. Caroline designed us some posters and we've got them up to create interest. Netflix is interested, but they want the pilot before they make a commitment. This would be our first series, our first major venue online, and would probably open the door for all of our future movies to be streamed. Netflix has given us until late summer to film the pilot. Gray is already reading the script, and Bart, I know you have, too. What are your thoughts?"

"That its heavy on seduction and low on action," Bart said. "It's thin. We need to hint at a backstory for the character, he's all flash and no substance as is. What is he supposed to be doing, other than seducing women? That's all he does in the pilot."

"And it's two women," Nicole chimed in. "I don't see if women will find it sexy that he's got two simultaneous lovers. That would work in the reverse, though, if we had a female and two males."

"Maybe not with male viewers," Giorgio, Pandora's legal lead chimed in. "I wouldn't like my wife having an incubus sneaking into her bed at night."

"Or my twin daughters," Mark added. "Though they've already

seen the posters and asked if they can meet Gray. They're sixteen, to give you some perspective."

"Teen viewers are good, but we need to capture adults, primarily women from twenty to fifty. If women don't watch this, we'll lose over half our target audience. Nicole, what other ideas do you have?"

"The female leads are weak; one's compliant from the beginning, the other's a ditz. We need a strong female lead. Maybe this movie should be more about how hard it would be for an incubus to seduce a woman in today's modern society? I think we need to play up the issues seen in other movies, with a supernatural being's nature being at odds with monogamy, even if the being wants it. If you think about it, an incubus is almost like a vampire. He can't feed from the woman he likes exclusively, or he'll kill her. That's lonely. We need to repackage that loneliness into romantic tension and longing."

"I think you're onto something, Nicole. Any other thoughts? Anyone? Speak up."

"Maybe romance should be secondary, and the sex not a given," Stacy offered. "Series thrive on conflict and action, in my opinion. We have the problem of monogamy. Why not make him on the run from a demon hunter? Say this incubus demon made a mistake a few years ago and killed a woman, and so every week he's moving around, travelling. It would make for excitement and explain why he can't have a long-term love. He's got to have some powers, right?"

"What powers?" Debbie prompted. "Anyone?"

"Seduction," Leri said in a purring tone, looking up at Debbie and Sheila in turn. "Incubi's chief power is to make their prey—

sorry, lovers—unable to say no. So he should have enough charm to get his way in nearly everything. Like you say, he's supposed to be what men would aspire to. So let him be witty and romantic, good at most everything, well dressed, and ready to save women who cross his path in distress. They're grateful after the fact and feed him their energy. He travels each episode so there's always a new woman and a new adversary, with the hunter always on his heels, maybe coming to blows now and again. Change that up for a few episodes with a woman who searched him out to get his help, or a woman who loves him. Hell, you could even have a woman who's suicidal who tries to get him to love her to death."

My God, I should have hired this woman years ago. "Brilliant. Nicole," Debbie said. "Can you look at all the ideas just discussed here and make the pilot a bit better?"

"Sure."

"Great, please give me a rewrite by the end of the week. Anyone else?"

"Are we going to do releases this year in conjunction with wine with Triss Vineyards?" Bart asked. "I've already been asked about the Incubus wine, as we had some of that last year at several functions. It seemed obvious that we'd use some for this year." He had spoken to Debbie, but his eyes were on Rack, who up until now hadn't spoken, only stared at Leri the times she spoke.

"Yes," Debbie said. "Mr. Triss will furnish us with wines for *Dare to Tell* and *Hell to Pay*. My thoughts are maybe a white for the first, and a blend for the second. But I leave that to our master of wine. And yes, we'll need some Incubus for the fall to help with the launch of the pilot episode. Please get me some ideas and meet with me in early February."

Rack nodded, jotting notes.

"I have a question," Bart quipped. "Why is he always Mr. Triss, and you call us all by our first names?"

Because I can't remember his assumed first name he told everyone here, but I know it wasn't Rack. "Just an in-joke," Debbie said fakely. "Anything else?"

There was silence.

"Thanks, everyone. Leri, come to my office, so you can meet with Sheila and I."

~

Leri followed Debbie into her office, Sheila shutting the door behind them. Leri intoned some words, then casually sat across the desk from Debbie. "So how've you been?"

"What was that?" Sheila said, as she and Debbie took their seats.

"Just a warding spell to make sure we weren't overheard. I'm surprised, Debbie, that you leave so many decisions to your team and only give them a few pointers to guide them."

"I never liked being micromanaged," Debbie said, picking up a pen. "I deliberately pick people for my team that I can delegate to who can give me results. You seem to be one of those people. Thanks for coming to work with us, I already can see you're going to be an asset."

"I never worked in films, but I enjoy them," Leri said, adjusting her skirt. "I just report to you both, right?"

Sheila nodded. "If you have any questions, you can see me. We can go to my office after this to discuss more of your responsibilities."

"I'd rather get started right away in trying to get locations, if that's okay? But I'm willing to come to your office this afternoon to meet." She smiled. "I want to get you something today, especially as you can't move any further on *Dare to Tell* until you decide on a location."

"You have a spot in mind?" Sheila asked.

Leri nodded. "There's a couple places I'm thinking of, but I haven't been there in years. I need to find out if the mansions are still standing, and then if renting them for a movie would be possible. I'd think that if we could shoot everything in one place, that would be easier than just using the outside and having to create a set of the inside here in the studio."

Debbie nodded. "You're right. Yes, please check out the places you are thinking of, and get with Sheila to get her feedback."

Leri turned to Sheila. "How is three pm? That should give me enough time."

"Good."

"Since you put a ward up," Debbie said. "We understand from Titus that you've…run afoul of Devlin for some reason. We won't ask your business, but we do need to ask you to tell us if he discovers you're working here. We won't volunteer this information to him. We are going to have to tell him you are an employee if he asks directly."

"I understand," Leri said coolly. "I'm not going to make trouble between you and him. I don't think he'd care if I was here, really."

"Titus indicated that the falling out was pretty severe," Sheila supplied.

"You want to know, obviously, so here it is: I helped a relative who made some bad decisions. He's not a good guy, but he's family. Because I helped him, he was able to make worse decisions, and he wouldn't listen to me when I tried to talk him out of acting on them. Titus imprisoned me as a result. He let me out on the condition we have a few months' separation." Leri took a deep breath. "I love my husband, but I also need some time and space to think about what I want. So here I am."

Debbie thought of Myrrh imprisoned in rock. "He bound you in a magical prison?"

"Bastard sent me to Hell," Leri said spitefully. "While he also rescued me after a week, I'm not exactly grateful to him. I helped put him where he is, and I get no credit."

"Asshole males," Sheila assented, nodding.

"Now that you know, I'm going to go do what you hired me for," Leri said, standing. "Thanks again for this opportunity. Sheila, I'll be at your office door by three." She waved her hand, then left by the door.

We now employ a paroled felon of Hell Debbie wrote on her pad, then held it up to Sheila. They both burst out laughing.

"In all seriousness, I do like her," Debbie said, tossing the note in the garbage. "She's going to be a help for sure."

"I think she'll be fine, too."

"Myrrh told me last night she's not going to be around as much," Debbie said. "So it's good Leri's going to be here. I feel safer. Are those interviews for new hires arranged for tomorrow?"

Sheila nodded. "Yes, there are some good candidates. Thanks also for saying what you did about *Origin of Fear*. I still really want to do that."

"With the actual haunted house sunk, I think we'll need a new location though. Maybe you can ask Leri about that, find something? If the house itself no longer exists, why be afraid to make the picture? We can't draw attention to something that's destroyed and underwater."

"Great." Sheila beamed. "I'll talk to her about that today." She paused. "There was something else though that I needed to talk to you about."

"Before you start, I have something I wanted to say, too," Debbie said bluntly. "About any new scripts you look into this year for next year's movies. I know there's been a new focus in "realistic" pictures, with characters that have a lot of shades of grey. While I agree that shows a high degree of authenticity, I want to stay away from characters that aren't either discernably good or evil. I also do not want any script approved for the coming two years that doesn't have an upbeat ending, unless it's a straight horror movie. I put *Origin of Fear* into that category, I expect it to end on a thrilling scare. But *Dare to Tell* purposely ends well. That's where I think we should go."

"That may lose us a lot of market share," Sheila said slowly. "What you're describing is the current norm now in independent movies, to have dark subject matter, dark heroes, and dark endings. That ties into what I was going to say: that *Everlasting* movie about that art-loving woman who sells her soul? We would need to either shoot it on the cheap with only a few unknowns and do a limited release in only the biggest cities, or else scrap plans to make it. I don't think the picture will draw audiences. The lead is weak and unsympathetic, and the average person doesn't visit galleries, or have much interest in art."

What she means is the movie will be hard to make a big profit from. "We got into motion pictures because we wanted to tell stories that meant something," Debbie said. "How does reaffirming that good is questionable in people make viewers feel better about their lives?"

"I'm not sure, but it's the current trend."

"And I'm not saying our characters have to ride off into the sunset hand in hand smiling for every ending," Debbie said crossly. "But I've had enough of watching people that struggle and do their best to be moral and noble in their choices getting shit in return, while those that scheme and backstab are made out to be the winners of the tale. Because that isn't really what happens in real life; I don't believe that." *At least, not anymore.* "I believe in karma, that if you pay good forward you will get good back. And if you do evil over and over, you'll get a shitstorm eventually."

"Then I guess we're in for another rough year," Sheila quipped, grimacing.

"You and I already paid for what we had to do to get Pandora where we are," Debbie said quietly. "We're lucky to be alive, Sheila. We're luckier still that we're both demon-free, and survived, because everything I've been told says that we should both be dead."

Sheila nodded once, biting her lip.

"We need to stick together, and keep our heads down this year," Debbie continued. "That means quality pictures, but not ones that draw attention with either deaths or on-set accidents. We can't afford any attention, either from the police or…religious vigilantes."

"I think we can manage that, with the new people Rack is interviewing for security, Leri working onsite, and Shaker making an appearance now and again. But Gray's a demon in *Incubus*, and the meeting we just had identifies him as a protagonist for the series. How are we going to spin that?"

"Sex," Debbie said, finally grinning. "A lot of sex." She sighed. "All kidding aside, we need to be true to his nature. He's fun-loving and very sexual, which taken with nothing else makes him seem shallow. We have to show that longing that Nicole mentioned, and give him some nobility with plot devices. Hell, if writers can make an assassin seem gracious for multiple seasons in *Burn Notice*, we should be able to use the same formula."

"Hmm," Sheila said. "Why not use Leri's inspiration and add an intro at the beginning of the pilot that Gray was in Hell and escaped?"

"Sounds great," Debbie said, flashing a wide smile. "This is going to be one of our best years yet."

~

The lone male figure pushed aside a low-hanging branch, studying the derelict mansion. *Looks fine. But looks are often lies.*

A thin long forked tongue poked between his lips, vibrating as he scented the air. *Nothing. No scent of human, no scent of anything non-human. Chasing my tail here in the swamps again for Dev. Story of my life.*

Debbie grimaced, then made a note for Sheila with her red pen. *We can't just launch into Lash appearing, he's got to have a better introduction. Maybe halfway through a fight scene or something.*

This was supposed to be the final scene of the script of *Hell to Pay*. It read like a rough draft, with all the exciting pages missing. *Fuck, why is this such a mess? It's like a bad dream.*

This new rewritten final scene of *Hell to Pay* had Lash investigating a mansion that his boss had bought to demolish to turn back into field. It happened to be the home of a woman who went missing years ago. The scene was Lash approaching the house, going inside, and walking around the remains of her bedroom, musing on the woman she was, and finding some overlooked clue before Morwen stumbled on him. *Slow, utterly contrived, and worst of all…boring. But if I write that Sheila's going to be pissed off, and it'll cause another fight. I'm going to have to meet with her and come up with a better idea. I know we just went over it last week and rewrote it. This isn't how the script is now at all…*

Realization dawned, just like that. *This is a dream.*

Debbie wrote *bring back the bar scene and add a verbal exchange with another patron, then Morwen walking in,* yawned, then put aside her laptop. *Enough for tonight.*

She turned off the light, then lay back. Just as she was drifting off, she felt a hand touch her intimately.

"Vassago?"

"Who else." He chuckled, stroking her.

"I thought it might be Shaker," she said pointedly, moving away.

"I thought you might be lonely."

"It'd be different if you wanted me for me," she said, turning away. "But it's just about the seduction."

"I have to eat, too," he said, spooning her. "I just feed on energy instead of food."

"Go feed on someone else."

"And I do want you for you," he said, kissing her cheek. "You make me work for it." Instead of moving to touch her, he moved away, rolling onto his back. "But I'm okay to fast, if you're not in the mood. Do you mind if I stay?"

Debbie looked over at him. "Why?"

"Because I don't sleep with anyone, ever. Or cuddle. Or really even talk."

"I'm not looking for another relationship. I'm already in one."

"I'm not looking for a relationship, just a little intimacy."

Debbie reached over and felt for his groin, grasping his swollen penis as he let out a surprised grunt. "That feels like a lot of intimacy."

He hugged her. "Just kiss me. Please?"

Debbie opened her mouth to protest, but his lips were there, meeting hers. Surprisingly, he didn't grab her, just kissed her gently. When she didn't protest, he began kissing her face, her throat. As her breath quickened, he kissed lower, but still outside her clothes, his kisses chaste.

She reached for his cock, sliding her hand up and down the shaft, rubbing the tip. Immediately it moistened, then grew slick as he stiffened still further.

"Yes, please touch me. Please."

Debbie worked him in her hand slowly, enjoying his silky yet firm hardness, as the last inches of his manhood filled out. She stiffened suddenly, as she felt his finger slide between her moist lips, teasing her swollen clit. But his movements were slow, achingly slow, as he moved back and forth, rubbing the slick hot flesh.

"I love that you want me, even when you say you don't." He kissed her still chastely.

"Roll over," she said, pulling away.

Obediently, he did, his cock standing up at attention. Debbie straddled him, but carefully, setting her swollen clit down against his shaft, so it was trapped between her and his body. She pulled her nightie over her head, then leaned down over him, pressing her breasts to his face.

Eagerly, he brought his hands up, cupping them and pressing them to his face, turning his head to nibble first one, then the other. He sucked the nipples, first hard, then tracing them with his tongue, then flicking them gently.

Debbie moaned, but fought the urge to move, his hot cock beneath her hard as bone. But the temptation was too great, and she moved up, letting the hard phallus spring up, as she settled it against her moist lips.

Vassago thrust up eagerly, burying himself with a grunt, then began to thrust slow and deep, as Debbie rode him, her hands splayed on his chest as he gripped her breasts. They built slowly, drawing out the moment for all it was worth, then coming hard.

Debbie finally stopped him at six orgasms. "I'm too tired. I can't believe you can get it up after a day of working."

He followed her into the bathroom, as they cleaned up. "That's work and eating. This is…intimacy."

"It's a lot of intimacy," Debbie said, as he followed her back to bed. "You've been here every night for a week, Vassago." *And your stamina is nothing short of amazing.*

"I like you," he said, clasping her hand in his.

"Why does…why do you feel better than other men? Are you different, um, differently formed?"

"No." He chuckled. "I use a different angle, and I'm not in a hurry to come. Most all males are, whatever make or model of beings they might be. Hurrying puts you all over the place and doesn't feel good on the receiving end."

Debbie laughed. "I never thought of that."

He was silent.

"Why do you come back? You already know I'm not lonely, with Myrrh and her murder staying here."

"I am," he admitted, squeezing her hand. "Shaker told me how it had been for him, when he was Jett. I didn't believe him, thought he was just downplaying fame. But people expect the character they see onscreen. Worse, they're angry if you aren't really that person. But don't think I'm changing my mind about *Incubus*, I want this opportunity very much, to work with you."

"Why?"

"Because you're doing a series, not a single movie. I hoped that you'd do for me and the other incubi what you did for demons as a whole, show that we aren't one dimensional. That there's not really black and white, there's a lot of gray in between." He paused. "That's why I took Gray as my acting name." He hugged her. "I'm not trying to come between you and Shaker, please don't think that. I'm here to comfort you and take comfort. I know Shaker wants to come back to you, and you want him to. I'll stop coming, when that happens."

"Love the double entendre," Debbie teased, tossing a pillow at him with a smile.

"So can I stay the night?"

"Sure."

Debbie opened her eyes, then cast a look around her. The three hellhounds were sleeping soundly, undisturbed. *That's the seventh dream I've had of Vassago in as many days. But I'm not low on energy, so it's unlikely it is him visiting me, and probably just my imagination and lack of sex. Still, I'd better check with Myrrh the next time I see her.* Debbie rolled over and went back to sleep.

CHAPTER FOUR

February

"DEBBIE, YOU HAVE YOUR DOCTOR'S OFFICE ON LINE ONE."

Ugh, you'd think they could send a text or something to remind me of an appointment. That has to be it. Debbie scanned her day planner, and sure enough, there was an annual physical there for tomorrow. *Good they called, or I'd never have made it, I had that meeting with Rack about the wines going right up to it.* "Put them through."

Debbie confirmed the appointment, then hung up the phone, dictating a short text to Rack asking him to cut their meeting short tomorrow or reschedule. Then she hurried to put on her coat, grabbed her laptop, and headed for the door.

For once, Debbie welcomed her commute, to give herself uninterrupted time to think. Shaker hadn't visited this month yet, contrary to his promise of arranging things with his human mistress so that he would be more available. Debbie didn't know how to take that, or if she should push. She went over the last few weeks, in her mind, trying to remember the literal words he'd said about when he'd next see her. *No real confirmed day, or even month. He misses Valentine's Day this year, he's going to be sorry.* Letting out an annoyed breath, she headed inside to find Myrrh in the living room, watching Netflix.

"How was your day?" she said, hanging up her coat. "Did you make me dinner?"

"It was fine, and no," Myrrh said, with a yawn. "But I can step out for some takeout, if you like, just tell me where."

"How about a few chopped salads, heavy on the meat? Anyplace is fine."

"Alright." Myrrh grabbed her purse, then vanished. She reappeared about ten minutes later, handing a salad in a plastic clamshell to Debbie. "Here you go."

Debbie began eating, and Myrrh put the other salad into the fridge, then sat down with a large container of fried chicken strips and sauce. Several crows cawed, then soon twelve of them were sitting in the kitchen around the two women, watching eagerly.

"I'm feeling the pressure," Debbie said lightly. "Are you going to feed them?"

"Come on, you, go out," Myrrh said grumpily. "Everyone out!" The crows cawed in irritation, but they left the room en masse.

"They're feeling the winter blues," Myrrh said, wedging chicken in her mouth. "Spring seems like it's here one moment and gone the next."

"I was never what you'd call an outdoor girl, but I know what you mean," Debbie agreed, forking up some salad. "I'm looking forward to the summer as well. But we've got a long way to go until then. It's barely the second week in February."

"I know what happened, at your family cabin," Myrrh said suddenly. "Titus let me know. If you go up there again, I will come with you."

She's talking about my attempted suicide this past fall. Debbie flushed slightly, struggling for composure. "I'm not in the same frame of mind as I was then," she said finally, annoyed at her hesitation. "You don't have to worry. But I'd appreciate the company, sure. I don't think I'll be going until this summer, at the earliest."

"It's not just for the company, although I and my crows would enjoy being near a lake. You still have enemies, Debbie. Just because you're not bound to a demon anymore doesn't mean that demonkind as a whole has taken you off their radar."

Debbie shifted uneasily. *I thought that's exactly what it would mean.* "Speaking of that…will there be any attempts by anyone else to try to bind me? I really am enjoying not being, um, tainted."

"Probably," Myrrh said, after a moment. "Rack's not going to try anything, or any of the others that are Shaker's allies. But I'm not sure about the new ones, like Mr. Gray there. You seem to have become friends."

"We aren't friends."

"Really?" Myrrh said with twinkling eyes. "I was under the impression he gave both you and Sheila an audition. The two of you together. One not exactly…private?"

Last fall, when Gray linked with me and Sheila in dreams. Shaker was a voyeur, watching the action. Debbie looked away, blushing. "How did you know about that?"

"Never mind. I know he's not a regular visitor, or you'd be too exhausted to leave your bedroom. I really don't think he'd try to bind you, either, that's not an incubus's style."

"So you're just teasing me."

Myrrh chuckled. "I enjoy watching you flush, yes."

"Saying that I trust him in my bed but not otherwise sounds foolish, doesn't it?"

"Foolish but truthful." Myrrh smiled. "I know what you mean in saying that, and as far as that goes, I think he's fine to be trusted that way. Nothing's hidden; Shaker's aware and approves."

"Approve is probably too strong a word," Debbie said, making a face. "I don't approve of him being intimate with his Mistress. But then neither he nor I made the rules here, we're just trying to live with them." *Ugh, I sound like a total slut and Shaker a player.*

"It really doesn't matter; I'm not judging you. But if you do take another lover besides Vass, yeah, it'd be wise to let us all know." Myrrh finished her chicken, then got to her feet. "I'm off, do you need anything else?"

Yeah, I need Shaker back. "No, thanks."

~

Debbie groaned as she looked at her watch. *I've been waiting thirty minutes. Shouldn't this be over by now?*

"Ms. Deal, please come with me."

Debbie followed the woman into the waiting room, then had her blood pressure and weight taken. *You make any jokes like "gained a bit, have we?" and I'll scream.*

The woman exited with the usual pleasantries and Debbie was left to her thoughts. *You have to announce the new hires later this month. Mark said that Eugene is working out great, and the first footage I've looked at for work here at the studios is excellent. Sheila said Leri did some good work on locations, but that she'd see me tomorrow in the afternoon to discuss them, we're supposed to be heading over to the Black Rose to use up the last credits I have. I hope she made up with Song or it's going to be awkward.*

Althea was a good choice for Editing/Cutting, she's already done some great work with Jett's old footage and given me a good idea of what we need to do with Brady to finish Destiny in the Ashes. *That reminds me, Brady's supposed to be flying in for the weekend, I'd better text him to find out when I need to pick him up.* She made a face. *I also have to decide if I'm going to honor my offer to let him stay at my house while he finds a place to live. But he's had close to three months now to reconsider his rash decision to drop his life and move out here next to Rhonda.*

Jay Nightingale and Wren Flicker came highly recommended for the CGI, best of all they don't need to be full-time, just a flat fee for specific pictures, given we know exactly what we need. We're waiting on a price for the two movies this year, and I need to get with Nicole about those possible rewrites of the Incubus series.

Debbie's phone rang. Debbie swore, then padded across the floor in her bare feet to her purse. "Yes?"

"Mrs. Black," a sultry voice purred. "So glad I caught you. Your office said you had left for the day."

"Yes, I'm at an appointment, so I'm afraid I may have to call you back."

"I'll just take a few minutes. I apologize that I haven't contacted you before now. I was travelling over the holidays, and January was a bit too…eventful."

The way he says that, he was doing something naughty and wants me to ask. "I trust everything worked out satisfactorily. You might have heard that Titan Pictures is no longer one of our rivals."

"It is satisfactory for now, yes," Devlin said with content. "But there's always room for higher ascents."

He's enjoying this too much. "What can I do for you, Devlin? Other than to congratulate you again for being nominated for best original score for *Immortal Confessions*. I was surprised, even though you're clearly talented. Independent pictures don't always do very well at the Oscars."

"Thank you. I heard Jett was also nominated. Will you be going to the ceremony?"

"I hadn't thought about it," Debbie answered, mind racing. *He's right, as the widow I should go. I had better book a seat by phone tonight.* "But yes, I should go."

"I will send an emissary in my place. As I said, I have been overly busy lately."

That's right, Shaker mentioned something about Devlin having a baby? But a vampire can't have children that I ever heard of. Maybe it didn't work out? I better not mention it. "If you give him my name, I'd be glad to meet with him."

"I enjoyed making the movie with you and your team," Devlin continued. "But I won't be able to work on future movies in person. I have set the money aside I promised to invest and am waiting only for the scripts before releasing it to you. I called to ask if they are ready?"

I'm ready to be seen. Where's my doctor? I'm freezing in this paper gown. At least talking to him is keeping my mind off it. "We have two movies, *Hell to Pay* and *Dare to Tell.*" Debbie elaborated on the plots of both movies, giving some details. "We've shot a few scenes and have CGI lined up, also. I have every reason to hope we can release both this year."

"Fabulous. Send over the scripts tonight if you would. I can give you my answer by next week."

"I'll do that." Debbie heard the knob turning. "I'm sorry I have to go. I'll call you back after the appointment." She hung up.

~

"*Give your body what it needs.*" *What the hell does that mean?* Debbie thought as she dressed. "At least the blood work was good."

"I think I might fit your needs," Shaker said with a grin, as he appeared next to her. Debbie let out a yell, and then smacked him on one broad shoulder. "What the hell are you doing here? You don't contact me for a week, then you pop into my doctor's appointment?"

"Just being the dutiful spouse," Shaker said, mock-affronted. "I'm here to defend your right to eat cheesy poofs with abandon and inform your doctor that you are the right size."

"You are not funny." Debbie's eyes narrowed, and she bared her teeth with a sarcastic grimace. "I have gained weight, according to the doctor. I need to go up a size, most likely."

"I know," Shaker said more gently. "But it's okay. I love you and I love your body, just as it is."

"You're ripping off Bridget Jones," Debbie snorted.

"Maybe so, but that doesn't mean it's not the truth." Shaker hugged her. "I do think you're beautiful, and I don't want you to be a scrawny bone woman that looks like the wind would blow her away, and is uncomfortable to lay with, literally."

Debbie laughed. "Now we're getting at it."

"You've been good?" Shaker said, his expression turning serious. "No problems? This is just routine?"

Debbie nodded. "I feel fine. But where have you been?"

"Being the picture of a dutiful, hardworking spouse, as I said," Shaker murmured, nuzzling her. "Except for the conjugal relations. I have wholly neglected them." He slid his hand down along the outside of her breast. "Believe me, I plan to remedy that soon."

Debbie pushed him away and continued putting on her clothes. "What does soon mean? Valentine's day is Saturday. That's the day after tomorrow."

"What would you like to do?" Shaker offered. "I'm free all day. We could see a movie, or stay in bed, or go out to dinner. Now that I have a job, I can give you things again."

Debbie finished sliding her shoes on, then went to him, hugging hard. "You already gave me everything, remember? You left me all your money, which rightly belongs to you. I'd rather have you spend more time with me than buy me presents."

"Tell me when you'd like me to arrive on Saturday, then?" Shaker kissed her forehead. "We'll make a day of it. I know better than to think you won't have some work to do, though, so I need to know when you'll be free."

"Shit," Debbie said. "Brady is flying in this weekend. I have to pick him up on Saturday. He's...well, he might be staying at my house."

Shaker blinked. "Can't you offer to get him a hotel?"

"I didn't offer to have him stay with me in the first place,"

Debbie said in irritation. "That demon impersonating Sheila did. But he's family and Jett had just died; I didn't see a way to refuse." She sighed. "Maybe he has a dog allergy."

"Miss?" There was a knock at the door. "If you're dressed can you leave the room? There's another patient we need to set up."

Debbie grabbed her purse and stalked from the room. Shaker followed her, none of the people they passed reacting with anything other than a smile or a greeting. *He must be wearing a glamour.* Debbie walked to her car and got in the driver's side. Shaker got in the passenger side.

Shit, I better call Sheila and ask her to send those two scripts to Devlin. Debbie made the call, and Sheila assented she'd email them immediately.

Debbie turned to Shaker. "I'll ask Brady to get a hotel, if I can work it into the conversation. Otherwise I'll tell him I have a dinner appointment Saturday, and that I'll bring him some takeout. I don't see a way though that I can rescind the invite after everything that's happened." She considered Shaker a moment. "Titus said you were building a house. Why don't we just go there afterwards?"

Shaker snorted. "I could take you there. I do want you to see it. I thought to offer that if Song and Sheila were still staying with you. But I didn't want it to seem like sex was my end goal in coming to you tonight." He held up his clawed hands. "Yes, I admit I want you. I think about us in bed every night, and if you want to give permission, I'll rise to the occasion right here in the parking lot, in this car." He winked at her. "I want more than one night, though, Debbie. And I want some time after, too." He paused. "I know this situation is more than most human women would want to deal with, and I truly wish that I didn't have to be bound to another woman to stay here in this world and out of Hell. But we agree that it's better to have another woman as my official Mistress, who bears all the dangers of being linked to a demon, don't we? It's safer for you, not to mention a more secure situation for all you and I have built and hope to achieve with Pandora, too."

Touched, Debbie began to tell him to come home with her right now. But jealousy reared up inside her, and other words fell out of her mouth. "Won't your Mistress interrupt that? I assumed that you've been gone so much because you were serving her."

The insinuation wasn't lost on Shaker. "There aren't going to be anymore commands for me to bed her," Shaker stated. "I've pretty much got her command not to so much as bring up the subject or even touch her at all in passing."

"Pretty much" isn't solid. Debbie raised her eyebrows in disbelief. "How did you manage that?"

Shaker smiled. "My Mistress is impetuous, but also very prudish, given she's got three full-time lovers. So long as I tease her occasionally and give her attention when she needs it, I think that order will stand indefinitely." He smiled wider. "Rash behavior is our favorite human trait among demons because it often leads to bad decisions."

Debbie ignored his barb. "So if you're not talking about sex or having it, then what kind of interactions do you have? You said she told you to hunt down some guy?"

"The one behind several attacks. His name is Valerian. He's an old vampire, one with a fang to grind, if not all four. He's after her because he's at war with Devlin and Danial, because they are allies with Lash, who has been his nemesis for close to a century now."

"What started all this?"

"Valerian was killing children. Lash took issue with this and burned him with magical fire, scarring Valerian for eternity. He was handsome once. They have been enemies ever since, and their war through the decades has caused a lot of collateral damage."

"Deaths?"

Shaker nodded. "Buildings burnt, lives destroyed, beings of every race and age killed and hurt."

"Will this Valerian be coming after me?"

"No," Shaker answered. "Although I am going to go after him."

Debbie gaped at him. "Why the hell would you do that?"

"It's my Mistress's sole command. Valerian is also allied with a demon who isn't going to leave us alone. You remember Azaroth?"

"Fuck. That was Dante's demon, right?"

"How quickly they forget," he quipped. "Yes, the one I sent back to Hell. He likely jumped at the chance to serve Valerian, I'm sure he wants another crack at Lash. And us."

And I thought I was out of this. "We need to prepare, both of us."

"No, we don't," Shaker amended. "I do. Valerian isn't my enemy, and he might retaliate if I attacked him directly. But my order was only to find him. I'll do that and report his location if I'm successful. But this vampire knows a fair bit of magic himself; his way has always been acting through others and letting them take all the risk. Azaroth won't attack us directly, he's going to stay close to Valerian. You aren't in danger."

"You just said Azaroth wants vengeance."

"I'm sure he does, but he wants to stay out of Hell more. Look, what I'm trying to say, and doing a convoluted job of it, is that I plan to look for this vampire during the weekdays. I'd like to spend the weekends with you, if you would like that. I want our relationship to continue. I miss you. So give me an answer. Do you miss me?"

"Yes," Debbie said, reaching across to him and kissing him. "I miss you. And yes, I'd love for us to spend weekends together."

Shaker began kissing her harder, making her believe he might try for a parking lot tryst after all. *The lot is fairly empty anyway, why not?*

Debbie's phone rang shrilly.

"Damn it!" Debbie dug it out of her purse. "Hello?"

"Mrs. Black," Devlin said. "I had a chance to skim both scripts and would like to give you my thoughts. Can we talk?"

"I'm just driving home," Debbie said, looking over at Shaker. "I'll put you on speakerphone while I drive, is that okay?"

"Of course. Just tell me when you're ready."

Debbie covered the phone. "Do you want to teleport home, maybe get a bath running or grab some food? Myrrh might be there but probably there's just a single crow on watch."

Shaker nodded and disappeared.

Debbie started the car, set up the phone and drove out of the parking lot. "I'm set Devlin, go ahead."

"I found the experience of sharing my life story…cathartic. I have a colleague who went through his own ordeal. I've asked him to write down a synopsis of his own tale and call you to book a meeting to present it."

Debbie thought fast how best to discourage Devlin from the idea, then remembered her team's inquiry about a sequel to *Immortal Confessions*. The historical vampire movie had been a blockbuster, and sequels were all the rage now, across all genres. If the story had similar characters and storylines, it could reap Pandora a significant profit, provided that Devlin's colleague could be either be persuaded to produce the movie, or they could reuse many of the costumes and studio sets with minor alterations. "Is he as good a storyteller as you?"

"Better," Devlin admitted grudgingly. "If you enjoy underdog tales."

"The moviegoing public does and that's our market," Debbie assured him. "Please have him call me and book a meeting when he's got the story written. I'd be excited to hear his ideas. If it's a compelling story, we can turn it into a script for a movie."

"Thank you. Now about these two new movies. *Dare to Tell* sounds interesting, but seems to lack any male-female interaction, as written. Is that purposeful?"

"It's a gothic horror tale. There's some insinuation that one of the ghosts cares for the protagonist, but no there's no romance."

"Hmm. I think it sounds good but would like to see a few scenes on tape before committing. Can you send those to me?"

Wow, he's a hard sell. "Sure."

"*Hell to Pay* sounds exciting, but I flipped ahead to the ending, and it seems a bit abrupt for the amount of exposition leading up to it."

Debbie waited, but Devlin didn't go on. "We needed a finale, so we asked for the author to write one."

"I'd encourage instead for you to use the initial script. A good story shouldn't be rushed."

He doesn't sound interested in either film. "There's also a haunted house story called *Origin of Fear* that we're just beginning work on and hope to shoot for next year. It's supposed to be on an island. We have someone at work looking at locations."

"Fear always sells," Devlin assented. "Let me put in a call to my people, ask if any of them know of a suitable island mansion within their borders."

"We also are looking into local places within driving distance. I'm talking condemned ruins here that could be purchased for next to nothing. For the script the house is supposed to be half flooded on one side. But with the lack of water in the last few years it will be difficult to find someplace where we would be able to set something up to flood a house, and if we buy one that has been flooded near a river, we have to film just the outside because we couldn't risk someone getting hurt. Ideally, we could find an area adjoining a body of water and build a house set near it which we could film part of the movie on and then flood the house to film the rest of the movie. These kinds of problems are why we need more time to work on *Origin of Fear.*"

"You may want to look at somewhere near the coast? No, you need freshwater. Hmm. A major river floodplain possibly? I can alert my colleagues near the Mississippi to report if they have such a house in their domain and ask for digital pictures."

"It's almost as if you'd rather we focused on *Origin of Fear,*" Debbie said slowly. "Not what I expected."

"I like them all," Devlin disagreed. "The last is just the only one where I might be of some behind the scenes help. Humans enjoy being scared, so long as the lights come back on at the end." He chuckled darkly. "While I like the plot of *Hell to Pay*, please be careful what you portray onscreen, in terms of what is evil and what is not. I understand there is a vampire who perishes that is part of the supernatural team."

That's what his reluctance is about? "They won't show onscreen the death of the vampire, only allude that the spiritwalker killed him. The only death shown in detail will be the destruction of the spiritwalker. That's some kind of skull wreathed in smoke with tremendous strength and speed. The end explains it as an entity sent by a sorcerer which originated from the tortured soul of a demon-possessed human."

"That's a bit too true to life for film," Devlin stated. "Knowledge is power, Debbie. I'd advise you to alter the spiritwalker's origin, while still being plausible."

Lash must have spoken to him, told him about the weird scripts we got with the false author names, and how the stories in the scripts mirrored true-life events he and Shaker had personal knowledge of. "We strive to show all sides to make our characters as real as possible, with good guys having flaws and weak points, and villians being both reasonable and intelligent," Debbie replied. "But be assured the vampire will be shown to be a good guy, his death a motivation for revenge. As for the spiritwalker, we may alter the ending again. I'm waiting to see what the CGI team I hired can do. There's always the option to leave the spiritwalker's actual creation process vague."

"Very good," Devlin said heartily, a slight lisp to his words, Debbie envisioned him smiling with fangs bared. "Keep me apprised. If you are willing to shoot the ending first and let me view it, along with the vampire death, and approve both, I'll agree to back this movie."

"I'll send you what you asked for," Debbie agreed. *But with or without your backing we are making both movies. And I will have the final approval.*

"Sheila sent me an email congratulating me on the nomination," Devlin said, changing the subject. "She asked how I could sing with my fangs, and not show them when singing. Please tell her the answer is years of practice as a bard. You both know the story now."

Is he always this full of himself? Debbie rubbed her eyes. *I'm almost home. When I am, I'm ending this call.* "I'll tell her. Was there anything else?"

"Yes, I wanted to offer my condolences. I've experienced my own losses. I'm glad to see you back in the saddle, so to speak."

Was he talking about Shaker not being bound to her anymore or her miscarriage? Or Jett's death? "Thank you."

"If I can be of service, please contact me. Otherwise I'll wait to see those scenes. Adieu, Debbie."

Thank God. "Goodbye." Debbie hung up, parked her car, and went to the door, unlocking it. Shaker was there to greet her, taking her coat and tossing it aside with her briefcase and bag. He pressed his body to hers, the hard length of him already eager against her.

"Did you get the food?" Debbie asked, breaking the kiss for a ragged breath.

"Yes, but I'm more hungry for you." Shaker led her to the bedroom and undressed her, kissing her face, then her bared skin as he unveiled it. "You're more beautiful that I remember." He touched her breasts lightly, cupping them, then circling the hardening nipples with his fingers. "Your breasts are perfect. That doctor doesn't know what she's talking about. Do not lose one damn ounce."

Debbie giggled, then reached down for his loincloth, pushing it aside. His penis was almost purple, fully engorged. "You look larger than I remember."

"The same but thank you." Shaker lay down on the bed, his hands roaming Debbie's body, rubbing and squeezing, their breathing faster in the cool air.

Debbie stroked Shaker's cock, enjoying the soft skin of the

swollen head, and the eager grunts he couldn't quite keep from uttering as she ran her hands over him. Impulsively, she pushed him on his back, then dipped her head between his legs, taking the wide tip in her mouth, running her tongue over the small opening.

Shaker bucked slightly, running his clawed hands in her hair. "Oh, yes. Please please. Please take me deeper."

Debbie carefully slid him deeper, worried she might gag. But Shaker stayed absolutely still as she fellated him, the throbbing of his organ increasing as she stimulated him.

"Enough," he said, expelling a breath as he gently withdrew. "Climb onto me. I need to feel you around me."

Debbie mounted him. Sliding her now wet channel over the wide moist head, feeling the tip of his cock widen her as he slowly pushed inside. Deeper and deeper he pushed, until the length of him was sheathed inside her. Shaker gripped her, his clawed hands making small indents on her flushed skin. He began to move her, thrusting up to meet her hips. Debbie ground against him, taking all he had to give, eager to receive him.

"I'm not going to last," Shaker grunted. "Are you close?"

Debbie moved faster, rubbing her clit on the root of his cock as he drove into her. The climax was there suddenly with no warning, the luscious feeling washing over her, engulfing her in its intensity.

Shaker waited until she'd stopped coming, then held her hard against him, as he pistoned against her, bellowing his pleasure as he came.

Debbie sank down onto him, still joined. "Are you done?"

"For now," Shaker said, hugging her close. "I really missed you. I'm so glad to hold you again." He kissed her nose, then flexed inside her lightly. "And to be held by you."

Debbie squeezed him lightly with her vaginal muscles. "I missed you, too. But I'm starving. What did you get?"

"Burgers, fries, and chocolate cake for dessert. I meant it when I said you shouldn't lose any weight." He kissed her. "And you need to keep up your energy level."

Debbie laughed, and then shrieked, as he began tickling her.

~

"So Delvin will sponsor the movies?" Shaker asked, as they shared the enormous piece of cake.

Debbie nodded. "But he wants final approval. I don't like that. I feel like he thinks he's in charge."

"He's used to being in charge," Shaker supplied, putting down his fork. "You get that last bit."

Debbie ate the last morsel, then took the plate and forks to the kitchen, returning with the wine bottle. "So what do you think of this? Rack called it Spiritwalker. I don't usually like white wine, but there's something compelling about this."

Shaker took a sip. "It's got a good body. Very nice."

Debbie lay back against him contentedly. "I'm glad you're here."

"I'm glad to be here. And I meant what I said about weekends. Tell me when I should get here."

"I'll get back to you, as soon as I coordinate with Brady."

"Are you ready for bed?"

"I'm more than ready. Come here."

CHAPTER FIVE

February

"WILL YOU JUST COME ON," DEBBIE MUTTERED, HAULING
Sheila behind her up to the counter in the Black Rose Spa. Song
was waiting for them, her expression aloof.

"We're both scheduled for a wrap or massage, haircare,
manicure, pedicure, and a facial, please."

"Of course. Follow me." Song led Debbie and Sheila to the
back area, then indicated two doors. "Please enter and undress to
your bare skin. I will send in someone to do your wrap, Debbie. I'll
be doing Sheila's wrap myself."

Sheila shot Debbie a look of disaster, then followed Song into
the room. Debbie stifled a smile and went into her own room. After
undressing, she put on the robe and slippers, and sat waiting.

Vassago Gray entered in a black shirt and dress pants. "Fancy
meeting you here," he said with a grin.

"What are you doing here?" Debbie asked, frowning.

"C'mon, you know I freelance here," he replied, as he began putting on some soothing stream music, and lit a few candles. "I don't have any appointments today, though, and Song's shorthanded with Xerxes out this week, so I told her I'd do you." He grinned. "If you don't mind, of course."

Do me, indeed. "Do you really have professional training in massage? I really need that, rather than just a wrap."

"As a master of massage? Eons, literally." He laughed. "Well, maybe not really that long, but I promise not to leave you disappointed." He showed her the tray of bottles. "We have the same options as last time, but also a few new ones, like the frankincense and myrrh, the black cinnamon, and the raspberry torte."

"I'll try the frankincense and myrrh."

"Ok, then lay back on the bed on your stomach, and relax. Tell me if anything I do hurts." He lowered the lighting. "Is that comfortable for you, or would you like an eye mask?"

Debbie giggled, then shook her head. "It's dark enough I don't see how you're going to massage me, no pun intended."

"Relax," Vassago soothed, his hands on her bare calves. "You're here to rejuvenate and refresh yourself. I'm going to stop talking now."

Debbie waited for him to try to kiss her as he began giving her a massage, or even to casually touch her sexually as his hands roamed her body. But Gray was all business, working her muscles until they gave way beneath his insistent pressure. After, he applied the lotion, working the light musky spice scent into her skin. When he finished, Debbie was nearly asleep, every inch of her pliable and logy.

"Turn onto your back," Vassago whispered. "I need to get your front. Stretch your arms out at your sides."

Debbie did as he asked. Vassago rubbed the lotion into her breasts, all down her legs and even into her upper thighs without so much as a stray pinch.

"'That was wonderful," Debbie groaned happily.

"You were very tense. I have to ask, how is my pilot coming?"

"Very well," Debbie answered. "But don't you have an agent that you're working through? He should be telling you timelines."

"Shaker advised me not to use an agent, since they might have me try to go to a competing studio. He said the best thing was just to work with Pandora…and you."

No wonder he's here then, the guy has no income with the pilot not being shot until next month. "Vassago, I'm sorry. Why don't you come to the studio next week? I'll get you at least some walk on parts in either *Hell to Pay* or *Dare to Tell*, or both."

"I don't want charity," he said a bit stiffly. "I want to earn my way."

"You will. We do want you for *Incubus*, we just had to do a big rewrite. We have to make Netflix so interested in the pilot that they can't refuse to sign the series."

"I understand that, which is why I'm willing to wait for you, Debbie," he said with a wink. "Please don't think I'm destitute. I enjoy working here. And once Valentine's Day is over there will be a line here for my services of women whose lovers let them down yet again on their big day."

"Damn, Vassago," Debbie commented. "You're pretty hard on the male species for being one, aren't you?"

He shook his head. "Men can be more obtuse than any other male in the animal kingdom. It's not usually a secret what women want. And then there's always the surest-yet-least-used-way a man can find out: ask." He looked over at her. "What facial would you prefer: mint, pumpkin spice or lavender?"

I hope I'm not one of those disappointed women come Sunday morning. "Lavender," Debbie answered distractedly.

Debbie pushed her self-pitying thoughts aside as Vassago cleaned her face, then moisturized and clarified and moisturized again. "Would you like a brow shaping?" he offered at the end. "Your eyebrows have a good natural shape, but they're wide. I could narrow them. Or I can just do a general shaping, pluck out the stray hairs."

"The latter. I never liked the 2mm think brows that some women wear, they look fake and unnatural. I'm not that delicate."

"I'd say not," Vassago whispered. "You're more a Valkyrie. Hold still." He adhered a few sticky tape pieces around Debbie's eyebrows, then pulled them off quickly.

"Ow!"

"Sorry. Hold still, I have the other side to do too."

Debbie wanted to squish her eyes shut, but she held still until he ripped that tape off too. *God, it felt like my entire eyebrow came off!*

Vassago smoothed on some cream, and the stinging sensation went away. He then turned his attention to her hands. "This is just to prepare you for your manicure, Sasha likes if I get the skin softening ahead of time."

"Is she new?"

Vassago nodded, his hands still massaging lotion into her other hand. "She's nice."

Debbie wanted to ask what kind of supernatural being Sasha was, but deemed it too intrusive. "How has business been? I'm glad to hear Xerxes came back."

"Business is okay, but it's a lot slower than last year at this time. Song had to take care of Sheila a lot last fall and winter, then again last month. She didn't have much help here, except for me. She had to cancel more than a few booked appointments." He half-smiled. "That's when I learned all this facial stuff, to help out. I was the only one who didn't abandon her. But even with my talents, there's only so much one man can do." He grinned.

"I didn't think how much Song had to give up to take care of Sheila," Debbie mused. "I should have offered to help her out more, help her find more workers."

"From what she said, you helped a lot, letting them stay at your house. Sheila would have been dead if you hadn't taken the situation in hand."

He's referring to hiring that hitman Gore to watch the house, so he was there to defend us the night the priest attacked. "I still wish she would've told me about how things were here."

"Let it go, business has picked up a bit, and we'll build it back up in time," Vassago said cheerfully. "Now off you go, Sasha will do your hair and nails and feet. I'll leave so you can get dressed. Enjoy the rest of your day."

"Ok, but please do come by the studios about those bit parts," Debbie called after him as he left the room. *He didn't try anything at all, I feel like such a fool for believing that he would when he's obviously a professional. It's me that's acting unprofessional, thinking he'd make a pass at his workplace. I've let my dreams take over my reality.* Irked at herself, Debbie dressed, then went out to the front of the spa. Sheila was already there, getting her nails dried under a heat lamp by a large squat woman with nails so long they resembled claws. *Wait, those are claws.*

"Debbie, hi," Sheila called happily. "I feel great. You look great! Did you hear Xerxes is back? What are you going to have done to your hair?"

"I'm not sure," Debbie answered, plopping into a nearby chair. "I hadn't even thought about my nails."

"Look at the racks of color on the far wall," Sasha said, without looking up. "Choose enamel or regular acrylic, then sit back and let me pamper you." She smiled, bearing a mouthful of large and blunted teeth. "You haven't had a proper pedicure and manicure until you've had an ogress do it."

～

"Delightful," Debbie drawled, as the duo exited the spa into the dusk. "I love my new strawberry blonde streaks." She waved her fingers. "And my dark red enamel. That ogress Sasha was right, that's the best damn pedicure I ever had."

"It's a good color for you," Sheila said, shaking out her new bouncy curls. "I'm glad to have gotten the last of the platinum blond and bright red out. Gold blonde is where I'm staying for a while."

"It's a good color for you," Debbie agreed. "We should come back in two months. How was it with Song?"

"She was fantastic," Sheila said, a little reluctantly. "We're um, back together. I had her move into my bedroom last weekend."

"Why didn't you tell me?" Debbie asked, trying to keep shrillness out of her voice. "Why'd you give me that panicked look when you went in for your wrap?"

"Because I was worried you'd be worried about me. And I was right, you are."

"I don't want you to be hurt again."

"I don't want to be hurt, either. But she's a loyal lover and friend, whatever else she might be. I want her, Debbie. We're renewing our vows tomorrow together, actually."

Debbie scrambled mentally for footing. "You didn't invite me?"

"Well...we really never did get married, remember? I fudged the docs to protect Rhonda in the hope Song could return. And because of that, now Song and me can't get married, because she's not in Rhonda now, and I'm going against any kind of possession against a person's will. This will be a ceremony with us just as us. Please don't be offended, we aren't inviting anyone."

Love is complicated when it's not on a movie screen. Debbie hugged her. "Well, I'm very happy for you. Please enjoy yourself and let me know if there's something I could get you for a present."

"No presents. But a raise if Pandora could afford it would be good? It's been a few years."

"It has and for me too," Debbie said aloud. "Let's look at the numbers when we come back to work on Monday, okay?"

"Okay and thanks. Have a great weekend!"

Debbie waved, then hurried to her car, checking email. *Still no text from Brady saying when he was going to get here. What the Hell?*

~

Debbie yawned again, then glanced at the airport clock. *Why did this have to happen? I've been sitting here for three hours.*

Brady had called to say his flight was delayed and he wasn't going to be in until 2am Saturday. There was some superstorm mid-country that stretched from the top of Texas to Canada. Debbie had prayed it would just shut down the airport Brady was at so he'd be stuck there and she could enjoy Valentine's Day with Shaker, but no luck: Brady had gotten the last flight out before the airport closed, but because of headwind and whatever else, the flight wasn't getting in until 4:30 am. Now it was nearly five, and they still hadn't announced the plane was officially unloading.

"Finally!" Debbie exclaimed, as the gate sign began digitalizing, the flight number appearing. She got up and went to the gate, as people began appearing.

"Debbie!" Brady called, as he hurried down the walkway. "I'm so sorry about this." He hugged her hard, then kissed her on the cheek. "Let's go, I just brought my carryon and backpack. I have the rest of my things coming in a week care of the studio."

"Your things? Everything?" *So he really did ditch his life back East to move here permanently after all. It's probably good Myrrh's not going to be around a lot, he'll be my houseguest for a while at this rate.* "Here, it's this way, my car is right out there beyond those doors."

"I don't have that much. I should be able to rent a small apartment and fit everything. I would have driven, but I heard that Rhonda's worse."

"She is?" *Sheila said nothing. Maybe she hasn't been to see Rhonda? But that's her legal wife, so the institution should be calling her first, not Brady.* "I'm sorry, I didn't know. What's happened?"

"She's become withdrawn, instead of raving like she used to. I'm not sure, but I'm going to see her tomorrow."

"Let's get to my place," Debbie said, opening her car door. "After we both get some sleep, we can go from there."

~

"Shaker, where are you?" Debbie fumed. *5pm on Valentine's Day and he's not answering my thought calls or calling me.*

"Debbie?"

"Brady," Debbie answered. "I'm in here." *He must be back from seeing Rhonda.* "How was your sister?"

"She seemed okay to me. Maybe a little quiet? She said that Sheila had been to see her, offered her a divorce if she wanted one." He paused. "Rhonda said she didn't remember ever getting married to Sheila."

"Um, I think they talked about it, but that Sheila signed paperwork to protect Rhonda after she...fell ill," Debbie stammered. "There wasn't a ceremony."

"That's what I thought. Rhonda...well, she wasn't making any sense. She wasn't hysterical, but she wasn't...I don't know."

This is not what I wanted to be dealing with on Valentine's Day, of all days. But if I don't deal with it right now, it'll bite me in the ass later for sure. "What exactly did she say?"

Brady rolled his eyes, exasperated. "She accused me of giving her a drug to make her compliant right after we got here that changed her personality, even her sexual orientation. That she never liked women before coming here to California with me for Jett's wedding, only men. That I'd tricked her into a marriage along with Sheila, that we'd put something in her food to make her like women as well as men. That we'd given her some kind of mind control drugs, and that the doctors at the hospital were still giving them to her."

None of that's true; Rhonda's just looking for a scapegoat to explain her bisexuality. Debbie breathed a sigh of relief. "So she's come out now, then, so to speak?"

Brady nodded. "She admitted that she cared for Sheila, and that she didn't want a divorce. I'm not sure that's true; I think she understands that its Sheila's insurance that's paying for her to stay there. She's also grateful that she's off the drugs and booze. The rest of the time she seemed...disjointed. Halfway through a sentence she seemed to reverse her thought or forget what point she was making." He held up his hands in frustration.

"Did you talk to the doctor? Is there a plan to get her to the point she can get out and live a normal life?"

"Not with how she's acting, no. She'd need a full-time caregiver; she can't hold a job or cook for herself. I wouldn't trust her not to light a candle in a room and accidentally put it under the drapes or her own hair," Brady said harshly. "Rhonda was always self-destructive; its how she got into drugs in the first place. It's like she lost that drive to destroy herself and can't find anything else to replace it."

I'll have to bring this to Shaker, get his ideas on how to handle it. If he ever gets here. "I can go with you next week to visit her, if you want? I'm sorry, I haven't visited her there, and she's my sister-in-law, I should."

"You didn't know her that well, and what you knew of her wasn't exactly endearing," Brady remarked. "But yeah, please come with me. I feel bad saying it but I'm already dreading going back."

"Of course," Debbie said, nodding. She put on her jacket, opened the sliding glass panel then walked out onto the deck, closing the door behind her. *Shaker where are you? Answer me!*

Out on the back lawn in the trees, a few shadows flitted. *Some of Myrrh's murder.*

Brady opened the glass door. "Debbie?"

"Yes?" she answered, turning to look at him.

He came out onto the deck, looking uncomfortable. "I just wanted to ask if you wanted to go out and get some dinner. I know

I'm not Jett, but he wouldn't want you spending your first Valentine's day without him alone."

Debbie made herself look right at him. "Um, Brady. I'm not. I have a date."

Brady looked shocked and angry for a moment, then frowned. "With who?"

"No one you'd know," Debbie muttered, looking away.

He folded his arms over his chest. "Please tell me it's not that Henry guy who proposed to you before?"

"Are you crazy?" Debbie sputtered, wheeling back toward him. "He's the one who put Sheila in a coma and nearly drove Pandora into bankruptcy. I hope he's still in jail."

"Then who? Your new *Incubus* star, Gabriel Gray?"

"Look, Brady, I know you're my brother in law, but that doesn't give you the right to tell me who to date, or when I'm allowed to start. You're right, my husband wouldn't want me to sit home crying today. And no, it's not anyone working at the studio right now. He's not an actor."

The doorbell rang. The three dogs emerged from the shadow near the couch and ran for the door, barking.

"I didn't know you had dogs." Brady said, confused. "They've been so quiet all day. You must have a dog flap on your ground floor backdoor."

Hellhounds don't need a dog door. "This is Pitch, Baroness and Pike," Debbie said hauling the animals back from the door and opening it. She accepted the huge bouquet of red and black roses in a crystal-cut glass vase from the floral deliveryman, then shut the door.

"Well, at least he's a gentleman," Brady said after a moment.

Debbie walked past him back to the kitchen, placing the flowers on the table. She grabbed the attached note and read it.

Meet me for dinner. Be out front in five.

"Brady, help yourself to whatever's in the fridge and kitchen," Debbie said. "There's HBO and Netflix on the television. Don't worry about the dogs, they're used to coming and going. Bye!" She breezed past him, and he called after her, but she was already through the door and running into Shaker's open arms. "Go now!"

Shaker teleported them instantly, Debbie's heels sinking into the sand. "Where are we?"

"The Breakers of Palm Beach," Shaker said, gesturing to the massive hotel behind them. "I have a reservation for us for two." He held out his hand.

Debbie took it. "This is a beautiful place." They walked up onto the concrete lower beach view terrace, then through a few small hallways and into a beautiful greenhouse-style glass hallway running the entire side of one wall. Everywhere glamourous couples were eating dinner or having a drink, and one man had just gotten down on one knee to propose to his date.

"This is spectacular!"

"Wait until you see the dining room."

Shaker led her into an expansive room of two tiers of tables and low overhead lighting. As before, almost all the tables were full. Shaker walked up to one that said reserved and pulled out a chair for Debbie.

"Are you sure this is ours?" Debbie said, sitting down.

"No," Shaker said. "But I did reserve a table for tonight, and this one looks the nicest for us."

A waiter came running up. "Can I help you?"

"Yes. Please bring us a bottle of the best Malbec you have here, and a plate of some cheesy appetizer."

The waiter looked about to speak, then smiled quickly. "Right away, sir."

"Who does he see you as?" Debbie asked, shaking her head and smiling.

"Brad Pitt."

Debbie began laughing, and clapped her hand over her mouth, glad of the noise all around her. "Then who am I?"

"Just yourself," Shaker said, taking her hand and kissing it. "You look beautiful."

Debbie looked down at her simple red knit dress. "I'm a little underdressed for this crowd."

"Not with those earrings," Shaker said with appreciation. "I'm so glad you wore them."

"Of course I wore them," Debbie said, squeezing his hand. *I remember the night you gave them to me.* She moved her head slightly, letting the carat ruby drop earrings sparkle in the light. "I wanted tonight to be perfect!"

"It will be," Shaker assured, taking her hand. He rubbed his finger over her onyx ring and wedding band, Debbie noticing his own band was in place. "Happy Valentine's Day, wife."

~

"That has to be the most luscious meal I ever had," Debbie said happily, as Shaker and she walked along the beach hand in hand watching the lights out on the water of boats offshore. "Thank you again, it's been memorable."

"Not yet it hasn't," Shaker whispered, then suddenly around them everything shifted as he whirled her in his arms, setting her down on a beach that was almost devoid of light. The air was noticeably warmer and more humid.

"Where are we?"

"Our beach," Shaker said, hugging her tightly. "Where we were those first times together, back when we first met." He took her hand. "Come with me, I have everything arranged."

Shaker walked her up the torchlit path, then teleported her again into the open- air mountaintop villa. "It sounded a lot more romantic to walk by torchlight here until I saw how far it was from the beach to the villa." He chuckled. "So Brady made it after all?"

"Yes," Debbie answered. "He got here on the red eye this morning. He's planning on staying with me until he finds a place."

"I thought you seemed in a hurry to leave," Shaker commented, tossing another log on the outdoor fire. "Do you want to open us a bottle of wine?"

"Another bottle?" Debbie teased. "I have to warn you I may end up falling asleep."

"That's okay," Shaker said, staring at her with a small smile for a moment. "I want some time just holding you."

Debbie brought out some red wine from the rack in the kitchen, Shaker retrieving an opener from a nearby drawer. Grabbing a few glasses, they settled next to the fire with the bottle.

Debbie poured them each a glass, handing one to Shaker. "Here." The air was cooler up here, with a breeze off the darkness below rising up, dense and moist. "Is that a forest down there?"

"Rainforest mixed with regrowth of other trees. Used to be a palm oil plantation."

"Nice," Debbie said, admiring the sea of blackness. *I'm glad it's gone back to nature, but I'm also glad I'm up here away from any of the wild animals.*

"So tell me all the news."

Debbie filled him in on Sheila, Song and Rhonda. "Is it normal for her to act how she's acting, disjointed?"

Shaker nodded. "She's used to Song being in control, after that long a possession. The person she was merged with Song's personality in the months they were together. You might say that Rhonda misses Song."

"Now you're just being evil. There's no way a human would miss the demon possessing them."

"And you're being naïve, Debbie. Rhonda acted like a disobedient child, and her actions were well on their way to killing her. Song, to her, is a conscience that suddenly came into being that stopped her from her destructive habits. Got her off the drugs, the cigarettes, and the alcohol, made her eat well, sleep enough, and exercise regularly. How hard is it for a person to keep to a new diet, or fitness regime, or a new resolution? How many resolves get kept? Few, because it's easy to go back to your old routine when the decision is yours alone. But say you had someone else saying 'no, you can't do that anymore'. How much easier would it be to stay on track?"

"You're evil," Debbie said, sipping her wine. "Mostly because you always make whatever bad thing you're championing seem perfectly reasonable and the most logical choice."

"I wouldn't advocate possession for you, my dear." Shaker flashed a winning smile. "But tell me, is Sheila giving any of the same symptoms that Rhonda did? I'll bet she's not."

"No, she's not. She's also against possession now completely."

"Whomever grabbed her was not a novice, to hold Sheila. Your friend isn't the type who's usually possessed; she's too bold and outspoken, a fighter. If she hadn't been attacked by Henry and been already in a coma, it would never have happened."

"If she hadn't been linked to two demons, it wouldn't have happened," Debbie corrected. "She was already feeling a tendency toward bad acts, she told me herself. That weakened her self-reliance, made her doubt her reasoning. She likely didn't fight the demon taking hold of her because of that. By the time she was aware of what was happening, it was too late."

"You may be right," Shaker said, after a moment.

"I know you don't want to acknowledge that aspect," Debbie stated. "But it's there. I do love you, Shaker. But I'm glad that you have a new Mistress, too."

"Sometimes you're glad," Shaker said sarcastically. "Sometimes you're not. You can't have everything, Debbie."

"I know," Debbie said, putting down her wine and leaning in against him. "I'm glad of what I do have. I'm glad you're here with me now."

Shaker rumbled something under his breath but put his arm around her. "How is Myrrh?" he said finally. "I hope you didn't leave Brady with her. She'll get annoyed and make him part of her flock."

"Not likely. He doesn't need redemption. Myrrh told me about her murder, about where they came from and why they serve her. Do you think they really get redeemed and go to Heaven?"

"I can't say," Shaker said. "She's not that old, really, only about two hundred. So not many of her flock would have gotten to redemption point or passed on to date. None of her crowmen are demons I know, to my knowledge." He paused. "I know what you might be thinking, and the answer's no, I'm not going to be joining her flock. I am who I am. If this was a romance, there'd be a big sacrifice on my part likely killing me close to the end and yes, I'd go to heaven and then be born again for you to find as a mortal man in the last scene."

"We already did that last year," Debbie quipped. "You died, left me your money and a new movie, and came back to be my lover by New Year's."

Shaker chuckled. "Now who's being evil? You know it's not the same."

"I know." Debbie hugged him. "I'm happy you're here with me."

"Good."

"Myrrh said she was going to be busy and away a lot. I haven't been home much myself since we have a lot of projects this year." She filled him in on *Hell to Pay, Everlasting,* and *Dare to Tell,* leaving out *Origin of Fear.* "*Destiny in the Ashes* will also come out in December, if we can get Brady to finish those couple scenes. I don't want to offend Brady, but I'm not sure how to deal with him. I didn't know very much about Jett."

"I can always help Brady cooperate," Shaker said, after a moment.

"I'd rather not do that, if there's another way," Debbie said delicately. "Once you left him, he'd remember what happened while you possessed him."

Shaker seemed to mull that over. "Not necessarily," he said finally. "I could close his eyes, so he couldn't have the visual reminder. But you're right in that when I left, he'd think he was going crazy, because he wouldn't remember any actions or the passage of time, and everyone I came in contact with as him would remember him. Plus the footage from *Destiny in the Ashes* would be there, of course."

Debbie sighed, then took another sip of wine. "Hopefully, he'll finish the movie, and then decide after a few weeks that this isn't the place for him. He seems too nice of a person for showbusiness."

"I agree that staying with you is no place for him," Shaker said, hugging her against him. "Remember if worse comes to worst though, the offer's open. I put too much into the picture to have it never see the darkness of the theater."

"You and your odd sayings," Debbie said, watching the flames. "So I have to ask, are we spending the night here? I have my cell phone, but I'm not sure it will work here."

"It won't. And don't worry, I'll take you back tonight if you want."

"I don't want. Brady's all set to give me a speech about dating too soon."

"We need to hook him up with a woman," Shaker said, after a moment. "Preferably one who will help him to decide to move back home."

"That'd be great, but no one comes to mind," Debbie said. "Unless you know of someone?"

"Give me time to think." Shaker kissed her cheek. "I may come up with something." He sighed happily.

Debbie leaned back against him and watched the fire, content.

~

"Shaker?" Debbie grunted, opening her eyes. For a moment she was terrified that he'd left her alone at the hilltop villa with no way home. But then she recognized her own bedroom, and the shifting hellhounds as they stirred in the blackness around her.

"Sorry, good dogs," she said, patting them each in turn. "I didn't know I was home." *The last thing I remember is sitting with Shaker in front of the fire.* She turned on a light, then staggered to the bathroom for a glass of water.

There was a note on the counter. "Had to go, sorry. Will be back tomorrow morning if I can." There was an S scrawled at the bottom.

His Mistress must have needed something. "Damn her," Debbie growled, then got herself the water and drank it. Irked, she went back to bed.

In the morning Shaker had still not returned. Debbie showered and dressed, then opened the bedroom door tentatively. The door to the guest room down the hall was still closed. Grateful, she hurried to the kitchen, fed the three dogs, and brewed some coffee. She was just enjoying it when she felt arms around her.

"Morning, gorgeous."

"Brady?" Debbie turned and narrowly avoided his lips. They landed instead on her jaw, as she moved away from him. "What are you doing?"

"What are you doing?" he replied, offended. "Last night you were in my bed and happy to be there. Then you snuck away in the night and this morning you're acting like it never happened?"

"I was out most of the night," Debbie corrected. "I was not in your bed. I got home before dawn and went to my bed. The three dogs were the only ones that slept with me last night, and that's the truth."

"We slept together last night," Brady said, hurt. "I can't believe you're denying it."

"Show me some evidence of that," Debbie countered. "Any

evidence. Because the dress I was wearing was on my bed this morning."

"You got home angry and said you were slipping into something more comfortable. You went into your bedroom and came out naked. Then we went back to my room. We made love several times, then fell asleep."

"I was with my boyfriend most of last night. I'm telling you I didn't see you at all after I came home."

"You came home in the middle of the night, furious at your so-called boyfriend. He'd left you because he had some emergency."

That part's true, though furious is too strong a word. "That didn't happen."

"I suppose that you don't remember telling me that I should make a stage name for myself like my brother, calling myself Pitch Black, instead of Brady Black?"

"Brady, I have a dog named Pitch! Why would I suggest that same name, even if yes, I admit it's catchy together with your last name?"

"I don't know why you're doing this," Brady said, shoulders slumping. "I really thought we had a good time. You're just trying to deny it because in the light of day you think you made a mistake."

Nope, I narrowly avoided one. "Look, you must have had a vivid dream. I'm glad if you enjoyed it. But I really didn't sleep with you. And as much as I want you to work at Pandora to finish Jett's scenes, maybe it would be best if I helped you find another place to stay for now."

"I can't deal with this now, I need to go see Rhonda," Brady said spitefully. "I'll talk to you later." He stalked out.

"What a mess." Debbie looked at the three dogs at her feet, all wagging tails at her. "I don't suppose you can tell me what happened here last night? I'd be willing to pay in bacon."

The dogs wriggled happily but didn't answer.

Just then the phone rang.

"Shaker, this had better be you." She picked up the phone. "Hello?"

"Hello. Is Brady Black there?"

He gave out my number! "Who's this?"

"This is the Lavern Institute and Healing House. It's about his sister, Rhonda Bernard. There's been an accident."

"Oh shit. We're on our way." Debbie hung up the phone, then yelled for Brady, as she looked for her car keys.

CHAPTER SIX

February

DEBBIE RUSHED THROUGH THE DOUBLE DOORS AT THE entrance of Lavern Institute, Brady at her heels. Sheila was waiting at the counter, upset.

"What happened?"

"Rhonda had a stroke, or something," Sheila said, hugging Debbie, then Brady. "Thanks for coming."

"You said 'a stroke or something'," Brady said curtly. "They don't know which?"

Sheila looked at him, annoyed. "They went into her room and she was sitting there, her face all contorted. She wouldn't answer any questions and wouldn't eat. They've got her on an IV now for fluids. They're going to give her a few tests."

"Tests for what?" Brady persisted.

"To find out if she's in a vegetative state, or if this is some kind of temporary coma."

"From what!" Brady exploded. "I was here yesterday to visit her, and she was okay! She can't just have gone into a coma!"

"Look, the doctor is coming, and he can talk to you, Brady," Sheila said, looking at Debbie in confusion. "I just know what they've told me, which isn't much as I just got here."

"Fine," Brady said, pushing past her and Debbie. "I'll go ask someone who knows something."

"What's up his ass?" Sheila said, after he'd gone.

"He thinks he slept with me last night, and is angry I told him he dreamed it," Debbie explained, rubbing her eyes.

"Are you sure nothing happened?" Sheila prodded meaningfully.

"I was with Shaker last night, most of the night," Debbie said. "Besides, I think I'd remember."

"Depends if it was memorable," Sheila quipped, then laughed.

Debbie smacked her shoulder. "That's not funny. He's really pissed off."

"Look, maybe you have a succubus haunting your guest bedroom," Sheila offered. "Or an incubus that's bisexual. Have you had any vivid sex dreams you thought might have been real?"

Debbie blanched, her face whitening. "Yes, actually. But I looked for key...items out of place the next day from the dream and they weren't out of place."

"I was just kidding. Brady obviously just hoped to hook up with you. Be flattered."

"You be flattered. Maybe he has a thing for his sibling's spouses." *And kidding or not, I need to question Vassago Gray on Monday. I've put it off too long already.*

Sheila snorted, then changed her expression as the doctor and Brady neared.

"Mrs. Blanchard. Your wife seems to have come out of her state. We aren't sure what happened, but she may have had a slight stroke."

"Why do you say a stroke?" Brady asked.

"We can't say what might have happened." The doctor shrugged. "We have done tests since the orderly reported her state at breakfast, and there was no change initially, now she's talking again and has motor skills. We'll watch her carefully for this coming week."

"I'm not sure that's best for her," Sheila said smoothly. "I trusted you with her care, and you haven't kept me in the loop." She glanced at Brady. "I'm her spouse. You've been calling my brother-in-law instead. I'm not sure what your problem is with lesbians, but my wife isn't going to be your guinea pig. Please get me discharge papers ready. I'm going to be taking Rhonda out of here."

"That's not a good idea," the doctor started.

"You can't take her home, Sheila!" Brady sputtered. "You have to work. Rhonda's in no condition to be on her own!"

"Why don't we all go and see her?" Sheila snapped. "Doctor?"

"She really shouldn't have visitors," he retorted. "But I can't stop you, as her spouse." He turned. "Follow me."

"What are you doing?" Brady hissed to Sheila.

"What I should've done a while ago," she retorted. "Stay out of this, Brady."

Debbie followed Sheila and the doctor down the hall and into another wing through a monitored electronically locked door. They went into the fourth room on the left. Rhonda was there in bed. She stirred when they entered, then sat up and smiled. "Sheila."

"Hi, baby," Sheila said, sitting on the bed. They embraced.

Rhonda looked at Brady. "Hi, bro."

"This isn't comatose," Brady said, glaring at the doctor. "She seems better than she has in weeks!"

Rhonda's eyes looked over and met Debbie's, then she winked.

Debbie started, drawing back. *Song's back in her.*

"Do you want to go home?" Sheila said, still hugging Rhonda.

"I'm feeling pretty weak," Rhonda said, moving back and pushing her hair out of her eyes. "And I need a shower. But yes, if they can pronounce me healthy, I'd like to go home."

"At least three days," the doctor stated. "We need to make sure you're really okay. Most people don't come out of a stroke with better verbal skills than before."

They do if they got their demon back, Debbie thought silently.

～

"We should talk," Debbie said, when she and Brady got in her car an hour later.

"Look, I'm sorry for earlier," Brady said, looking out the window. "I, um, remember something from the dream that I realize is not in my room this morning and would be, if what I remembered had actually happened." He cleared his throat. "I also remember using all my condoms in my wallet, and they're still there. So you're right, it didn't happen."

But you still want it to, don't you? "Good. I wasn't sure what to say to convince you." She paused. "I'm surprised about Rhonda. But she does look a lot better."

"She does, but none of it makes any sense." He rolled down the window, breathing deeply. "I hate hospitals, the smell worst of all." He turned back to her. "Rhonda was always a pain in the ass. I was glad she met Sheila, and I'm still glad. But I'm seriously thinking of suing that doctor. He seems to have no idea of what's really going on with her."

He has no idea of what's really going on with her. Neither do you. "I think it's one of those medical problems that doesn't have a clear diagnosis. I'm just glad she's better. You said once that she had drug and alcohol problems, indicating that it was a long-term issue. Maybe she's got some brain damage from that, and it contributed to this happening. The idea of suing is great if it makes you feel better, but I don't see where they did anything to Rhonda that might be considered malpractice."

"You're right," Brady said, after a moment of silence. "I'm just angry."

93

"Do you want to finish the picture?" Debbie said bluntly. "*Destiny in the Ashes*? I need to know, Brady."

"I told you last night I would," Brady said softly. "I meant it then. Yes, I'll finish it."

"Do you want to be billed as Pitch in the movie, and not Brady?"

"No," Brady mumbled. "Every time I hear that now, I'm picturing your dog."

"How about Cole, instead?" Debbie offered, thinking rapidly. "Or Coal, with an "a"? It's a play on words like Jett's acting name was and also a man's name, too."

"Hey," Brady said, perking up. "Yes, that's an excellent name."

"Great, then I'll take care of it, Cole," Debbie said, flashing him a smile.

"Do you still want me to find an apartment?" Brady asked.

"I'll help you find one," Debbie said kindly. "We're family, after all."

∽

The next morning, Debbie drove Brady to the studios. She lent him her car to transport the 30-something boxes that had arrived at a storage facility, then went right to Sheila's office, slamming the door.

"What is it?" Sheila said calmly.

"Song's in Rhonda," Debbie whispered fiercely. "If you were going to do this, why didn't you do it before Brady arrived? He's thinking of suing the doctor."

"Because Rhonda didn't go into her fugue state or whatever until Sunday early morning," Sheila shot back, eyes narrowing. "I and Song went to the hospital together. I sent her in to see how Rhonda was while I went to the front desk. Song reported that Rhonda had "shut down" and wasn't responsive. So she went back

94

into her to see if she could get a response. Apparently, Rhonda didn't fight at all, and gave up control willingly."

"And you believe that?"

"I have no reason not to. Song was with me when Rhonda stopped responding. She didn't cause this." Her tone softened. "Rhonda wasn't the most stable woman to begin with, Debbie. On her own she would've lived in that institution the rest of her life. Do you think that's better than the life that she can live with me and Song?"

Her rationale sounds just like Shaker's. "I'm not going to protest, because it wouldn't do anyone any good." Debbie sat down opposite Sheila. "I asked Shaker about this, and he indicated that Rhonda might need to be repossessed." *God, I sound like I'm describing a car.* "Brady told me about how she was when he visited. It sounded like she was in trouble."

"So how was Valentine's Day?" Sheila asked, changing the subject. "Did Shaker get a furlough?"

"We had a good time. But he had to leave early."

"Maybe he should possess Brady," Sheila offered. "If Brady is willing? He doesn't seem to have a very strong personality, in spite of all his posturing with the doctor."

Debbie's mouth fell open. "I can't believe you just said that! You just told me you weren't pro-possession a few weeks ago."

"Look, I admit I don't know Brady that well," Sheila said, putting up her palms. "But he doesn't seem to have any drive, and some very questionable actions. He's just moved across country to what, do a walk on part in a movie that will last at most two weeks? He's making moves on his dear departed brother's wife and seems happy to live in his brother's house rent free with no contributions of any kind without telling you what his plans are for the future. It sounds to me like he wants to step into Jett's shoes, and into your bed."

He does, he even want's his own tradename. "Even if I wanted that, which I don't, Shaker wouldn't go for it."

"Wouldn't he?" Sheila poked. "It wouldn't be like it was with Jett. Brady could be a willing participant, like Rhonda."

I'm not convinced she's willing. And nothing you say is going to convince me. "Brady wouldn't believe me if I told him about it, and even if I did, I'm not sure he'd be willing. Shaker's powerful, Sheila. I think the relationship he'd have with anyone he possessed wouldn't be…equal. Brady needs to find his own place to live, and I told him I'd help him find an apartment."

"Look, I'm not trying to tell you your business," Sheila said finally. "But if you don't want him as a lover or a problem, then we should hurry and shoot the scenes this week and next, and then send him on his way. Don't help him find an apartment."

"How exactly am I supposed to do that?"

"Tell him it's not working with him living in your house rent free with no long-term job, and that we're sorry but we can't offer him any more work because he's a bad actor. Have Shaker use a glamour and come over and tell him to leave as your new lover. I don't care, just get rid of him."

"Duly noted." *And a lot easier to say than to do.* "Now, since I'm here, do you have any updates for me?"

Sheila nodded, handing her a folder. "Here's the house that Leri found to shoot *Dare to Tell*. It's a few hours north of Los Angeles near the Angeles National Forest, in Flintridge, California. It belonged to Robert Thomas Moore, a poet and businessman."

"What was his business?"

"He raised foxes for their fur and made millions off their pelts. In his spare time he collected birds and mammals. The collection at the time of his death was something like 50,000 specimens."

"So he electrocuted and skinned millions of foxes for money and for fun he suffocated and poisoned other animals and birds for trophies by the thousands. Charming. He deserves to be in hell, not hanging around here on Earth."

"He donated his land on his death to the Audubon Society. It's now over 1600 acres. His house though, Sunny Gables Estate, is for rent and I checked, we can shoot *Dare to Tell* inside it. It's got everything the script asks for: seven bedrooms, a creepy master bedroom that Moore supposedly died in, a staff guesthouse that we can have the heroine living in, a bar, a library, and even supposedly some secret passageways. We'll just have to have a set or greenscreen here with the house being at the top of a town looking down on it, to shoot the outside shots."

"When can we begin shooting?"

"The house does most of its business as a haunted tourist trap in the fall, so their spring schedule is light, and right now they've got nothing booked until June. So if we hurry, we could have most of the scenes shot in the next couple months, ending right before their first appointment. I told him to hold the house as a rental tentatively for us as I wanted to talk to you first."

"Do it, that's fantastic. Announce it by email today to everyone on the team and ask Eugene and Mark to check it out ASAP, I want them there by Friday with the heroine shooting the first scenes. Keep me apprised of the progress. Anything else?"

"Leri also found a good location for the outside of the house." Sheila tossed Debbie a picture. "This is another house a few miles south of Sunny Gables, its outside looks a little more intimidating. The owner said he'd take a couple thousand, and as far as he was concerned, he'll sign the deed over to us. It comes with a few acres of land."

Debbie looked at Sheila, incredulous. "What? Why? This house looks a little rough, but unless it's a shell, it's worth far more than a few thousand dollars. But yeah, take him up on his offer and buy it."

"You haven't heard the best part! This house is near a depression, so if we get a good rain, there'll be some water near it. We can maybe fudge that into a lake." Sheila grinned. "We'll be able to work on *Origin of Fear*, if the weather cooperates."

"It's a little eerie, how well this is working out," Debbie mused, then shrugged. "But this is great news. Anything else?"

"Oh, I have your tickets too for the Oscars," Sheila said, digging in her desk. "They were sent over this morning." She handed them to Debbie. "It's not great seating, but you'll have a decent view of the stage."

"There's two of them," Debbie uttered. "I don't suppose you want to go?"

"No, Rhonda and I'll enjoy watching you accept the trophy on Jett's behalf," Sheila teased. "Why don't you ask Gray? He's here on one of the sets where *Hell to Pay* is shooting. He said you told him to get a walk on part, so we have him in some heavy makeup as one of the characters that gets killed in the opening scene."

A necessary evil. "Good," Debbie said, turning. "I need to talk to him."

~

"Okay, places people! Remember, use the house shot in the background on the screen just for reference, this is just a short scene that takes place on the lawn. The scenes that take place on the lawn and in the house later in the film will be shot over on set two, as well as Cassy's character of Morwen coming out of the river from swimming as a wolf and changing into human form. The group is just coming together to head out on a job to kill a demon. This is one of the first scenes of the movie, so makeup and expression have to be perfect, for a third of you it's the only time we really see you before you're dead."

"Thanks a lot, Bart," an actor in a fedora and tan suit sniped. "We read the script."

Debbie turned to Sheila, who had come with her. "Okay, explain who everyone is. I see that Cassy Knight's there playing the lead werewolf, Morwen."

A sharp reprimanding bark sounded out of sight, ending with a questioning howl.

"*Orn, wanting to know where I was,*" came the voiceover in Cassy's voice. Cassy came on screen dressed in jeans and sneakers and an oversize T-shirt with a plaid shirt over it, her hair in very long blond dreadlock-type braids.

"Orn is Morwen's lover, another werewolf," Sheila whispered. "We got Guy Hammerhelm to play him. He's that stunt double Idris Elba used to use?"

Cassy headed toward the house, as a voiceover stated "*The pack's house. My pack, even if that included a human now.*"

"Here comes Apex, he's the guy in the hat who's the sorcerer," Sheila said.

"Still doing the braids?" the actor in the tan suit and fedora said snidely, striding up to Cassy. "You look like some kind of half-assed Scottish warrior in your pants and plaid, Morwen."

"That's...shit, that's Gray," Debbie exclaimed. "That's not a walk on part, Sheila."

Sheila shrugged. "We'll have to ask Bart."

"Better than a mobster, Apex," Cassy cracked. "All that's missing is your Tommy gun. When are you going to realize that its 1945, not 1925?"

Gray adjusted his hat, aloof. "It matters to have a little style. Come on, the others are waiting out front. Pete's going to brief us." He smiled. "Jay told me that the mark this time is a demon."

Cassy followed Gray across the side yard, as another voiceover sounded. *Even though we were prepping for another job, I was at ease. Alone, I would have worried about the tables being turned, about being killed by what I had been hired to hunt down and kill. But with my team, I never worried. They had my back and I had theirs. That was just the way it was.*

"That's Maximillian Goth playing Pete, the vampire leader and Guy as Orn the werewolf, who I mentioned earlier," Sheila said. "He was the one who used to be a faerie in the original script."

"*Pete was our leader. It was a given that Apex would follow his style. The younger man looked up to him. Even if their age only looked to be a few years difference, Pete was much older, being a vampire. Darwin was also there, his expression eager. But he'd only been with the team for a few months, on short successful runs. He had no idea how bad things could get if something went wrong.*"

"Darwin is the teen boy, Killy is the teen girl. Empath werewolves," Sheila added. "Heath Bannock is the boy, the girl's some relative of Cassy's who's hoping to break into film. That guy coming from stage right is Jay, another vampire. We got Sam Waters to play him, he makes a good tough guy."

"Don't you ever wear anything but a sour expression?" Sam mocked, whacking Cassy on the back. She growled at him, letting prosthetic thick fangs show. He growled back at her with a fanged smile of his own with delicate vampire fangs, then sauntered over to talk to Maximilian.

"Same kind of fangs we used in *Immortal Confessions*. They're remarkably easy to wear, the actors just have to practice talking so they don't lisp. I asked Devlin about that, actually."

"He said to tell you that he'd had practice as a bard for centuries," Debbie whispered back.

Guy came over to Cassy, his expression troubled. "*Orn's worry bothered me, because he never went into a job with anything but surety. He wasn't blood—the usual term most werecreatures used to describe a close relative—but he was the closest thing. We'd grown up together, fending for ourselves on the streets and bedding down with the coyotes at night. Looking back, it was surprising we'd stayed intelligent and not gone over to animal, where life was more brutal but a hell of a lot easier. Some of that was we'd had each other. But finding this group of hunters was what had given us our purpose. It had saved us.*"

"This is a lot of voiceovers for the beginning of a movie with the actors just standing there," Debbie mentioned.

"Can't help it, we can't afford to show all the backstory."

"Maybe have CGI make a short section of the baby werewolves toughing the streets? I'd at least like to see the option."

"Okay." Sheila scribbled it down.

"Do you know anything about the mark?" Cassy asked Guy.

"Don't call it that, remember?" he said gruffly. "Apex and Pete had a hissy fit last time you did. We don't kill people. We kill things that murder people like us for fun."

Cassy rolled her eyes. "I didn't mean anything by it, Orn. Why do you have to overthink everything? I just wanted to know some info."

Guys's gruff expression broke into a tired smile. "Sorry. I just don't want us anything but solid. The thing we're going after this time is a demon. And he probably has friends."

"So? We've killed demons before."

"Yes, and we lost 2 pack members doing it. I don't want to lose Darwin. He's just a kid, even if he acts like he's wise. Or Killy—"

Cassy grimaced. "The things we hunt always go for the empaths. You know that. Darwin knows that. So does his sister, Killy."

"Knowing it and escaping with ease is one thing. Having a demon get hold of you is another." Guy's tone was haunted. "You and I both saw what happened to previous empaths, Morwen. I don't want to see another one ripped apart."

The voiceover began again. "*I didn't want to talk anymore about the realities of the job. Hunting with our group gave us better odds at success. It didn't get rid of the danger. Nothing could.*" "I trust Pete, Orn. He'd never take on more than we could chew."

Guy let out a breath and nodded, his shoulders relaxing. "I know, Morwen. I'm just worried. We've had a really good run these last six months, ever since Apex joined us. The longer it lasts, the more I worry about it ending, about what might happen."

"Cut!" Bart yelled. "Okay good first run. Now go back and do it over. Cassy, this is your lover, show a little affection, maybe a smile for Orn."

"Should a woman warrior be showing affection when she's heading out to kill a demon?" Cassy called out. "It seems to me from the voiceovers she's thinking more about surviving."

"Point taken. Scrap that," Bart said, annoyed. "Gray, you're a sorcerer here, not a model. Give us an expression that says more danger than fun-loving scamp."

"Got it," Gray called back. He noted Debbie and gave her a quick salute with a smile.

Bart had them run through the scene a few more times, then called for a stop. "Okay, that's good, and I like what I'm seeing. Everybody take a break, but make sure you're over to Set 2 by ten thirty, that's a half hour from now. We'll do this scene for real, then do a few more that take place outside the house. We'll break for lunch about one, then Cassy, Guy, and Heath, I want you back at Set 2 for the later scenes around the house. Gray, you also need to show up, but you'll need a costume change and a lot of fake blood applied, so show up as soon as that's done. Thanks people!"

Everyone began heading offset in various directions. Debbie motioned to Gray, who held up a finger with an earnest expression as he was talking to Cassy. He excused himself, then came over to her.

Think of him as Gray and not Vassago. Keep it professional. "I see you've got a speaking part."

"Yes, the actor who was supposed to play Apex backed out." Gray grinned. "I'm very lucky."

Did you have something to do with that, is the question. "You are. Good luck with the part. Walk with me."

Gray fell in place beside her as they left the set, heading back to the offices. "What's up?"

"If I needed to know if I'd been visited by an incubus, how would I tell?" Debbie said pointedly, stopping and looking him over. "If he didn't look like himself that is and wore someone else's form."

"What a sly fiend," Gray teased, his eyes flashing. "I'd expect the usual manifestations of sexual completion. I hope that there was completion?"

Debbie stepped close to him. "Don't fuck with me, Vassago Gray. Did you come into my dreams?"

Gray just smiled. *Let's just say I came in your dreams,* said his voice in her mind. *You enjoyed it enough for three women.*

The crowmen, that was him. All three of them were him. I didn't put it together at the time, but it is also likely why Morwen said what she did about him being my lover. "And all those dreams of you visiting me as an incubus?"

"With the first dream, I wanted to see if you were open to a little dream action, and you were. I was myself after that, because I wanted you to want me for me."

Debbie flushed, thinking of all the things they'd done in dreams and all she'd shared. "You gave no sign that my dreams were real that day at the spa!"

"Because they aren't real. They're just dreams, my mind touching yours. There's no reason for us not to enjoy dream sex and still be professional colleagues."

Yes there is. But that can wait. "Did you visit this weekend and seduce Brady?"

"A succubus seduces men. An incubus seduces women."

"But many hold that a succubus and an incubus are but two sides of the same demon," Leri purred, striding out from behind a prop. "Myths hold them both to be beautiful but able to change form, seducing their victims. They visit at night, but often can attack through dreams, without being in the room at all."

She came out of a shadow like the hellhounds do, I'd swear it. "Leri, hi," Debbie stammered.

"Yes, and we're also supposed to crush people," Gray said sarcastically. "Incubi derives from the words meaning "to lie upon." But that's all crap. Modern science has defined that panic crushing experience as deriving from sleep paralysis, not demons. Most of the accusations through centuries were because some woman got impregnated by a guy she wasn't supposed to be screwing and gave the excuse that a demon impregnated her as a get out of jail free card."

"But they didn't get out of jail free, did they, most of them?" Leri pushed, shadows seeming to gather around her. "Those desperate women? They got burned as witches, or devil worshippers." She turned to Debbie. "You know the supposed origin of incubi? They are the children created when a demon male lies with a human female."

That can't be. That's impossible. I would have had an incubus for a child? Debbie looked at Gray in horror and surprise.

"I'm not your son," Gray said softly, taking her hand. "I'm much too old, Debbie. Don't mind Leri, it's her way to cause trouble."

"It's you that are causing trouble," Leri hissed, holding up an accusatory finger. "Someone did come to Debbie's house Saturday night. Myrrh's crows reported a figure slipping in. Myrrh investigated it and found signs of a night seducer. You say it wasn't you. Fine, then tell me who it was."

"She doesn't want trouble. She was called because of the man's loneliness and desire. I had nothing to do with it!"

Leri held up a hand, black fire gathering in it. "Tell me, Gray. Or I will burn you down and find another incubus to wear your current form for Debbie."

The shadows near Leri swirled, and a cloaked figure ghosted out of it in a long black dress. It was a woman, veiled and hooded, but her eyes were unmistakably feminine.

"Namaath," Leri said, lowering the threatening Hellfire. "Why didn't you just say it was you? I wouldn't have caused a fuss."

Namaath dropped her veil. "I go where I'm called." She turned to Debbie, her face more lovely than any supermodel Debbie had ever seen. "Please forgive the intrusion, I didn't think anyone would mind, so long as I was not seen."

I don't know who this is, but she must be someone of prominence.

As in not someone to piss off. "It's no trouble, Brady's a consenting adult and he enjoyed himself," Debbie said bravely. "He just thought you really were me, and it caused an issue when he tried for a repeat performance."

Namaath nodded. "I see. If he calls to me again with his desires, I'll make it obvious it is a dream." She began to fade from sight.

"Wait!" Debbie called.

Namaath's form re-solidified. "Yes?"

"You are the most beautiful woman…um, female I have ever seen. Why not just be yourself?"

Namaath laughed, the sound rapturous even to Debbie's ears. "Why, because he wanted you most, human." She disappeared.

Leri let out a breath. "Almost stepped in it there. I had no idea it was her."

"Who was that?" Debbie asked.

"One of the four mothers of demonkind," Gray said. "Allegedly. Accounts differ."

"And your mother, Gray," Leri said, shaking her head. "Just tell me next time, I don't like having to manifest Hellfire and not use it, it's a huge waste of energy."

"Your mother ever wants a walk on part in your series, she's got it," Debbie commented. "Though it probably wouldn't be a good idea, because any man that saw her would lose interest in all the other actresses in the series."

"Namaath isn't interested in films," Gray remarked. "She just came to visit me. She won't be staying." He stalked off.

"Stay out of my dreams, too," Debbie called after him.

"Are you sure?" Leri said with a smile. "Gray does know how to show a lady a good time."

"I'm sure," Debbie said pleasantly. "But I'm after more than a good time." *Fuck, I did forget to ask him about going with me to the Oscars. I can't ask him now. Damn it!*

"What about babies?" Leri offered, shadows swirling about her once again. "Vassago can offer that, too."

"I don't want any more pregnancies that end in miscarriage," Debbie said harshly. "And I really don't want any child that isn't Shaker's."

"Dutiful and wise," Leri said, nodding once. "If you change your mind, let Gray know. He could arrange a sperm donation from Brady, with no one the wiser. Or another male of your choice." Leri strolled away, as Debbie tried to form a reply, trying to find words and failing.

CHAPTER SEVEN

February-March

DAMN IT, I SHOULD HAVE GOTTEN THIS DRESS IN ONE SIZE BIGGER. Debbie took a shallow breath, her movement restricted because of the Spanx she wore. *But I do love how this looks.* The long gown was a one-strap red wine burgundy silk sheath with an irregular hemline. *What's a few hours of being uncomfortable compared with being thought unfashionable? No contest.*

She fashioned on her ruby drop earrings and examined herself in the mirror. *Older but hotter.* Debbie laughed, then grabbed her bag with the tickets. "Brady, are you ready?"

She walked into the living room. Brady was there waiting on the couch, and he turned just his head as she walked in. "The picture of perfection, my love."

Something is...off. "Brady?"

"Not quite," Brady said in Shaker's voice. He smiled widely, baring his pointed rows of demon teeth. "But I'll do my best to escort you tonight. Better than he would, certainly."

"Why are you doing this?" Debbie swallowed hard, leaning against the doorframe for support. "Tonight of all nights?"

"For the best reason there is," Shaker said, as he got up, putting his hands in his pockets. "Because I may never be up for another award like this one, ever, no matter how long I live. If I do win tonight, I want to be there to collect the statue, and to give my speech." He chuckled in rumbling bass tones. "Don't worry, I'll keep it short and put in a plug for Pandora."

Debbie didn't move. *Shaker, you do this to Brady, and he'll know. He'll know you were in Jett, he already suspects about Rhonda!*

"So let him know," Shaker said, holding out his arm. "What's he going to do? Who's he going to tell that would believe him?" He laughed. "Besides, he's not going to tell anyone anything now."

Debbie crossed her arms over her chest. "We can't do this."

"Why are you being so difficult this year?" Shaker grimaced, putting his arm down. "I sometimes wonder that you're the same woman I married."

"Because Brady is a decent man at heart. Jett was a bastard who loved no one and thought only of himself, when he could think clearly around the alcohol and drugs. He'd betrayed Pandora…and me."

"How do you know Brady's a decent man?" Shaker questioned. "Because he told you? For a woman of Tinseltown, you're sometimes incredibly naïve. Let me give you some facts, Debbie. Brady didn't move out here and leave his life behind—he fled. He was fired from his job for drinking on his lunch hour. He doesn't have his own car because he's had so many DUIs that they took his license away."

"That can't be true. You told me last year that he, out of his whole family, was the rock that held it together, that he didn't drink or do drugs. I believed that he was a good guy because *you* told me he was a good guy. I've been giving him an easy time because he's been through a lot." *And because I felt guilty about what we did to his brother.*

"Brady didn't do drugs when you first met him, but he enjoyed his alcohol. He just had to keep his shit together to take care of Rhonda. Then he met a few people at Pandora's party last year. Remember Nelson, who was part of the plot to kidnap you? He also happened to be Jett's drug dealer, as well as servicing a few other of our addicted personnel. He hooked Brady up with a few free samples of cocaine and ecstasy. Jett's little brother returned home with his new toys and a thrilling new-found freedom of life without Rhonda. The drugs amplified Brady's little drinking problem, which quickly became a burning need that destroyed his daily routine. He's staying with you because he's broke. His car got sold for legal fees to keep him out of jail. He sold all his furniture just to buy the plane ticket out here."

This nightmare can't be true. "Do you have any proof at all to back up your claims?"

"I thought you might require some paperwork," Shaker said, withdrawing a paper from his pocket and handing it to her. "Here's his most recent ticket, which he got while driving your car to the storage facility. You'll notice your plate number is noted. You might also notice that it says he's due in court next week? Violations of California Vehicle Code Section 12500a are punishable by up to six months in county jail and fines of up to $1,000. But driving without a valid license usually turns a misdemeanor DUI into a felony. A felony means jail time, as in years." Shaker's eyes flashed red. "I wouldn't have minded Brady just lusting after you or trying to become me, because I know you'd never look at him twice. But I do mind him fucking up a picture I gave my life to finish, when all he had to do is show up for a few days sober."

This is a real-life nightmare that just gets worse and worse. Debbie crossed to the couch and sat down. "It's my fault. I invited him here to that party."

Shaker sat down beside her, taking her hand. "Brady's fuckup isn't your fault any more than its your fault Jett was the mess he was. Brady had a lot to deal with handling Rhonda all these years. One of the reasons he came here when his life fell apart wasn't to help care for her, it was because he knew you were alone and that you had helped Jett get his life back. He desired you, but he also wanted what he believed you could do for him. Namaath saw that right off, which is why he believed her dream to be real. She told him exactly what he was wishing to hear."

"We also took Rhonda off his back. Apparently, she was the only thing keeping him a good boy."

"We had no choice. We had to protect what we were building. Rhonda got everything that she wanted and more, just not exactly the way she thought she was going to."

"Fuck!" Debbie shouted, closing her eyes and putting her head in her hands. "ARGH!"

Pike, Pitch, and Baroness came running from the kitchen growling, then went over to Shaker, tails wagging.

"No squirrel for you tonight, good hounds," Shaker said, petting one after another. "But I'll bring you some next week, promise." He looked back at Debbie. "This is the only way."

Debbie looked over at him, her eyes swimming with tears. "And what are we going to do when we run out of brothers?"

"We'll cross that burning bridge when we're on it," Shaker answered, standing. He offered his arm again. "Come on, sweetheart. We're going to be late, even teleporting."

〜

"The Oscars are everything I imagined," Debbie said, as they were seated. "I can't believe I'm really here." *Keep focusing on tonight. You can do this.*

"We're far enough from the stage you should believe it," Shaker grumbled good naturedly. He pointed out a few of the stars sitting around them, then the lights went down.

They waited through several awards, then Debbie felt Shaker tense as the list of nominees were read, including Jett's name.

"And the winner for best actor in an action movie is...Jett Black!"

Debbie let out a scream that was drowned out by the thunderous applause, then Shaker was getting up and offering his arm to her with a huge grin. Debbie walked down the long aisle with him, and up to the podium, where an actress in a glittering gown held out the golden statue to Debbie.

"I hope you prepared a speech," Shaker whispered.

Holy. Shit. Wing it. "I'm honored to accept this award on behalf of my husband, Jett. I know he'd have been thrilled to win, and I'm just sorry he's not here." *Shaker, I've got nothing else, so jump in!*

Behind her on the big screen pictures of Jett were being shown, stills from his various pictures, from the beginning of his career to *Smoke and Ashes II.*

"We also want to thank everyone here who made Jett the man he was," Shaker added. "He was a good brother to me, and a fantastic husband to his wife Debbie. But his one goal in life was to make movies that people enjoyed, and to be recognized for that. You've done that tonight for him, and we thank you."

"Thank you," Debbie echoed, to thunderous applause, holding the award aloft.

"As you may know, Jett died during filming of *Smoke and Ashes III*," Shaker went on. "I'm proud to finish that film for my brother, knowing it meant so much to him. We love you, bro." He turned and blew a kiss to the screen pic of Jett.

"Thank you!" Debbie managed with a last smile, and then they were being directed to the side of the stage accompanied by more applause, as the next presenter headed for the microphone.

They slowly made their way back to their seats, Debbie's one hand clasping Shaker's tightly, while the other held the trophy.

Debbie sat down, her heart racing. *Shaker really won an Academy Award!*

Thanks for this, he said to her mentally, as she looked over at him. *I can take many things for my own, and create far more, see anything in the world and know immortality. But this I couldn't ever have gotten without you, my love.*

Debbie squeezed his hand. *I wouldn't be here without you, either, Shaker. I love you.*

I love you, too. He kissed her cheek, then they settled in to watch the rest of the awards.

~

"It's so nice to be home," Shaker said with a sigh, as he relaxed into the couch. "I only wish I had a day to keep you in bed."

"About that," Debbie said, getting up from the couch. "I may need a little time to ease into your new body. I wasn't attracted to Brady, as you know."

"I seem to remember one night when we both made good use of his human body," Shaker teased, cupping her ass. "And that you accommodated yourself to it quite fast."

Debbie slapped his hand away. "You'll remember that I made you come out of him for our second round, you old sinner."

"One of the oldest and most original," Shaker said proudly. He crooked his finger. "Why don't you come back and sit on my lap. We should properly celebrate this night."

Debbie smiled, but stayed where she was. "I'll need a few days to adjust to see him as you." *I mean it.*

"That's okay," Shaker said, looking up at her winsomely with his arms folded under his head. "I am going to need a few days to get this body in shape. It's craving alcohol badly, and the withdrawal's not great, either. That's why I called Catarella tonight from my cell during the intermission, to prep him on the court appointment. We need him there tomorrow on Brady's behalf." He groaned. "It does suck how anyone easily accessible to demons always has all this baggage."

"Are you going to check into an addiction treatment center?" Debbie asked.

"I didn't with Jett, because he hadn't been convicted of anything. But Brady's got a record, so the judge might say he has to. The thought of hours of group therapy, no sex, and repeated tearful confessions to my higher power is enough to chill even a demon's ardor." Shaker lost his smile. "Which brings me to the bare bones. Once Catarella deals with the court, I will be here on the weekends, and I'm guessing with my Mistress not calling on me, I'll be able to get Brady clean and sober, and also get the movie scenes shot during the weeks."

"What about you having to look for that bad vampire, Valerian?"

"I am going to scrap that," he said heavily. "I can't risk any harm to my Mistress, which is what would happen if I found him and tangled with Azaroth. I can't go looking in this body because after tonight's award ceremony I'll be recognized, which would lead back to you and Pandora. We can't risk Brady getting killed like Jett did. I also can't leave Brady for any real length of time for a while, unless he's asleep and guaranteed to stay asleep. We'll arrange that if we need to."

He took her hand. "I would like to sleep near you, but I can't risk my own desire, especially fighting the cravings Brady has." He kissed her hand. "I'll go to his room. Goodnight, my love."

"Goodnight." She kissed him on the lips, then shot him a smile as he grabbed for her and missed.

"Tease."

"I'll make good when you're well," she said, blowing him a kiss and heading to her room. "Goodnight."

~

In the morning when Debbie came into the kitchen, Myrrh was already there, a crow on each shoulder, talking to Shaker. Another crow sat on the table, trying to sneak some bacon off his plate.

"You're sure this is a good idea?" Myrrh said. "You remember what happened last time."

"I thank you for that," Shaker said kindly, putting his hand over Myrrh's.

I guess they're friends now. "Good morning," Debbie said more gruffly than she meant to. "Good to see you, Myrrh."

"I had a report that you screamed, and that Brady was still here," Myrrh said with a shrug. "I thought maybe Gray had entered him. I was surprised to see Shaker."

"I was surprised that you went to Leri about Brady getting seduced by a succubus, but didn't mention it to me at all," Debbie retorted. "Who is Leri to you, Myrrh? A relative?"

"She was a mentor of sorts, over the years," Myrrh said finally, drinking coffee. "I went to her because it was Brady that was seduced, not you. You're not in a relationship with him. I thought that Leri could find out if there was a rogue demon looking for a way into your circle. She did. You couldn't assist in this, Debbie. But I did plan to let you know today, yes."

Perfectly logical, but it annoys me anyway. "Okay, but don't keep me out of the loop next time," Debbie said, irked.

"Leri is in a position to stop a demon if needed," Myrrh said bluntly. "Even to drive one out by force. You aren't."

I am, actually. Debbie cleared her throat. "I'd like you to put a ward on my home, Myrrh. Something so that any dreams I have, I see exactly who is in them, not some magic glamour."

"Okay," Myrrh said, glancing at Shaker. "Do you want to do that, or should I?"

"Go ahead," Shaker said with a wave of his hand. "I'm tapped out this morning."

"It will be done by tonight," Myrrh said, standing. "Debbie, I've got to go. I just wanted to say congratulations on the awards. Pandora will get some attention now."

"Awards?"

"Devlin won for his score for *Immortal Confessions*," Shaker announced. "When we were late coming back from intermission, because of my cell call running long. I'll have to call Devlin later and congratulate him once he's up."

"Later," Debbie said, also standing. "Come on. We've got to get to the office, Catarella is waiting for us."

~

"A mulo is the evil spirit of a dead person that was killed who haunts its lover or the person it feels responsible for its death. It's a Romany word for ghost which also equals vampire, and it's supposed to work like an incubus but is said to cause early death—"

"Nicole, why are you telling me this?" Debbie said in exasperation, looking at her closed office door. She'd sent Shaker to the bathroom as he said he felt awful. *Where is Catarella? We only have an hour to meet with him this morning before we need to be at court, and we have no idea what we can do to keep Brady out of jail.*

"I'm telling you because I think we can use a mulo as the chief villain in *Dare to Tell.* I've come up with nothing to rival the spiritwalker from the other film, but I think this has a lot of possibilities."

"Wait, *Dare to Tell* was a finished script. How could we possibly not have a decent villain?"

"Because the script leaves it ambiguous what exactly is haunting the mansion, or why it doesn't hurt the medium. I also think we can work this mulo into the story. The ghost views the teens that went missing as responsible for her death. They are, in part. The first person it kills is its former lover, years before."

"I don't quite follow you," Debbie stated. "But I do trust your judgement. Go ahead and use your idea. Alter the script and shoot a few scenes, and show them to me, I would like to watch the filming, but I can't be certain of that. By the way, Devlin still needs the vampire death scene and ending scene clips from *Hell to Pay*. Can you get that put on a DVD and sent over to him via FedEx? We need his approval before he'll release any more money."

"Congratulations on the award," Nicole replied, smiling. "You and Brady looked great onstage. I'll get to work on this right away and will arrange for the DVD to ship to him by the end of the week."

Hell, they've already got us as a couple. Well, maybe that's not a bad thing. "Thanks, Nicole."

Catarella pushed open her door. "Debbie, sorry, I was stuck in traffic near an accident. Where's Brady?"

"In the bathroom. Please come in, he should be back shortly."

"See you later," Nicole said to them both, blatantly curious. She left, bumping into Shaker as he entered. "Sorry."

"Good to see you again, Nicole," Shaker grinned.

Nicole looked at him oddly, then walked quickly away. Debbie raised her eyebrows at Shaker.

He gave her an innocent look. "What? She met Brady at the Halloween party last year. It's not my fault she doesn't remember."

"Lock the door," Debbie said. "Catarella, what have you got for us?"

"Good news and bad news," the lawyer said. "First, let me tell you the law, then my strategy."

"In California, when a person is arrested for DUI, their license will be suspended thirty days after the arrest. They request a hearing, etc. etc. But Brady didn't have a valid license in California. He's charged with drunk driving without a license, and so is facing two separate criminal cases."

"We are so fucked," Debbie said, leaning back and closing her eyes.

"Wait," Catarella cautioned. "Now, California Vehicle Code states that driving without a valid driver's license is illegal. You are considered to be driving without a license if you were never licensed in any state, or failed to renew your expired license, or are a resident of California, but do not have a California license, or are ineligible for a California driver's license. They will argue that Brady's case falls under the fourth description. I will argue it falls under the third."

"Now, while driving without a license can be charged as an infraction, when combined with a DUI arrest, it will likely be charged as a misdemeanor. That usually means a few months of jail time, up to six months, or more likely a thousand dollar fine."

"We can pay the fine, but I need not to go to jail," Shaker said.

"Wait, I'm not finished. Now, the court has to prove two things to convict you of a suspended license, Shaker: that you drove a motor vehicle while your driving privilege was suspended or revoked; and that you knew that your driving privilege was suspended or revoked."

"Brady knew both," Debbie said. "Didn't he?"

"The first statement only requires that the prosecution show that you were driving when you didn't have a license. But the second statement is harder. The law says that a driver knows he's suspended if he got a DMV notice in the mail, AND that the driver received it, as in it didn't get returned to the DMV as undeliverable. But Brady never filed a forwarding address for his mail. So the notice was mailed, but it was returned to the DMV as undeliverable in his home state."

"How do you know this for sure?" Debbie asked.

"I have friends in low places," Catarella winked. "So I think I can get the driving without a license thrown out, which means no felony charge. But the DUI is harder, especially as Brady's license was revoked in his home state of South Dakota because of his drinking and driving. But more on that later."

"Now, a first-time DUI is a misdemeanor in California. If convicted, Shaker will need to face a sentence of between forty-eight hours to six months in county jail, a maximum three hundred and ninety dollar fine plus additional penalty assessments, and up to six months of mandatory license suspension. In addition, he will be required to enroll in a minimum three-month alcohol program and pay a hundred and twenty-five-dollar fee to the DMV for reissuing his license. Oh and you will be placed on probation for three years."

"I'm beginning to think Brady's going to have to go it alone," Shaker groaned. "I'll grab him after he's out of prison. This is overload."

"Remember I said that Brady's license is from South Dakota? That state happens to be the least strict out of all fifty states. It has no minimum sentence for either a first or second DUI, although a third DUI is considered a felony. There is no administrative license suspension, no vehicle impound, and no mandatory ignition interlock device required. Brady did get two DUI's, but not a third, which is why he didn't go to prison in South Dakota. He did get his license suspended, but it was because of running stop signs and lights while he was drunk with the first DUI's. There's no record of Brady getting an official DUI before coming to California."

"So you think you can get him out of all of this?" Debbie said skeptically. "You're stringing together a bunch of technicalities."

"Technicalities are what lawyers are for," Catarella said, his eyes flashing red. "And keeping allies out of trouble." He shook Shaker's hand. "It's good to see you again, Shaker. We should leave now for court. I'll speak to you in thoughts during the hearing, follow my lead. We can win this."

"Okay," Shaker said, glancing at Debbie.

~

"That judge basically said he would make sure I never drove again," Shaker groaned, when they left the court. "He was extremely pissed."

"Of course he was pissed off," Catarella joked. "He knows you're guilty, and he can't truly punish you."

"A sentence of a week in county jail, a three hundred and ninety dollar fine plus another three hundred dollars in penalty assessments, six months of mandatory license suspension with another hundred and twenty-five dollars to reissue plus three years' probation hurts plenty," Shaker said gruffly. "What can we do about the three-month alcohol program?"

"The only thing I can think of to do is detoxify your system with a little magic," Catarella stated. "Coupled with a blood transfusion. They'll take your blood in jail right when you get there, because they'll assume because the judge ruled your ticket as a DUI conviction that you're going to have withdrawal. They need to know how bad it will be, to give you drugs to counteract that. We need to show that not only are you not in withdrawal, but also that your blood is healthy and shows no signs of persistent alcohol abuse. If we can get that documented on your first official blood test, I can make a successful case to overturn the DUI."

"Is that possible?" Debbie asked. "To really clean out his blood to that extent?"

"It is, but it's going to be painful. Here I gave that good speech about missing Jett and being overcome my first day here and drinking his last fifth of a bottle of Jack Danial's I found in his things," Shaker lamented. "And then in my grief not realizing how much I'd drunk. That since my brother's death I'd given up drinking, that this was just a relapse. That I wouldn't even apply for a license for three years, as a show of good faith. Even with all that, I still have to shed blood."

"You laid it on a little thick," Catarella reproved. "But that's fine, it made for a great written record. It also helped that the police officer who issued the ticket didn't show up in court to testify today." He glanced at Debbie. "They usually don't for most tickets, a little-known fact. Brady wasn't really drunk when he was ticketed driving your car, he was just at the legal limit. But he wasn't familiar with the streets I'm guessing and so was breaking erratically, enough that a cop tailed him and pulled him over. The ticket noted that Brady was pulled over for irregular driving. Coupled with the breathalyzer test, it was enough for a DUI ticket. But that's also why he wasn't arrested. Likely the cop told him he had to stop driving for an hour, knowing that Brady would be well under the limit by then."

"Yes, the policeman told Brady to stay pulled over for a half-hour," Shaker said. "I checked Brady's memories. The cop also didn't let him see the result of the breathalyzer test, which legally he's supposed to do. Brady knew he'd been drinking and so didn't demand to see it. Possibly one of the reasons the cop didn't show up to court today was because the ticket was on thin ground."

"Thank you," Debbie said, clasping Catarella's hand. "You work miracles. I thought we were screwed."

Catarella's eyes flashed red as he winked. "That's why you have me on retainer."

"Thanks," Shaker said, holding out his hand. Catarella shook it, then walked away.

"Do you think this will work?" Debbie said, watching the lawyer drive off. "Tell me the truth."

"It should. Brady isn't ever going to have a drinking problem again, or a drug problem, and he's about to get a strong work drive as well. Maybe he'll even find out he's a natural actor." Shaker laughed.

"I'd feel sorry for Brady, but he could've killed someone," Debbie said, hugging Shaker. "And he obviously wasn't going to stop, as he didn't even think he had a problem."

"I'm not looking forward to jail," Shaker grumbled. "But at least I'll be out in a week. Then we can start filming Brady's walk-on parts, and get the movie finished." He hugged her tight, then kissed her cheek. "Ask Myrrh to stay with you this coming week, okay?"

There was an urgency to his words. "Did you look ahead again?"

"Yes," Shaker said. "Mostly for myself, to make sure that I could serve my Mistress and be there for you at the same time. There'll be some dicey moments, but I can work it out."

"So why should I be afraid to be alone?"

"Because we've got a couple other adversaries about to arrive on the scene," Shaker whispered. "And these ones are brand new."

~

"And that's all he said?" Myrrh shrilled, making her crows caw and flap their wings on their perches around the room. "Brand new adversaries, no details, names, dates, descriptions of dangers, nothing? Old demons, they're always such cryptic bastards."

"Yes. So will you stay with me this week?"

"Of course," the faerie concurred.

"Good," Debbie said, handing her a glass of wine, and taking a big sip of her own in relief. "Will you tell me about Torren?"

One blue and one red eye fixed on her. "Just out of the blue, you're curious?"

"I could hint or try to work it into the conversation, but I want to know, so I decided to ask."

"He was my Oathed One."

"Like in Devlin's movie, *Immortal Confessions*? A vampire marriage?"

"Oathing isn't really a marriage; it can be one-sided possession, or a partnership. Much of that depends on the vampire. Torren was one of the good ones, honorable and fair, even with his love of the black arts."

"He did black magic?" *That's a great character, a vampire that does black magic. We should try to work one into* Incubus *in a bit part.*

"Yes. But when we met, Torren was a human soldier, not a vampire. This was many years ago, near the coast of…a fairly large city."

"You don't want to tell me where and when?"

"That's not important. Besides, it's my story. There was talk of a war, I don't remember why. Probably the usual, with powerful men preening and getting their feathers ruffled, then having to push back so everyone knew they were the strongest. Anyway, talk was they would land on the coast. They weren't fighters, or so it was said, being more concerned with their fancy clothes and facial hair than the quality of their swords. That statement wasn't true, but the people of the coast thought that they didn't need to worry about the invaders. They instead planned a celebration, as it was the start of the New Year. They held a street party, with fireworks and roasts. It was one of the largest celebrations I can remember, but I couldn't tell you what they ate, or even what songs they sung. What I remember most was the gold dust. They had given out packets of the stuff pressed into star and moon shapes. Children had thrown some into the harbor water, and there'd been more in the fireworks. It turned the water glittering and swirled with gold. I remember being there at the edge and using a stick, and being amazed at the beauty, and that leaders would waste such wealth."

I should be taking notes, this paints a great setting for a scene. "How old were you?"

"Old enough to see the first ship crash ashore in fog and know that there were enough men still alive after it wrecked to be a danger." Myrrh smiled. "Torren was one of those men."

"What happened then?"

"As you might imagine, the people of the coast went into full flight, especially as more ships landed. The soldiers storming ashore had one thought besides plunder, and that was women."

"Did Torren…did he, um, have sex with you?"

"After a few close calls, he was the one who found me. And yes, we started to, but then the people of the coast rallied, and we were caught in the middle. He teleported us a few miles away to safety. I didn't know what that was then." Myrrh smiled. "But I've always been a quick study."

"Was it love at first sight?"

"I told him he wasn't handsome, after he alluded that I was a whore. Being a virgin at the time, I didn't appreciate that." Myrrh laughed. "He dropped his glamour, revealing his tall, dark, and handsome self."

"Can you show me what he looked like?"

Myrrh waved her hand. An image of a willowy, dark-haired man solidified, his face noble with high cheekbones and piercing eyes. "That's how I remember him looking."

"And?"

"We passed the rest of the night with him teaching me simple spells. When he woke me in the night from sleep, I let him finish what he began earlier."

"You 'let him finish'?" Debbie let out a laugh.

"Okay, okay, I touched him and asked him to, alright?" Myrrh grinned. "You remember your first time. I was sore the first time. The second time was better. The third was even better. But he told me the next morning...." She stopped.

"Told you what?"

"He said, 'I'm here for you,' as we lay there together in a blanket. 'You're the reason I was called, because you're right, they're afraid of you.'"

"What are you going to do to me?" I asked him.

"Bind you into rock," he admitted.

"And you're really going to do that, imprison me?" I asked.

"'You need training to control your power,' he said. 'We're in the middle of a real war here, no matter that this battle was much about nothing.' He said it would last for years, and he was right, it did. He said, 'Your people will decide that your power should be used against their enemies and you'll beat them back for a while, but there'll be too many, and you'll be killed eventually. It's better to put you into the rock for now. When you emerge, you'll come into a much more stable world.' I struggled up, fighting him, and said, 'You're talking about imprisoning me like its nothing!'" Myrrh paused.

"And?" Debbie said shrilly.

"He said, 'I won't leave you there alone. I'll go into the rock with you.' He left me for a time after our night together, and when he returned, he was a vampire. I never asked but always wondered if he went and got himself turned on purpose, in order to live through my imprisonment with me."

That's unbelievable loyalty. "How was he sure you'd both get out eventually?"

"He left clues. And in time, people followed them and broke us both out."

"He sounds very brave."

"He was," Myrrh said wistfully. "He knew the time of his own death. It made him somber sometimes, but also able to really enjoy life, knowing that in really bad times that it wasn't going to be the end of him, or us. I clung to that, to him knowing what was going to happen in time to warn me, to him finding a way to stop it. I got used to him being there. And then he wasn't one day. It was the single greatest loss of my life."

"That's why you have the nickname the Queen of Swords," Debbie said quietly. "For your eternal grief."

"The widow shieldmaiden, yes," Myrrh assented, drinking her wine down. "There's worse names out there to be known as."

"Thanks for telling me," Debbie said, wanting to hug her, but unsure if the woman would want her to.

"Thanks for listening," Myrrh said, smiling, opening her arms to Debbie. "And yes, come and hug me if you like. I'm not as forbidding as I come across. Some of it is so long being alone, and spending time with my crows."

Debbie hugged her tightly. "You know you're always welcome here with me. I'm glad to know you, Myrrh."

Myrrh hugged her back. "I'm glad to know you too, Debbie. Very glad."

CHAPTER EIGHT

March-April

"You know, I didn't think it could work out," Debbie said, leaning back in her chair. "But you were right, it did."

Shaker stood before her, his expression pure sexual smolder. He was dressed in Jett's outfit for "Smoke" Storm of black leather jacket over an oiled chest, ripped jeans with a chain hanging off the back, a large knife in its sheath at his belt. His black hair was still too short for a ponytail, but it had been cut in Jett's style. His blue eyes roamed over Debbie slowly. "Yes, it did. You don't have to tell me you like what you see." He grinned. *You're so aroused I can scent you.*

Yes, you're hot. "How did you do it?" Debbie said. "Brady didn't have much of a physique going in."

"It's a glamour," Shaker explained, shifting his feet and hooking one thumb in a pocket. "But I've already begun an exercise routine, and soon the muscles will be real. As painful as the blood transfusion my brother performed was, it did more than clear out signs of the drug and alcohol damage; it also helped with the withdrawal symptoms. The doctors at the prison gave me a full physical, and I passed enough that Catarella's got me out on bail while they fight over overturning the DUI. I'm glad though that the parts Brady needed to do were just walk on. This body is not up to battling evil just yet."

"That's too bad," Debbie said coyly, batting her eyes. "Because I'd hoped we could celebrate tonight, seeing as today's scenes were the last ones we needed to finish the movie."

"It feels good to be done," Shaker said. "But I'll miss Storm. He was a fun character to play."

"Well, you may get the chance to play him again…if you want," Debbie offered.

"We're not going to make a fourth movie?" Shaker said in surprise.

"No plans for that. But I did hear from Netflix. They are still considering the *Incubus* series. They said they would be "more predisposed" to say yes if the series contained Smoke Storm as the antagonist."

"What?"

"Gray's the incubus, a demon. We have him doing good works each episode, but he's still a demon. Storm's a demon hunter. It just makes sense to put a well-known, well liked character in the series to help it stand apart from the other competing series that contain only unknowns. That he's the 'bad guy' in the series should also be great for ratings, we can show some of his ruthlessness. He views the world as black and white, and Gray will show him a shade of… um, grey."

"Wow," Shaker mused, ignoring Debbie's quip. "They really want me? Even knowing that I'm not Jett, I'm Brady?"

"Cole," Debbie corrected. "Cole Black, remember? I got several calls in the last few weeks from Bart. He's incredulous that you've never acted before, because you've been so professional and seem to "read his mind" to give him what he wants. He personally put in a good word that we hire you for future movies. He's on board completely with casting you in *Incubus*."

"And Gray's good with this? He's not going to mind my shadow looming over him on his series?"

"I think he's really relieved," Debbie said. "He doesn't have to carry the series anymore, if you're involved. Smoke's a beloved character, and you're bringing him to life when he's supposed to be gone forever. Your inclusion can only help the series."

Shaker nodded. "Then I'm in."

"No, you're not," Debbie said seductively. "But would you like to be?"

Shaker gave her a look of surprise and blatant desire. "You're sure?"

Debbie nodded. "Why don't you lock that door and come over here?"

Shaker chuckled, then walked easily to the office door, locked it, then came back to the desk, walking to stand in front of her. "At your service, ma'am."

Debbie shook her head slightly, then opened his belt, pulling down the zipper constraining the bulging denim. The moist head of his erection peeped just over the band of his underwear. Debbie pushed down his jeans and underwear, cupping his ass in her hands. *Mmm, those tight muscles feel so good, rock hard against my hands.* She brought him closer, then bent her head, taking his penis into her mouth, circling the head with her tongue before slipping the length of him into her throat.

Hellfire, that feels good, Shaker groaned in her mind, as he moaned aloud in the room. He only let her do a few more strokes, then stopped her. *You do any more and I'm going to come, and I haven't waited to have this fantasy so long to have it over so quickly.* He helped her to her feet, then embraced her, thrusting against her lightly as his mouth devoured hers. Debbie reached down, squeezing his shaft in rhythm as he kissed her.

I need you. I need you right now, he said inside her mind. *Touch me again.*

Debbie stroked him faster, making him break the kiss and arch his back in a cry of want. With a ragged breath, he shoved with both hands, pushing all of her papers off her desk onto the floor. Debbie expected him to put her on the desk, but instead he sat on the edge, then beckoned to her.

Glad I had the foresight to wear a garter belt today. Debbie put her arms around him as he lifted her, then scooted back onto the desktop so he lay atop it, her straddling him.

"Letting me stay in charge?" she said huskily, pushing his leather jacket aside to run her hands over his chest.

"It's your desk." *You do a lot for me. I want this first one to be all you. Let me hear you scream!*

Debbie aligned him, then welcomed him with an eager groan as he slid home. *I can't scream, someone will hear me. But the feel of your thick head pushing inside me, Oh, I've wanted that for so long...*

"Scream," he said, putting his hands on her hips. "I put a ward up. Believe me I'm going to."

Debbie began moving her hips, rubbing against him as she took him in again and again. His hands slid up from her hips under her shirt to her breasts, cupping the mounds outside of her bra before pushing the material down to let her breasts hang free.

"You missed that, didn't you?" Debbie raised up slightly, then pushed the hot nubs closer to his face.

"Fuck yes," Shaker said hoarsely, grabbing one breast and bringing it to his mouth. He bit lightly, then sucked on the hard nub, his other hand finding her other breast, squeezing the hot flesh before he suckled that one too.

"I'm going to come, I hope you're close," Shaker panted, his hands returning to her hips to trap her against him as he pushed deeper.

Debbie splayed her hands against Shaker's chest, rubbing the oiled skin as it bunched up under her hands.

Debbie began rocking faster, the feel of his mouth and hands like an electric current straight to her groin. She could feel him tightening beneath her. Trying to hold back as long as he could. She felt him begin to come and it brought her to climax, yelling, bucking against him as he spilled himself inside her. Debbie finished her climax and began to sink down against Shaker's chest. With a grunt he was off the desk, helping her to stand and then spinning her to face the desk. Debbie put out her hands quickly, bracing herself on the edge.

"My turn," Shaker whispered. He pushed aside her panties, then pushed himself in slowly. *I love how you're always so wet for me.*

"I love how you're always so hard for me," she breathed, looking at him over her shoulder. "Now take what you've wanted for so long."

"I am going to take it," Shaker said, pinning her hips against the desk. He began to thrust gently, as his hands went up again to cup her breasts. "I'm going to take you and spill myself inside you again, because I've thought about doing this since that night I first met you here." Without another word he began pumping fast, his hands slipping down over hers to brace himself. He came with a guttural yell, sagging for just a second before sitting in her chair, pulling her down on top of him. He began moving again beneath her, his semi-hard cock again elongating.

"Hell," Debbie said, trying to catch her breath. "Out of practice my ass."

"I built up my stamina in the last few weeks," Shaker panted. "Scream for me again, Mistress."

"I'm not your Mistress," Debbie said, even as his voice saying the word filled her with a thrill.

"You're always my Mistress," Shaker said, filling her in long strokes. "And us together just like this is always my one desire."

~

"You and I were lucky that my secretary had gone home," Debbie said, her complete satisfaction radiating from her in a warm afterglow. "We'll have to wash these clothes tonight."

"I can get them sprayed with stain-be-gone, if you want to start the shower?" Shaker said, sliding his hand over to stroke her thigh.

"So you're not done?" Debbie said lightly.

"Not by a long shot."

~

"Okay, I can't move," Debbie groaned, half-laying on Shaker's chest as they snuggled on her bed. "But I need some chocolate."

"Demon to the rescue," Shaker said, gently pushing her aside and padding out of the room. Debbie dozed off before he returned. She was awakened by Baroness leaping on the bed, Pike right behind her. Both of them licked her face.

"Hey," she sputtered, trying to sit up.

"Down," Shaker said, coming in with a plastic container containing a brownie with chocolate frosting, Pitch trailing him. "Sorry, but you didn't have any chocolate in the kitchen. I had to toss on some clothes and go out and get this."

"Thanks," Debbie said, as he slid into bed still clutching the brownie. Together, they finished it off in a few bites.

"It's so good to eat food again without having to do a spell," Shaker sighed. "We'll have to go out to celebrate our anniversary and get a dessert tray or something to bring back."

"About that," Debbie said. "I thought you could only eat human food when you were possessing a human body? That otherwise it was a diet of only blood and meat?"

"Titus showed me a spell he'd concocted to basically let someone unable to eat food consume it, then teleport it out of them before it made them sick. I told him he should publish it in Spell Review. That magazine only comes out once every five years, but his spell has a lot of applications that most any non-human that

knew magic would find useful. They'd pay him in gold, I'm sure."
Shaker scooped up a blob of fallen frosting with his finger. "Sorry, I
thought I'd told you about that spell."

*That's right, you did last year. When you were going to eat your new
Mistress's chocolate chip cookies she made for you when you got injured.*
Debbie made a face.

Shaker looked over at her, non-plussed. "Isn't it pretty obvious
that I haven't been getting any action, sweetheart?" He grabbed her,
tickling her until she gasped for breath, and she was laughing so
hard her eyes were leaking tears.

"Stop! Stop it! I can't breathe!"

He hugged her to him. "It's so good to be with you here like
this again." He nuzzled her neck. "Even your jealousy feels good."
He bit lightly. "Although you've no right to be jealous, with Gray
coming to visit you in dreams."

"That was once, and I didn't know it wasn't a dream," Debbie
said defensively. "That's why I had Myrrh put the ward in place on
the house, to make sure that wouldn't happen again."

"The ward will reveal him for who he is, not bar him from your
dreams," Shaker said pointedly. *A thin line that still leaves you room
for some significant bodily intrusion.*

Debbie frowned. "Why are you trying to make me feel guilty
for something you gave permission for?"

"Why are you trying to make me feel guilty for something you
gave me permission for?" Shaker said right back. "Tit for tat." He
reached around and tweaked her nipple.

"Hey," Debbie said, knocking his hand away. "Okay all right,
you're right, I shouldn't be making you feel guilty." She pushed hair
out of her face. "I guess it's because she's not like me. A woman who
was a corporate executive…well, I know I could be better than she
was in pretty much every way. You said I was a good Mistress, fair
and kind and tough when I had to be, but practical. But this new
girl…she's a woman that bakes cookies for her demon. I never did
that for you."

"No, you didn't," Shaker said quietly. "But you also never felt guilty about being my master and commanding me and otherwise abhorring everything I stand for. This Mistress doesn't want me, Debbie, not like you do. Believe me on this. She's…she's a woman of faith."

Debbie laughed aloud, then saw his expression. *Shit, he's serious!* "How in Hell does a woman of faith get bound to a demon?" *And isn't she worried she's going to be damned?*

"Needing protection from a Hell on Earth situation and seeing no other way out. The usual reason." He paused. "But I was talking about our anniversary. Let's go out, we can get a big lavish dinner with that dessert takeout I mentioned, then go see a scary movie and throw popcorn at each other, then we can come home and make love." He kissed her ear. "And you can call in sick the next day."

"How are we going to handle us?" Debbie asked. "You staying here initially and showing up at the awards ceremony with me isn't going to be questioned. But us seen out together on my wedding anniversary obviously in a non-platonic relationship is going to raise some eyebrows, even in this town."

"Hmm. Okay, we'll celebrate at home on the actual day. And that weekend before, we'll go out. That would be the 23rd-24th. Sound good?"

"Yes," Debbie agreed. "It sounds perfect."

"At some point we'll have to come out, so to speak," Shaker murmured. "But I agree, that can wait." He paused. "I don't think we should move to immediately get married, either. We should wait at least a year or two. Unless you conceive, in which case we can legalize things."

Debbie's eyes almost popped out of her head. "You go from pillow talk to heavy subjects. But overall I think that's a good plan." She shifted her body nervously, snuggling closer against him. "Do you think a baby is possible? I'm a year older."

"We'll have to wait and see," Shaker rumbled in her ear. "We're going to enjoy trying, that's for sure."

~

"How can it be April already?" Debbie said, as she and Sheila walked to their cars. "Mid-April, no less?"

"Every day is a step closer to summer," Sheila said happily. She turned to Debbie, exultant. "Song is going for fertility checks, Debbie. If it works, we're going to try to have a baby."

Debbie blinked in shock for a moment, then hugged Sheila hard. "Congratulations. I hope it works for you."

"You haven't said anything," Sheila prodded. "But I'm guessing you and Shaker are trying too?"

"We aren't," Debbie said nervously, looking at her hair in the car window. *It's a good thing I'm headed to the Black Rose next week, my roots are showing. Maybe I need to go darker again, this blonde makes the dye job over-obvious.* "If it happens, we'll celebrate, but I'm not going to obsess over it."

"Good," Sheila agreed. She grinned. "What if you and Song were pregnant at the same time? That would be so wild."

What would be wild about that? She's a good ten years younger, and probably will have an easier time. Debbie closed her eyes and made herself take a deep breath. *Get ahold of yourself and stop being jealous. They're happy, be happy for them.* "Did you choose a sperm donor?"

"I was actually thinking about asking Gray," Sheila said awkwardly. "If he could provide some. I'm worried if we get a donor who isn't part of our circle that they could somehow endanger us or try to take the baby. I'd prefer an anonymous donor." She smiled. "And Gray could ensure that the baby daddy is handsome and smart."

"But can you trust him?" Debbie said, stopping in her tracks. "For something as important as this?"

"I'm not sure," Sheila said softly, looking around for anyone listening. "I do trust him as part of Pandora. But having a child is really important to both Song and me. It's the next big step for us, really the biggest step there is. I want us to be happy. Speaking of happiness, congratulations on your wedding anniversary. It's a year next Saturday."

"Yes, Shaker and I are celebrating at home that weekend. I never thought last fall that things would have worked out so well for us both, Sheila." She hugged her friend. "Black Rose this Friday, remember." *I want to look good for Saturday's big date night.*

"I'm not forgetting. Every time I look in the mirror my roots remind me." Sheila laughed. "Goodnight!"

Debbie moved off to her car, stopping off at the grocery store, then a local restaurant for takeout, then came home. Shaker helped her carry in the bags and trays. "Wow, it looks like you bought out the store."

"I knew the fridge was empty, and I didn't think I'd have time after work tomorrow," Debbie explained, putting a chocolate three-layer cake on the counter. She also took out a bag of flour, a bag of sugar, some vanilla, a bag of chocolate chips, and a pack of butter. "I knew we had eggs, or I would have gotten them, too."

"You're planning on baking?" Shaker asked, his expression carefully neutral.

You raise those eyebrows a millimeter at me, you're going to be wearing this flour. "I can negotiate million-dollar deals, I think I can bake cookies," Debbie said primly. "But you'll have to get the recipe you want me to use. I've never used a cookbook in my life before."

"That will be a problem. There's no way my Mistress will give hers to me."

He must want her cookies, or he'd have said just to get a recipe off the internet. Debbie turned to him, irritated. "What you mean is if you tell her you want your wife to make you the same cookies she did, she's not going to give it to you."

"No, she doesn't know about you, and I don't want her to,"

Shaker rumbled in bass tones. "Think of her as a special needs child with attention deficit disorder; she needs to think she has all my attention and any perceived deficit will cause our arrangement to devolve into disorder."

"Ha ha," Debbie snorted. "I'm not suggesting you ask her. Just go take a picture of it with your phone. You must know where her cookbook is."

"There's a problem with that. I have to appear to her as how she met me. She sees me as Brady she's going to have a bunch of questions, and I'll be bound to answer them, which sooner or later will lead her to you and/or Pandora."

"What if she calls you, and you have to go?"

Shaker produced a bottle of pills from his pocket. "Valium strong enough to put me out like I had severe narcolepsy. The catch is if it's when I'm working at the studio, then you'll have to cover for me somehow. I'll feign sickness and go to my trailer and send you a telepathic message."

"It's not great, but it's a plan. Ok. How is filming going, by the way? Bart told me he pushed you to put in for a bit part in *Dare to Tell*?"

"More than a bit part," Shaker said proudly, as he put away the last of the groceries. "I'm the love interest for the heroine, the owner of the decrepit haunted mansion that she goes to live at." He beamed. "Bart told me to study up on Jane Eyre, to mimic some of the behavior of Ed Rochester."

"Have you ever read the book?" Debbie asked, pouring them both some wine.

"No, have you?" Shaker said, feeding the three hellhounds some pieces of meat. "I thought we could google it sometime this weekend."

"We probably can get a copy of one of the movie adaptations online," Debbie mused. "That's a good idea of Bart's. But the script has no romance, and the owner of the house is supposed to be off camera except for one scene."

Shaker shrugged. "I have a bunch of scenes I'm in but there's nothing lewd. My take is that they are going for that happy ending you said you wanted for all films this year, which includes hinting at a romance between me and the heroine." He held up his glass in a silent toast, then drank some. "Good idea, in my opinion. Most of the highly watched movies in history have good endings where characters have not only growth but some resolution that fits with the growth they experience."

He's really excited about acting again. And about guiding Pandora's path. "What about a death of meaning?" Debbie said with a hint of sarcasm. "Did you add one of those as well?"

"Have I annoyed you for some reason?" Shaker asked, setting down his wine.

Debbie shook her head and sighed. "No, I'm just being bitchy. I'm glad that Bart sees you're an asset, and I'm happy he expanded your part. But he didn't tell me he did that, and neither did Nicole. I'm the CEO and I'm out of the loop."

"You did tell them to do what they thought was best along the lines of your directives," Shaker pointed out. "I think they're trying to do that." He picked up his wine. "And yes, they do have a death of meaning, but it's not a death, really; the most helpful ghost in the house ends up being consumed by an evil spirit, that mulo Nicole mentioned to you. He has a choice to go on to Heaven, and instead stays to save the heroine."

"Hmm, that's different and good," Debbie said approvingly. "You're right, I need to not micromanage. I guess I'm more suspicious than I used to be, after finding out members of my team last year were enemies in disguise." She finished her wine, then set about pouring them both another glass. *Just a half each, I know we both have to be to work early tomorrow.* "Speaking of enemies, you said we had new ones. What did you mean?"

"I saw Pandora joining with another production studio on a joint movie." Shaker's expression was dark. "At least one of the two people who came to see you were demons."

"Can you tell me any details? What they looked like? Why you think they are enemies?"

"The woman was a blond, the man was a brunette, both dressed well, but old-fashioned attire. Almost all of the time you get images with this kind of magic, and no sound, as in no dialogue, so it's hard to tell what's happening. I think they're enemies because looking ahead again beyond that point where I saw them meet with you, I didn't see either of the humans again. But the demon, whomever it was, appeared again, sometime in what I'm guessing was midsummer. At least, you were wearing a summer dress, and I was in my Smoke outfit, probably on-site filming. There was an old house nearby, and a pond."

"And the demon attacked?"

"No, it was watching you. I seemed to be running through lines and oblivious to surroundings. You were on your phone and didn't notice it."

"Are you sure it's an enemy then? If we are making a movie with this demon, or its human host, couldn't that just have been the movie? Did you see a camera crew?"

"No crew, but yes, there could have been one. Point of view is a real issue in foreseeing the future, like the no sound, seeing only from one direction for a few seconds gives a very limited view about who or what is actually there and what they're doing. But if the demon was there to help make the picture or watch me practicing, why was its focus on you and not me? And what's that old house?"

How can you tell its focus was on me from what you saw? Debbie rooted through her bag, bringing up the picture of Sunny Gables. "This is the house where we are shooting *Dare to Tell.* Could it be this one?"

"No. The house I saw was more derelict. And there was a pond next to it, or at least the edge of some kind of water. Maybe even a huge puddle?"

A shiver crossed Debbie's shoulders. *It's that house I authorized Sheila to buy, the one she was offered for almost no money.* She steeled herself, passing him the other photo. "Sheila bought this house for another movie, her pet project. Is it this house you saw in your vision?"

Shaker glanced at it, then at her. "Yes, that's the one. What movie are you making?"

"*Origin of Fear*," Debbie said heavily. "The horror movie about the island haunted house called Latham's Landing."

"I told you not to make that movie!" Shaker ripped up the photo of the house and threw it down. "Why are you going ahead with it?"

"Look, I understand your reasons for not wanting to make the picture. But you're thinking of what you know about the actual house, and what you went through because of your personal connection." *At least, I'm guessing that's your reasons, as you've never really explained your aversion to the house.* "We are using a different house on a different side of the country to shoot the picture, and the actual history isn't mentioned at all in the movie, Shaker. We don't have to mention this is based on a real house, it's not something we would look up for a script. This is a typical haunted house story: teens go to visit, and one by one they get killed. There's no mention at all about any demon that's bound there–"

"But Sheila mentioned one to you," Shaker interrupted. "She even said his name was Rigor, and that Latham made a pact with him. She talked about the water freezing and thawing, and the room of glass that lights when the house is actively hunting victims. Do you understand that this is why places that are steeped in evil go on spreading evil year after year? Because there's always some new people who learn about the place and then think they can go and investigate or discover treasure or proof of life after death or other bullshit. They arrive and get ensnared. If they're lucky, they just die. If they aren't lucky, they either get trapped there to haunt the place forever or infected and sent out to catch others. Either way, they propagate the cycle. The more real information is out there, the more reason people will have to look for the real house."

"The author's name was fake, as was the author for *Hell to Pay*, the movie that Lash said was aimed at him," Debbie said. "Initially you worried this was an enemy making a point to you that he knew what you were, but because he's included in this, I think it's something else." She paused. "Could it be that this is coming from Valerian, that vampire you're supposed to be hunting? A warning to you not to interfere with him, saying he knows where to strike back if you attack?"

Shaker gave her a look of awe, then nodded once. "Yes. He's very much a man of puzzles and games, and this would be his style. But these two scripts were sent to you almost a year ago. I was enjoying myself then with you and Cyrus was watching me intermittently, but my leash was very long. What reason would Valerian have had to warn me in this way then, before he was my enemy? If this script was a warning, why not make it clearer what I'm being warned away from?" He shook his head. "It would fit completely with Valerian if it had arrived this year as a warning not to pursue him. But it arrived last year. I still think that whoever sent it wanted us to make the movie to draw people back to the house."

"You're a demon," Debbie said quietly. "If what you theorize is true about drawing attention to the house and we make the movie, then we are helping evil. I don't want to do that. Yet you say that's what you are supposed to be doing when you're out walking the Earth. If we do this, isn't there a chance that you might get a pass and be allowed to stay here?" She looked at him meaningfully. *With me?*

Shaker looked at her. "It doesn't work that way," he said finally.

"Doesn't it? If the demon there really is your father, why aren't you eager to see him, or to free him, if it is a prison? You're close with your brothers."

"I don't want to talk about this, Debbie," Shaker intoned, his eyes pits of fire.

Debbie ignored him. "Is the demon you see in the future your father?"

"I don't know!" Shaker bellowed, throwing his hands up in the air. "I feel him, yes I think it's a him, I can't be sure. I can't see him. But whoever it is, they're watching you, Debbie. That can't be a good thing, regardless of anything else."

"Please," Debbie said, going to sit on the couch. "We need to talk about this."

"Why can't you just trust me on this?" Shaker said, but he did come and sit next to her.

"Because I need to understand. And to understand, I need you to talk to me." Debbie took a breath. "I'm not trying to dredge up bad memories. But your father was not at our wedding, and you're upset it was possibly him watching me. I conclude from that he's not on good terms with you and that if he were to arrive here, he would be our enemy. Is that right?"

"I don't know," Shaker said, after a bit.

"I want to trust you," Debbie said, laying her hand on his arm. "I do trust you. But with what you're telling me, I'll just be afraid of anyone coming to meet with me. I can't work and live in constant fear, Shaker, especially when I'm not sure what's a real danger, and what might be nothing."

"Premonition isn't accurate, always," Shaker murmured. "Yes, it does usually make you more fearful of the future. But that fear is useful, it could save your life."

"But what kind of life is it if I'm always looking over my shoulder, clutching a bottle of holy water in my hand? And that's if the demon doesn't just pay someone else to kidnap me or kill me with a regular weapon like a knife or a gun."

Shaker pulled her close, embracing her tightly. "I'm encouraging your fear because you are mortal. I don't like to mention it, I know you're sensitive about getting older. To me you are very fragile and can die so many different ways so easily." He kissed her brow. "I didn't understand this when Lash mentioned it to me a year ago, about his lady love. But I understand it now."

"Lash has a lady love?" Debbie said in surprise.

140

"Yes, and there was an incident, she almost died. He had a chance to turn her into a weresnake like him, but he didn't, worried she would hate him. But now he's worried she might be killed because she's only mortal." He drew back from her slightly. "I don't suppose you'd consider becoming non-human, one of the werecreatures? There are many animal forms to choose, not just snake or wolf. I can't advocate for becoming a demon, or a vampire, and there's no way for you to become a faerie, or a goblin, or any of the other races. But you could become were."

Debbie shook her head. "I really want to stay human. Besides, how would that help? Creatures like Lash aren't immortal."

"No, but they do live a longer life, and they can heal injury, like a bullet wound, or a knife. Even decapitation, if their body parts are pushed back together in time."

How did we go from the possibility of baking cookies to a discussion on disembowelment in the space of an hour? "Shaker, I appreciate your concern, and I will be careful. But I want to stay human, at least for now. If you're so worried, you mentioned once that Titus had made Lash some kind of magical aid to help him stay safe. Why don't you make me one of those?"

"I can ask," Shaker said, after a pause. "I will ask, tonight."

"Good," Debbie said. "If you don't want to talk any more about Latham's Landing, that's fine. I'll show you the script of *Origin of Fear*, there's no mention of Rigor, or about Latham's pact with a demon in the movie. Yes, Sheila got that information, but I'm not sure where she got it, because it's not in the script. I'll ask her about it next week, when we're alone, and ask her to leave all of that out of the movie. We can make up some fictional history for the house." She paused. "You should know that the actual house got completely flooded and fell down, that was why I pushed Sheila to find another set, and why we didn't begin shooting last year. It belongs to some retired police chief who now also owns all the shoreline as well and has banned anyone from coming within fifteen feet of the water. Well, he also flooded the house completely, so water covered the island and the whole first story. A few months later the house apparently fell down and is now covered by water. So there's nothing left for anyone to go looking for if we make this movie."

"Really," Shaker said, visibly relieved. "I hadn't heard that."

"Really," Debbie said, getting up and going back to the movie file. "I think it's possible that someone wanted to bring attention to the house as a last-ditch effort. But we delayed making the script. We'd bought it, so they couldn't offer it to anyone else. Then the island got flooded and whatever power was pushing this movie got extinguished." She handed it to Shaker. "See Sheila's notes, these are before she..." *Before she was possessed.* "Shaker, I noticed but forgot to mention, the demon that possessed Sheila last year, it worked on all the movies we had in progress, except this one. This script wasn't touched at all. What do you make of that?"

"Whomever it was, that demon knew the real story behind the island and didn't want to mess with it," Shaker replied, paging through the file. "Thanks, I'll read the script over this weekend." He sighed. "Seeing these notes and the picture of the house mostly in water, I really don't see why you couldn't make the movie, if you really are going to shoot somewhere else and make those changes leaving out the demon history. But please don't go out to the house you bought without me, unless you take Myrrh. Okay?"

"Good," Debbie said in relief. "And okay, I won't go there without you or Myrrh. Now let's start our weekend, we deserve a good Saturday. Why don't you ask one of your brothers to get a copy of that cookie recipe you want and drop it by? Tell them I'll give them some of the cookies if they do."

Shaker laughed, rooting in his pocket for his phone. "Okay, but you'd better make a double batch."

~

"These are delicious!" Titus said, grabbing another. "Just as good as..." He trailed off, looking at Debbie. "Better than anyone else's."

"Good save," Debbie retorted, carefully transferring cookies to a baking rack with a spatula. "Thanks also for the rack, Titus, I didn't know these would cool better this way instead of the counter."

"One of humanity's kinder inventions," Rip said, putting a few cookies in a bag. "I've got to run, but thanks for inviting me." He flashed a smile at Debbie, then disappeared.

"I also must go," Titus said, taking Debbie's hand and kissing it. "Thank you for this, I love baked goods. Anything with chocolate or any pies." He smiled. "Any time you need another recipe stolen, call me. I work for generous shares." He also vanished.

"Who knew demons were such softies for warm gooey desserts?" Debbie said, putting the last batch of cookies in the oven.

"I could have told you, if you'd asked." Shaker ran a hand down her back, then patted her bottom. "Our most wicked dream is a happy housewife baking us good things to eat dressed in a teddy and some high heels."

"And you were doing so well with the compliments," Debbie said, throwing him a disdainful look. "Try again."

"We all want strong women not afraid to share their thoughts who are our equals in every way, yet deign to smother us with their love and warm flesh, and sprinkle in some cookies once in a while?"

"Better." Debbie turned off the stove. "Shall we make some popcorn and go try to find an adaptation of Jane Eyre?"

"Yes," Shaker said, grabbing a handful of cookies. "I can't totally neglect my work, even for you."

"Hmm, well that was pretty good," Shaker said, as the credits were rolling. "I can be gruff and cold and then turn on a dime and be romantic and lustful. Yet I wouldn't have guessed he had a mad wife in the attic, he played it pretty cool."

"Your character won't have a mad wife in the attic. Audiences today take a dim view of bigamy."

"Rightly so," Shaker said, kissing Debbie. "One wife is enough for anyone. Care to call it an early night?"

"I thought we were going to go out?"

"Well, we already had an early dinner, and a movie. I just thought naturally that bed was next."

"Okay, but I want to go out in May. Maybe back to the Breakers?"

"Anything you want, my Mistress. Anything you want."

CHAPTER NINE

May-June

DEBBIE YAWNED, THEN GOT OUT OF BED, CASTING A LOOK back at Shaker sleeping entwined in the covers. *He's better than an electric blanket, I'm going to have to turn down the thermostat once summer gets here.* She slipped on a silky robe and slippers, then headed to the kitchen.

Debbie smiled in relief, flipping over the calendar from April 30th to May 1st. *I can't wait for good weather!* She called to the hellhounds, putting down their bowls of meat as the trio came racing out of the shadow of the trashcan, knocking into one another in their haste. "Hey, be nice, there's plenty to go around."

Debbie started the coffee, then put in two bagels to toast, and poured some cereal into a bowl. *I'm still full from last night.*

Shaker came out just as she was putting her dishes in the dishwasher dressed in his robe, his expression hopeful. "Did you make me anything?"

Debbie motioned to the toaster. "Your bagel's in there. I thought you might want some of your leftover steak on it."

"Yes." He arranged his meal, then warmed it in the microwave. "Don't you want any meat?" he said, sitting down to eat. "I'll share."

"I'm pretty full. But thanks."

"So tell me what Sheila said when you got your hair done." Shaker quickly ate a few bites of meat. "I like the brunette with the red streaks, by the way."

"Thanks," Debbie said, twirling a lock around her finger. *It's getting long, I need to cut it next time.* "She said she didn't remember telling me about any demon bound to the Latham's Landing island, much less give him a name. I didn't know what to say, so said that I thought I'd heard that somewhere. She said no, the script was what they were sticking to, no changes. I didn't want to push, so just said, okay, I must have got it wrong, and changed the subject."

"So she doesn't remember."

"Or I misremembered."

"I don't think so," Shaker said. "You told me what she said some time after she told you, but I recall that what you said had a lot of real-life details, not just the name Rigor. You couldn't have known those things by yourself. I think the demon that possessed her either blocked that knowledge from her waking mind or was the one that told her in the first place. Do you remember when exactly she mentioned this to you?"

"Early last year? March maybe?"

"Then well before she was possessed. So the demon must have blocked out the memory like it never happened, which is why Sheila never mentioned it." He ate another few forkfuls. "So that demon and its team weren't behind these scripts. Hellfire, it would have been so much better if they could be attributed to that demon."

"Could you question her," Debbie asked. "Well, hypnotize her? If what you're saying is true, she must have met with the person or being who gave her the scripts. Maybe they weren't submitted at all?"

"Not without possibly hurting her mind, and causing a relapse," Shaker said. "If a demon tampers with memories, it leaves a ragged scar. Besides, I'd only see what she saw. Whomever gave her the scripts likely was wearing a magical disguise."

"We're back to square one," Debbie said sarcastically with a grimace. "This is not how I envisioned our anniversary."

The doorbell rang.

"Must be the flowers?" Shaker said with a smile. "I ordered you some. Stay here, I'll go get them."

"When you're good, you're good," Debbie sunnily called after him.

There came the sound of the door opening, then Shaker speaking, then the door closing.

Eager to see her flowers, Debbie got up. Grinning, she went towards the front door. "I hope they're red and black, like—" Debbie stopped abruptly, her face flushing, as she beheld her mother and uncle, Shaker standing behind them holding a large bouquet of red and black roses.

"Hi Debbie," Stuart said nervously. "I realize we should have called first. Kallia did mention that. I thought you might be too distraught to answer the phone."

"What are you doing here?" Debbie managed, folding her arms over her chest.

"Your wedding was a year ago today," her mother stated.

"Yes, and you missed it. You never sent a card, or even a text. But you thought you'd show up a year late? To what? Give me condolences on being a widow?"

"It seems you found a replacement fast enough."

"Hey!" Stuart shouted, holding up his hands. "Cease fire, ladies." He turned to Debbie. "It's my fault. I saw the order come through for flowers for you, and thought you'd ordered them for yourself. I didn't want you to spend your wedding anniversary alone and miserable. I told your mother I was coming to visit, and encouraged her to come, to try to mend fences."

Shaker laughed. The other three stared at him. "Sorry, but I'd forgotten that the Tennison family supplied flowers," he commented. "Still it's good to see you both."

"Who are you?" Kallia asked coolly.

"Brady Black, otherwise known as Cole Black," Shaker said, extending his hand to Kallia. "Jett's brother." When she didn't move to take his hand, he leaned in, grabbed hers, and shook it heartily. "Glad to meet you."

"Brady, yes, you were at the wedding," Stuart said, offering his hand, which Shaker shook. "Good to see you. You look great."

"Thanks, I've been working out. I'm working at Pandora now."

"Another actor?" Kallia asked snarkily.

"Just starting out," Shaker beamed. "But I'm told I'm a natural. I've even taken the professional name Cole Black."

"Why are you staying with Debbie?" Kallia continued. "Are you too poor for your own apartment?"

"Tactful as always," Debbie murmured.

"I'm staying with her because we're a couple," Shaker said cheerfully. "With luck you'll be a grandma soon, Kallia."

Debbie's mother's eyes nearly popped out of her head. "What?"

"What is this?" Stuart said, looking from Debbie to Shaker. "Debbie, are you really a couple, or is this some kind of joke to get back at us for showing up with no warning?"

"It's not a joke," Debbie said tartly. "I cared for Jett and would have been happy to live the rest of my life with him. But he was murdered. I grieved and moved on. No, before you ask, I'm not getting married again right away. But yes, I'm in love with Cole and yes, it's serious."

"And you're okay with this?" Kallia said, staring at Shaker. "This woman is your boss. And your sister-in-law."

"All women are the boss of their men, if their men are smart about keeping a happy home," Shaker quipped. He looked at

Stuart. "Debbie's right, I'm serious about her. I care about her and want to make her happy, and right now that's living together. When she's ready for more, we'll take the next step."

"Are you pregnant?" Kallia asked shrilly.

"Maybe," Debbie said slowly, relishing the horror on her mother's face.

"If we do get pregnant, we'll let you host the baby shower," Shaker said, grasping Debbie's hand. *Let's not make this worse, dear.* "Now do you want to sit and have some coffee, or would you rather snipe and screech about things that don't really matter?"

Stuart looked at Shaker, then burst out laughing. "You know, you're just like your brother. I liked him right off, too. Welcome to the family, Brady."

"Thanks," Shaker said. "I'll go get the coffee. Would you like any sugar?"

"No," Kallia said stiffly. "We should leave and let you get back to your morning." She turned and headed for the door.

"No," Stuart said, blocking her. "Brady and I will go out and have a drink. If he's so serious about Debbie, I want to know more about him. You two are staying here and talking to each other."

"Why are you doing this, Stuart?" Debbie stated.

"Because it's past time that this family came together," he said angrily. "Your mother needs you, and you need her. Don't waste the next years being angry for things that don't matter."

"It matters that she didn't come to my wedding!" Debbie shouted.

"What matters is she's here now," Stuart yelled back. "Stop being a child, and start being a woman...and a daughter." He motioned to Shaker, who gave Debbie a smile of encouragement before heading for the door.

Shaker, you're dressed in your robe! Debbie thought to him.

I'll wear a glamour. Call me if you need me, I'll come back, came his reply as the door closed.

149

"Do you want to sit?" Debbie said to her mother. "I need to put on some clothes."

"I'll get some coffee," Kallia replied.

Debbie dressed in some leggings and an oversize top, put on a little makeup, and then returned to the kitchen. Kallia was drinking her coffee and eating one of the chocolate chip cookies.

"These are good, almost like homemade. Where did you buy them?"

"I baked them from scratch."

Kallia gave her an incredulous look. "You don't bake. Or cook."

"You don't know me," Debbie said with finality, sitting down with a fresh coffee. "I'd say it's been years since we had a heart to heart, but we never really had one, ever. Now why are you really here?"

"I'm here because I thought that you might feel badly on your first anniversary as a widow," Kallia said tentatively. "Stuart was right, we saw the order come in for the black and red roses to be delivered today, and that it was your home address. I thought you'd ordered them for yourself."

"Why would you think that?" Debbie said loudly.

"Because this is my first year as a widow, too," Kallia said softly. "And I felt bad on your father's death anniversary. I ordered myself some flowers, knowing he would have wanted me to."

I never thought of her caring for Dad…or being capable of pain. "I'm sorry."

"We didn't know you had a new beau. If we'd known that the order came from him, we'd have just filled it and said nothing. But the name ordering it was Black. We thought it was you that placed the order, not Jett's brother."

"Why were you filling the order anyway?" Debbie asked. "I'm guessing Brady ordered them through the local FTD or maybe Teleflora."

"We filled the order for your wedding flowers," Kallia said, offering a small smile. "Where do you think those places source their flowers, especially the more exotic ones? I still think red roses streaked with black are an appalling choice for a wedding. But we are the only growers that can supply custom colors to turn one side of the petal black while retaining the original rose color on the reverse side." She paused. "I hope it was a beautiful day for you."

"Hang on," Debbie muttered, rising and going to the living room bookcase. She grabbed the envelope Sheila had given her months ago and brought it back to the table. Quickly, she checked the pics to make sure there were no shots of anything paranormal, then handed them to her mother. "It was. Here's a few shots Sheila took."

"What a setting," Kallia said in appreciation. "That's a fantastic replica of Stonehenge."

It is Stonehenge. "Thanks. And thanks for the flowers. As you can see, they were beautiful."

"I'm sorry I wasn't there," Kallia said, her eyes misting up. "I should have come. But I was stubborn. I convinced myself that it was better if I wasn't there."

"I was stubborn, too," Debbie admitted. "But I hoped you'd relent and come."

"I'll come to the next one," Kallia said, offering a tentative smile. "Brady seems very smitten with you."

"Okay," Debbie said, nodding.

"So when did you start baking? You always said you were never going to cook, that you were going to make enough to either order takeout or hire someone to cook for you."

"Since I found a life outside work." Debbie noticed the three hellhounds peering from around the side of the living room door and beckoned. "Come."

Kallia turned quickly. "Who's here?"

The three hounds drew back out of sight.

"Treats," Debbie said, going to the fridge and getting out some cut up meat chunks. "Treats!"

Baroness appeared from under the table, prancing out of the

small shadow, while Pitch and Pike ran in from the living room, tails wagging.

"Dogs? You have three dogs?" Kallia said in befuddlement. "How did I not see the one that was under the table?"

"They're very quiet." Debbie fed each of the dogs a chunk of meat.

"You've never had a pet in your life. Where did you get these? And why do they have those ugly metal collars?"

Damn, I forgot the glamour Myrrh put on the dogs, so it appears they are owned. "They were a gift from a friend, all rescues." *From Hell.* "The collars look like metal but they're fabric." *I hope if she touches one it feels like fabric...*

"You're a workaholic, Debbie. When do you have time for walking a dog or paying them attention, much less three?"

She's never had a dog, either and suddenly she's the champion for animal rights? The unkind thought brought sudden inspiration. "You might have heard last fall that the CEO of our biggest rival, Titan Pictures, got indicted for dogfighting. Pandora volunteered to fund the rehabilitation of the dogs seized in the raid. All of them were successfully helped into new homes."

"I heard about that. I was surprised then, too."

"I...um, I got pregnant, back last spring," Debbie said uncomfortably. "As a present, one of Jett's close friends got me a dog. I called him Guardian. I originally thought of him as just a safety precaution. Then over time he became more than that. He... passed on last fall, right after Jett died."

"And your baby?"

"I miscarried."

Kallia rose, and came over to Debbie, bending down to hug her. Debbie saw her coming and braced herself to tell her mother not to hug her, or feel sorry for her, or touch her. Instead she dissolved into tears.

"I'm so sorry, honey," Kallia said brokenly. "I'm most sorry you had to go through it alone. I failed you in your darkest hour."

Instead of feeling worse hearing her mother's words, Debbie felt a protest stirring within her. *I wasn't alone. In my darkest hour, I had Myrrh. That's when she arrived and helped me turn things around. Don't say that, you'll just have to explain more.* "I'm okay, Mom."

Kallia tittered. "Now I know you're not okay. You haven't called me mom since you were five."

"I didn't think you wanted me to," Debbie said reluctantly, separating from her mother's embrace. "You were always so formal. You were busy a lot with the business, and clients, so I called you Mrs. Tennison around them."

"Where do you think you get your work drive from?" Kallia scoffed. "Not from your father. He was a good man, husband, and father, but never businessman of the year. He was happiest when he was on the golf course or walled up in his study."

"Is what Stuart said about you being overworked true? Are you having a hard time by yourself?"

Kallia raised her chin proudly. "I ran the business pretty much alone most of my married life. Your father worked hard with me when your grandparents were alive, but he wanted to sell the business after they passed. I'd grown to love it by then and refused. He didn't protest even though selling would have given us a windfall, but he did begin leaving the big decisions to me alone after that." Kallia smiled. "I discovered I liked that, being the boss instead of just the assistant wife. Yes, Tennison Flowers has become more of a burden over the years. I don't move as fast as I used to, and I get tired earlier in the day. But I enjoy it, and it keeps me busy. Stuart also helps out quite a bit."

I'm more like my mother than I ever realized. "So, no plans to retire?"

"No. But I don't want to talk about me, I want to talk about you. Tell me in what other ways you've changed, Debbie."

How much should I tell her? Leaving out the demons is a given. "If you want the long version, we're going to have to switch to something stronger than coffee at some point, because we'll be here well into the evening."

"That's okay," Kallia encouraged. "I have a lot of catching up to do." She gestured to the counter. "I see you have some wines there I've never heard of."

"These are some of the cult wines we buy to market our movies," Debbie said, coming back with three bottles which she put on the table one by one. "This is Footsteps on the Stairs, a port wine, the first port we've gotten from Triss Vineyards. This is Incubus, a red that's been called hedonistic with a great finish. And this is Spiritwalker, a white wine with a great body."

"Fabulous." Kallia said. "We can have our very own wine tasting."

Debbie peered at her mother closely. *This is so out of character for my mother, I can't believe it's her.* Debbie got up and got them each three wineglasses, then poured a little of each wine into a glass before replacing the stopper. "Hold on, I think I have some crackers, too." She got out a plate, and put some crackers on it, then also added a big wedge of gouda cheese. *Thank goodness I did buy out the store.*

"You asked how I changed," Kallia said as Debbie sat down. She grabbed a cracker. "After your father died, I stopped trying so hard to be perfect, and started focusing on making myself happy. Many of our friends are sick with chronic illnesses, or already dead. I'm active in my community and church, I eat healthy usually–this morning notwithstanding–and I exercise. Right now I want to spend some time with you." She grabbed her glass of Incubus. "To mothers and daughters getting to know one another."

"Um, Amen," Debbie said, raising her glass to clink it against her mother's glass. *I didn't ever think bridging the gap with my mother was possible, or that it would happen. But I'm glad it did.*

"Now tell me all about your life," Kallia said, sipping her wine. "Give me all the details!"

"I can't believe that went as well as it did," Debbie said, sinking down on the couch after Kallia and Stuart left. "I don't remember sitting with my mom for that long without an argument. I never remember drinking with her. How was your talk with my uncle? You must have been gone five hours."

"Okay," Shaker said with a shrug. "He asked the usual questions: was I a lout or a gambler or a loser or a swindler or a cheat? I assured him I only had the most honorable intentions toward you."

Debbie raised her eyebrows. "I suppose you didn't mention the desk incident in my office?"

"So licentious," Shaker chastised. "Don't make me bend you over this table for a repeat performance, little lady."

"Now who's teasing? So everything went okay?"

"Pretty much. He still thinks that you should come and help with the family business. He said your mom's a workaholic, but that without your father she's running herself into the ground."

"My mother alluded to long hours, but said she appreciated them as they helped keep her active and strong," Debbie commented. "I did promise that we'd visit in October. They ship out a lot of flowers for the holidays, and that's right before the busy season, but after most of the summer and autumn weddings are done."

"I'm fine, as long as we stay in a hotel again and I don't have to go to church."

"I think we can do that."

"So do you think she liked me?" Shaker asked.

"I think they both liked you," Debbie said, taking his hand in hers. "But I love you and I like you, and you like and love me. That's what matters more."

"I think the May staff meeting went well," Debbie said, as she and Sheila walked to her office. "Though we shouldn't have waited until practically the last day of the month. We are ahead of filming on *Hell to Pay*, about halfway done. The CGI effects so far look great and are under budget. *Destiny in the Ashes* is all finished, and the editing's almost wrapped. How is *Dare to Tell*?"

"Almost no progress, but not for lack of trying. The casting isn't going so well, most of the people we were interested in working with either want too much cash or have already committed to other projects. But we have a few people lined up for auditions this week and next. I extended the rental of Sunny Gables for another two months. We have been able to shoot all the background scenes we needed, like the intro of the house, and Shaker's solo scenes, plus some scary moody pieces with the two people we do have cast as ghosts. We can use them to flesh out the movie."

"Good. How is the pilot of *Incubus* coming?"

"Gray can begin filming the pilot of *Incubus* as soon as *Hell to Pay* wraps, and Shaker's already done his bit parts for that pilot separately. In fact, I think Gray only is needed on the *Hell to Pay* set this coming Monday, then he's done. The small bit parts with just the other characters have already done rehearsals, so they are ready to go, they're just waiting for him."

"Good."

"It's a good move getting Brady/Shaker involved with *Incubus*," Sheila approved. "We've had inquiries about him ever since you two appeared at the Oscars together. In fact, there's a meeting I booked this morning that I wanted you to sit in on, because I think that we have another studio interested in working with our biggest star."

"What?" Debbie stopped in her tracks. "Who?"

"Dark Angel Pictures," Sheila said, making a face. "The ones that bought those couple films last year which you didn't care for, and also tried to buy the two we snagged and are shooting now."

"Who are they? Refresh my memory."

"They make sort of Lifetime Mature movies with a paranormal

slant. Remember the potential script about the witch who lost her child or something, then gained a new one somehow? I don't really remember the premise or the name, only that they bought it before we had a chance to reject it."

Debbie cast her mind back. "I remember it had a bad title. *What Matters Not*, that was it."

"Well, it wasn't successful," Sheila said. "But others of their lineup have been. They called this meeting. I think it's because they want to collaborate with us."

"Why?"

"It's the new strategy. A bunch of indie studios go in together on a film. They can afford a lot more advertising and a bigger budget, so more people see the film and they all get more revenue, and more publicity for their own studio and other lone works."

"You think we should do it?"

"I think we should see what they have to say."

Debbie followed Sheila into the conference room. A woman with blond hair and a man waited there.

Debbie stopped in her tracks. *Shaker, the demon you foresaw is here now.*

I'm coming, came his mental reply.

"Who are you?" Sheila said in confusion, looking at the pair.

Debbie's eyes widened in sudden fear. *Shit! Shaker, get here! Vassago! Rack! Get to the conference room now!*

"I'm not sure who he is," the woman said with a shrug aimed at the man. "I'm Autumn Silver, and I'm here for my appointment to audition for the lead in *Dare to Tell*."

Rack entered the conference room heading for Debbie, followed by Vassago Gray. "Ms. Silver, so glad to make your acquaintance. I'm sorry, but you're here in Pandora's office area. The director Bart is expecting you on the studio lot, he wants your audition to be on the set today. I'll be happy to take you to your audition."

Ms. Silver nodded hello to Debbie and Sheila, batted her eyes at Gray, and followed Rack out.

"Who are you?" Debbie demanded.

"Mr. Perry, from *The Star*?" The man held out his credentials. "I'm here for an interview with Mr. Gray about his upcoming series *Incubus*. My editor set it up." Perry looked at Gray. "Is here good?"

"Yes," Vassago said, looking at Debbie curiously. "Unless you were going to use this room."

"Damn it, I asked that the Dark Angel people be shown in here when they got here," Sheila fumed. "That damn doorwoman."

Shaker? Debbie sent out mentally. *Where are you?*

Come to the lobby, came his reply.

"They're in the lobby," Debbie said, tapping Sheila's shoulder. "Come on."

~

"Now that we're all here," Debbie said, looking across the table at the platinum-haired woman. "What did you want to discuss?"

"First, let us all be open," the woman breezed. "Shaker, it's good to see you again."

"Ms. Grim," he said, nodding. "You already know of Debbie, Pandora's CEO. This is Sheila, Pandora's VP."

"Good to put a face to a name," Ms. Grim said, flashing a smile of shark teeth. "I know you're busy, so I'll be quick. As you are aware, I represent Angel Pictures. We primarily do television movies, usually drama with a paranormal or supernatural slant."

"Yes, you're our newest script rival," Sheila said, her expression fake pleasantness. "I thought it was Dark Angel Pictures."

The woman's eyes narrowed, annoyed. "Just plain Angel Pictures, for now. We would rather not be rivals. I'm here as an emissary to ask you to be allies."

"Allies how?" Debbie asked.

"We'd like to help produce some of your movies, to get a

toehold into theaters. In turn, we'll offer you some help in the television streaming market."

"Why do you think we need your help?" Shaker asked.

"Because every independent studio needs help in these times. Sixty years ago there were a handful of stations, and everyone with a TV watched the same things. Thirty years ago there were thirty-some channels and people had their favorite shows they had to sit and watch when they aired, because no one could figure out how to program a VCR successfully. Today we have ten major streaming services, and more being added all the time, all of which have their own original programming. Cable has its own shows, as do the premium channels and those also have their own programming. Other countries have their own versions of cable which also have their own original programming. It's entirely possible today to spend considerable money with well-known players and not get an audience, because your tagline or photo or fifteen second video doesn't grab their attention in the two seconds that you have as people skip by your promo on their homepage, or you simply aren't licensed on the best platform for your genre."

"You paint a bleak picture of the industry," Debbie said.

"It is bleak," Ms. Grim stated. "Theater chains are also jumping on the subscription bandwagon in an attempt to fill seats. It remains to be seen if this will stem the losses in revenue they are currently sustaining. Only the biggest movies are packing theaters, and indie movies are not exempt from this, no matter how well they are reviewed."

"Your focus right now is TV," Sheila interjected. "Ours is movies. Given what you just said, why would you be keen to get involved with Pandora when your studio seems in a better position to make a profit in the future?"

"Because your new focus on horror movies is the only genre in theaters still bringing in steady income. People would rather be scared in the dark together than at home alone. Historically, horror movies came out in the summer and in the fall, and otherwise were pretty rare. Now in any given week of the year, normal means there's at least one scary film in the theater roster. You're also going above the normal genre films of serial killer/slasher to examine what good and evil really means. Some might say you are redefining the line between the two." She paused. "I went to see *Absolution* in its limited release last year and loved it."

"Thank you," Debbie said. "What are your terms?"

"We'd like to feature Shaker aka Cole Black in at least one TV movie. We will put up money to help with marketing and promotion of *Destiny in the Ashes*, and also put 200K towards another future movie of your choosing, provided the genre is straight horror and that it either features Shaker or another bankable star. We will also put another 200K toward the *Incubus* series, provided that Netflix does agree to pick up the series."

"And you don't want any money in return? Excuse me but this seems too good to be true."

"We are angels, after all," Ms. Grim said with an evil smile. "Just a different kind of angel. This is our offer. If you refuse, we will take our capital and simply use it to buy a studio. I understand Titan Pictures is up for grabs."

"Titan was sold off in pieces," Sheila grated out, her eyes daggers.

"Yes, and we quietly bought most of the pieces: the lots, the studios, the office space, and the warehouse of props," Ms. Grim answered. "You accomplished a lot in two years. If you can do it, so can we. We can make our own foray into movies without you, and likely become your competitor, as Titan was. We prefer not to."

I'd rather buy them out, Debbie thought to Shaker. *Will they go for that? You know this demon.*

No, she won't. But this offer sounds like a good one. My vote is to accept.

"If we agree to this, we'd want to know we could trust you," Debbie said. "We'd want you to give us a written contract to lease the studios and lots to us that you bought from Titan for at least five years. Only the ones you aren't currently using, that is."

"Agreed. But they will be used for films for either television or theaters that we collaborate on only, not any lone movies of yours."

"Agreed. We'd also need meetings quarterly to discuss new joint acquisitions and those projects we already have in progress, as well as to coordinate promotion and marketing for the ones that are completed."

"My people can meet with your people on everything but the new acquisitions and fill us in later. For new projects, you and I should meet with our respective VPs quarterly to discuss potential pictures, decide on the ones we both feel will be worthy, and then frame out the particulars, like your lot or ours, your director or ours, etc."

This could work. But it's bigger than anything we ever did before. "I need to run this past my legal team. But I'm definitely interested."

"Good," Ms. Grim said, standing. "I'll send you over a proposal in the next week to look over. I will expect you will be able to give us an answer by the end of the month?"

"Yes," Debbie said, also standing and putting out her hand. Ms. Grim shook it, then shook hands with Shaker and Sheila.

"Wow," Sheila said, when Shaker and Debbie had returned to Debbie's office. "This is big, Debbie. Really big."

"Exactly what I was thinking," Debbie replied. "Shaker, you said you're for this deal. I thought you said that Ms. Grim would be an enemy?"

"I don't really call the demon in Ms. Grim a friend," Shaker answered. "But she's generally a female of her word. Why she wants to partner with us is what I'm not sure of."

"It could be that Angel Pictures didn't have that much luck last year," Sheila said, looking at her phone. "They had a net loss, not a big one, but a loss. I'm guessing, but I think it's because they don't have a star of their own tied to the studio; they've used mostly unknowns in their pictures. Their list of upcoming films online doesn't have anything on it as of today."

"Hmm. Look into this, would you, Sheila?" Debbie stood. "I will tell Catarella and Giorgio to expect the contract and ask them both to review it and look for loopholes." She turned to Shaker. "As much as I want to believe Angel Pictures just wants us, I think they may be after you and your star power."

Shaker shook his head. "My turn to be humble. Jett maybe, but Brady's still an unknown, even if I am playing Smoke."

"Could they be hoping Devlin will back a picture that they come up with, and so are just looking for an infusion of funds?" Sheila suggested. "Demons aside, business is business. Possibly they are just trying to survive."

"I guess we'll find out," Debbie said darkly.

"Debbie?" came her secretary. "Mr. Gray is here to see you."

Sheila and Shaker got up and headed to the door. As Gray entered, Shaker stopped in front of him. "Remember," he rumbled forbiddingly. "This is the waking world, Vass." Then he strode away.

"Guess I got warned," Vassago Gray said with a smirk as he shut the door. He looked at Debbie under lowered lids. "Should I lock it?"

"You wouldn't keep him out if you did," Debbie replied, aloof. "Now what did you need?"

"I just wanted to tell you that the reporter, Mr. Perry? He asked a lot of odd questions along with the normal crap."

"Like what?"

"Like was I scared to work here because of Jett's death, or the accidents last year. If you were really a cougar. If I'd felt any weird feelings or seen any ghosts."

"'If I were a cougar'? You've got to be kidding."

"That's what I thought. I said no comment to a lot of it, because Shaker said not to act like anything upset me and to keep smiling."

"When did he give you all this advice on being a celebrity, by the way? You don't exactly come to the house when he's home."

"I'd be happy to have a threesome any night he's willing–"

"Not going to happen," Debbie interrupted curtly. "Answer me."

"Back last fall, when he recruited me for Pandora."

"He recruited you? He told me you approached him."

"He put out the word among demons that he was looking for a handsome male who knew how to be sexy, intelligent, and was willing to cooperate."

"He used those words? 'Willing to cooperate'?"

"Verbatim."

"Hmm." *Is Gray supposed to be willing to cooperate with Shaker or me?*

"I went to see Shaker, told him I was interested in his offer. He talked to me for a few hours and gave me the rundown. I told him it sounded good, so he told me to come and see you. And you know the rest."

"I don't see why you feel you had to tell me this."

"To be blunt, it seemed to me that Mr. Perry is connecting the dots."

"Explain."

"He's not a priest, and he's not out to vanquish demons, or even targeting Pandora," Gray said. "But he's fleshing out a picture that a demon hunter could take one look at and know instantly for what it was. I was as vague as possible about the incidents that happened here before me, like the deaths of your former partner Rebecca, her husband Paul, his son, Dante, the deaths of Jett, the priest turned actor Cahill, the supposed bombs, Sheila's attack and subsequent coma…you get the idea. But a lot of that is public record now. If we have a few more incidents like those here, we won't be dealing with solo hunters. We'll be dealing with an army of them."

"And your opinion is?"

"I think you're right in diversifying movie subjects. I heard about the deal Angel Pictures is offering, and I think you should do it, because their focus is on more drama with happy endings, and less death and mayhem. I also think you should begin doing one non-supernatural movie each year."

"That's not where our target audience has been. We lose the death and paranormal mayhem, we likely will lose our forward momentum."

"That's a rote answer," Gray whispered, coming forward to lean on her desk. "Yes, you might be right, but isn't it worth switching gears if by doing so you can fly under the radar?"

"Can you get to the point and stop with the euphemisms?"

"Fine. Here's bluntness: Brady is becoming a copy of Jett. That's good for the studio. But when you're seen together as a serious couple, that angel Rafael is going to come back with another demon-hunting priest in tow. Shaker got a pass for bringing in that sorcerer's soul last fall, but if he's sent back to hell with nothing to show for it within a year, he's not going to get out again so easily."

How does he know about all of that? "You don't know that's true, any of it."

"Truth doesn't matter. What matters is perception. My perception when I see the two of you together is that Jett is back. A hunter doesn't need to know about Shaker or any of us others to be attracted. The likely explanation that you sold your soul to have Jett returned to you will be believed by a demon hunter. That will make Shaker a target. If they try a holy water test or a cross against his skin, that'll show him for what he is. And then you'll have a repeat of last year."

"You're making the hunters sound stupid, which in my experience they aren't. Brady is Brady, not Jett."

"Brady was a drug addict and an alcoholic like his brother; now he's reformed and healthy and acting like a pro even though he's had no training. He's living with you and in a serious relationship with you exactly like his brother was. Jett died about six months ago, and you met Brady at your wedding, didn't let him stay with you then, and invited him to visit right after Jett died. He immediately dumped his life and moved out here within three months. Even by Hollywood standards that's a fast romance."

"Maybe I always harbored a crush on Brady, because he was a version of Jett that was much more innocent than my former husband," Debbie said smoothly. "Maybe we were thrown together by my husband's tragic death, and formed a bond born in mutual grief. And maybe it won't work out in the long run, but we're happy together now. Or maybe I just like men with black hair and blue eyes in my bed."

Gray smiled and nodded. "Very good. Very good. Now memorize all that, because you're going to get the question within the month from Mr. Perry if not others."

"And what was your big suggestion on how to avoid demon hunter attention?"

Gray stroked the back of her hand, withdrawing before she could react. "I was going to suggest you be seen with me in public. If you date both your stars, you'll break the pattern. Cougars aren't going to raise red flags with a demon hunter." *And I like that you called to me when you thought you were in danger today.*

"You're more of a target, you play a demon, not a demon hunter like Smoke," Debbie rebuffed, moving out of arms reach. "Nice try, but no."

"But I'm a good demon," Gray said in sultry tones, winking slightly. "You already know from experience, Debbie."

"There's no such thing in my experience," Debbie said coldly, standing. "Goodnight, Gray. I'll see you Monday."

CHAPTER TEN

"I LOVED YOU TELLING HIM THAT, ECHOING MY WORDS ABOUT no good demons," Shaker laughed. "He does have a point about the pattern we're making. But I don't think it's as serious as he made it out to be. He really just wants to be in your bed for real, not just in dreams occasionally."

"He's out of luck," Debbie said affectionately, leaning back on Shaker's lean naked chest. "I already have a man in my bed."

"A fully capable one, too," Shaker teased, his hand reaching down to stroke her mound. "If you'd like another demonstration, I'm at your service."

"I'd love to, but I think you'll have to give me until tonight to recover." She patted his muscular thigh. "What else can you tell me about incubi?"

"I supposed I could get you a copy of the other books of the Bible, the ones that were taken out before King James published his version," Shaker mused. "There's some really good stories in there. The Book of Jubilees has Cain marrying his sister. The Gospel of Mary Magdalene is very feminist; she was first among men and women, independent and strong-willed. Or there's the book of Nicodemus, which details Jesus's decent into Hell."

"I just want to know what you know about them."

"The angel Uriel is on record as being against the mating of human and angel, which is supposedly the origin of the incubus and succubus," Shaker replied. "That's why he lobbied for the Great Flood, to kill off the crossbreeds." He cleared his throat. "Here shall stand the angels who have connected themselves with women, and their spirits assuming many different forms are defiling mankind and shall lead them astray into sacrificing to demons 'as gods', here shall they stand, till 'the day of' the great judgment in which they shall be judged till they are made an end of. And the women also of the angels who went astray shall become sirens." He paused. "I forget the chapter and verse, but that's in the Bible. You'll have to Google Uriel to find out exactly where. Many flood myths exist in various texts and civilizations, usually caused by a deity in anger for some evil on Earth, though the Internet supposedly says that there's no evidence of a whole planet flood. I guess there are possibilities of a comet hitting the Earth to cause a planetwide tsunami, but it's more likely that different civilizations had their own flood myths from localized flooding, or perhaps from finding the fossils of marine life buried in their lands."

"I don't care about all that," Debbie said, exasperated. "I want to know if our child would have been an incubus, like Gray."

"No, in short," Shaker said, his expression uncomfortable. "A regular human can't have a demon's child."

"Stop talking around the question. I hate it when you do that, say a bunch of words that seems like you're answering me but tells me nothing new or relevant. Now...you impregnated me while possessing Jett. Would the child have been an incubus if it had lived?"

"Not for certain," Shaker said finally.

"Why are you being so curt? What don't you want to tell me?"

"Having a child with a demon taint is very difficult for a

female," Shaker admitted. "It's almost impossible for a demon not possessing someone to have one with any female: the demon energy of the child is too much for the pregnancy to go to term. For a demon possessing a human, it is easier to breed with any female, because the demon energy that goes into creating the child is diluted. Yes, many children born of a possessed male and a human female have the possibility of being succubae or incubi. I would have needed to help you carry the child to term with the aid of magic."

Was this part of the reason I miscarried before? "You and I are trying right now," Debbie said loudly. "Don't you think you should have shared this with me sooner?"

"I didn't want you to say you didn't want to try again," Shaker murmured. "I thought if you knew it would be difficult, you'd tell me you didn't want to try."

"You're right," Debbie said coldly. "I don't want to try, knowing this. I'll call and get some birth control pills from my doctor on Monday."

"Alright. I'm sorry."

Debbie turned on her side away from him and didn't reply.

"So this is the proposal Ms. Grim sent over," Debbie said, as she read. "What's this movie that they refer to that they want Shaker to do?"

"It's called *An Unconventional Christmas,*" Sheila said, grimacing. "Pure rom-com, contemporary, no paranormal at all. They want Shaker to play the pro bono, Earthjustice-employed lawyer who finds romance again with his wife, a high-powered CEO, through the very clever efforts of a service called Ms. Romance."

"Ugh. And this movie will sell to networks?"

Sheila nodded, a small smile on her lips. "Christmas romance movies are highly watched from fall all the way through the winter, and networks line up scores of them. I'm not sure it will be memorable, but it's clever enough that it will sell to a network. Plus, Shaker aka Brady will be exposed to a brand-new group of viewers who might not see our regular movies, so we can expect that our previous films he starred in will have increased downloads every time the TV movie airs on television."

"Hmm, that's very good, then. I see a note from Catarella and Georgio that both say that the contract looks good to them." She took up a pen and signed the back page, then dated it and handed it to Sheila. "Can you please have this sent back to Ms. Grim?"

"Of course. I do have some bad news though."

"What?"

"That house we bought to film Origin of Fear? Remember how it was near a depression, and I hoped to use that to fill with water, so we could pretend it was the lakeshore? Well, a very big rain system went through that area, though it missed pretty much everywhere else here. The same thing that happened to us with *Absolution* two years ago happened again. The house really is flooded now."

"That's great! Can you go out and shoot some scenes?"

"We could, but it will be tight. Of the five students that make up the main cast, we have only three that could drop what they are doing and go out there to do some filming before the water recedes. Even then, I'm not sure how safe the house itself is, especially now that the foundation is sitting in water. But I do want to try getting some scenes from outside the house, just to see how they look."

"This sounds like good news, not bad news. What's the problem?"

"The problem is that I was waiting for *Hell to Pay* to wrap, so Bart would be free. He's almost done, but now that we've signed Autumn Silver to star in *Dare to Tell*, he wants to go right into that. I think she's banging him."

I can't say much, when it looks to the world like Brady is my lover.

"Tell him to take a day this week and get some shots at the house," Debbie said indulgently. "We're ahead of schedule, and we do need to know if it can work. But verify the house is safe before letting any of the actors near it, we can't afford to get sued. Okay?"

"Okay," Sheila said happily.

~

"Shaker?" Debbie called as she got home. "Are you here?"

"He's not," Myrrh said, as she stepped in from the deck, one of her crows on her shoulder. "I think he's out getting you some special dinner. I take it there was a fight?"

Debbie put down her purse, then sat on the couch, the three dogs wriggling happily and trying to lick her face. "Down! Yes, you're good dogs. It wasn't really a fight. I just wasn't aware that it was so hard to have a baby with a…with Shaker. He told me that it would be really difficult. I'm wondering now if my miscarriage was because of that."

"Probably," Myrrh said, sitting beside her. "Most cross-species mating is because of love, and much of it is unfruitful, to the pain of the would-be parents."

"Why didn't he tell me that explicitly?"

"I don't know. What did he say?"

"He said I'd have said no. Which is what I told him last week, after he admitted that. We haven't spoken about it since then. He's been gone most nights, and I've been trying to figure out how to handle this." Debbie let out a breath. "What I'm saying here is that he let me risk my life and didn't tell me about the danger."

"Perhaps he thought he could mitigate it?"

Debbie cast her mind back over the events of the last year. "I don't remember him saying anything about it being dangerous, but I thought someone else did allude to that, maybe Song? Wait it was Terian, that's Titus's son. He said he had a baby with a human woman. But he's only half demon. He said Titus helped her deliver safely."

Myrrh nodded. "Titus helped you, as I remember, as well, after you miscarried. He's good at healing."

"Why would I need healing, though? Women miscarry babies and are able to heal themselves."

"Demon babies tend to be born with their true nature in full force," Myrrh said slowly. "They can rip their way out of their mother's wombs. Even if they come out the usual path, the mother is often torn by their talons. Healing is a necessity, unless they are cut to remove the child."

I am definitely not trying now. But yes, that's what Terian said, that his wife had their child by Cesarean. "There is no way I'm doing that. He should have told me."

"Did you talk about having a child?"

"When I got pregnant, it was kind of an accident," Debbie admitted. "I didn't think about Jett, well...jetting into me and making a baby." She forced a smile. "I'm sorry, I'm being crass because I'm tired. Let me say goodnight and go take a shower."

"Actually, I am here on a task that can't wait," Myrrh said, holding up a small white pebble. "You asked Shaker for a talisman to resist magic. Here it is."

"Why are you giving it to me and not him?"

"Because he had to ask me for it." Myrrh smiled. "He's a great sorcerer unto his own, but only I can create this."

Debbie took the stone, rolling it in her hand. "Why?"

"Because I'm the Magicbane," Myrrh said. "It's made from my body. That is bone, not rock."

"You're giving me a piece of your bone?" Debbie said, wide-eyed. "Where did you get it from your body?"

"Little toe, usually. That's easy to heal."

"*Usually!?*"

"Of course. This isn't the first time I've made a talisman for someone, though you can count the number of people that have them on one hand, and they are all family, save one," the faerie answered. "I made him pay through the nostrils for his, though. But it made the difference between life and death for him more than once." She drew a small knife from her belt. "The best way to make it most effective is to insert it under your skin. It will form a layer of scar tissue around it, in time, but I'd still advise putting it in a place where you have a layer of fat that isn't usually compressed, such as under your arm, or your inner thigh."

I can't put it on my thigh, I'd be self-conscious. "Under my arm, please."

"Look away as I cut. It will hurt, but I'll heal you after. Ready?"

Debbie nodded, pressing her teeth tightly together as she shut her eyes. Myrrh sliced into the inside of her arm near Debbie's armpit, then came the pressure and pain of something being forced into the wound. Myrrh began murmuring, and the pain slowly faded.

"There," Myrrh said. "How does that feel?"

Debbie felt the underside of her arm, where the hard lump bulged just beneath the skin. "Odd."

"You'll get used to it, in time."

"You said you made these only for family," Debbie said slowly. "Except for some guy. But I'm not your family, Myrrh." Her brow furrowed. "Am I? Is that why you came to help me last year?"

"Yes," Myrrh said, resigned. "You're too clever for your own good, Debbie."

"Answer me."

"I'm related to Shaker," she said finally. "You're his wife. You're family."

"Are you his child?" Debbie asked. *And if you are, what does that make me? Stepmom to a daughter who is a hundred years older than I am? And what faerie is Myrrh's mother? Leri? Some stranger that Shaker's never mentioned to me, not that I'd want to know...*

"I'm your friend," Myrrh said, standing. "You're good for him, more than you know." In a swish of dark skirts, she was gone.

I need a drink and I need one now.

When Shaker arrived close to an hour later, Debbie was on dregs of her second glass of wine, and in a much more relaxed mood. But she still only let him set down the two bags of takeout on the table before asking, "Is Myrrh your daughter?"

"Pour me a glass," Shaker said, sitting down. "We can talk as we eat."

Debbie poured quickly, and then sat down, not touching the food in front of her.

"Yes, she's my daughter," Shaker said, in between mouthfuls. "and before you ask, I didn't really know the faerie that carried her, or about her, until a little while ago. I didn't have any part in her upbringing. I can't take any credit for the amazing woman she has become."

"She is amazing," Debbie murmured. *Damn it, I can't yell if he didn't know, and I can't be jealous if Myrrh's the product of some one-night stand. But this does put into perspective why he trusted her after meeting her and explain that tender scene I witnessed with the two of them a few months ago. He was thanking her for looking after me.*

"I'm glad you agree. Now eat something. Myrrh healed you, but your body will still need extra calories to recover losing the blood."

"How did you know?"

"I smelled the blood."

"Were you going to tell me?" Debbie asked tentatively. "About her?"

"She asked me not to."

She must have asked her crowmen not to, either. That's why Bawdir refused to tell me and referred me back to Myrrh that day I asked him. "Why wouldn't she want me to know?"

"I got this food especially for us," Shaker said pointedly. "Please, eat some, Debbie, while it's warm. I can't tell you Myrrh's mind, she's a force unto herself. And no, I didn't ask her to watch over you last year, because I didn't know about her then. I met her that day I came to see you, and she was here standing guard." He chuckled. "I think she put that ward on your house on purpose, so I couldn't get in magically that night I came to reunite with you."

"If she doesn't like you very much, why would she like me?" Debbie pressed. "I'm only her stepmom. Which is pretty weird, by the way, with her being so much older than me."

"Think about this as you gaining a daughter and a friend in one person," Shaker answered, finishing his meal. "That's how I see it and that's how Myrrh sees it. She doesn't expect you to be her mother."

"Who does she expect me to be?"

"She expects you to be you. And that's who you should be, because that's who you are."

Stymied, Debbie began eating her cooling food, her thoughts churning. *That's why she came to rescue me from the demons, faced down Celia's ghost, and put the tracking spell on me.* "I should pay her for the magical charm, at least. A gift basket doesn't quite cover it."

"I think she'd like that. Faeries love gold especially. Perhaps get her some doubloons."

"Okay." *Especially with this, I don't want to talk to him tonight about us not trying for a baby.* "Where have you been all week?"

"Fixing up your father's cabin," Shaker answered. "You said you wanted to go up there starting in June, and I said I'd help. I built you a better dock to sit on, and a sunken stone path from the house to the water, and a deck off the back of the cabin, so you can sit and watch the sunset."

"Why didn't you tell me?"

"I thought you were angry with me and needed some time." Shaker put his hands on her shoulders. "I'm not angry if you don't want to have my baby anymore. I'm not with you to procreate. I'm here because I want to be with you."

"That's what I want, to be with you," Debbie said, reaching up a hand to clasp his. "But I think it's too risky…at my age." *There, I said it.*

"Did you get the pills," Shaker said, crouching behind her and ruffling her hair. "I stopped tonight and got some condoms, in case you didn't."

"You're really okay with this?" Debbie looked up at him quizzically. "And yes, I got them. I've been on them a week, I'm protected."

"I'm a demon," Shaker said, oddly somber. Then he smiled. "I'm not the ideal father, just for that. I know you would make a good mother, you're protective and fierce and ruthless and loving. But I'm okay just having you. You're enough for me to be happy." He touched her cheek. "I will say this, though saying it makes me jealous: if you want to have a human baby that is not mine, I'm okay with you asking Vass to inseminate you. I know him too well to think he hasn't offered."

"He has, more than once," Debbie said coolly. "I told him no."

"Are you sure?" Shaker asked. "Though the delivery system is via demon, the sperm will be completely human. He could also—"

"No," Debbie interjected. "At least, not right now. You don't have to tell me I don't have much more time; I know that already. I will think about it, because you're right, if I'm going to, I have to do it soon. But I just need more time to consider it."

"Okay," Shaker said, as he turned away.

"It's beautiful up here," Myrrh said, as she and Debbie unpacked the car. The hellhounds were running about chasing anything that moved, howling up a storm. The crows were flying around, looking over everything, roosting here and there, several down by the water already hunting for food.

"It is," Debbie said in appreciation, looking at the deck and the stone walkway down to the new dock. "Shaker outdid himself. He said he could build, but this looks professional."

"He is a master builder," Myrrh said, dropping the cooler on the kitchen floor. "Now what?"

"Put the groceries away," Debbie said, as she opened the fridge. "Aww." She took out the little bag of chocolate hearts wrapped in red foil. A note was on it that read *Eat with Impunity*. Debbie unwrapped one and ate it, then replaced the rest of the bag. After she and Myrrh unpacked the groceries, they both sat in the sun, drinking water and reading.

"I've never understood modern spellbooks," Myrrh said, closing hers. "They're all 'do what you will' and 'harm none' and 'hope for the best'. Real magic is dark and requires ritual and sacrifice. You can't get real results without real sacrifice. I should just incinerate this garbage."

"How dark is the magic you do?" Debbie asked, putting down her own book on social politics. "Can you do anything with magic?"

"I'm half demon and half faerie, with a little goblin and other magic mixed in. Mostly demon magic is destructive, where faerie magic is transformative. I can do healing, defend myself, attack others, disguise myself, create magical doorways, and burn the evil out of demons, at least temporarily. Not anything, but close." Myrrh laughed, Debbie joining in. "In fact, I made you something." Myrrh held out a small bag.

"I'll owe you more doubloons," Debbie said, taking it. "Thanks."

"No, you were kind to pay me, and I am grateful for the money, but this makes us even."

"What is it?" Debbie asked, holding up the small crystal-like mirror on a chain.

"A shadowbringer. It will create light in a dark place and create a shadow in a bright place that has no darkness. I did it so that wherever you are, if you need them, your dogs can come to you."

"Thank you," Debbie said a touch anxiously, looking over to where the three dogs were dozing in the sun, Pitch on his back with his legs in the air. "But I don't want them hurt."

"Your last hellhounds stood between you and the demons that

attacked you," Myrrh said quietly. "They bought me time to find you. You may need that time."

"Can I be teleported against my will, now that I have your talisman on my person?"

"It will resist you being teleported, yes. But a strong enough entity could do it. You're wearing your ring, and it retains the tracking spell, that's another safety net. The magic nullifier now inside your body is more for a spell which is cast on you than for challenging unwanted magical travelling. Yes, any spell cast on you will fail."

"That's a relief," Debbie said, laying back and closing her eyes. "Is there a reason you're so worried?"

"I just thought that you were thinking of getting pregnant," Myrrh said carefully. "I wanted to make sure you'd have safeguards in place."

Debbie debated staying silent, then told Myrrh about what Shaker had said. "Do you know about the incubus insemination process?" She paused. "I don't want to give birth to an incubus, Myrrh. Or any kind of demon."

"I believe that Vass could give you a purely human child, if you agreed to let him have sex with you. But he'd definitely want to have sex for a while, as in more than one night, so you'd have to go along with that until he delivered the goods, so to speak."

"I know," Debbie said, shifting uncomfortably. "He's a great lover, but I really don't want anyone but Shaker. And I'm not sure how long he'd require me to agree to."

"The other shoe is that you'd have to trust Vass implicitly. Can you trust him like that? I can't say personally, I don't know him. I'm used to trusting almost no one."

"So am I," Debbie said grumpily. "I don't like depending on someone I don't know that well to create a life with me. That's another reason I think I should forget it. Lots of women are happy with no children, and I never even considered it until I got pregnant the first time. I wonder how much of my longing is me really wanting a child, and how much is really just that I want a do-over that ends differently."

"I'm not a good one to ask," Myrrh offered. "I never considered children. Faeries have a hard time of it, and half breeds like me a harder time still. Torren was an infertile vampire. There was almost a magnitude less than zero chance of a pregnancy."

"But would you have had one, if you had a viable option?"

"I'd have tried," Myrrh said finally. "I miss Torren. I'd have liked to have something of him besides his belongings, something of ours together."

"But the child will not be Shaker's," Debbie uttered. "I think that's my deciding factor, Myrrh. It won't be our child. It will just be my child."

"Shaker can help you to raise it, as Brady. That's safer for the child, to not be part demon, and for you, too. The child doesn't have to be his blood to be his."

"Down deep, I'm not sure that Shaker wants a child not his own," Debbie said. "Especially now that I've told him I don't want to try to have his."

"Debbie, we can go round and round with this and not get anywhere. If you're asking me, I say you have to think about if you want to try. Remember, no matter what Vass says, he can't guarantee you'll get pregnant." She paused. "It's possible that the miscarriage scarred your womb, because you were carrying a demon baby. You might not be able to get pregnant again. But if you want to try, then do it."

I've annoyed her for some reason. "Alright," Debbie said. "I have another question then. What can you tell me about Uriel?"

"The angel Uriel? Supposedly handsome as in blond with blue eyes, energetic, purposeful, oval face, medium sized, not bulging with muscle but more compact and lithe. It was said that the devil or his forces sought to impregnate human women to create more warriors for Hell's uprising, knowing they would mature fast. But when the deed was done, the females gave birth to males with dark hair and colored wings not white—"tainted men", who were "predisposed to evil, not good", and were not angels. Supposedly each coupling brought forth not one or two, but closer to a dozen. They were "shapechangers, able to take flight." Despised of Heaven, they instead swelled the ranks of the devil, and almost all became full demons in time. They were the precursors for most demons." Myrrh turned and looked at Debbie. "I'm assuming you're asking me because my crowmen fit the description of Uriel's dark tainted men, especially with the note about them being able to fly."

"No," Debbie said, her mind trying to quickly commit to memory everything Myrrh had just said. "Shaker talked about Uriel, that he was an angel who was against angels and humans having sex because they spawned incubi. But you just said he was in Hell's uprising."

"Honestly, I'm not sure," Myrrh said. "There's not a big volume of tomes that tells the history of all the magical bigshots in the history of the world. There's little written down about angels except in the Bible, and as you know there are a lot of versions of that book. Paintings of angels weren't done from life, but from the artist's imaginations, and so are completely unreliable. I've had others accuse me of working for the devil over the years, especially after seeing one of my crows in human form, so I'm familiar with what I quoted to you. But I've heard other stories, about Uriel guarding heaven, that he's supposedly the angel that warned Noah about the flood. He supposedly condemned the half-breeds into being succubae and incubi, but that doesn't mean he didn't have a part in making them. There's supposed to be a lot of angels. My guess is that there's more than one with the name Uriel. And that the whole passage was made up by someone who didn't know what they were talking about."

~

That night, Debbie felt someone crawling into bed with her. "Shaker?"

"Unless you were expecting someone else?"

Debbie embraced him, kissing him with abandon as her answer. Their lovemaking was brief and fast, leaving them spent and gasping.

"I'm decided," Debbie said, still panting. "I'm not going to try to have a child."

"Are you sure," Shaker said, hugging her. "This isn't the decision I expected."

"Did you foresee something?"

"Something I obviously misunderstood." He kissed her brow. "But I'm glad to be wrong in times like these."

"I knew you didn't want me to do it. I didn't want to do it. So why do it?"

"Because it's the only way to have a child."

"We can adopt, if it comes to that," Debbie said stubbornly. "I want you. I love you. *You, here with me. I don't need to try to chase other women's dreams. This is what I want. You are what I want.*

I'm here with you, came his loving answer in her mind.

"Please make a ward yourself tonight for here, as well as home. I don't want anyone in my dreams but you."

"If you insist," he said. "Vass is going to be disappointed. He bet me a hundred dollars you'd say yes by the end of the year to insemination."

"You bet on this of all things?"

"I took a vow to you, 'til loyalty should fade," Shaker whispered. "I know mine is lasting. And I would bet everything that I have that yours is, too."

∾

The next morning, Debbie awoke alone. On Shaker's pillow was a note that said *be back later.* Debbie got up and watched the dawn rise as she sat on the deck with morning coffee and a Danish, the sky golden and pink, clouds reflecting the fire of the sun. She was just going to head back inside when she caught sight of a crow watching her from the new walkway.

"And what's your name?" Debbie asked, holding out a piece of the Danish.

The crow cawed, then flapped closer, alighting near her. Ignoring the offered treat, it picked up a stick and scratched a word into the dirt.

"Sheila." Debbie fought herself not to recoil. *This is the demon that kidnapped me, that planned to possess me, the one that possessed Sheila!* "Why did you do what you did?"

The crow wrote *had to.*

"Can't you transform and just talk to me?"

not allowed, the crow scratched.

Debbie went inside quickly and came back with a pen, some stone coasters, and large pad of paper. She put the coasters on the paper to weigh it down, then handed the pen to the crow, which snatched it with its beak.

"Who was behind the attack? The truth."

The crow dropped the pen and shook its head once.

She won't tell me. That must mean it was someone still free who isn't also part of Myrrh's murder. Someone who is possibly still dangerous to me. "What did you hope to accomplish? Did you really plan to become me?"

The crow nodded once, cawed, and did a little dance that could have had no meaning other than fiendish glee.

Debbie resisted the urge to grab a deck chair and kill the creature. "Why?"

The crow grabbed the pen again in its beak. *To make movies.*

"*Everlasting*?" Debbie said, thinking back. "Or *Dare to Tell*? Or *Origin of Fear*?"

The crow dropped the pen, looking nervously around.

"Which movie?" Debbie pressed. "*Everlasting* is on hold, I'm not sure we can make a profit from it, though with the right cast and a more dramatic ending it could work. We are making *Dare to Tell*; the script was excellent. Shaker is going to star, as is a woman called Autumn Silver."

The crow drew a smiley face.

Now for the million-dollar question. "Did you write those scripts yourself?"

The crow made a big checkmark on the paper, then dropped the pen and cawed again.

"Did you write *Origin of Fear* and *Hell to Pay*, also?"

The crow nodded.

Finally, some progress! "Why?"

The crow scratched some more on the paper, paused, scratched another line of words, then one more before stepping back.

"Everlasting=life," Debbie read aloud. "Your life? Your life story, you mean? Why you became a demon?"

The crow nodded, then pointed with the pen to the other two lines.

Debbie ignored them. "You know things about Latham's Landing no one else knows. But you deliberately didn't work on the movie you wrote. Why?"

The crow dropped the pen, cawing at her in anger, then took off in an explosion of wings. Debbie saw Myrrh coming. She grabbed the paper hastily, stuffing it in her pocket. "Good morning."

"Good morning. I hope none of my crows were hassling you, I told them no begging for food and no stealing trinkets, or they wouldn't be allowed to come back."

"Why don't they spend more time as winged men?" Debbie ventured. "I look around and see a lot of yardwork I would be glad to pay them to do."

Myrrh looked at Debbie oddly. "They are serving me to earn their way out of Hell, and this time here is their holiday for the work they do for me at my estate. Plus they are always on guard, even here. You want them to do yardwork, too?"

That was completely lame. Debbie flushed. "It was just a thought. I'm sorry."

"Only Bawdir is allowed to assume human form outside of battle at this time. The others must remain crows, to reflect on their evil ways and repent. They are forbidden from any behavior that a normal crow wouldn't perform." Myrrh's eyes narrowed. "Did one of them do something?"

"Just cawing at me, when I tried to give it a piece of Danish," Debbie lied. "If you want one, there's another in the kitchen, help yourself."

"No, thanks. Are we heading back today? You have work Monday, right?"

I hadn't planned to go back until Sunday. But I need to call Shaker now and talk to him, and I can't here, or Myrrh will find out about that crow's communications. "Yes, later today. Something's come up that I need to address immediately."

~

"What do you think it means?" Debbie murmured, showing the crow's paper to Shaker.

"Maybe I should just ask Myrrh to question the crow myself."

"I think it's odd she never offered us the option," Debbie thought aloud. "And that we didn't ask for that, or even think about it until now. Don't you?"

"I assumed the demons that kidnapped you were associated with the demons that were working with Cyrus, my former captor, and his vampire employer, Michael. The demons were all sent back to Hell, Cyrus included, or became part of Myrrh's murder. I didn't think that we had anything to learn of value from the demons that became crows."

I'm missing something here. "And Michael?"

"He's still at large, but being hunted," Shaker said uncomfortably.

Why is he so nervous? "Could he be behind this?"

Shaker shook his head. "He's very old-fashioned, I doubt he watches movies or even knows what's current."

Debbie eyed him. "What are you holding back?"

"Remember Valerian, the bad vampire still at large? Well he was in league with Cyrus. Michael was his lover."

"Which doesn't help. None of this fits together, Shaker. It's like a two-sided puzzle with missing pieces."

"In any case, consider this: Myrrh wouldn't have let us question her crows, even if we'd wanted to. Also, that crow that talked to you did so in defiance of her rules."

Debbie nodded. "She said that her crows had to repent and act like avians, not former demons."

"Her process of redemption has them free from both God and the Devil, for now," Shaker explained. "When the crow said not allowed, I think that's what it meant."

"What about the rest? *Hell to Pay* is a story out of Lash's past, he said so, but that's got nothing to do with me. Or it could mean the place Hell is the crow's past, as it's a demon from Hell. We're making *Origin of Fear*, it's one of our future movies. But none of those statements is news to me. Why make a big deal to write them?"

Shaker put the paper aside. "I guess we'll find out in time."

On the paper under *Everlasting = life* was written *Hell = past* and *Origin = future.*

CHAPTER ELEVEN

July/August/September

"OKAY, THIS IS THE BIG SCENE. THE HEROINE IS READING A diary of the owner's grandmother found in the old house, and she discovers the identity of the killer who slipped through time. The spirit possessed the father and made him kill, then passed to the son and made him kill also."

"So how does that relate to the recent killings in the movie?"

"She's going to discover that the spirit intends to possess the grandson as well. He hasn't so far because the grandson hasn't fallen in love. But he is starting to with the heroine. That's where the title comes in: she has to dare to tell him that his father and grandfather were killers and make him believe that in time so that he doesn't get possessed himself."

"Seems a small climax."

"Not for us, we discuss demons and possession regularly, but we're not normal people anymore, Debbie. For normal people, they'd be worried about getting believed."

Debbie chuckled, her eyes on the woman as she suddenly clutched the book, as her bedroom door slammed by itself. "So Autumn Silver's working out okay? She seems like a great actress."

"A rising star," Sheila commented as Shaker burst open the bedroom door and proceeded to yell at Autumn for slamming it. "One infatuated with our new star, Cole Black."

Debbie narrowed her eyes, noting the way Autumn lit right back into Shaker, accusing him of slamming the door and scaring her on purpose. The scene ended in some hot and heavy kissing before Bart called cut. "This looks a lot more romantic that I remember it being. Did we rewrite the script I approved?"

"Devlin's suggestion, remember? He's only agreed to back this after we added more of a romantic aspect."

"He's not what you'd expect of a vampire," Debbie said, catching Shaker's eye and beckoning him over. "He did release the money for *Hell to Pay*, right? We're nearly done with filming it and so far, Pandora's paid for everything."

Sheila nodded. "Yes, the money's been deposited for both movies in an offshore account. We've got more cash than we've ever had before. That reminds me, Angel Pictures sent over three new scripts for you to look at for co-projects, all are projects they have given the green light to. They want your answer before posting to their website."

"That's a relief, that they have more projects in the pipeline. I hope they're solid. Please get me a copy of each, I'll take them home tonight." Sheila kissed Shaker as he came close. "Hi. How's your day?"

"Good, I'm getting kissed a lot," Shaker teased, then avoided Debbie's swat. "Seriously, Autumn is a very good actress, and very professional. I'd be for doing more films with her, if she's interested."

"I'm sure she's interested," Debbie said icily, looking over to where Autumn was staring at Shaker. The actress averted her eyes at Debbie's look.

I'm only interested in you, came Shaker's mental reply. *Care to take me to your office, so I can prove it?* He winked at Debbie.

"Shaker, will you come with Debbie and me to see the house we bought for *Origin of Fear*?" Sheila interrupted. "We have a group shooting there today. The water at the base of the house receded enough that we could check the foundation and it was safe. California is forecast for drought the entire rest of the summer, so I want to get the finale of the movie shot before the waters recede. That's the last of the shots that need the outside of the house, all the others can be shot on stages in the studio."

"Sure," Shaker said. "They're breaking for lunch now, and they won't need me for the rest of the afternoon, they're doing shots with Autumn and some of the ghosts."

I could tell Bart to add a scene with Autumn kissing one of them. Debbie tossed the thought aside and smiled at Shaker. "Can you teleport us, and just check everything is safe? Sheila left her car there; we can drive home after."

~

"This is really a great setting," Debbie said, the huge house looming over her. "I don't want to get carried away, but it's clearly a solid structure. Hell, we could even fix it up when this movie is done and shoot another film in it."

"It's pretty creepy," Sheila offered. "If we shoot another movie here, it would have to be a horror movie."

"What's to say we couldn't have a sequel to Origin of Fear, if it does as well as we think it will?" Debbie walked closer to the house tentatively, worried there might be some loud bangs. The remaining scenes being shot were of two college students, a girl and a boy, running from ghosts inside the house, then outside, where they tried to lock them inside the house. "I thought they all died at the end. Did you already shoot those scenes, Sheila?"

Sheila nodded, not moving from where she was. "There's a twist to the script ending. But yeah, they all die at the end, and become ghosts there. We could do a sequel, sure, but we'd need other actors and actresses and a different plot."

A sudden bang sounded, but it was above their heads. *Thunder.* Debbie and Sheila looked up to see dark clouds racing towards them, blocking out the sun.

"Damn it! They forecast only 10% chance of rain today!" Sheila put her jacket over her head, as she ran towards the car, rain pelting down hard. Debbie made a move to follow her, then stopped. The camera crew were grabbing their things and abandoning the camera's after covering them with tarps. But the actor and actress inside hadn't come out.

They're being smart and staying inside under cover, what I should be doing. Debbie ran for Sheila's car. By the time she slammed into the backseat, she was soaked to the skin. She was about to ask Sheila if she could call Song back to teleport them home when she noticed the man in the passenger front seat, wet hair plastered to his neck. "Hi."

"Debbie, this is Eugene," Sheila said. The man offered his hand to Debbie, who shook it awkwardly over the seat. "He's been out here overseeing filming."

"Great! How's it going?"

"We've got all the shots we need," Eugene said. "Don't worry about this, by the way. Showers seem to spring up here often, we usually get one every day we're here." He smiled. "Probably why the water's still high near the house."

"But you'll be done after today?" Debbie asked, looking out at the deluge. *This seems a lot more water than just a shower.*

"Yes."

He just stopped talking. Debbie looked at the front seat. Sheila was missing, but Eugene was still there, looking at the house. "Eugene, where'd Sheila go? I didn't even hear her get out."

"There they go," Eugene said softly, pointing at the house. The actor and actress had emerged and were trying to bar the door behind them. "Watch and see just how it really happened."

Debbie got out of the car, rain lashing her face instantly. "Hey! Hey! The cameras have stopped." The kids ignored her, both of them now fleeing off the porch and splashing though water which unbelievably was almost to their waists.

This can't be, it just began raining! Debbie waved her arms. "Over here! Can you see me?"

"I can see you," a sepulchral voice intoned. Debbie looked over to see the car had vanished, as had everything familiar except the two kids, who were trying to swim away from the island house and had been swept under huge whitecaps on a narrow lake. She was on a shore outcropping now across from the house, waves crashing at her feet. Beside her was Eugene, his face waterlogged and pale as a fish belly, his eyes missing. "There's no escape. Not even when you're dead."

Debbie let out a shriek and flailed. She fell and hit the ground hard.

"Debbie?" Sheila and Shaker were there at her side, their expressions worried.

"I'm alright," she said, accepting their help to stand. "I...I don't know what happened. Some kind of waking dream." She looked across to the house, which sat on dry land. The filming was done, the actor and actress heading to their cars, the camera crew packing up everything. Sunlight bathed everything, with no clouds in the sky. Eugene came out of the house and locked the door behind him, then gave a wave to Debbie and Sheila before heading off with the others to the camera vans.

"Debbie?" Sheila asked.

"I'm okay. I do have a tagline for our Origin of Fear poster, though. Have it read "There's no escape...even when you're dead.""

189

"Are you going to tell me what really happened?" Shaker asked, as he shared some wine with Debbie on her deck. The hellhounds were below, chasing a ball Shaker kept throwing. Pitch and Pike were faster, but Baroness kept using shadows to jump ahead of them and grab it first. She returned to Shaker proudly, and he tossed it again for her.

"I don't know what happened," Debbie said. "I already told you about what I saw. Obviously, none of it was real."

"None of it had lasting effects," Shaker corrected. "It might have been that demon's way of making contact with you."

"Why scare me?" Debbie said. "It's kind of pointless."

"Maybe to test your mettle. Maybe just to see what you'd do." Shaker sipped his wine. "Don't go back to that house again without me. And don't go inside for any reason."

"Okay, but that seems extreme," Debbie replied. "It's a really good setting."

"Leri worked a bit of magic on it, to make it more forbidding-looking. She also knows how to call a storm. I think Sheila may have asked her to make it rain regularly there, until they were through filming."

I should give Leri a raise, she's gone over and above in Location. I'll do that on Monday. "Well, they are done, all that's left is to do the scenes on sound stage," Debbie said in relief, filling their glasses again. "We're doing really well on timing, no problems like last year. All the ads have been booked, no problems with theaters. After last year's success they're asking us to take more weeks, even. It's great."

"Did you look at the three scripts Angel is offering?"

"Maybe later," Debbie said seductively. "I have a different pastime in mind for our evening."

"Please call our accounting service and arrange a 10% raise for Leri White," Debbie told her secretary, as she arrived Monday morning. "Who's my first appointment?"

"Adeline in a few minutes, Mr. Triss at ten, Mr. Nightingale at eleven. Your afternoon is free; you said you wanted to go attend a screening of the finished pilot episode of *Incubus*, that's at one. You had calls from Angel Pictures regarding the three scripts they sent over, from Mr. Gray who asked for an appointment at 4pm if you were free, and from your doctor's office, that said they called in your prescription."

The birth control refill I asked for. I wonder if Song is pregnant yet? "Kaitlyn, please also tell the accounting service that Sheila needs a 10% raise as well."

"If you're doing raises, can I put in for one?" Kaitlyn asked boldly. "I'm still at my starting salary."

Debbie looked at her in surprise. "Yes, for 10%. Please also assemble me a list of all direct employees ASAP, their salaries, and when they last got a raise. I was supposed to do annual reviews last fall and never did. I need to remedy that."

"Thanks so much, Mrs. Black," her secretary beamed. "I'll get you those figures before this afternoon." She closed the door.

Debbie checked her voicemail, where another message from Angel Pictures waited, asking about the scripts. *They're really pushing, I wonder why?* Debbie rooted in her bag for the scripts, scanning the names as she put them in a pile on her desk. "The Perfect Moment, Her Frozen Heart, and Night Music. Hmm." *I'll have to see if I can read through them today, between meetings. At least one of them.*

Her secretary buzzed her. "Adeline is here."

"Send her in please."

The door opened and shut. Debbie looked up with a welcoming smile that quickly faded. Instead of the dark-haired promotions manager, a blond woman with silver-streaked hair stood there in a long pastel dress. Debbie grabbed her bottle of holy water. "Who are you?"

"My name is Rene," the woman said, sitting down. "I mean you no harm. I just came to thank you for your assistance last year."

Leri appeared near Debbie's desk, wreathed in her swirling shadows. When she saw Rene, she relaxed. "Glad I didn't manifest the Hellfire." She turned to Debbie. "You know each other?"

"What are you doing here?" Rene asked haughtily, getting to her feet.

"Excuse me, but this is my office, so I ask the questions," Debbie interjected. "Rene, what are you here to thank me for?"

"I understand that you were the one that passed on news of the ambush in New Orleans, right before New Year's Eve of this year," Rene said, her eyes still on Leri. "You saved a lot of bloodshed, and possibly the lives of two children. So I'm in your debt."

I repeated to Myrrh what I'd heard the demons say when I was kidnapped. She left right then to tell someone, after bringing me home. "You know my, um, kin-daughter, Myrrh?"

Rene smiled. "Yes, she's become a trusted ally." She looked back at Leri, frowning. "Unlike some. Farewell, Debbie. Rest assured that I'm taking care of Shaker's sustenance, so he doesn't draw attention to himself or to Pandora. Take care." She disappeared.

"Always thinks she's the cream and I'm chaff," Leri complained. "Her magic is just as dark as mine."

"Thanks for coming," Debbie said. "You must have felt her arrive?"

"As a rule, only Shaker teleports into your office or even on company grounds so anyone other than he, I check it out," Leri said. "Which is why I was there the day Namaath came here to visit Vassago Gray."

"Thanks for being so alert," Debbie responded. "You've been going over and above. I approved a raise for you today."

"Thank you," Leri said in surprise. "I'd better get back to Sheila." She disappeared.

Adeline entered, as if she'd just been announced. "Good morning, Debbie."

"What do you have for me?"

"The promotional bags you wanted for *Dare to Tell* arrived." She handed one to Debbie. "We put the silhouette of the house on the front, its windows glowing, on a black background, with the tagline, "Evil never rests.""

"Wait, this is the wrong house," Debbie said. "And this says, 'There's no escape. Even when you're dead.'"

"I'm so sorry, those are the ones for *Origin of Fear*," Adeline said, flushing. She handed Debbie another bag, this one with a silvery grey house looking down on a town, misty screaming ghosts swirling around on a dark blue background. 'Evil Never Rests' was in block letters across the bottom.

"These both look great. Tell me why we're going for totes this time? We never have before."

"There's a big push on the coasts, California included, to phase out plastic bags. So people have to buy tote bags, or they have to pay for paper bags or carry their groceries in a box. It makes sense that we do totes for all our new movies from now on. The totes wear out over time, so people won't turn down a new one, and its free advertising for us with them using it out in public places. I have additional bags ordered and here already for *Destiny*, *Incubus*, and *Hell to Pay*. I also ordered extra and have put out a memo companywide for all employees to contact me for a free bag."

"That's fantastic. Can you get me one of each?" *I'd forgotten that plastic bag ban was coming up; this is an ingenious move. I'd better give her a 10% raise, too.* "What else?"

"The website is doing steady business in downloads. I've got pens, T-shirts, and other promo items ordered and ready to go with the same logos. I've also got a website contest running once a month to give away some small prop from a movie, like a signed still photo, or a costume piece. So far that's only getting a few hits, but I hope that interest will grow in time."

"Great. Is there anything else to go over?"

"No, other than I need you to sign a check to pay for the Incubus bags. The site I ordered them from is complaining that they never got paid."

Debbie's brow furrowed. "Do you have the invoice?"

Adeline handed it to her.

"I'll take care of this. Thanks again."

Adeline left.

Debbie checked the clock, and saw she had a good fifteen minutes before Rack Triss arrived. *Time enough to sort this out.*

~

"So our accounting firm said they had two credit card digits transposed?" Rack stated in disbelief. "That's all it was?"

"That's what they said. I made sure I got a confirmation, so the bill's paid. I'll have to check with accounting, I'm not sure how that happened, but if someone listed the wrong numbers once, they could do it again." Debbie let out a breath. "So what do you have for me?"

"You've already seen and tried Spiritwalker, Footsteps on the Stairs and Incubus," Rack said, producing two bottles. "Thanks for sharing them with your mother, by the way, she placed an order for fifty bottles of Incubus for her company Christmas party, which cleared out the rest of our stores of that. This is Lifeblood, a Malbec with a very peppery taste, and Island Song, a cabernet-Malbec-shiraz blend. Try both and see what you think."

"I love the labels," Debbie said, looking at the island silhouette on Caribbean blue water with white music notes interspersed with blowing leaves. "I'll try these this week and get back to you on Friday. Do we have enough of the other wines already approved for our movies releasing this year?"

Rack nodded. "Yes, though I may need to outsource for some wines next year. Partnering with you has been extremely lucrative for Triss Vineyards. Our sales have tripled in two and a half years. We're now selling out of vintages before the correlating movie completes its run in theaters. All of the previous movie vintages are all sold out, and reselling on wine sites for twice their original price. In short, we can't keep any stock on our shelves."

"This is great news, but what does it mean for future movies?"

"I have other demons and humans I know in the wine business. I'll let a few of them know that I am looking to source rare or complex wines and offer a partnership. I think we can get enough support and product that we shouldn't have a shortfall. I have also begun to create larger batches. If we can bridge the gap between this year and say three years from now, we'll be fine." He cleared his throat. "I'm operating from the supposition that Pandora will continue growing as it has been."

"All signs point to that. Thanks again, Rack, for coming that day in the conference room."

Rack looked bewildered. "Of course I was there, I had been looking for Autumn Silver, when she missed her appointment on set. I'm still not sure how she got up in the conference room."

So he didn't hear me call for him mentally. "Thanks for all you do. Was there anything else?"

"I was initially against Leri working here, as I told you at our last meeting," Rack said standing up. "But I have to admit I was wrong. She seems to be working very hard." He nodded once, then left.

"Debbie, Mr. Nightingale is here."

Debbie looked at the clock and groaned. "Send him in."

So the CGI budget is bigger than expected, because of all the ghost effects on Dare to Tell. *Maybe I should look into hiring a ghost.* Debbie put down the scripts, then sighed. *All of them are decent*

scripts, but they are all romances. She looked at the clock, then bolted to her feet. "Shit!"

Two minutes to one, Debbie entered the screening room. Shaker waved her over to the seat beside him. Debbie just sat down when Vassago entered and sat right next to her.

"How are the scripts?" Shaker asked, ignoring Vassago.

"Romances, though one has vampires, and another has witches and sorcerers," Debbie replied. "But all three look solid."

"I'm not sure I can play a vampire or a sorcerer," Shaker said. "Even if I am the latter to some extent."

The lights slowly dimmed, and the movie began. In the darkness, Debbie felt Shaker take her hand. She squeezed, then turned her attention to the screen.

~

"That was great," Debbie said, as the lights went up. She turned to Shaker, only to see Vassago holding her hand. She snatched it back, but not fast enough that it wasn't noticed by her team. "What are you doing?"

"Keeping the home fires burning," Vassago said cheerily, as people began coming up and congratulating him on his performance.

Shaker must have had to leave again, damn his hide. "You were great," she said coolly to Vassago, then left.

Gray followed her. "Are you free now?"

Irritating or not, he's going to be one of our main stars. You have to be polite. "Yes," Debbie said, turning to face him. "What did you need?"

"Just an answer. Why don't you want me?"

"You're not Shaker, and I love him, not you. I don't want the baby you can give me, because it's not his. I want a life and a love with him, I don't care if you're talented, or the lover of all lovers that there ever was in the history of the world. You aren't him."

"I guess that's pretty clear," Vassago said grudgingly.

"Good, I meant it to be."

"Alright, I'll stop pursuing you," Vassago said. "You know where I'll be if you change your mind."

~

"So he really said that, and now avoids you?" Sheila asked, as Sasha put the finishing touches on Debbie's nails at the Black Rose. "You haven't talked to him since late July? It's the second week of September."

"He's an enigma." Debbie shrugged. "And a great actor. Some of him not seeing me may be he's working long hours shooting the rest of the *Incubus* episodes. I'm so thrilled Netflix agreed to the series." She turned to Sasha, the ogress. "Is Vassago still working here?"

Sasha nodded. "He's here every day or half day he's not shooting pictures. Lately it's been half-days once a week and more than a few nights." She smiled, showing her blunt teeth. "There's quite a demand for Incubus Treatment at the Black Rose. So much so that women don't mind coming in at odd hours to work around Gray's acting schedule."

I never get tired of seeing that smile. It should be frightening, but she's such a kind creature. "That's good," Debbie said in approval. "I heard it was an expensive treatment, so Gray must be making good money."

"More than he's making at Pandora, I believe."

"That can't be true. Why is he making films then?" Sheila asked.

"Everyone's got to live their dreams," Sasha said with a shrug. "Mine was to do nails and hair, and not be the monster I was supposed to be. Maybe Gray also wants more than what he is."

"Come on," Sheila said, standing. "We've got to get to that staff meeting. See you next month, Sasha."

"Tell me why we're having it so late in the day?" Debbie said, as they hurried to Sheila's car.

"Because you're on vacation next week, I'm gone the following Monday to go with Song to the baby doctor, and then the team members' vacations start."

"What happened to vacations in August," Debbie muttered. "At least Bart's taken all of his, so we can finish the last scenes of *Dare to Tell*. Have you heard how Althea is doing with the editing of *Hell to Pay?*"

"You can ask her at the meeting. But I have no reason to believe that both movies won't release on schedule."

"Good. It's such a relief that this summer is going so smoothly, compared to last year."

"Okay, people," Bart called. "Kate hears a noise in the bedroom she's been in, watching TV. Handsome man is in her bed, dressed in a grey suit with a sheen. Gray, that's you. Everyone get in place. Action!"

Gray smiled. "I'm so glad you're ready for bed." He extended a hand.

"You shouldn't be here."

"I couldn't stay away," Gray implored, beckoning. "You said you needed some comfort. I'm here to give you your massage, nothing more."

"A house call?" she said sarcastically, raising her eyebrows.

"Who said women needed to come to men all the time?" Gray said, patting the bed. "Please, come here and lay down. I promise I won't do anything you don't like. Just tell me to stop when you're relaxed enough."

Kate shook her head, then went to the bed and lay down on her stomach. "Aren't you going to ask me to undress?"

Gray began massaging her feet, working out the kinks of the

day with his deft hands. Kate was soon groaning in pleasure. When his hands moved up her legs, rubbing the muscles sore from a day of wearing heels, she sighed happily.

"Let it all go," Gray soothed. "You deserve to be pampered."

He worked upwards, grasping her buttocks in his strong hands, working the muscles. Then he continued upward, touching her sides, the tightness in her body giving way to relief. He lay out each arm and stretched and pulled, relaxing her wrists, and fingers, then moved to her neck, moving her head slowly around in all directions. When it was over, Kate was limp on the bed, a smile on her face.

"I'm so glad you're relaxed," Gray whispered in her ear. "Now lie still. I need to apply the lotion."

Kate turned her head to protest. "Remember, nothing I don't want."

He slid off her crushed velvet shorts trimmed in lace. "Remember, face down."

Carefully, he applied some scented lotion, rubbing it firmly into her skin. The fragrant heady scent was intoxicating, bringing thoughts of sex to her mind unbidden. "What is that?"

"Frankincense and Myrrh oil." He continued rubbing it into her feet. "I'm glad you like it."

That's what he rubbed on me, Debbie thought as she watched the scene unfold. *I remember how good it smelled. How good his hands felt working my body.*

"I love it," Kate murmured.

Carefully, Gray removed her top, still lying on her stomach, then began rubbing oil into her back. He ended at her neck. "All done."

"My front isn't done."

"I wasn't sure you wanted that."

"If you can be professional."

"Of course." Gray put more oil on his hands, then began to rub it into her breasts, tweaking the nipples as he smoothed

199

around the erect nubs. By now Kate's breath was rapid panting. "Finished."

"There's one more place you didn't apply oil."

"Because you don't need any lubrication here," Gray said silkily, stroking her upper thigh. "And no massaging, at least, not with my hands."

Kate grabbed the oil bottle from him. "You lay on your stomach. I want to repay you."

Gray did as she asked. Kate disrobed him as he had her, then carefully rubbed his body with the oil, enjoying the firm hard muscle under her hands. She kneaded his buttocks, rubbed his back, then touched him on the shoulder. "Roll onto your back."

Gray did as asked, his smile inviting. He wore a small piece of cloth covering his parts: standard for a scene like this, which would be cut to ensure that the camera never saw the cloth and he appeared naked in the finished film. "Please Kate, touch me."

Debbie closed her eyes, imagining Gray rolling over, herself as Kate with the oil before him. Instead of a careful cover, his cock was revealed in all its glory, proudly rising above his pubic hair.

Debbie took the bottle of oil, lubing up the organ. She stroked it, enjoying the way his face contorted, the desperate lunge of his hips pushing into the slippery flesh of her hands.

Gray grabbed hold of her, pulling her onto his lap. He grasped a breast in each hand, his oiled skin sliding on the soft mounds. "So full and beautiful. So ripe." He kissed her neck. "I can't get enough of these. I imagine them when you're working in the office, when I get a glimpse of camisole, or one of your push up bras."

"I hate those. They aren't made to move in. I drop a pen and reach down to get it and I strain not to fall out."

"I imagine you popping out," Gray said, suddenly pushing down her bra to bear her breasts. He devoured first one and then the other, Debbie's hands in his hair. "I imagine me doing this." He suckled her, then bit softly. Debbie cried out. "I imagine you protesting, that you have a meeting, that I'm naked and have to get out of your office."

"And?"

"And I kiss you." He kissed her. "I let you feel my penis, how hard it is, how much it needs to be inside you. How much I need to be inside you, pleasuring you, feeling the tightness of your body welcoming mine, welcoming what I'm going to do to you–"

"Cut, cut, cut!" Bart yelled in fury. "Gray, where is your mind? You're supposed to be pretending you're getting a hand job, then we cut to the phone ringing with a desperate warning that Storm is on his way, out for your blood. And Cassy, what are you doing? Kate's not supposed to be atop the incubus, she's supposed to be teasing him with only her hand. You've all but given in to him! It's like the both of you were about to have sex on camera!"

Debbie flushed, then excused herself from the shoot, deliberately not thinking until she was a few blocks away in her car, heading home. *Did he pick up on my fantasy? He must have. I'd better not go to any more shoots, at least ones that involve sex scenes.*

CHAPTER TWELVE

October

"I'M GOING TO BE GONE A BIT THIS MONTH," SHAKER SAID, glancing on the calendar. "I know for sure tomorrow night, and possibly later in the month."

"Did your Mistress have her babies yet? Doesn't it affect them, being bound to you?"

"Yes, she did, and no, it didn't. But as you discovered, Rene the sorceress has been handling my…favors."

Choosing people for you to consume you mean. Debbie pushed the thought from her mind. "Later in the month, as in Halloween?"

Shaker nodded. "Devlin and his brother Danial always have a party that night, on Halloween. My Mistress has to attend, and its expected I'll be on call. Nothing may happen, but I'd need to respond immediately if something did happen. So I think it's best for me to let Brady sleep the night away, and go out of this body, just in case."

"I think that's a good plan," Debbie agreed. "But what about the Night Carnival we're planning at Pandora for Halloween? If I show up without Brady, it will be assumed that we had a fight or are on the outs."

"People still get sick in this millennia. I can call in sick the few days before the party, so no one thinks anything of it."

Debbie nodded, disappointed.

"I'll make it up to you," Shaker promised. "Besides, Vass will be there. He's right that being seen with him will make it less obvious how close we are. Dance with him a few times, if you can. But otherwise just have fun. Rack and Triss will be there, I know you haven't seen them at all this year, except for at work."

"We haven't seen John and Madeline, either," Debbie answered. "The last thing I heard was that he sent a check for investment in *Immortal Confessions*."

"Which earned him back his money and then some," Shaker continued. "I'd guess another check will be forthcoming, if you tell him he can invest in other films. Just give The Chalet a call or send over a roster of this year's movies. I think he and his wife will love *Dare to Tell*. But I thought we weren't looking for investors, because we were flush with Devlin's money?"

"Don't mind me," Debbie said, ruffling her hair and wishing now she hadn't cut so much of it off last month. "I'm nervous about seeing my mom, you know that's also the end of this month. What if you need to be gone during the time we're there? I can say you're sick for a day, but not for the whole visit."

"Don't worry," Shaker soothed, hugging her. "It will work out. Trust me."

～

"Debbie, hi!" Kallia said, hugging her daughter. "I'm so glad you've agreed to come visit! Stuart's finishing up at work, but he'll be along for dinner later."

"How's the flower business?"

"You're staying Monday through Wednesday, right? I planned to take you for a tour tomorrow morning, if ten's okay?"

"That's perfect," Shaker said, caressing Debbie's arm. "We'll have time for a big breakfast."

I'm sure that's not all you're planning on eating tomorrow morning, Debbie thought to him.

We have to make sure to burn some calories, don't we? came his teasing reply. *You do want my abs to still be lean when you run your hands down my chest.*

You read my mind. Did you bring your Storm outfit? We can recreate my office scene on the dresser.

Of course. I'll even quote you some lines, my Mistress.

The next morning, Debbie was impressed by the sheer volume of the flowers that the Tennison greenhouses were producing. "You said you have five more of these ½-football-field-big greenhouses in this state alone?"

Kallia nodded, touching a rose leaf. "We've grown to meet demand. The economy is getting better. When there's a recession, flowers used for decoration are often the first items to be cut, and we have to turn to funerals and weddings to get by, along with the regular holidays like Mother's Day, Valentine's Day, Christmas, and Easter. This year the orders are pouring in, for everything from children's birthdays and nursing homes to conferences. We've even added a new branch to the business, creating gardens for hospitals that have regular inpatients. These are flower gardens mixed with vegetable plants that produce food that is consumed in the hospital."

"Mental hospitals," Shaker commented to Debbie. "Growing is good therapy. Rhonda appreciated the one at her hospital."

What an odd thing for him to say. "Maybe we should order some flowers for Pandora's bigger parties?" Debbie mentioned, fingering a few carnations that were bright shades of orange. She turned to Kallia. "Do you have a minimum order to deal with businesses?"

"Unless you want something custom like those black and red roses, setting up an order through your local shop is likely a better deal," Kallia said apologetically.

"Now wait," Shaker said, stopping. "How about instead of cut flowers, Pandora actually puts in a small garden in one of the studio lots? It wouldn't have to be big, just a few plots of flowers and some vegetables that could be tended. I think the staff would appreciate vegetables that were grown right there"

"It would require a full-time gardener, since your growing season is so long, and your rainfall is so sporadic," Kallia said, forcing a smile. "You'd also have to modify whatever site you chose to accommodate the plants' needs for sunlight and soil depth. I can't recommend it, I'm sorry."

What is up with you? Debbie thought to Shaker, giving him a curious look.

Shaker shrugged, his expression apologetic.

～

"You've been quiet all day?" Debbie asked, as Shaker and she returned to their hotel in the late afternoon. "Though thanks for enduring my mom, she prays before every meal, and then spent the rest talking about business. I think she's taken solace in religion now that Dad's gone."

"I was thinking about coming back here, and having you all to myself," Shaker said, grabbing hold of her. "Why don't you put on that special outfit that you've been carrying around in your purse so I wouldn't see it and join me in the bedroom."

"I didn't think you saw," Debbie giggled, then nodded. "I'll be right in."

Debbie entered the room a few minutes later. Shaker didn't let her get to him before he was up and moving, his hands already reaching for her breasts. "I love the pink lace."

"I wasn't sure you'd like it," Debbie breathed, then gasped, as his wet, cold hands slipped the lace down to bare her breasts so he could cup them. "You're cold."

"I wanted clean hands," he murmured, massaging her breasts. "I love your breasts, the way they're so full and soft. The way you wear those push up bras that make them stick out." Shaker moved in front of her and went to his knees, sucking one breast, then the other. "Lay back for me. I want to taste you."

Debbie lay on the bed. Shaker grasped the lacy thong, pulling off the panties then pushing her legs apart, the feel of his slippery tongue licking her vagina one minute later.

"Oh," she groaned, her hands in his thick black curls. "God, that feels great!"

Shaker didn't answer, his mouth busy as it licked and slipped into her, caressing and teasing.

Finally, Debbie stopped him. "Please, I need you. Don't keep me waiting."

"You're still on the pill?" he whispered. "I didn't see them when we unpacked."

"Yes," she breathed. "I'm safe."

"Good," he said eagerly, stripping off his pants and kicking them away. "I don't want to wait one more minute. I can smell how excited you are and its driving me crazy."

The push of his hard cock into her was fast, but she was wet and ready for him. He began thrusting immediately, his kisses wild with abandon.

"Damn you're needing," Debbie moaned.

"I just need to know you're mine, that you want me, that I can make you come," he panted. "Now yell out your climax like the bad little girl you are. Let the whole damn hotel hear you!"

Debbie rode the wave of his desire, embracing the first stirrings of orgasm, pushing hard for the escalating white-hot orgasm. She screamed as it broke over her, then filled her lungs with another breath to scream again as Shaker bellowed his release.

"I hope no one works here that knows my mom," Debbie said, as she lay back on the sheets trying to catch her breath."

"I hope someone does," Shaker said in satisfaction, snuggling her close. "I want everyone to know how good we are together." He kissed her. "And I just enjoy the naughtiness of it."

Debbie laughed, nuzzling him. "I do, too."

Debbie and Shaker got through the next breakfast, the tour of yet more greenhouses, and a five-course lunch at her mother's favorite restaurant. It was at the dessert course that the curveball finally came. "Church is tonight at six," Kallia said. "Will you meet us at the church?"

Wednesday evening services, I completely forgot! "I can come," Debbie said quickly. "But Brady needs to handle a conference call." *Shaker, say something! Make up something believable.*

Kallia looked from Shaker to Debbie. "On your vacation? About what?"

"I'm a recovering alcoholic," Shaker said, looking very guilty. "I haven't touched a drop in six months, but I got stopped by a policeman back when I was drinking. Though our lawyer successfully fought the DUI conviction, I agreed as part of the settlement to go to AA. I need to check in with my sponsor tonight." He offered a tentative smile. "If it ends early, I'll try to meet you, but I didn't want to promise anything."

Good save. Debbie squeezed his hand.

"That's very responsible," Stuart said, though his expression was concerned. "Are you off drugs too?"

"Stuart!" Debbie said sharply, making others around them look over in curiosity.

"He's only asking because he's worried for you," Shaker said to her. He turned back to Stuart. "I did take them once, but I'm off them now. The death of my brother really threw me for a loop, especially when Rhonda got put in the institution. I got on a dark path. I'm off it now, and I don't intend to ever get on it again."

"Thanks for being so frank with us," Kallia said, after a moment. "I didn't expect that."

"I want to be part of your family," Shaker said, shrugging. "You should know who I am, so there's no surprises down the road. I'm serious about Debbie, as I told you back in the spring."

"I was going to say that you had wine with dinner," Stuart said slowly, looking at the table. "But I see now that your water glass is empty, and your wineglass is full."

"I hope at some point to be able to drink socially," Shaker said reluctantly. "But that's going to be a while. I'm serious about staying sober right now."

"You're not what I thought," Kallia said, motioning for the waiter. "But I approve. Do you want dessert?"

"Yes," Shaker said, then smiled innocently at Debbie. "I'm hoping to really indulge tonight."

~

"Are you nervous about my mom and uncle?" Debbie asked, as they walked back up to the hotel room. "You seemed a little off tonight. But that was a great save at lunch. You were smart not to drink."

"A little nervous." Shaker got out of his dinner jacket. "Do you want me to just stay here, or work it so I get to the church in time to pick you up after?"

"The latter, if you can manage it?" Debbie suggested, rifling through her clothes. "It'll have to be the rose dress. I don't have anything else left that's clean."

"Wear it, it looks great," Shaker said, embracing her from behind. He kissed her neck urgently his hand reaching down to cup her thatch and squeeze. "Though I think you look better naked."

"What has gotten into you?" Debbie whispered, as his fingers slid beneath her panties and began rubbing circles around her clit.

"I want to get into you, sweet wife. Hurry, we have just enough time."

~

Debbie genuflected as she entered the church with her mother, relieved that there was no electrified feeling or buzzing in her ears. They sat down together in a pew near the back, her mother looking through the pamphlet to mark out the songs ahead of time in the hymnal.

"Debbie," the priest said, stopping briefly as he headed to the lectern. "So good to see you. I'm sorry also to hear about your husband. You've been in my prayers."

"Thank you," Debbie said.

The priest continued to the altar, and the service began. They were in the middle of the second song when the door opened and Shaker slipped in. Debbie looked at him in surprise, then full shock as a man entered behind him. "Rafael?"

Shaker and the angel came and stood near Debbie, Shaker picking up a hymnal after looking at Debbie's. He found the right page, then passed it to the angel, who began singing. Debbie was staring at them both so hard she found it hard to concentrate on the song and remained standing a few seconds after everyone around her sat down.

Shaker, what is going on? How are you in here?

Shaker didn't reply. Aware of Rafael watching her, she took Shaker's hand and held it, as the rest of the service passed uneventfully.

When it was over, Debbie and Shaker headed to the back, but were blocked by Rafael. "I'm glad to see you have both mended your ways," he said gently. "Go in peace." He disappeared.

Debbie looked at Shaker. *What is going on?*

There was no answer.

OMG. "Brady?

~

"How long?" Debbie asked, when the couple was again back at their hotel. "How long have you been here? Where is Shaker?"

"I'm not sure," Brady said defensively, sitting on one of the two chairs at the small table. "I woke up and he wasn't there. He hadn't said anything to me, or wrote out a note, if that's what you're asking."

"No wonder you…um, he didn't answer me mentally." Debbie paced, then stopped still. "Wait, which morning was it that you woke up and he was gone. This morning?"

Brady made a small smile. "Yesterday morning."

Ugh. I slept with you, not Shaker. Not once, but twice. "Why didn't you say something?"

"Why?" Brady shouted, apoplectic. "Because I wanted my body back, Debbie! Do you know what it's like to not have control of your own body? How could you do this to me?"

"You're an alcoholic and drug addict that's made a mess of your life, and you were going to mooch off me the way your sister was planning to mooch off Jett and me, Brady. You lied to me and tried to get me in bed. You never had any intention of finishing *Destiny*. You were just hiding from the police. I don't feel sorry for you! And I don't owe you squat!"

"Do you owe Jett? What about what you did to him? My brother's dead because of you!"

"He'd have been dead from drugs and disease instead if he hadn't known me. I'm not apologizing for Jett. He was an asshole."

"An asshole you used."

"Look, I don't want to talk to you," Debbie said, grabbing her purse. "You can stay here or do whatever, but I'm leaving. I'll see you again when Shaker comes back." *If he comes back.*

"Don't go," Brady said, letting out a breath. "I'm not sure why he's gone, but it could be something bad. He'd want you to stay here, to be safe."

"I thought you were weird, when I met you," Debbie said, looking for her car keys. "But you're insane, telling me in one minute that I'm despicable, then in the next worried for my safety."

"Hey, I'm part of your life, whether you want to admit it or not. I'm part of his life, and he's part of mine, too...whether I want to admit it or not." Brady held his head in his hands. "It's hard to separate his needs and wants from my own needs and wants, after him being in my head for so long."

Maybe he has gone insane. Debbie sat down. "Do you want a drink?"

"No." Brady ran his hand through his hair. "I mean, I do, of course. I'm an alcoholic. But with him not here to limit my drinking, I'll have more than I should. That's why I haven't drunk at all since he left me. I meant it tonight when I said I wanted to stay sober."

Debbie studied him. "Thanks for what you did today, what you said to my uncle and mom. And for what you did with the angel, Rafael."

"Is that who that was? I hadn't ever seen him, but he seemed to be too interested in me to be a stranger. He saw me outside the church and made a big point of asking if I'd go in with him."

"He mistook you for Jett, I think," Debbie mused. "He wanted to see if you were still possessed. You coming into the church and taking part in the service convinced him you weren't. Thank you for that. Even if you didn't mean to, you might have saved your own life." *As well as taken Rafael's attention off of us.* She filled him in briefly about what had happened with Rafael's demon-hunting priest, finishing with Gore's saving her life. "I didn't think he'd still be hanging around here." She glared at him. "I would have told you, if I had any idea you were...you."

"That's good," he said sarcastically. "Is there anything else I should know?"

Maybe I should play for time, in case Shaker's on his way back to me? "I can give you some of the background of the last two years, if you want? You've probably heard about the accidents and the people dying."

Brady faced her. "Only if you're going to be completely honest." His eyes narrowed. "I can guess at a lot of things, from the discussions you've had with Shaker, or things that others have said to him. But I'd like to know what really happened."

Debbie grimaced, but told him about Paul, Dante, Rebecca, Cahill, Harp, Jett, Guardian, and the other Pandora employees that had betrayed her. She mentioned briefly how she met Shaker, their deal to save Pandora, and how they had fallen in love. She left out everything else, including everything with Sheila, Rhonda, and Song, as well as Myrrh. "I think that's everything. Oh, and there was a guy, Henry, that first year, he asked me to marry him. I should have told him no right away. Instead, I delayed, and he found me with Jett. He's been angry ever since. It finally escalated to his attack on Sheila which put her in the coma. He's in jail, I think."

"And my sister?"

"You saw how she was at my wedding rehearsal. Yes, we got someone to keep her out of the way. Before you act judgmental about it, remember that she was completely out of control and you were at your wit's end."

"I'm not going to criticize," Brady said, after a moment. "I just want to know if she's herself now, or if a demon's in there holding her prisoner."

"All I can say is that I think Rhonda's happy now. She's pregnant, if you hadn't heard."

Brady managed a smile. "I never thought I'd hear that and be happy to hear it. Good for her." He paused. "You have had your fair share of enemies. Shaker believes Angel Productions has something bad waiting too, but he's not sure what."

"Are you privy to his thoughts?"

Brady shook his head. "No, but I listen in to conversations when he lets me. Initially I did it hoping to find a way to break free of him." He glared at her again.

I want to ask what being possessed by Shaker is like, but if it's bad, I don't want to know. "I'm not sure what to say."

"I'd say I was sorry about the sex, but I'm not," Brady said tightly. "He lets me see most everything that's going on if I want to see it, except the sex. When he has sex with you, he blocks me. I get the first few kisses, then nothing."

"He's a demon," Debbie offered, feeling lame. "He enjoys torturing you because he knows you were interested in me." *That's why he asked about the pills; he didn't know if Shaker would have been expected to wear a condom.*

"Well, I'd be more cooperative if he would give me a little. Endless teasing coupled with forced celibacy for six months straight left me close to insane."

Maybe that was Shaker's plan. "Brady, have you seen his Mistress? The woman he's bound to?"

Brady shook his head. "He's kept me asleep before now when he's left me, or he's gone and back so fast that I didn't have time to do anything before he returned. I'm assuming she's calling him those times. I hear a voice in my head...um, our head that calls his name."

"Does he ever say her name?"

"No. He never thinks about her, really." He met her eyes. "What he's said to you is true. There's no relationship. He's always thinking about you."

That would be romantic, if this situation wasn't so bizarre. Debbie steeled herself. "Brady, I get that this hasn't been ideal for you--"

"That's an understatement."

"We needed you to finish *Destiny*. You know that Shaker's done that and has been asked to work on *Incubus*. He's done the pilot, and a few other episodes. We'll hear soon if the series is going to be picked up, but it looks very favorable."

"Yes, I know."

"Do you want that as your future?" Debbie asked. "To be Pandora's star, and possibly my life partner? To live with me and be Shaker's human vessel? Or do you want to be cut loose?"

"You have no reason to do that," Brady said nervously. "You are just as ruthless as he is, it's probably why you're such a good power couple. I could expose you, or even turn you and Shaker in to that angel. Why would you offer this?"

"Because I meant what I said, too, the night of the awards. Do you remember?"

Brady nodded. "You were against him possessing me, until he told you what I'd done."

"I was angry, and I was looking for the quickest solution to the problem," Debbie admitted. "I didn't think about you, other than finding a way to control your mess to finish my movie. Shaker did both; he's a good actor, and he can keep you off the drugs and alcohol, because he's not an addict." *Damn it, find the right words!* "I haven't always been moral in my choices; the world is hard, and I have to be harder. But I can't unhear what you've told me. If you don't want to go on like this, tell me now."

"There's no way he'll leave willingly, you'd have to exorcise him," Brady muttered. "He's happy to be acting again, and to have my body to enjoy you with. He's excited about *Incubus;* he can't give up my body and still play Storm."

He's right, Shaker won't want to do it. But will he if I ask him? "Just answer me."

"Yes, I want out," Brady said. "But like I said, I don't see where it matters."

"It matters to me, Brady. I am not going to be able to look at your face for the next however many years and know you're trapped

in there against your will, and that you don't want a life with me."
And the idea of ever being intimate with you again is revolting.

"It would be different if you wanted a life with me," Brady said gently. "I...um—"

His clumsy attempt at a romantic overture brought Debbie's rage to the forefront. "Not ever," Debbie interrupted with a sneer. "Don't worry that you're going to be more than a hiccup to us. Yes, will a transition be hard? I'm sure it will be. But LA is full of addicts and we should be able to locate another down on his luck wannabe actor that Shaker can reside in. And you can go home to South Dakota or wherever and become the drunk you were born to die as, just like your brother."

Brady stared at her in rage, breathing hard. "Okay. Then yes, I want out."

"Good, get out please," Debbie said, handing him a fistful of cash. "Get your own room, I don't want you here tonight. Here's your ticket, too, you can fly home, or you can trade it in for someplace else."

"I worked for you for the last six months," Brady said coldly. "I want my share of that money."

"You know, I'm glad this happened," Debbie said, as she wrote him out a check. "I don't want you around me, seeing the kind of person you are." She handed it to him. "Goodbye."

"Five hundred dollars? I made ten times that!"

"Shaker was and is the only reason you weren't in jail. It was his pain and blood that bought you a way out when there wasn't one and gave you a clean record free of DUIs. It was his skill and effort that earned the money acting. Consider that a rental fee, especially as he left your body in so much better condition than he found it!"

"You bitch!" He stalked off with his luggage, slamming the hotel room door.

Debbie closed and locked the door, then sat down on the bed in a state of shock. "Now what am I going to do? Damn it, think!"

First, you have to get back to the house. Brady left his keys at home, but he'd be able to convince Sheila that he needs to get in, and he'll know where the stash of money is. He put his paychecks in my account for the most part, but he did buy a new car; I need to get that title and put it in my safe deposit box. He also might have an extra key, so I should just change the locks. Debbie called the airport and found out the earliest direct flight to California was leaving in two hours. She arranged to switch her seat to the earlier flight, then debated cancelling Brady's. *I should, it would delay him. But suppose Shaker returns and possesses him again? I'll leave it.*

Who else might he approach for money or assistance that would help him? The other demons would know, wouldn't they? But I didn't know, and I had sex with him. But I just thought he was nervous from having to be around my mom and all of her faith. Fuck!!

"Think, damn it, recrimination isn't going to help you!" *Start packing, you need to check out immediately. Fuck! You need to get the rental car!* Debbie tossed all of her belongings into bags as fast as she could, then hurried downstairs. Checking the parking lot, the place where the rental car had been was empty. She handed the desk clerk her credit card and the two room keys. "I'm checking out." *I also need to check my own credit card statement in case he knows the numbers. But Brady should have his own cards.* "Have you seen my boyfriend? He was supposed to meet me here."

"He came down and left a while ago in your car," the desk clerk said apologetically. "I'm not sure where he went."

"I can guess," Debbie said, signing the statement. "Can you call me a cab? I need to get to the airport. It's an emergency."

~

"How could this have happened?" Sheila said for the fifth time. "Shaker's always so careful, he never had any trouble with Jett."

"It's that damn mistress of his," Debbie swore, as she lugged her bags to the check-in counter. "He's afraid of her finding out about his other life. And now that life is gone because he didn't just be honest with her."

"I don't think it's as bad as that," Sheila consoled. "Shaker should be able to find Brady and repossess him. Then he'll teach him a lesson, so he never gets out of line again." Sheila laughed.

"You aren't hearing me," Debbie said curtly. "Brady is a fucking asshole, a leech, a drunk, a letch, and a slimeball. I don't want to ever see his face again. I don't care who's wearing his skin."

"What are you going to do about *Incubus*? Or *Destiny*? If you really aren't going to work with Brady, then our star is gone, Debbie."

"We'll have to stick to Vassago Gray," Debbie said heavily, as she moved up in line. "He's what we'd planned to do anyway this year. Storm was only supposed to have a bit part on the series."

"What about Angel Pictures?" Sheila said, her voice rising in pitch. "Part of the deal that we brokered has Shaker doing their Christmas picture as Cole Black!"

"Shaker is going to have to find another vessel," Debbie said, handing the ticket to the lady at the counter. "I'll have to call you back as soon as I'm home. Bye." She smiled at the counter woman. "I'm sorry, but I broke up with my boyfriend this morning and it was a violent encounter. He was in the seat next to mine for the return flight home this afternoon, so I moved up my flight to this one. I know it's not routine, but can you just verify that he's not on this same flight out? I understand if you can't give me any more info than that, I'm just scared."

The flight attendant's eyes flicked to her coworker, who was busy trying to upgrade an irate family of five to first class, then back to her screen, then up at Debbie. "He's not on this flight, don't worry."

"Thanks," Debbie said in real relief as she boarded the plane.

The welcoming sight of three crows that were waiting for Debbie as she drove into her driveway brought tears to her eyes. She got out, then beckoned to them. One flew over to her and cawed expectantly.

"Please get Myrrh," Debbie said. "I need to see her immediately. Something's happened to Shaker, he's missing."

The crow nodded, then flew off, the two others following. By the time Debbie had stepped inside with her bags and locked the door behind her, Myrrh stepped through a magical doorway behind her. "What happened?"

I think this is the first time I've seen her look anxious. "Shaker went somewhere and hasn't come back. He left Brady, who pretended to be him and…" *had sex with me* "…um, I found out last night." She rubbed her eyes, then looked at her phone. "It's time to get up and I haven't been to bed yet."

"Go get some sleep," Myrrh said. "I'll go and see Titus right now and find out where he is. How long has he been missing?"

"At least two days."

Myrrh turned back to Debbie, incredulous. "And you just noticed now?"

"He was acting weird, but we were with my mom and uncle. I was nervous too, acting unlike myself," Debbie said, defensive. "We had to be careful what we said, and I was so worried about it going well that I wasn't paying close attention."

"You should have been able to feel the lack of Shaker." Myrrh shook her head. "You're still demon-blind."

"I really don't need criticism right now," Debbie retorted. "Either help or don't help, but don't tell me what I should have done. I'm well aware I didn't handle this well, any of it." She bit her lip, wanting to destroy something.

"For what its worth, Shaker's okay, wherever he is," Myrrh said, turning away again. "Titus would have told me if he'd been sent back to Hell, because the shock of it would have hurt his Mistress, and Devlin, Lash and Danial would all be in an uproar."

"What?" Debbie said, in dawning comprehension. "Are you saying that his Mistress is Devlin's Oathed One?"

"And Lash's mate and Danial's Oathed One, as well," Myrrh said. "Didn't you know?"

CHAPTER THIRTEEN

October/November

DEBBIE MADE A "POST-BRADY" LIST, AND BEGAN CHECKING things off, cancelling off their shared card, saying it had been stolen. She was just hanging up the phone when Myrrh reappeared. "Shaker is in Florida, at a hotel called The Breakers. His Mistress had some kind of epic fight with Lash, and she asked Shaker to take her there. With no guards, he stayed to watch over her."

"That unbelievable bitch," Debbie fumed. "Why didn't she just call one of her other guys to come and be with her? Or go to their houses?"

"Lash cohabits with Devlin, as his master guard. Danial, I'm not sure. I think she wanted some time alone."

"She 'wanted some time alone'?" Debbie screeched. "That bitch has ruined my life with a fucking whim! A fucking whim! Brady's gone, the deal with Angel Pictures will fall through, and Pandora's going to fold! This is a goddamned repeat of last year! And I fucking walked into it all over again, I fucking believed everything was going to be okay when Shaker said he could balance being her demon and being my life partner."

"He's a demon," Myrrh said. "What did you expect him to tell you? The truth?"

"I said, I don't need any criticism right now," Debbie grated, seething. "I already know I'm a fucking idiot, I don't need you to spell it out for me."

"I don't think I've ever heard you swear so much in so short a time."

"Do you have anything helpful to add, or not?"

"I went to The Breakers and told Shaker what happened. He said to tell you he was sorry, and that as soon as he was free, he'd track that 'son of a bitch Brady down and return to you.'"

"Did you tell him I didn't want that?"

Myrrh nodded. "He didn't believe me. He said he'd come and see you first, though."

I hope he's delayed some. I'm too exhausted for a big fight, and we're going to have one. "Thanks, Myrrh. I'm sorry to have unloaded on you."

"I put up a barrier that will alert me if Brady comes here," Myrrh said. "But I'm guessing he won't. He knows Shaker could easily repossess him. He likely went home and lost himself in a bottle."

"It doesn't matter," Debbie said, picking up the phone. "I've got to call and get a locksmith out here. Do you want to have dinner later?"

"I'm under the impression that Shaker will be here sooner rather than later," Myrrh said. "He was only waiting for Lash to arrive to take over guarding his Mistress, which should happen within the hour."

"I hate that woman. I fucking hate her."

"From the little I know of what happened to her these last few years, I would pity her instead," Myrrh said, making another magical portal with a wave of her hand. Through it was glimpsed an overgrown garden in the first rays of dawn, some crowmen at work among the greenery. One of them waved. Myrrh walked through, and the door vanished.

Debbie took a shower, then went out on the deck with a glass of water, the dogs laying at her feet. She was still there when Shaker appeared an hour later.

"I'm sorry," he whispered, embracing her. "Forgive me."

Debbie didn't answer, pushing him away.

"Why aren't you in bed? Myrrh said you were exhausted."

"Because I didn't want to do this in my bedroom."

"It's our bedroom," Shaker said, taking a step toward Debbie. She retreated two steps.

"I can't fix this if you won't tell me what happened. Myrrh said Brady didn't make a scene, that your parents thought he was me. But you found out. Did you bribe him to play along?"

"He did that on his own. He must have learned acting from you after all."

"Look, I've also been up for close to two days now, and you look exhausted, even if you don't want to admit it. So let's go to bed. Don't worry about Brady, I'll track him down over the weekend and make him wish he'd never been born and be back in time for shooting on Monday."

"I don't want you to track him down," Debbie said. "I never want to see him again. He's a piece of shit." *And you are, too.*

I can't believe you said that to me.

Debbie felt a flash of Shaker's hurt, then it disappeared. "Tell me what he did. I have never seen you this angry."

"I believed you had all of it, everything, under control! Instead you just left and now everything is in ruins!"

"TELL ME WHAT HE DID!" Shaker boomed, the glass in the panes rattling.

"He pretended to be you," Debbie said bitterly, tears coming to her eyes. She fought them back, blinking hard. "In all ways, okay? I should have known when he asked me if he needed to wear a condom." *I should have known when the sexual undercurrent was missing, and his comments weren't cleverly appropriate, and when he stopped responding to my mental texts. I didn't know until he walked into the church alongside Rafael.*

Shaker's eyes radiated flames, and he appeared near her, pulling her into a hug. 'I'm sorry, I can't say how sorry. I will kill him for this. I was pissed off at Vass just for his dream subterfuge."

As much as she was still furious, feeling his arms around her and his assurance tamped down her anger.

"I'll pull his soul out and take it to hell. The next time I have to leave, my body—and it is MINE—will just lie there until I return. I may need to be gone again, and I won't risk you. I'll also make sure to teleport my body home before leaving, so you don't have any complications."

"Complications?" Debbie shrieked, pushing him away again. "This goes way beyond complications! Brady told me that you'd let him see and hear everything that was going on around you, so he's really well informed about our lives and our past. He also said you'd blocked him during sex, which was what prompted him to screw me over literally."

"I thought he'd go insane like his brother," Shaker said, eyes narrowing. "I forgot that as Jett I'd been hunting my own kills, and also handing out death and dismemberment to your enemies, where Brady only witnessed the energy transfer that Rene arranged, and the sporadic raw meat meals. Of course I blocked out the sex! Did you want him to experience it with us?"

"No! I didn't want him at all! He was never attractive to me, Shaker."

"Then I'll take Brady's body and do some magic to mold his face to look more like Jett looked. We can tell everyone I had plastic surgery."

"Shaker, you aren't listening to me! Brady is gone, he doesn't want any part in our lives or acting or any of it! He's out."

"Not by any estimation is he out," Shaker growled. "I put too much effort into this to be sidelined by a twerp like him. I'll leave now and take care of things. You will never have to speak to him again, Debbie. I'll leave his soul in tatters for the hellcats and Takers to fight over."

"You go to possess him, then don't come back," Debbie said heavily. "I mean it."

Shaker stopped still. "What are you saying?"

"I don't want a life with asshole Brady. I want a life with you, but I don't see a way. You're trying to do what you did last year, serve two masters. You can't be hers and mine and cover all the bases."

"We can have that life. Your attitude is the only thing that's standing in the way."

"My attitude?"

"Yes, your new righteous I-want-to-be-moral-and-just-and-still-have-everything-I-want attitude, Debbie! It doesn't work that way. You want miracles, and you never care how they happen at the time, but later you guilt yourself up. What happened to the power woman I pledged myself to, who saw what she wanted and went after it, damn the consequences?"

"That was before my best friend almost died. Before I almost died! I can't check constantly to see that the man I'm in bed with is you, and not someone else! I can't trust you to be there when I need you when you keep taking off without telling me!" Debbie's eye narrowed. "Why didn't you just tell me you were leaving? I'd have had you teleport us both home. It would have taken 5 minutes, tops. Then none of this would have happened."

"You mean you wouldn't have had to face Brady's accusations," Shaker retorted, now angry himself. "I don't understand why you're so surprised about any of this, Debbie. You knew he was an asshole before I possessed him, that's why you agreed to it. You also knew he wouldn't be happy about being possessed. You were aware I might need to go at the drop of a hat if I was called, too."

"Yes, but not that you'd be gone for forty-eight hours with no word. What was so important, by the way, that you couldn't pick up the phone and call?"

"That's my fault. I expected to be gone a few minutes tops. But she asked to go to Florida. It was a perfect storm from then on in: the hotel she planned to stay in was gone, even the bar was gone, there were no pay phones, and there was no cell reception. I had to relocate her to another hotel."

"Yeah, Myrrh told me. The Breakers. What a coincidence."

"I took her there because I'd just been there with you, so I knew where everything was, and was able to get a comped room pretending to be Brad Pitt again. It's not like I had my wallet, or my phone. I couldn't risk coming back and picking up Brady's body, because when I got down there, she'd ask who I was possessing."

"She really doesn't know you've been acting these last two and a half years?"

"Devlin's hesitant to tell her about the movie *Immortal Confessions*, seeing as it's about him and his first love Anna, and he did all the work making it in the time she was being held a prisoner by Michael. Sooner or later she's going to see it listed online and recognize his life story, but he asked me not to say anything."

"Why didn't she just pay for her own room?"

"She didn't have her wallet, either!"

"You stayed there in the room with her? No wonder it slipped your mind to call me."

"No," Shaker grated. "I spent the night outside her room, guarding the door."

"You couldn't find five minutes to call me?"

"There was some other demon there, possibly more than one. I was afraid if I relaxed my guard the slightest bit, it would show itself and pick a fight. It's an old trick to send someone to fight the guard while another sneaks in to kill what he's guarding. I spent most of those two days I was gone watching her like a hawk, and reciting protection spells."

225

"Look, I just flat out don't believe you. But even if I did, this just proves what I've said, that we can't make a go of this."

"The only reason we can't make a go of this is you!" Shaker thundered. "I can get Brady back here, and you can have it all: the deal with Angel Pictures, the *Incubus* series, and me as your partner. Or you can stick to your priggish ways and throw it all away for some morality that you'll regret by tomorrow." His eyes glowed. "Because you will regret this, Debbie, as soon as Pandora begins its downward slide. You'll call me to come back. Whether I do or not isn't a given, not after this. Your loyalty to me seems to have faded to pretty much nothing, from where I stand."

"My being loyal to you isn't an issue!"

"I say that it is!"

"I love you," Debbie said, wiping away her tears to face him. "But I can't do this rollercoaster anymore."

"You'll regret this," Shaker said, then disappeared.

Debbie regretted what she'd said to Shaker the next morning, when she awoke. "I had to do it, though, Pitch," she said as she petted the three dogs. *I closed my eyes to what was going on long enough. It isn't worth having Pandora Productions if the price is putting someone else, even an asshole, in a living Hell they can't escape from.*

When she got to work, she called together Rack, Vassago, and Catarella, and told them about Shaker's release of Brady, leaving out most of the details. "Because of what happened, I'm not sure if Shaker will return in another guise, or as himself. Please let me know if he comes on the premises. I also want to be informed immediately if Brady arrives here for any reason. Technically, Cole Black is supposed to shoot his last scenes for the fourth episode of *Incubus* on Monday."

"Of course," Rack said, and stood. "I'll be in with the wine samples later for *An Unconventional Christmas*. I have a red and a blush for you to try."

"I'll be in my office," Catarella said, also standing. "Brady wasn't anything but an employee, so I don't have any legal papers to draw up because of your separation. I will inform payroll to hold the check he would have gotten today, and not mail it without talking to you first."

"Are the three of you staying?" Debbie said bluntly, stopping them in their tracks. "I need to know if I can count on you. Shaker recruited all of you. This is different than him being sent back to Hell last year, even if I haven't said that explicitly until now. Are you willing to work for me?"

"Every couple has spats," Rack said almost cheerfully, as he headed to the door. "I'm staying regardless, but I won't be surprised to see Shaker come back." He left.

"I'm your lawyer, and his," Catarella said. "But you're offering me steady employment. That's rare. You should know that demons usually can't even hire themselves out as an assassin, or find any kind of regular work, because no one knows for sure when they'll be called away. I'm here forever." He grinned a smile full of too-long teeth, then also left.

"And you?" Debbie said to Vassago, as he moved closer to stand in front of her desk.

"I told you I'd be here for you." Vassago shrugged. "Though I also won't be surprised to see Shaker and Brady come back, in time. He really seems happy here with you."

Debbie swallowed tightly, her teeth clenched. *Hold it together.* "We were happy." She looked up at him. "Were you ever in a long-term relationship?"

"Not long, no," Vassago said, shrugging. "Incubi are the fathers of one-night stands. I wanted to try recently," he said meaningfully. "But the lady wasn't interested."

"Vassago, I look about twice your age, I'm human, and I've officially got demon baggage. You're charming, handsome, and about to have your own hit series. Don't tell me that I'm your dream woman to boot, or you'll get me in the throes of…whatever."

"You'll be in the throes of 'whatever'? Sounds kind of radical for you, doesn't it?"

"Ha-ha, you're so funny."

"This is clearly a time for holding and not talking," he said, moving closer and taking her in his arms. "Sorry."

Debbie leaned into him, glad to feel arms around her. *Tell me he'll come back.*

He'll probably come back, Vassago answered in her mind, to her surprise. *He does care about you deeply, or he wouldn't have given me that warning. It's demon code not to ever show something means anything to you to another demon, because it's taken for a sign of weakness.*

"I'm sorry," Debbie said, separating from him. "I didn't mean to ask you that, I just was thinking it."

"Part of your demon baggage," Vass said, hugging her again. "I like it very much, actually. Most humans are uncomfortable speaking their minds, their true thoughts. They like to hide. I like that you're not afraid." He kissed her cheek before she could pull back, then turned away. "If you change your mind about dinner some night, just send me a text."

Debbie awoke suddenly, opened her eyes, then looked around carefully, relieved as she had been the last few nights that only her hellhounds were with her in bed. She dressed in her robe, then the four went out to the kitchen. Myrrh was there with a crow on her shoulder, yawning. "You know, you really should be safe on your own. I'm going to leave you with a few crows tonight to keep watch. If anything happens, I can just make a magical doorway and come to you."

"Myrrh, I had another dream," Debbie mentioned, as she made coffee. "I knew it was a dream because some of what was said wasn't what would happen in real life. But I need to make sure that this was just a dream. No one was there with me?"

"You have asked me every day this week, and five times previously, and every time I assure you, no, the dreams you're having are all your own," Myrrh said, yawning again. "You just miss Shaker. Now that you're watching *Incubus* episodes being filmed, you're enticed by Gray. He is sexy, even I think so."

Makes sense, last night was another repeat of that lotion massage scene. "Would you let him into your bed?"

"Sure, if he wanted me," Myrrh said, obviously surprised. "Incubi are some of the best lovers there are. But he's interested in you, not me, or he'd have made a play by now." She winked. "Though if he visits me, he's going to be in for a rough ride. Faeries are notoriously hard to satisfy."

Debbie's eye bugged out and she looked down quickly to stop from spewing her coffee. *Definitely another side of her I never knew about until now.* "I just never have seen you as, um, available," Debbie managed. She put a box of donuts on the table. "Help yourself."

"Probably most males don't," Myrrh said easily, taking a donut and feeding a piece to her crow. "That's okay. I like my solitude."

"Have you heard from Shaker?" Debbie asked.

"I think he's at Devlin's estate, brooding," Myrrh said. "Titus said he couldn't find Brady."

"I'm not sure if I want to find him or would rather never see him again. But I'll have to contact the police in a few days, if he doesn't turn up."

◇

"Brady is here," Rack said, when she arrived at work Monday. "He's shooting the scenes he's supposed to."

"Is Shaker here, too?"

"He was here." Rack gave an apologetic smile. "He also contacted me and asked me to contact him immediately if Brady showed up for work."

There's no point yelling at him. "And?"

"Go see for yourself. It's a war of nerves and daggers are drawn."

Debbie hurried down to the set. Vassago saw her coming and beckoned. She went over to him. "Where is Brady?"

"He's on camera," Vassago said, pointing. There was Brady, choking a ragged looking made-up demon with small horns, demanding information about the incubus he was hunting. "And I have to say, it's a good thing that actor isn't a demon, he'd be smoking."

Debbie blinked, then stared. Brady's expression was determined, but it was definitely Brady, not Shaker. "I don't see anything different?"

"That's because you aren't a demon," Vass explained. "Brady's glowing with belief and also blessings. He must have been in church this morning or taken a bath in holy water. I'm serious, it's hard for me to look at him for very long. No way can I touch him, even if the scene asks for it."

"You shouldn't have any scenes of hand to hand fighting until the finale. Did he say anything at all to you?"

"Nothing out of character." Vass smiled. "Shaker was here and tried to pounce on him but was repelled by all the God-power. I've never seen him so angry. He left after his fifth try."

Shaker can't blame me for this; Brady must have gone to a church right from the hotel room. But what's he doing here? She signaled an assistant. "Please tell Mr. Black that I need to see him, when he's finished here."

~

Brady strode into her office a few minutes before five, his expression venomous. "What do you want?"

"What are your intentions? I expected never to see you again."

"I had a contract with Pandora to fulfill doing bit parts in the rest of the first series of *Incubus*, and I've done it," Brady said, then smiled evilly. "That was the last contract I had with you. Now I'm going to work for Angel Pictures. I've already signed a deal with them for that Christmas movie." He looked down at her. "They said I was a great actor, a natural."

Debbie laughed sarcastically. "Trust me, you're not that good an actor."

Brady sneered. "I fooled you, didn't I?"

Don't punch him, he'll have you arrested for assault. "Only because I was distracted. Shaker's a complete package of brains, brawn, daring, and seduction. You're just not, and likely weren't ever. How can you act believably like an alpha male when you never were an alpha male?"

Instead of a retort, Brady looked hurt. "Shaker wasn't an actor, either, when he first started. Even Jett had to learn to be cool. Besides, I need money, and this is a lot more than I ever made for a lot less work."

"It's a lot of work," Debbie said caustically. *I can't believe I had sex with this asshole.* "You'll have to make yourself do the two-hour-a-day workouts, now that you don't have Shaker to make you stick to them. And no showing up drunk or high, or they'll fire you on the spot."

"I know the routine, I lived it every day for the last half a year," Brady huffed, finally showing anger. "Unless you have something to tell me that pertains to future work, I'm leaving."

"Debbie," a voice hissed from behind him, as Lash swaggered in, his black leather creaking. "I was in the neighborhood and wanted to see how my movie was coming."

"Your movie isn't even on their radar," Brady said gleefully. "She thinks it's garbage."

Lash looked affronted. "Shaker, you'd better watch your shit."

"That's not Shaker," Debbie put in. "He is an asshole, though."

Lash considered that, shifted his feet, then planted his right fist in Brady's stomach. The handsome man bent double, then fell to his knees.

"I didn't break your ribs this time, but you mouth off to me again, and I will," Lash hissed at him. "Now get your pansy ass out of here." He turned to Debbie, as Brady began to try to get to his feet. "You're finished with him, right?"

"Yes, we're finished."

"We are. I'm never working with Pandora again." Brady cast Debbie a look of hate, then staggered out the door.

Lash watched him go, then turned back to her. "What he said about my film, is it true?"

"No, I don't think your movie is garbage, we just don't have a star to portray you." *Sheila is still trying to find a way to spin the weresnake protagonist into someone that people will see as a hero.* "In fact, we are setting up the last few scenes of *Hell to Pay* to lead into your character. We hope that will whet audience's appetite for your movie."

Lash cocked his head, weighing her words. "What if *Hell to Pay* doesn't do well?"

"We have our marketing on this hard to see that it does. Your character kills the spiritwalker and saves Morwen, the heroine. There's no way that you won't be cheered at the end. And unlike that jerk who just left, you know how to be an alpha male, Lash. Yes, we reworked your scenes, but most of the dialogue we plan to leave as is. It's coarse and there's a lot of swearing, but there's also a lot of raw emotion in your rough draft. We think that will resonate well with modern audiences."

"Good," Lash said, putting his feet up on one of her end tables. "So what's with that guy? I thought you and Shaker had a thing, and he was in Jett?"

"And I had no idea you had your own steady girlfriend and a

new baby," Debbie said quietly. "Congratulations. I'm glad you two made up."

Lash jumped to his feet, all lassitude vanishing. "Who told you that?"

"I'm just making the point that we aren't friends who share personal stuff."

"Hell, that's like using a slap across the face to wake someone up in the morning," Lash said gruffly, sitting back down. "But okay, I don't need to know your business, and I'll keep my own. Thanks for the congratulations."

"Thank you for punching him," Debbie said. "I've wanted someone to do that for several days now." She sighed. "I'm sorry to be bitchy, Lash. I just had things fall apart when I thought everything was settled on a good course."

"It's been a fall for things getting FUBAR," Lash hissed in agreement, standing. "I hope things get better for both of us. If you want his ass kicked again, just call me, I'll do it for free." He gave her a lopsided smile, then sauntered out.

"Why did I think that a costume party would be fun?" Debbie lamented, looking at Sheila. "And what are you supposed to be again?"

"I'm a sheep," Sheila said, holding out white wooly mittens. "Song is Little Bo Peep." She beckoned to a slightly pregnant woman in a cute blue dress and pigtails.

"You have to pick something cute when you're pregnant," Song beamed. "Thanks for the crib you sent over, we hadn't gotten one yet."

"You look fabulous," Debbie said, pushing away a flash of jealousy. "I should have gone for cute too."

"You look wonderful as Maleficent," Sheila argued, snapping a photo of Song and Debbie. "Here, we need to get one of all of us." She began scanning the crowd.

"May I be of assistance?"

"Hey, Devlin, I didn't expect you, but you're welcome! Yes, can you please take a picture?"

Debbie posed with Sheila and Song for a few pictures, then turned to the figure along with Sheila. "Devlin, I didn't expect you. Hi." *His own party must have gotten over early?*

"Sheila, we have to go now," Song said urgently. "I'm going to be sick!" She ran off in the direction of the bathroom.

"Excuse us," Sheila apologized, then ran after Song.

And here I was envying her being pregnant. Debbie turned to Devlin. "Who are you supposed to be?"

Devlin opened his arms theatrically, his dark velvet suitcoat shining with black gemstones. There was dark glitter sparking in his golden hair. "Pleased to meet you, won't you guess my name?"

"The devil. Very good." Debbie laughed. "Or should I say bad, right?"

"Evil is a point of view," Devlin replied. "But you know that very well, don't you Deborah Veronica Tennison?"

Debbie almost dropped her wineglass. *No one outside my mom and uncle knows my full name, not Shaker, not even Catarella.* "You're not Dev. Who are you?"

"I wanted to meet you in person. Shaker isn't the oldest of my legion, or the most formidable, but he's...enjoyable to watch. I heard your vows last spring and wondered how long they would last."

The Devil. Debbie felt herself begin to pee in terror and shifted violently, biting her lip to control her fear and her bladder.

"Very good," the figure nodded approvingly. "You control yourself well, Debbie. But I'd expect nothing less."

"Why are you here?" Debbie got out, her voice cracking.

"I came to tell you that I'm enjoying Shaker loving you, because he'll be that much more of a broken creature when you die, whether that's in a few weeks, or fifty years. But I hope you do live, my dear, because the longer he knows you and loves you, the more pain he'll feel when you are ripped away from him forever."

Brady, you're an asshole but thank you for reminding me. Debbie felt for the cross necklace she'd bought at an antique store yesterday and brandished the talisman at him. "Please leave, now that you've said what you came to say."

He dismissed the cross with a wave. "He and I are old friends. But as I've said what I came here to say, goodnight." He walked off through the crowd.

~

"I can't believe that I met the devil," Debbie said, downing another slug of wine. "Keep pouring, Rack."

Rack poured her another glass of Incubus wine. Song had alerted the other demons to their master's presence before leaving the party with Sheila. Rack, Vassago, and Mrs. Triss had come over to make sure she was okay, once the coast was clear.

"I'm sorry we couldn't do more, dear," Mrs. Triss said, hugging her. "Drink up. Calm down and relax. Overall this is about the best message you could have hoped to get from him."

"I'm sorry I didn't come over," Vassago said, hugging her. "But there's nothing I could have done against him, anyway."

Shaker would have tried. Sorry, sorry, to anyone that heard that. I'm just still scared. Debbie finished her wine, then handed the empty glass back to Rack. "I'm okay, thanks. I think I'll call it a night."

"We all will, it's nearly midnight already," Vassago said. "Let me take you home."

"I thought you meant drive," Debbie said, when they teleported to her door. "How did you know where I live?"

"Because I've been here before," Vassago murmured, trying to kiss her. "But you know that, Debbie. We could have arrived inside, but there's a barrier in place. If you let me in, it will break, though."

Did Myrrh make the ward breakable in case I reconsidered? Debbie hesitated a moment, then shook her head. "I'm sorry, Vass. I can't."

"What is it that you're so worried about me doing to you in there in the dark?" he murmured seductively. "I've already done it all, we've done it all, Debbie." He kissed her cheek, then her throat. "I've gotten flashes from you of your fantasies about me. They distract the hell out of me when I'm trying to act." He kissed her chin, as she dodged his lips again. "Right now, I can see what you're thinking. The things you have me doing to you shock even me. It's incredibly arousing."

"Yes, I find you really attractive," Debbie admitted. "But I can't go from one lover to another, not in real life."

"Then at least let me into your dreams again. What can it hurt?"

"Both of us, if I'm not serious about a relationship with you," Debbie stated. "You've got it all, Vass. Don't settle for a piece of a woman's heart when you can have a whole one."

"Okay," Vassago said, raising his eyebrows, and turning away. "More time, gotcha." He vanished.

Debbie unlocked the door, then locked it behind her as her hellhounds ran up to greet her happily. "I dodged a bullet there," she said to them. "Chalk one up for loyalty."

~

"These last few weeks of November have been a series of events that just get worse day by day," Debbie said to her hellhounds.

"Do you want to tell me about it?" Myrrh asked from the doorway.

"Sure, come in and pour yourself some wine."

"Not tonight," Myrrh said, sitting down. "Tell me what happened."

"Well first, Angel Pictures tried to back out of our deal. Partly that's my fault, in the mess that happened in October, I never got back to them on their three scripts. They went ahead and got all three films and will make them by themselves. Georgio has said that's not reason enough for them to back out, but then Brady made good on his threat."

"He signed with Angel Pictures?"

Debbie nodded. "Technically he already had when I talked to him, so I'm glad I said everything I said, and didn't try to talk him into staying exclusive to Pandora. But he was our big star. Vassago is going to be a star, but he's unknown right now. He's volunteered to be in one of Angel Pictures' three new films, but they're making noise now that that might not be equal to what the contract stipulated. Giorgio and Catarella are fighting it, but I'm not sure even they can fix it. Angel Pictures has demon lawyers, too."

"What else?"

"I think it's going to escalate to threats," Debbie said. "I've gotten a knife in the mail this week, and a tourniquet the week before."

"Did you report these things to the police?"

Debbie shook her head. "The newspapers would hear about it. They've already heard about Brady leaving Pandora...and me."

Myrrh hugged her. "I'm sorry. Do you want me to contact Shaker?"

"No. But will you please be on call? I feel like something's coming."

"Of course."

~

When the moment came, it was on a perfectly normal afternoon. Debbie had finished reviewing some new scripts Sheila had given her and was just closing her computer when a figure slipped into her office.

What does Ms. Grim want? Myrrh, please come! "Can I help you?"

The woman stood before her, solemn. "The world is a certain way for a while. Maybe years. Maybe even a decade or two. Then people get older and things change subtly, shifting. The edges start unravelling, even as you try to hold them together with duct-tape desperation. Time passes and you wait for that small event that will mark the beginning of the end of how things were, and the start of how things will now be." Ms. Grim smiled. "That day is here, Debbie. You are Pandora's past. I am it's future."

"Like Hell," Debbie said, carefully opening her desk drawer.

"Shaker's onto other greener younger pastures, and your witch is occupied with a territory dispute. Don't reach for that holy water. Don't fight us. This isn't worth your life, Ms. Deal."

"My name is Mrs. Black," Debbie said, bringing up the gun from behind her desk. The shot found its mark, the demon's mouth an O of surprise as it fell sideways, the large hole in its chest smoking.

Myrrh appeared, then peered at the fallen demon. "Well, I guess there's no point in threatening to make her one of my crows."

"That's Ms. Grim," Debbie said, getting closer to look at the body. "I can't believe she attacked me so openly."

"Likely that demon just possessed her," Shaker said, appearing beside Myrrh. "Grim is short for Gigglegrim, a male demon. But he usually possesses females. What's that?"

Myrrh reached around the woman's throat, then held up a thin bar made of silver with some writing on it.

"What is that?" Debbie asked.

"That's latitude and longitude," Shaker said quizzically. "See the other side is a design of a compass." He yanked, breaking the pendant off the delicate chain. "I'll find out where this exact specified location is, and then go there and investigate." He disappeared before Debbie could thank him.

"C'mon," Myrrh said. "I'll take you home."

"Let's stop by the church on the way," Debbie said, grabbing her coat. "I need to refresh my holy water. Dipping those bullets as you suggested just saved my life."

~

Debbie looked at the tall thin dark-haired man before her. *He could almost be Torren, if he were a little taller and thinner. But he's too beautiful to be called traditionally handsome.* "*Immortal Reckoning?* Decent title. And it goes with your brother's movie's name. The only trouble is that people may not come to it, thinking they've already seen it."

"This manuscript has gone through several harsh revisions, just as I have gone through life changing events that molded and shaped me from the man I once was to the vampire I became." Danial steepled his hands. "I tried to be as clear and honest as possible."

"That may be," she replied evenly. "But I'm the boss of Pandora, Mr. Racklan. I have complete faith in my team. If they tell me a script needs a rewrite, then it needs a rewrite, whether it's the 1st or the 100th. As it is now…you're too much the victim."

The dark-haired man slammed his hand down on Debbie's desk, a deep crack appearing in the solid wood. "I am not a victim," the vampire hissed.

"Then stop writing as one," Debbie said, not backing down an inch. "You want your sequel to come off as well as Devlin's initial *Immortal Confessions* did, then you have to tell an exciting tale."

"I am telling you the truth!"

"Audiences aren't interested in the truth, they want a hero, one they can root for, one that never gives up, that turns the tables at five to midnight and not only saves the world and his girl but looks gorgeous doing it. You don't have to make it look easy, or leave out the brutal truths, Danial. But you do have to triumph."

He nodded thoughtfully. "I see. You are saying I'm focusing on the wrong bits, not emphasizing the triumphs and only the failures."

"Exactly."

Danial shuffled the papers, aligning them neatly. "I will rewrite and return. Please excuse my frustration, this is a new undertaking for me. I will pay for the desk, if you'll send me the bill."

"I'll do that," Debbie said. *Or someone will.*

Danial looked at her oddly. "Will you? Your tone suddenly holds no conviction."

"I'm not sure where I go from here," Debbie said wearily. "Correction. I'm not sure where I want to go from here. I always knew what I wanted, with one clear goal in sight. And now that it's happened, I feel like it's hollow, because the one person I most wanted to be here to share it with is gone."

"It is one thing to never have known love. You don't miss the lack of it, if you never experience it. But love ruins us. Once experienced, it is never enough not to have it." He patted her hand. "You won't believe me, but you will find love again, if you don't close yourself off. Time heals."

"Unfortunately, I don't have another century, as you do," Debbie said cuttingly. *Even if I did, I wouldn't find another Shaker.* "It's been good speaking with you."

CHAPTER FOURTEEN

December

"How is it the second week of December?" Debbie said to Sheila, as they walked to her office.

"Right," Sheila sighed. "I still have to get a holiday present for Song." She beamed. "Can you believe I'll be a mom by next March or April?"

Debbie gritted her teeth. *Be happy for her.* "You said there's no shower?"

"I don't have any friends outside of work, and my family disowned me when I came out to them," Sheila said bluntly. "I think the girls in the office are going to throw a shower after the new year. So you have a lot of time. Kaitlyn and Adeline are running it, they have the registry list."

"Why so late?" Debbie asked. "You'll have bought everything you need by then, right?"

"Um…I think it's because…" Sheila trailed off and looked down. "Because so much can happen before the baby's born."

You mean miscarriage. Like me. "I'll get a list from Kaitlyn. Thanks for telling me."

"I'll see you at the holiday party on New Year's," Sheila said quickly. "I'm on vacation the next two weeks."

"Sure," Debbie said, turning away.

Sheila grabbed Debbie's arm. "Debbie, thanks again for the raise. It means a lot to me."

Debbie turned and hugged her. "I'm happy for you. I'm sorry it's not more, but we'll need to look for another star next year, and they'll cost us a lot. As it was, I wasn't able to give out raises to everyone like I planned. *Including myself.*

"Thanks. You're my best friend."

"You're mine," Debbie said gratefully, separating. "Have a good vacation."

～

"Adeline, thanks for filling in for Sheila while she's out."

"No problem, Debbie," Adeline said. "We're all so happy that Sheila not only made a full recovery, but she's married with a baby on the way. I wasn't alone in thinking that Pandora was cursed, after everything that happened last year. But you were right that things would get better." She paused. "You're a great leader and an inspiration to me."

"Thanks," Debbie said awkwardly, pleased and a little embarrassed. "Now what did you have to show me that couldn't wait until Monday?"

"The first video ad clip for *Origin of Fear.* Althea's editing like crazy, and I know we aren't going to release until next summer. But you have to see this, I think it's going to bring the kids in droves." She put the CD into Debbie's laptop.

There was the shot of the house in the rain, the camera

climbing the walls, the suggestion of something just out of sight moving right before the camera crossed the spot it had been.

A sepulchral voice intoned, "Welcome to Latham's Landing, a cursed island mansion that dwells like a sitting spider on a long clear lake in the northeastern United States. The stones that make its skeleton are red granite, bleached in spots to white and pink. Lights form at night in its windows, though the electricity there has been off for some time. Winding out from the isle is a long narrow stone bridge that snakes to a house of glass known as The Sea Room. On some nights, The Sea Room also lights up, burning like a pyre of Hell as it welcomes in new victims."

Debbie got chills as the lights in the dark house in the water went on and off, then the ball of glass became a sun lying on the dark water, as a ragged scream of terror cleaved the air.

"How many have died on the shores of the island, or within the walls of the mansion is unclear. What is known are the many drownings in the waters just around the island. The shallow water is home to many hidden rocks ready to gore a boat's bottom. Winds tend to come up out of nowhere, becoming tempests of lightning and rough waves in mere minutes that overturn boats with childish ease. Time passes differently there, the hours slipping away like minutes."

Now there were shots of a couple boating, then a storm coming up, overtaking the craft and swamping it. The figures treaded water in crashing waves, then were dragged under, bug-eyed in terror.

"To those that spend the time to research the haunted isle, there is also one other troubling characteristic: the house *changes*. Return through a doorway you just left, and you may find yourself in a room that you've never seen before. What was once a wall may suddenly have a door...and the door you ran to for escape may suddenly disappear. Part of the house is sunken, or so the tales tell. But more than one fisherman has returned with his catch to report a house that sits up on dry land, no contact with water visible. The tides ebb and flow is what some say. However, no one who goes looking for the proof of that ever comes back."

Shots now of the house on dry land, and then suddenly waterlogged. Then to her horror, Debbie saw part of her vision as two people ran out onto the house porch, trying to bar the door, then waded out into the water, only to be drowned.

"Disappearances stack up back from the owner's time. Hans Latham was a shipping tycoon who made his fortune in transport. Some say on foggy nights they hear a clipper ship's foghorn sound on the lake. Others report a ghost ship covered with algae and flying tattered sails, crewed by a host of skeletons. It is hard to say really what is truth and what comes from fear. For the isle wears an unspeakable menace like a permanent cloak, and none who come close enough to see anything—and live to tell about it—ever tell all that they have seen."

A shot of a ghost ship crewed by skeletons, then a clipper ship that crashed onto rocks and disappeared. Again that ball of glass lighting the surface of the lake, and more tattered screams, as the lights in the house all came on at once.

"It is said that the island is able to sense your fears, to reach into your soul and see what most terrifies you...and bring those fears to life. Some people report dead loved ones beckoning to them from the shore. Others tell of haunting music floating on the breeze, plaintive and melancholy. But most report a shadowy male figure that waits on the shore appearing near dusk. He will not answer any mortal's call, and never leaves the shore. Not long after, a wind often springs up, storm clouds appear on the horizon, and the waves begin to heighten. Those who report seeing him—for most everyone agrees it must be Latham's ghost—don't fish those waters again, if they make it back to shore. For it is well known the island takes offense with those few that manage to successfully escape its storms, enacting terrible vengeance if they dare its waters again."

Here were rapid clips from the film: the kids running through the house afraid, interacting with ghosts and almost killing one another, one going under as they drowned, pulled down by a skeletal sailor.

"What exactly haunts Latham's Landing? Certainly Latham himself, and also possibly his wife, who died there. A woman is sometimes sighted near The Sea Room, dressed in flowing gauze with ribbons in her short hair. There are two reported sightings of a ghost child within the mansion, a boy with needle teeth who asks for his missing father. There are still more reports of a crying girl with long hair on the shore. She plays a flute stained with blood. Like Latham, it is said these spirit apparitions come in advance of storms."

A woman played a flute on the shore, blood spattering her clothes, the melody haunting. When one of the college kids approached her, she vanished. But the kid picked up the flute, very real blood getting on his hands.

"Strangers come from time to time, looking for paranormal activity. They usually say they have experience; that they know what is waiting for them out there on Latham's Landing. They bring along lifejackets, just in case they get marooned there. They quote that the police are available with an easy call to 911, and that they are not afraid of ghosts. They go, either with permission or without, sometimes sneaking out with oars in the middle of the night. We find their gear, their boats, sometimes even their personal effects. But we never find them. Not alive, anyway."

Here were some of the action clips, one kid kissing a ghost then suffering a heart attack as it turned into a monster, another kid pursued along a flooded bridge by one of the kids who had been drowned and reanimated.

"You want to go on to Latham's Landing? Go ahead. Yes, I'll rent you a boat. I've done my duty and warned you. I won't stop you, though I must insist you fill out this waiver, which says you are liable for any damage to the boat and equipment. Go on, the isle is waiting for you. It already knows you're coming. I wish you Godspeed where you're going, and I hope you get there. I don't think I'll be seeing you again. If by some 100-1 chance you do survive, you will not be the same. No one is, once they set foot on Latham's Landing."

Adeline shut it off. "What do you think?"

Debbie swallowed hard. *You came face to face with the devil and you're afraid of a house?* "I think it's great, I'm scared watching it. My only suggestion is to shorten some of the words, make it harder hitting."

"I can do that," Adeline said, standing up. "Have a great weekend, Debbie."

Debbie stayed until five, then got up with a sigh and put on her coat. "At least my good dogs are at home waiting for me." She turned off the lights and walked out to her car. She had no sooner touched the door then she was teleported, arriving in the middle of a busy road. She dived out of the way of an oncoming car, breaking her heel and skinning her knee as she fell down an embankment. The car's wheels ran over her briefcase, flattening it, and broke her cellphone to pieces.

Debbie looked at the spreading pool of holy water. "Shit." *Myrrh! Leri! Vassago! Rack! Oh, screw it. Shaker! Shaker!*

There was no reply.

Everyone is too far away, so they'll never hear me. I don't even know what state or country I'm in. Debbie hurried back up through the brush, heading for the road. Just as she climbed out of the ditch, a passing car was cleaved in two by the magical doorway that appeared in front of her. Through the portal an island house rose from a bed of fog and lapping waves, lights shining in all the windows. A dark figure seemingly made of shadow walked out from the house, coming toward the portal purposefully.

Holy shit it looks just like I imagined when I heard that scary promotion Sheila dreamed up. Help! Rack! Shaker! Myrrh! Vassago! Help! Debbie shouted with her mind, then yelled the names again as loud as she could.

"Be silent," a soothing voice said from behind her. Out walked

Ms. Grim, her form changing to that of a hideous gnarled tree-ish man, several demons behind him. They grabbed her arms, pinning them at her sides.

"What is this?" Debbie struggled, kicking.

"Payment for services rendered," Grim said smugly. "We get Pandora, to merge with Angel Pictures. And Rigor gets you, to call his son home at last."

"You'll have your sweetheart again, you should be happy," one of the demons jeered. "Look on the shore."

Debbie let out a cry. There on the shoreline, face down in the light waves, was Brady, still in his Storm outfit, unmoving. "Shaker's not even in him!"

"No, but he still wants to kill him as much as he will want to save you," the other demon sneered. "Too bad that we saved him the trouble."

The shadow figure was at the portal now, trying to cross and having difficulty. *He is still bound to the island.*

"That's what you get when you bless yourself so much we can't touch you," the other demon sniggered. "Water doesn't have to answer to anyone. Crosses and blessings don't protect you from drowning!"

They threw Brady into the lake and left him to drown. "Why kill him if you can't use him?" *They'll throw me into the lake to drown, too. Or maybe once the island demon touches me, I'll die anyway, if he takes my soul*

"Because Rigor got his soul, which goes a third of the way to fulfilling our end. And he's getting yours, too. 2 out of 3 ain't bad, that's what they say!" The demons evolved into laughing.

I don't want to do it, but I've got no choice. "Pitch! Baroness! Pike!"

In the space of a split second the three dogs came barreling out of the darkness of the ditch culvert, each slamming into a different demon. Freed, Debbie ran for the treeline, bracing herself for the sound of their death howls. Instead there was the sound of electricity snapping, and a trio of demonic shrieks. Debbie looked back to see the demons and the dogs had vanished, leaving only Grim, two more demons, and the shadowy figure which had managed to get one arm across the barrier, which had widened and lengthened to twice its original size.

"Nice trick," Ms. Grim said, grabbing hold of Debbie. "But there's no one to save you now." The demon let out an unearthly screech as its arm was severed, Debbie falling as she was pushed backward.

"Get back," Vassago said, standing over her, wielding Storm's sword from *Incubus*.

The two demons charged him. Vassago feinted and lunged, running one through and beheading the other. Both of the demons shrieked, their skin steaming as they dissipated into black smoke. Water was spilling now through the magical portal, the shadow figure standing in a spreading pool. With a triumphant horrific sucking sound, the figure stepped out from the doorway, water gushing behind him like a hydrant. Debbie stood up, the slimy water soaking her feet.

"Drop the sword," Grim said from behind Debbie and Vassago. "You're nothing but an incubus, your only power is seduction!"

The shadowy figure solidified into a figure in a dark cloak. It threw back its hood with one taloned hand, revealing a face that looked much like Shaker, except pitted and festering with evil. Red eyes looked her over eagerly.

"Rigor," Debbie breathed.

"Should have invited me to the wedding," Rigor rumbled, the bass crackling tones discordant and coarse with disuse. "But that'll be remedied now. You'll soon be calling for Shaker nonstop from the shores of my domain." He chuckled evilly. "He doesn't have the will to ignore you for long."

Anger filled Debbie. "He's ignored me just fine for the last month. You're making a mistake!"

Rigor went for Debbie and Vassago attacked him with the

sword, cutting into the robe's left side. The demon shrieked, grabbing Vassago, its talons sinking deep into his flesh. He lifted Vassago over his head to throw him through the doorway.

Debbie RUN! came Vassago's cry, the incubus changing form to a horned small creature with a lashing forked tail. It went for the demon's throat, tearing a gaping hole. Rigor bellowed. Taking hold of the creature in his hands, he ripped it in half, blood fountaining up.

Debbie went to her knees, her hands reflexively going to her ears as Vassago's scream of ultimate agony coursed through her mind. Off balance, she fell into the ditch, which was now flooded. Flailing for footing, she began climbing up the bank toward the forest, several splashes signifying something already coming after her.

With a raucous scream, the murder of crows burst out of the trees. They went for Grim, black wings flapping madly, several becoming men and women with black wings. Together, they lifted him and flew into the portal, towards the island.

"Go on, I can always use another demon on the Landing," Rigor croaked eagerly, reaching for Debbie.

A lightning bolt struck his hand, leaving a livid burn. The demon looked up in surprise as another bolt of energy hit his midsection, and another his left arm.

Namaath stood there, swirling shadows all around her flickering with red light, enraged. "You destroyed my son!" She hit him with another energy blast.

"Are you alright?" Myrrh said, helping Debbie up. "Go to the woods, call the dogs, they'll lead you home." She gave Debbie a push up the bank, then went to cross the ditch. She took one step in and went under.

"Myrrh!" Debbie shrieked, turning to wade into the water to help her friend.

"You had the element of surprise, but it availed you not," Rigor said, looming over a fallen Namaath, her shadows torn away, her face crisscrossed with burns. He picked up Vassago's sword. "You can join your son."

Dark and light blasts of energy hit Rigor, making him howl. Rene stood there like a warrior goddess, her pale blond beauty shining in the gloom, electricity cracking from her hands, Leri in her own nest of shadows beside her. "Titus sends his regards," Leri said, hellfire forming in her hands.

"You have no power over me," Rigor said. "In two hundred years of isolation and steady raw material, I've come up with a few tricks of my own." He gestured, throwing up both hands, an energy field forming around him. The women renewed their assaults with Hellfire and light energy, but the demon remained unscathed. He turned and came toward Debbie.

Debbie was feeling in the brackish water for Myrrh. She steeled her will and jumped in, her weight landing squarely on a red-haired woman as it broke the surface. The creature snarled at her with fish teeth, then bit into her arm. It let go a moment later, its eyes going white.

"Damn siren," Myrrh said, coughing as she emerged from the water, a bloody dagger in her hand. Bites covered both her arms, bleeding freely. "Come on, get out of the water, there's more of them down there. Blood draws them like sharks."

"You're not going anywhere," Rigor said, materializing in front of them.

"Let us go, grandfather," Myrrh said, blocking him from Debbie. "Go back to your domain."

"Child out of time," Rigor said almost kindly. "You're most like me, of all my kin. Proud to defy both Heaven and Hell in creating your own domain apart. Leave me to my prey, just as I have left you. Or suffer the consequences."

Rigor was suddenly lifted, then thrown back through the portal, his impotent yell trailing off as he landed near the shore on the rocks to the snapping of bone.

"Get back," Shaker intoned, heading toward the portal. He

grabbed up the sword. "We have to close the portal! Myrrh, call your souls!"

Myrrh let out a piercing whistle. The crows and crowmen who had crossed the barrier were flying hard, but as fast as they were flying the island was receding equally fast into the distance, the gush of the water through the portal lessening as it withdrew.

One crow hit the barrier, then another, cawing in desperation as their claws tried to scratch a way through. Shaker cut his wrist in a spray of blood, the droplets falling onto the portal door. Like acid, the surface bubbled and opened yawning holes, the crows bulleting through.

Titus appeared behind Shaker, both of them trying to hold the portal open.

"Bawdir, don't!" Myrrh shouted. "Leave him!"

All the crows were through but Bawdir, who was struggling to fly bearing Brady's body. His once black wings were white, shining like a beacon.

"Hold it," Shaker said, casting a look of pain at Debbie. He climbed into the portal, splashing as he hit the water.

"Shaker!" Debbie screamed.

Bawdir made it to the barrier just as there was a bright light coupled with a high-pitched whining. With a sudden crack, the portal snapped closed, Brady's body falling to the ground as Bawdir was cut in half, his upper body to his hips and his partial wings falling to the ground in a spray of blood. Titus let out a cry of pain, one of his fingers severed. A bloody hand also fell out of the portal, twitching.

"No!" Myrrh shouted, going to her knees.

There was the sound of sirens in the distance.

"Come on, we've got to leave," Titus said, picking up the still twitching hand. After putting it in his belt, he hefted Bawdir's remains gingerly. "Myrrh, you need to get Brady. I can't touch him."

"I should leave him here to get run over," Myrrh sniffled.

"Bawdir died to save him, though I'd have left him there, too," Debbie said softly. "C'mon, I'll help you. Titus, is Shaker okay?"

"He's safe onshore, but wounded," Titus said. "But don't worry, I can reattach his hand, and Leri can see to my finger. Devlin had to have felt that, he's going to be pissed."

Debbie looked around. "Where's Leri, Rene, and Namaath?"

"Everyone knows to disappear at the sound of sirens," Titus said, glancing at the car which was cut in two, the front squashed flat like a building had landed on it. "I can't wait to see how the police chief explains this."

~

"I'm sorry about Bawdir," Debbie said, putting a blanket around Myrrh's shoulders. "I liked him best of your flock."

"That's because he was the only one you knew by name," Myrrh sighed. "I know I shouldn't be sad. He died redeemed. I saw his wings were white, not even gray like they were last time I saw him in human form."

"You act surprised."

"I am," Myrrh said with a small smile. "He's my first success story."

Debbie gaped at her. "You mean that you've been doing your demon redemption program for years and this is the first time it has worked?"

"Heaven is very unforgiving, and it operates with a lot of rules that are biased, in my opinion." Myrrh defended. "I have no idea how much sin each of my crowmen have, or how easily each is forgiven. So I have no idea how long it will take for them to be forgiven by God." Myrrh smiled. "I just have hope that forgiveness for beings that strive to make amends is possible. Bawdir likely saved Brady because of all the blessings on him. It would be remiss of an angel to leave a blessed man on a demon-ruled isle."

"Rigor said he took Brady's soul."

"He did," Myrrh said. "But Brady's body was still alive, his life still flickering."

"How did he do that, if Brady was blessed?"

"That island is steeped in blood and curses. Blessings only work as long as faith in them lasts. Rigor's a master of working at a mind, warping it until it snaps. A pope could go to that island and succumb in a matter of days."

"I don't understand," Debbie said harshly. "Why should someone who did all the things Brady did be able to go and get blessed by a priest and be immune to demon attack because someone said some words. It's…unfair and unethical."

"He did die in the end," Myrrh reminded her. "And yes, his soul's still on the island, most likely. No matter how many prayers he had over him, I doubt any emissary from Heaven will be going there to get it back."

"Are the rest of the crows okay?"

"There is one that is unaccounted for," Myrrh said darkly. "The same one who wanted Pandora last year. She was obviously in league with Grim, who was also in league with Rigor. My guess is she flew to the island and hid there, though I doubt Rigor will give her or Grim much of a welcome home party after his defeat today."

"Why was he so powerful to overcome? And why didn't Shaker blast him?"

"Kin does not fight kin," Myrrh said. "It's a rule, you might say the one decent rule of Hell. That's why Rigor didn't just kill you or take your soul, he knew you were Shaker's wife. He wasn't just being a nice guy, offering you eternity imprisoned on the island."

Debbie repressed a shudder, petting the three dogs, that were lying at their feet, Pitch again with all four feet in the air. "Thanks also for what you did for the dogs. It was ingenious of you to put a homing/teleport spell into the new collars."

"I…remain touched that they mean so much to you," Myrrh said, blinking her eyes and looking away. "I've never known a human woman to embrace an inherently dark creature with love and affection. Or believe it could…overcome its own nature."

Is she crying? If she is, she won't want me to ask. "I didn't used to," Debbie said, sipping her wine. "Ironically, it was Shaker that made me believe it was possible. He's a demon and he still looks at a lot of things in a way we can't agree on. But I love him. I think any creature with intelligence makes its own choice on how to behave, choosing the light or the dark. I believe there's hope for forgiveness, too."

"I'm sorry I didn't get to you faster." Myrrh cleared her throat. "It took a few moments to contain the three demons who the dogs brought back with them, then use one of the collars to jump back to where you are. I'm glad you called for them. I was blocked from you completely, and I'm guessing Shaker was, also."

Vassago wasn't. And he came, though it meant his death.

Myrrh looked at Debbie, opened her mouth then shut it, looking away.

"Go ahead and respond to my thoughts, it's obvious to me you read them all the time," Debbie snapped.

"He must have really cared for you, is all I was going to say," Myrrh said, taking Debbie's hand. "He knew they'd kill him easily, just as he knew they'd let him walk away unscathed if he stepped aside."

"Shaker said it was impossible for demons to die," Debbie said slowly. "So is Vassago in Hell?"

Myrrh nodded. "Rigor destroyed his true body. I saw his remains when I was lifting Bawdir."

"Can he get another one?"

"Not for a long time. Incubi are pretty low on Hell's roster. And he died for what will be viewed a romantic noble reason. He'll likely get extra torture, not a commendation."

Debbie gathered herself. "If I was able to get him out, could you turn him into one of your crows?"

Myrrh laughed, then saw Debbie was serious. "I see his sacrifice left a mark. First, getting him out wouldn't be easy. Secondly, no, I wouldn't. Even with what he did for you, I don't think he could be redeemed in a hundred years. He's too carefree and fun-loving."

Debbie nodded. "You're probably right." *But that doesn't mean he deserves eternity in Hell, either.*

~

"Hello," Leri said, standing in the doorway of Debbie's office. "It looks like everyone has left but you and me."

"The Friday before Christmas Eve is usually a ghost town here," Debbie agreed. "What's on your mind?"

"I just wanted to tell you that I'll need to go part time next year," Leri said. "I'm going to be watching my granddaughter much more often."

"Congratulations," Debbie said politely. "Was she just born?"

"She'll be a year old soon, though she looks about three," Leri said happily. "All supernatural children age quickly when they mate with humans." She shrugged. "My daughter in law is human."

"Don't you approve?" Debbie asked. *Why is she telling me this?*

"It is she who doesn't approve that much of me," Leri corrected. "I have a chance to change her mind, so I'm going to try. The first step is free babysitting."

Well, it's nearly Christmas, everyone deserves happy endings. "Thank you again for all you've done for us," Debbie said, standing and rooting on her desk. "Here's your Christmas bonus, I wasn't sure where to mail it, as you always got your checks in person."

Leri took it, then looked at her, expectant.

"What?" Debbie said finally.

"I'm here for more than this," Leri said meaningfully. "I've also felt your thoughts these last few weeks, and the question you want to ask. So ask it."

"Can you put me in touch with Namaath?"

"Yes. Why do you want to see her?"

255

"She's the mother of Vassago. I wanted to ask her if she can get him out of Hell."

"She can. But I can, as well."

"Shaker warned me about you," Debbie said quietly. "He said there wasn't much you couldn't do, but what you'd ask in return would always be something I wouldn't want to give. Namaath has her own skin in the game, she should want to rescue her son."

"I'm resisting the urge to cackle," Leri said, chuckling. "You give me hope for the wisdom of humans, Debbie. As it happens, I'm heading to see her now. I'll ask her to see you. No strings."

"Thanks," Debbie said, then went back to work as Leri left.

There was a knock at her door, then Sheila opened it. "It's Friday, are you going home, or should I bring you a sleeping bag?"

"Soon," Debbie said tiredly. "Myrrh's left some crows on guard, so I don't have to hurry. It seemed like a good evening to catch up." She faked a smile.

"I know you've been down," Sheila said from Debbie's doorway. "Still no word?"

"Shaker's likely molding Brady's body into Jett's, in the hope he can return to acting," Debbie supplied. "Or he's healing his hand being severed, or maybe both. I'm looking forward to his return. But I'm not sure why he hasn't contacted me. It can't be a good sign."

"Look, if you're up for some fun, why not come to a wedding we're going to? It's tonight, and Song's teleporting us in."

"My first night out in months!" Song said, sticking her head in the door. "I can't wait. And I haven't seen Elijah or Harp since before I was pregnant."

Debbie's brow furrowed. "I don't think whoever's getting married will want me to crash their reception."

"Elijah would love to meet you," Song assured. "He doesn't have many friends, as in I can count them on one hand. Most people there will be people of standing in the vampire community."

"He's the groom?"

"Yes. He'll love you. So will the bride, Elle, she's demon friendly, if you treat her fairly. She's let me stay at her house before. Devlin will be there, too, as well as Danial. He paid for this big party, I believe."

Wait a minute. "Who is Elle to Danial?"

"His adopted daughter. Oh and Lash should be there too, at least briefly." Song tittered. "Danial and he don't get along. It's funny to hear the things they say to each other at parties. I confess I'm hoping for a scene, maybe even a fight."

Danial and Devlin together means that Sar will be there, too. Better make sure. "And Elle's mom?"

"Her adopted mom Sarelle will be there," Song said, thinking. "So will Rene, she's linked to Devlin now, too. I'm not sure if Shaker will be there, but you might see him."

Oh I'll see him. And get some answers. Debbie grabbed her coat. "I'm in. Can we stop by my house quick to change?"

$\sim$

Debbie walked in wearing her Oscar's dress to the Baltimore Ann Arbor Hotel ballroom behind Song and Sheila. "Wow this place is gorgeous."

"See, there is Elle and Elijah," Song pointed to a long table, where a bride with long blond hair down to her waist was sharing a forkful of bloody meat with the red-eyed groom.

"What is he?" Debbie whispered, putting her bottle of Incubus on the table piled with gifts.

"A dhampir, a half vampire, half human." Song pointed again, putting their wrapped gift beside Debbie's offering. "There's Devlin and Rene dancing. Ah, there's Danial and Sarelle."

Debbie looked over, expecting to see a warrior goddess. Sarelle was beautiful, but not as breathtaking as Rene, who was wearing a similar dress and resembled a young Michelle Pfeffer. *She has the same long blonde hair as Elle, but hers is dyed.* Debbie shook her head. *Stop being so petty. You're here to find out about Shaker. And maybe introduce yourself.*

"Debbie," Lash hissed, coming up to her. "What are you doing here? You're not on the guest list."

"She's with us," Song said. "She's hoping to see Shaker."

"I guess it's okay," Lash said, nodding. "Just don't start trouble, okay?"

"I'm not sure what you mean," Debbie said lightly.

The smile left Lash's face. "Stay away from Sar." He moved past them to the next people coming in the door.

"Well, I guess there goes my plan," Debbie said.

"Come over and meet Harp," Song said, taking her arm. "Have a glass of wine. You're here to have fun, remember?"

Debbie let herself be led away. The next few hours passed quickly, and enjoyably, as she nibbled on delicious food, including some chocolate chip cookies whose taste was all too familiar. She had a second glass of wine, and was standing by herself watching the orchestra, when Devlin came up to her. "Debbie, hello. Song mentioned you were here, so I wanted to greet you."

I hope he's not going to be full of himself again. Damn it, watch what you say, he's a big investor. "Hello, Devlin. I'm glad to see you. Did you know the devil came to my Halloween party and he dressed as you?"

Devlin's mouth fell open. "You're kidding."

"Nope," Song said, coming over. "I saw it myself. It was a great glamour."

"I'm honored," Devlin said, breaking into a grin. "What else can I say?"

"You can tell me who this is," Sarelle said from behind him, her eyes blazing with jealousy. She looked Debbie up and down. "I don't recognize her."

"This is Debbie Black," Devlin said. "She runs Pandora Productions, an independent movie studio."

"I've looked forward to meeting you for some time," Debbie

said smoothly, offering her hand. "Devlin is an investor of ours. And a very talented musician."

Sarelle looked from Devlin, who was shifting uncomfortably, back to Debbie. "Yes, he is."

"Excuse me," Devlin said, looking over at Danial across the room, who was signaling to him. "He's indicating there's something I need to help him with." Devlin headed away.

Debbie looked around and saw that Sheila and Song had also moved away and were watching her. *They're waiting for the big scene. I might as well get to it.* "Are you enjoying the party? Your daughter is beautiful."

"I'd say which one, but I know you mean the bride," Sarelle laughed, the motion making her harried expression vanish in a swell of happiness. "Yes, Elle is beautiful, and I'm so glad she's found Elijah. He loves her, and they'll be happy together. They already have a baby boy."

Debbie fought down a wave of jealousy. "I'm glad you're also back. Devlin was bereft without you last year."

Sarelle turned to Debbie in slow motion, her face going white as a sheet. Debbie thought for a moment the woman would strike her, then the moment passed.

Sarelle put the glass down with a bang so hard Debbie was amazed the wineglass didn't break. "Who are you? Tell me right now."

"I'm just who Devlin said I was—Mrs. Black. I was married to Jett Black, who passed away last year–"

"Oh, I think I read about that last year," Sarelle interrupted. "I'm sorry. Elle's father just died a few weeks ago, one of the reasons we had to postpone her wedding for the third time. He was my former husband." She twisted her wedding band, then her hand went to the two chokers at her throat.

"You're Oathed to Devlin and Danial," Debbie said. "Those are beautiful pendants, the fox and the bear."

"And what do you think of my scars?" Sarelle said in a ragged voice, her green eyes boring holes into Debbie's. "Everyone sees them, yet no one mentions them, because here it's a sign of respect. In the mortal world, strangers offer me pity, thinking I was attacked by dogs."

There is a terrible pain to her, like a woman on the edge. "I understand," Debbie said, taking Sar's hand in hers and squeezing. "I had a miscarriage last year. No one wants to talk about what happened, and everyone who has a baby, they're careful what they say. I feel like I can't stand if they mention it, but I also can't stand if they treat it like an elephant in the room."

Sar squeezed her hand. "I went through that myself, so I know what you mean. Please don't give up. Have you and the father tried again?"

"He's my husband. Yes, he wants to. I'm not ready," Debbie said, wanting her hand back and not willing to try to yank it out of the other woman's grasp. "I'm worried it won't work."

"You should try again. Don't give up. I love being a mother. Is the father a vampire too? Or a faerie?"

"No, a full demon," Debbie said, enunciating each word slowly. "His name is Shaker."

Sarelle's eyes bugged out of her head. Her hand tightened on Debbie's like a vice, and she screeched out "SHAKER!" at top volume.

The band went silent. Everyone turned to stare.

"Damn it to Hell," Lash swore, pushing past people, his expression murderous.

Shaker appeared, looked at Debbie, then at Sarelle. "I'm here, Mistress."

Lash reached them, going to Debbie. Shaker blocked him. "Get out of my way. I will not have my Mate upset, Shaker, she's been through enough."

"Stop," Sarelle said, throwing out her arm to block Lash. "Shaker, is it true this woman is your wife?"

"Yes," Shaker said in relief.

"Why the Hell didn't you say something?" Sarelle shouted.

Devlin came running up. "What is going on? You're frightening all the guests."

"If they were scared by a little screaming, they wouldn't have been invited to this party,' Sarelle said darkly, her eyes fixed on Debbie. "You came here to make me aware of you. You have. Now what do you want?"

Debbie took a deep breath. "I want you to let Shaker come back to me and live as my husband. I understand he's bound to you, and I'm grateful you kept him out of Hell. But he wants to go back to acting, and there's a body he can possess, to make that possible. I understand he also may need to drop everything and come to you in an emergency, and I accept that." She looked over at Rene, who had also come running up, followed by Leri and Titus. "And I thank you again for helping Shaker with his...sustenance."

"Does everyone here besides me know this woman and who she is?" Sarelle said, glaring at Rene, Devlin, Shaker, Lash, Leri and Titus. No one met her eyes.

"I don't," the bride said, striding up to stand next to her mother. "Why are you at my wedding? I didn't invite you. And you're upsetting my mom. Please leave."

"You know, Sarelle. I'd give anything to have a daughter like her," Debbie said, tearing up. "You should remember how lucky you are." She turned to leave.

"I'm okay," Sarelle said, grabbing Debbie's arm while blinking her eyes very fast. "This is just a shock. I had no idea. Shaker, you should have said something."

"What's going on," a gorgeous young woman said, striding up. "Mom?"

"This is my other daughter, Venus," Sarelle said. "Girls, meet Shaker's wife, Debbie Black."

~

"It was so good to meet you," Debbie said, hugging Sarelle hard. "And yes, please send me any recipes you have. I really like the chocolate chip cookies."

Sarelle smiled. "Thanks, it's my own family recipe. Please feel free to come and visit soon. You're family."

"I'm not," Debbie said, then looked at Shaker. "Am I?"

"You're related as Sarelle has been exposed to demon blood on multiple occasions," Titus boomed in Debbie's ear, startling her. "I gave her a transfusion of my blood. She's my kin by blood. You're my kin via marriage."

"Close enough," Sar said. "Bring Myrrh, I'd love to meet her. I didn't know Shaker had a daughter." She glared at him. "You are to be more forthcoming from now on."

"Yes, Mistress."

"Goodnight," Debbie said, as Sarelle and her two vampires walked away, Lash following them, still shooting dark looks at Debbie.

"I have to go as well," Shaker said, hugging her. "But I'll be with you as soon as I can." Before Debbie could respond, he teleported her home, and left her in her house.

"Pitch, Pike, Baroness!" Debbie called, setting down her bag. "Come out. Treats all around!

～

Later that night, Debbie felt a light blackness touch the edges of her mind, then looked up from reading to see Namaath hovering outside the window. Debbie opened the glass. "Hello."

"Good evening."

"Are you okay to talk, um, hovering?"

"Your kin-daughter has warded the property well, I can't even get close enough to pull you from the window," Namaath said. "Now what is it you wanted?"

"Can you get Vassago out of Hell?"

"Yes, but it wouldn't help him," Namaath said miserably. "His body is destroyed beyond healing. He's not a demon as Shaker is, able to regenerate a new body when he is let out of Hell. Incubi live forever and their domain is this world. He was such a gentle boy."

"Is a new body all he would need?" Debbie asked.

Namaath shook her head. "No, because when he was forced into Hell, he ceased to be an Incubus. Now he's a regular demon, albeit one almost at the bottom of the food chain."

"You're saying he needs a Mistress."

Namaath looked at her sharply. "Are you volunteering? I thought you'd sworn off demons."

"He died for me," Debbie stated. "That means something. I'm not going to just leave him there if I can help him. But no, I can't give my soul to free him."

Namaath nodded. "There is one other way, but it's painful, very painful. And he'll still need a body."

"I think I know someone who can help us."

"You want me to what?" Rene asked, her French accent heavy in her confusion. "Titus said you called, but I thought it was to talk to Sar."

Debbie gritted her teeth, then went over to lock her office door. "Create a body for Vassago. You said you had done it before, with Sar's help."

"Yes, with some raw material. It's not like I have human bones and hair and skin laying around to work with. The process takes time, months usually."

"Can you do it?"

"Why do you want this?"

"Vassago saved my life. If he hadn't delayed him, Rigor would have taken me to the island. And Shaker might have been trapped there, rescuing me. Sarelle, your 'sister' as I understand from her, would have either been pulled in also or killed outright if Shaker had been trapped."

"Yes, you're right that he inadvertently saved her as well as you. Do you think you can get Vassago out of Hell yourself?"

"No. Namaath said she can, though she tells me I'll have to do something painful."

"You know, you are much like Sar, in your quest to do what is right at all costs," Rene murmured, watching her. "I have more of that in my character now, from all the time she and I have spent together." Rene held up a hand. "You don't have to remind me again. I told you I owed you a big favor, for your information that you told Myrrh and she passed on to me. I will make a body for Vassago, though I can't guarantee it will be handsome as the old one was."

"Can you make him a temporary vessel, so he can get out of Hell now?"

Rene laughed. "You are a treat in your boldness. Yes, I have just the form. I will speak with Namaath, our coven is tomorrow night."

~

"Sit still, and don't bite your tongue. This is going to hurt."

Debbie gritted her teeth, pain wracking her. *It feels like she's tearing out one of my organs!*

"There," Namaath said, a shining piece of light in her hand. She dropped it in a silver locket, then shut it. "When I emerge from the portal with him, hand this to him." She handed the chain to Debbie.

Debbie waited by the portal spot for hours, trying not to fall asleep, alternately nervous and so tired she had to switch positions to stop from falling asleep.

A vivid spectrum of lights shone through the floor, then a ripping noise like tearing of sailcloth. Namaath's hand emerged. "Debbie, pull him!"

Debbie flailed getting up and fell. She crawled to the edge of the portal, then looked down into a fiery abyss. Figures were swarming Namaath, who was protecting a burnt hollow of a man, his eyes shut tight. Debbie reached in and grabbed the figure's arm and pulled with all of her might. He didn't budge.

"Debbie hurry! I can't hold them!"

Put the chain on him. Debbie grasped the chain, trying to loop it over the figure's head, but it wasn't long enough. The figures swarming Namaath stopped still for a second, then all came for Debbie.

Debbie shoved the chain in the figure's mouth, which finally got a response. The figure gagged, saw her, and lunged up into her waiting arms. *Debbie?*

"Pull!" Rene said, appearing near Debbie, her hands reaching for Vassago's torso. Together they hefted him out, as Namaath went under the massing crowd of figures. Vassago landed full on Debbie, knocking her head against the floor and making her see stars.

Rene shot Hellfire into the midst, helped a well-singed Namaath out of the portal, then closed it.

"Last time I attempt a rescue alone," Namaath said grumpily, looking at her scratch-covered skin. "I just healed up from wounds from Rigor."

"Easy to fix," Rene said, blue healing light beginning to shine from her hands.

"What about Vassago?" Debbie said, sitting up. "Where is he?"

"Adjusting to the new body," Rene said, as she finished healing Namaath. "I'd give him some time tonight alone, before calling him." They both vanished.

"And faeries call demons cryptic bastards." Debbie looked in all of her rooms but saw nothing out of place. Leaving the three dogs sleeping on her bed, she took a shower, then settled down to read.

There was a noise from the living room.

All three dogs looked up and growled. Then Baroness gave a slight whine and began to wag her tail.

A sleek hound, larger than the other three, came trotting into the room, and sat down.

"Vassago?"

Rene said it would teach me some humility. Namaath said it would teach me to sacrifice myself for a human.

"Are you okay?"

That depends if you have some room in that bed for me. The dog grinned at her and wagged his tail hopefully.

"Sure," Debbie said. "Everybody move over." *Note, buy a king-size bed tomorrow.*

Vassago curled up and fell asleep almost instantly near Debbie's side. The other three dogs curled up against him and Debbie and also fell asleep.

Debbie looked at them lovingly, then turned off the light.

Debbie awoke in dreams, arms around her. For an instant she struggled, sure it was some demon that had escaped the portal of Hell.

I am that demon, Vassago said in her mind, hugging her. *Thank you.*

"Are you hurt?"

"I'm okay, but would like never to go back," Vassago said, nuzzling her. "There's no hugging in Hell."

"Why'd you do that, sacrifice yourself?" *When there was no way you could win?*

"I was never a hero before. No one ever expected me to be one. No one ever expected me to be better than I was, an incubus whose only renown is being a good lover." He kissed her. "No one ever called me to come to the rescue. There was no way I wouldn't answer you."

"You shouldn't have done it."

"Shaker would have," Vassago said. "That's all I kept thinking, was that Shaker would have, so I should, too."

"I'm not sure he would have," Debbie murmured. "Not because he didn't love me, but he'd hesitate to give his life to buy only a few minutes." She hugged him. "Sorry, I'm sounding like an ungrateful bitch. Thank you. If you hadn't fended them off, I'd be there now on that island."

"Oh, I had an endgame," Vassago assured. "I knew he'd kill me. I knew it'd be painful. But my mother would hear my mental scream of pain, and she'd come. Between both of us, we'd buy enough time for Myrrh to get there."

And Shaker?

"I sent him a mental text *Follow me to Deb!* I knew he would, if he wasn't already there with you."

"Thank you," Debbie said. "I'm glad you're okay. Rene is making you a new body, but it will take time."

"Thank you," Vassago said. "No one has ever done anything like this for me before." *No one would have, either.*

"Your mom would have."

"She isn't pleased about what I did for you, and thought I needed some time in Hell to adjust my attitude. She thinks I've fallen in love with my character on the series and forgotten what's expected of a demon." He kissed her cheek. "Your offer to help me compelled her to reverse her decision." He kissed her again. "I'll be a good watchdog, until I'm rehomed in my new body."

"So you're happy?"

"Of course. I'm in bed with you," he teased. "This is what I've been wanting all year."

"We were already in bed," Debbie said, giving him a dark look. "In a dream like this one."

"Yes but you know it's me this time. You want me here. You gave a piece of your soul to make it happen." He kissed her lips lightly. "That makes all the difference."

"But I don't love you," Debbie said gently.

"I'm not here for sex." Vassago got out the words, then took a long shuddering breath. "I can't believe I can finally say that. And mean it."

Debbie looked at him, realization dawning. "Your mother said you're not an incubus anymore. You're a regular demon."

"I'm not sure what I am," Vassago admitted. "But my life revolved around sex when I needed it to eat and live. Now that clawing ache that was always inside me is gone." He kissed her lips again. "Not that I don't want you, because I do. Our lovemaking was fantastic. You're so open and bold."

"I'm glad for you. Glad for me, too. I won't have to worry about you draining my energy."

Vassago laughed. "I never fed from you, Debbie. Didn't you know that? I was with you for intimacy, just like I said I was. That's probably why your daughter Myrrh didn't banish me outright."

Debbie leaned in to kiss him again, and felt the dream fading. She opened her eyes. "Damn it!" Stymied, she got out of bed, then started her day.

～

Myrrh appeared, holding out her hand. "Are you ready?"

"Yes," Debbie said, taking it.

They appeared in a large overgrown garden adjoining an ancient orchard, the trees gnarled and twisted. Snow covered much of the land in deep drifts, though the path they walked was bare stones.

"I hope you'll let me come back in Spring," Debbie said, marveling at the huge stone mansion and outbuildings.

"It will be pretty again then, when the flowers bloom. Winter is the season of death."

"I have to ask, why did you wait to have this funeral," Debbie asked.

"Christmas may be a time of giving gifts, but it's also supposed to be Jesus's birthday," Myrrh said. "Bawdir was redeemed and is in Heaven, an angel once more. I thought he would appreciate us having a ceremony for him this day, instead of the solstice, or the turning of the New Year."

"Everything is ready," a man said, his black wings shifting.

Myrrh followed him into a very old chapel, a plain cross there on the altar. An urn rested on the floor before it.

"Death is before me today, like the recovery of a sick man, like going into a garden after sickness," Myrrh intoned. "Death is before me today, like the odor of myrrh, like sitting under a sail in a good wind. Death is before me today, like the course of a stream, like the return of a man from the war-galley to his house. Death is before me today, like the home that a man longs to see, after years spent as a captive." She lay her hand on the urn. "Enjoy your eternity, Bawdir. We were all graced to know you and will remember you."

Myrrh turned to leave, her crowmen already transforming into birds and taking to the skies. Debbie followed her outside. It was beginning to snow.

"That was it?" Debbie ventured.

"The crows can't take being in the chapel long," Myrrh explained. "I left it consecrated. I also feel an uncomfortable tingling inside. Besides, Bawdir is gone. What is left of him will wait there for spring, and we will till him into the earth." She turned to Debbie. "Do you want me to take you home?"

"My uncle and mother are hosting their annual party," Debbie explained. "I was invited but refused because of Shaker. I could have gone anyway but I think I crashed enough parties this year."

"You don't have plans?"

"Don't you want me to stay?" Debbie said, biting her lip. "You're my only family, Myrrh." Debbie took a breath. "You're my daughter. We should be together at Christmas."

Myrrh embraced her. "Of course I want you to stay…Mother."

Debbie and Myrrh stayed up late on Christmas Eve near a roaring fire, drinking wine and eating comfort foods, as they threw lighted balls for the four dogs to chase. In time, Myrrh led her up to her room, a cozy wooden room with no windows. "Sorry that there isn't a window, but the upper rooms with views are all terribly cold this time of year. This is the warmest room next to my own."

"Goodnight," Debbie said, giving her another hug.

Myrrh hugged her tightly. "Goodnight, Mother. I'll see you in the morning." She hurried away.

Debbie snuggled under the covers, the dogs around her. *I was wrong to envy Sarelle her daughter Elle. I have a daughter just as brave and fierce and loyal, I just had to be willing to see her.*

∼

Debbie got into bed wearily, the hounds all snuggling around her. "You know you'll have to vacate the bed if Shaker returns," she warned them. They ignored her, stretching out still more, until she was squashed into a sliver of the bed. *I really have to get a king size bed. Hopefully there will be some after Christmas sales.*

"Debbie," a voice called from the living room.

"Hello?" Debbie called. "Who is it?"

There was no answer.

Secure in the knowledge that the watching crows and wards were still in place, Debbie went out to the living room and turned on the light. There, standing before her in his Storm costume of black leather jacket, sunglasses, and ripped jeans, was Jett.

Shaker.

Who else? He tossed aside the sunglasses and grabbed her with a growl, his lips seeking hers feverishly.

Debbie kissed him back hard, her blind need eclipsing everything. *You did it! How'd you do it?*

Vass had nothing to fight for except himself. I have you and us. He took her nightshirt in both hands and ripped it apart, buttons dropping on the floor and rolling in all directions. "Very nice," he said, running a hand over the gold and dark burgundy lace of her camisole. "I see you've been consoling yourself with your charge cards."

270

Debbie grabbed his face with both hands and kissed him, her tongue teasing in, then darting away. *Stop talking and kiss me.*

"I'm merely making sure you know it's me," Shaker chided. "Though you should know my body well by now, just as I know yours." He ran his hands again over the lace. "If only I had some nipple clamps."

"What?" Debbie said raggedly, drawing back in alarm.

"Your nipples, my dear," Shaker said, taking one breast out of the bra, and folding the cup cloth under it, so it stood at attention. He kissed one lightly, then drew just the tip into his wet mouth, biting it gently before releasing it. "They've been lacking attention. You deserve a little bondage for the Hell you put me through, but perhaps clamps are too extreme. But some nipple chain might be just the thing. Ah, that's right, I have one in my pocket." He slipped a silver cord from his pocket with loops at both ends. Before she could stop him, he slipped both lassos over her nipples and tightened them, the sudden pressure making her take a sharp breath.

"There," he said in approval. "My bad little mistress who needs punishing." He gave a sharp pull on the chain making Debbie cry out. He then grabbed the chain and pulled it. Debbie went with him, protesting.

"Stop! They're too tight!"

"Not tight enough." Shaker pulled the little nooses tighter, turning Debbie's nipples purple. "There. I like to watch the chain swing between your breasts." *I'll like it more when you're riding me. Mistress.* He pushed the camisole off her shoulders, letting it fall. Then he eased down his jeans, baring his rigid cock in the nest of dark pubic hair. *Part your legs and welcome me home.* Shaker grabbed the chain and slowly sat on the couch, then pulled Debbie by her breasts to straddle him.

He rolled over on her, thrusting the length of himself inside in one long movement. Then he buried his face in her breasts, sucking the already tender nubs, biting gently. Debbie moaned, the feel of her tender flesh ultra-sensitive.

"Wait." He removed the lassos, massaging the nubs. Debbie breathed a sigh of relief, then a gasp as he stretched her nipples then reattached the loops farther in. "The more to suck on," Shaker said wickedly, beginning to thrust again.

Debbie's nipples throbbed now, the steady tingling almost like pain, but different.

God they're so full and soft, so big and beautiful. Shaker thrust faster, then stopped suddenly with a groan. He rolled over onto his back, then gave the chain another tug. "Ride me, Mistress."

Debbie began to move, but Shaker didn't let go of the chain. Her movements forward gave the chain slack, while backward tightened the chain, pulling both nipples. The sensation was new and utterly erotic. Too fast, Debbie was there, grinding home her orgasm in loud, sweet release. Shaker let out a groan just like pain, then rough grunts as his lust was sated.

Debbie went to move off him, but Shaker grabbed hold of the chain. "No, you're staying right where you are." He tugged the chain once more. "Now move, Mistress."

⁓

"Damn," Debbie said, massaging her breasts as Shaker removed the nooses from her nipples one at a time. "That felt amazing."

"Of course it did," Shaker agreed, grabbing her in a bear hug. "I wanted it to be the best for both of us, this first time back together."

"Are you back?" she asked tentatively. *Are we back together?*

"Do you want me?" he whispered.

"I always wanted you. I just had to draw a line somewhere."

"Even if it was across my heart, bisecting it in two?"

"I never meant to hurt you. I'm sorry for the things I said."

"I'm sorry you said them to me, too."

"Hey," Debbie said, annoyed.

"I'm sorry we fought. I can't say I'm sorry for what I said. I told you the truth." He paused. "I don't blame you for not knowing Brady was me, even if you still blame yourself. That's what was behind most of your anger, wasn't it?"

"And that you didn't tell your Mistress about who you really were and are."

"You did that for me," Shaker quipped. He took a deep breath. "I foresaw that, actually. My visions skipped over a lot of important stuff I neglected to see, like Brady coming to after I'd put him in a stasis, but it showed me that. Which is why I couldn't tell her when you asked me to; I had to wait for you to do it yourself."

"Nice save," Debbie complained. "Why didn't the magical stasis work?"

"Because I have a charm from Myrrh, also. Spending time in Brady, especially the magical transfusion of blood I did initially, it mixed enough of my essence in that he had a good resistance to magic. That's also why he ended up working for Angel Pictures, instead of just getting possessed again. Well, that and all the active blessings, the boy must have gone from church to church and gotten one every single day since getting back here. Thank God for Liquid Sin."

"So that's how you were able to take possession again? Titus was able to make some?"

Shaker nodded. "Sheila's off the cuff suggestion last year was an excellent idea. Titus worked on it himself for a while, then pulled in Leri. She's the best dark witch there is. I understand there were a lot of apologies for him sending her to Hell that Leri made him utter before she agreed to help him. Liquid Sin is a kind of liquid curse, able to bring all a person's flaws to the surface to overwhelm the good traits. Brady needed a lot of applications to get through the blessings. Even then, my skin crawled for a week."

"That must be potent stuff. All that work with Brady to keep him alive and work on him had to take enormous effort. Did you pay Titus, or did he help you because he's our brother?"

"Our brother," Shaker repeated, studying her intently. "Good. And yes, I consider having to reattach fingers over and above. I stole an object of power from Cyrus. I gave it to Titus."

"How is your hand?"

Shaker held it out for her. "You were fondled by it with no complaints. Applying a nipple chain is no mean feat with limited dexterity, never mind removing it."

Debbie swatted him. "So you're healed. Where do we go from here?"

"As you can see, I have possession of Brady's body. He doesn't need it, his soul passed out of it onto Latham's Landing. I've modified it some to look more like Jett."

"What will happen to Brady's soul?"

"Let's just say there will be a lot of moments in the years to come where he regrets saying he wanted out." Shaker grinned his shark's smile.

"Bawdir meant to save you, he thought it was you."

The smile left his face. "I would still be there in that house. It was only all the blessings and crosses and evil-repelling herbs that Brady had on him that let his body be rescued still breathing. Even then, Bawdir took a mortal wound saving this body."

"I know," Debbie said. "I'll miss him, he was a good person."

"Don't be sad, he's in Heaven, redeemed, what his goal was," Shaker assured. "No one with any taint could have scooped a body from the grip of my father."

"You're sure it was him? Rigor?"

Shaker nodded. "It was him I saw watching you that day you and I went there. We were alone for a few minutes, waiting for the cast and crew who were late on the highway. You had your waking dream a few hours later." He paused. "He must have engineered a way to make a portal off the island. Latham's been gone for close to a hundred and twenty years, it figures Rigor finally found a way off, at least for brief excursions."

"But you think he's still bound there?"

Shaker nodded. "If he wasn't, he'd have shown up just to make his presence known long before now. And he wouldn't have needed to make a portal that led from this world right to the island shoreline."

"I met the devil at the Night Carnival on Halloween," Debbie whispered.

"You did?" Shaker said in surprise. "What did he say?"

Debbie flushed dark red. "That you were free to act or do whatever, because being with me caused you more torture than anything he could do to you."

Shaker laughed. "Satan always did have a sense of humor."

"So what about your Mistress?"

"She's jealous, about what I expected. But she's also relieved, because she doesn't have to worry about meeting my needs."

"You should have told me she had three other guys. That she had children with all of them and is a workaholic to boot. I wouldn't have been jealous."

"Yes, you would," Shaker corrected. "And I did tell you she had three other guys, just not that she had five children. You just weren't in a mood to believe me."

"So she gave you permission to come back to me?"

"I'm to check in with her each week, and come if she calls, no exceptions. But yes, she's given permission. Devlin, Danial, and Lash aren't super happy, they think she's putting herself at risk. But as usual, she's reserved the right to choose her own path herself." He hugged Debbie. "I'm glad you're both going to be friendly, if not friends. It makes this all easier." He paused. "And how was the big holiday party at Pandora?"

"I don't know. I didn't go," Debbie said with a shrug and a grin.

Shaker blinked. "What?"

"I spent the holidays with Myrrh. It was wonderful, actually. I never had a female relative to do traditional things with like that. We went sledding, and skating, and cooked a few cookies, and walked at her place. And we spent a few days here too, streaming some series and drinking wine and eating and talking." Debbie paused. "She's an interesting woman."

"You're a good mom," Shaker said tenderly. "And no man could ask for a better wife."

"You know, I would have scoffed if you told me I'd be thrilled to hear someone say that," Debbie whispered. "But I am." She nuzzled him. "Are you going to give me any assurances about next year?"

"Hmm, like will it be easy? Probably not. Angel Pictures is missing its leadership. We'll need to act fast to take control. But I did go to the party, and so heard that our revenue was above last years. Sheila did a great speech. *Dare to Tell* just released, and it's getting a good share of the holiday crowds. *Hell to Pay* didn't fare as well, but it's getting a small cult following, Lash may get his chance to be a hero after all. *Destiny in the Ashes* didn't release on schedule, as Brady sued at the eleventh hour, stopping it from releasing. But I'll cancel that, and we can release next year."

"You're a good partner and husband."

"I know."

"So much for humility."

"How's this then? I'll love you and you'll love me, and we'll make good movies, and enjoy this life and each other and our dogs and our daughter."

"Good because the dogs are all there in the doorway."

Shaker beckoned, and three of the dogs came to him tails wagging. "Myrrh got you a fourth hound?"

"That's Vassago," Debbie said gently. "Rene's making him a new body."

"So she got you out of Hell," Shaker said gruffly. He looked again at Debbie closely. "I thought your soul looked a little frayed on one side. You gave him a piece."

Debbie nodded. "He saved both of us."

Shaker grimaced. "So he did." He held out his hand to Vassago. "Being a regular demon's a lot easier than an incubus. I'll show you the ropes. And you'll have it easy, having a piece of soul, as you won't have to find a Mistress or Master to serve."

One big happy family Vassago said telepathically. *I can't wait.*

EPILOGUE

THE SMALL HOUSE MADE OF STONE WAS CHEERY IN THE HEAVY morning fog, the lighted windows hazy glows in the dew-filled air. Titus appeared outside the front door, then knocked.

Leri let him in, her simple dress of blue cotton covered with blood and other fluids. "It's done."

Titus went into the main room, where a young redheaded woman lay very weak, still hemorrhaging blood. "Why aren't you collecting this?" he asked Leri, as he began working a spell to stop her bleeding. "Fairy blood is one of the most potent and useful."

"Because I've just helped her finally give birth, after two solid days of trying," Leri snapped. "I've had my hands full, Titus. I don't have the power to heal her."

"She's bad off," Titus said, working faster. "You should have called me sooner."

"She can't see you, or know what she really gave birth to," Leri hissed. "But you must save her, if you can."

"Let me work," he said gruffly. "Tend to the child."

Leri moved away towards a small wrapped bundle in an old wicker bassinet, as Titus began chanting.

~

Leri was feeding the baby the evening of the next day, when Titus appeared, looking haggard. "At least it's done," he said, sitting down heavily. "Though in retrospect it would have been better to kill her."

"She doesn't know anything, and she helped me, when she didn't have to," Leri snapped again. "Stop being a demon asshole and start showing some compassion. You're an uncle now."

"Yes," Titus rumbled, sitting near her. "Girl or boy?"

"Girl." Leri shifted the baby to Titus. "Myrrh, Shaker said Debbie wanted to call her. He said he liked that name, too."

"Then that will be her name," Titus said, kissing the baby's cheek. "Little Myrrh." The little girl immediately woke, looked at him with one red eye and one blue-violet eye, and began wailing.

Leri took Myrrh and began rocking her. The baby looked up at her seriously, then over at Titus, her mismatched eyes wary.

"She knows what I am," Titus said in surprise.

"She's something new," Leri said proudly. "Half demon and half faerie."

"With some human," Titus reminded. "Debbie was several months along when she began to miscarry."

"I still can't believe you were able to save the child," Leri said. She smiled down at Myrrh. "You are very lucky to have your uncle."

"It was only possible because she was part demon," Titus sighed, rubbing his temples. "And that using Shaker's foresight of the miscarriage, we planned it to happen at The Chalet, where John's power over time is strong. And that faerie's bodies are accepting of children not their own."

"We kind of have to be, being born with no ovaries of our own," Leri snapped, disgruntled. "It's helpful for not having children but having them requires magic. And a human egg to use."

"If Shaker hadn't warned us it was going to happen and when, we wouldn't have been ready," Titus rumbled. "But we were, and all went well. We were able to save her. Debbie will have in time her

279

own mortal child, or not. She would have died bringing forth Myrrh, even without the miscarriage. This was the only way to save both her and the child."

"You didn't know if it would work anymore than I or Shaker did," Leri accused. "I'm amazed it did. But now that it has, what are we going to do with her? We can't raise her here as Devlin will end up seducing her."

Titus laughed, and she glared at him. "That's not a joke. You know he will."

"Not this one, I think," Titus said. "She's going to be a force to be reckoned with. But you're right, she can't stay with us. She must not be known to be Shaker's daughter, not for some time, if ever. We must hide her, hopefully with an adoptive family that will both teach her magic and keep her safe, until she is old enough to watch out for herself."

"There's no such place," Leri said. "We are out of good fairies to ask for help."

"Then we'll have to ask some bad ones."

"No," Leri said. "What we need is to "pull a switch," the oldest trick my kind is known for."

"Take a human child and leave this one in its place?" Titus said. "You can't be serious. That would get discovered very fast, with all the DNA testing available."

"In today's world it would," Leri said slowly. "We have to take her back into the past."

"How?" Titus said, gaping at her. "That's a one-way trip for her and you, even if you do manage it. And to whom would we give her? They won't know she's part demon. They might harm her. Perhaps it's better to keep her here, try to raise her ourselves." He winked at her. "I keep telling you I'm open to more children."

Leri snorted. "I am too, if you carry and bear them. And no, Shaker wanted her safe. The safest thing for her is to be well away from our world, and Debbie's, too. In today's world she'll be discovered. The best thing for her is a wild frontier, someplace she can grow up where no one will be looking for her."

"We can't do that. She'll die."

"No, she won't. Myrrh is going to be powerful in a short time. She won't know magic instinctively, but she'll learn it easily." Leri murmured some words over the child, and the baby's one red eye changed color, becoming blue violet to match the other. "We have to give her that chance. You and I have the power to open a portal to the past, just not the strength to do anything else but hold it. We just need someone to take Myrrh through it."

"And return." Titus studied her. "Cheyenne is the only one with the power to do that, and she won't help us."

"She won't by choice. But she owes me a debt from long ago. I'll call it in."

~

Henrietta sighed, looking at the mess the pigs had made in the corn after getting free. "We've got enough trouble with Indians, we didn't need this, Lord."

"Henny!" her husband yelled. "Henny, come quick!"

Scared, the young woman ran in the direction of his voice, coming to him near the banks of a creek. Her husband was holding a young Irish woman, several arrows in her chest.

"Lay still!" the man said, trying to stop the bleeding.

"My baby," the woman gasped, blood leaking from her mouth. "Please, take care of her, please..." She trailed off, slumping.

Henny hurried to the bundle lying on the ground. A baby lay within, looking at her curiously. She picked it up, and it smiled at her. She cradled it, then looked down at the dying woman. "She have any money on her?"

The man made a face, then began to rifle through the prone woman's pockets. As he did, an arrow whistled through the air, hitting him in the neck. He choked, then fell onto the dying woman.

Henny screamed, and ran with the baby for the farm. She only got a few yards before an arrow hit her in the chest, and she fell to the ground, as the baby began to wail.

Natives came out of the brush and began to inspect the bodies. As one leaned in to the dead Irish woman, she shoved him away with a curse, getting to her feet, the glamour of death coming off her to reveal her long black braided hair, hide dress, and stern expression.

The natives backed away, some of them shouting she was an evil spirit, to go away.

Cheyenne grabbed the squalling baby from the dead woman's embrace, then turned to the leader. "Take me to your village now, to speak with your leader. Or I'll kill you and your entire war party." She held up her hand, blue fire burning from it.

The leader nodded.

A short time later, she was standing before the leaders of the village. "I come from the future," she said slowly. "I have brought you this baby. If you take care of her, she will grow up to be like me, and become your protector."

"You know our language, but we don't know you," the leader said. "And this baby is white, not like us."

"You will be exterminated in another hundred years," Cheyenne shouted. "All of this wilderness will be gone. Your way of life will be gone. You cannot stop it. But you can hide, as I hid my people, when the whites came. No, you don't know me, but I am blood of your blood, and I would save you from extermination, if I can." She laid the baby at his feet. "This girl will become a woman in time with great magical power. She can save you, if you save her now."

The chief held tight to his fear, not backing down. "She is not one of us."

"Teach her your ways. She is young, she will learn. Her name is Myrrh."

"I will take her," the shaman said, speaking up. "My woman and I have a baby of our own now who is almost weaned. She has milk to feed this child. We do not need her white name; we will give her one of our own. But if you do this, go, and do not come back. The girl will either become one of us or die."

Cheyenne nodded, as she watched him take the child to his tent and give it to his wife. The woman initially balked, but once she saw Myrrh, she accepted her happily, and began to nurse her.

"Go in peace, spirit," the leader said. "We thank you for your warning."

Cheyenne moved off, through the trees, looking back at the peaceful scene. Then she turned again, and hurried in the direction of the portal

THE END

~

Don't miss out on your next favorite book!

Join the Satin Romance mailing list
www.satinromance.com/mail.html

THANK YOU FOR READING

Did you enjoy this book?

We invite you to leave a review at the website of your choice, such as Goodreads, Amazon, Barnes & Noble, etc.

DID YOU KNOW THAT LEAVING A REVIEW...

- Helps other readers find books they may enjoy.
- Gives you a chance to let your voice be heard.
- Gives authors recognition for their hard work.
- Doesn't have to be long. A sentence or two about why you liked the book will do.

ABOUT TARA FOX HALL

Tara Fox Hall's writing credits include nonfiction, horror, suspense, action-adventure, erotica, and contemporary and historical paranormal romance. She is the author of the paranormal action-adventure *Lash* series and the vampire romantic suspense *Promise Me* series.

Tara divides her free time unequally between writing novels and short stories, chainsawing firewood, caring for stray animals, sewing cat and dog beds for donation to animal shelters, and target practice.

www.tarafoxhall.com

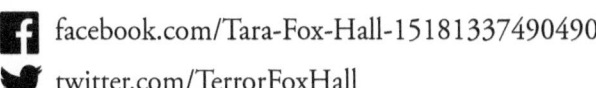

facebook.com/Tara-Fox-Hall-151813374904903
twitter.com/TerrorFoxHall

ALSO BY TARA FOX HALL

Multi-AuthorAnthologies
Her Frozen Heart in Frozen
One Perfect Moment in Propose To Me
A Love For Michelle in Second Chance for Love

Unhallowed Love Series
A Good Year
Year of the Demon
Year of the Incubus

Promise Me Series
Promise Me
Broken Promise
Taken in the Night
Taken For His Own
Immortal Confessions
Promise Me Anthology
Her Secret
Point of No Return
Lost Paradise
Dark Solace
Eye of the Storm
Tempest of Vengeance
Sundown & Serena

Hope's Return

Fate's Prison

Web of Memory

Forever

Freedom: Elle's Story

Immortal Reckoning

Novellas

Return To Me

Surrender to Me

The Oath

Night Music

Anthologies

Make Me Behave

Make Me Behave II

Latham's Landing

www.ingramcontent.com/pod-product-compliance
Lightning Source LLC
Chambersburg PA
CBHW022025240626
47154CB00007B/2273